Galileo's Telescope

DAVID HARRY TANNENBAUM

Red Engine Press
Fort Smith, AR

Cover art copyright © 2024 Ana (Kat) Gally Zelaya

Library of Congress Control Number: 2024945656

ISBN: 979-8-9895620-4-6

Disclaimers

Everything in this book is fictional, except for the below listed Facts, as well as the establishments frequented by Detective Leslie Hodges.

Fact One

Galileo (Galileo DiVincenzo Bonaiuti de' Galilei) made fundamental contributions to, among other disciplines, the sciences of motion and astronomy. He is perhaps best known for promoting his belief, based on the rotation of the planets and their moons, that the earth revolves around the sun—and not the other way around, as taught by the Catholic church.

Pope Urban VIII ordered Galileo to cease all public comments in support of this "heresy". Galileo complied with the Pope's directive—but only for a while. He published Dialogue Concerning the Two Chief Systems of the World. It was this "Dialogue" that caused the Inquisition to find him guilty of heresy.

Galileo's life was spared apparently because of his long-time relationship with the powerful Medici family.

Fact Two

In 1622, eight Spanish ships laden with gold bars and various other treasures, sank off the coast of Florida. One of those ships, the *Buen Jesús y Nuestra Señora del Rosario*, has recently been discovered and its treasure recovered.

Fiction

The possibility exists that one of Galileo's Telescopes could have been a gift to a Medici leading to the sparing of the Great Man's life. The possibility also exists that this very same telescope was among the treasures recovered from the sea bottom. It is also possible then, that as chronicled in THE SEMINAL SOCIETY— GALILEO'S TELESCOPE, that very same telescope could be responsible for the recent loss of a life! It's up to Sheriff's Deputy Detective Leslie Hodges to untangle the hows and whys of a mysterious death. Once again, the volatile world of the Seminal Society's billionaire art collectors is on our emerald-eyed detective's radar.

Lee County Acronyms

ASA   Assistant State Attorney
CIA   Criminal Investigation Assistant
COD   Cause of Death
DFU   Digital Forensics Unit
ROR   Release on Own Recognizance
RTIC   Real Time Intelligence Center
SOU   Special Operations Unit (SWAT)

Dedication

This book is dedicated to the memory of my friend, Barbara Ann Appelbaum, who passed away in recent months. Barbara was a gifted art conservator, becoming a Fellow of the American and International Institutes for Conservation. In addition, Barbara was a noted author, chamber music violist, artist, puzzle aficionado, and spreadsheet queen par excellence.

Among the objects she worked on over her long career was the dress worn by Marilyn Monroe when she famously sang "Happy Birthday" to President John F. Kennedy.

May Barbara's memory be a blessing to all who knew her.

GALILEO TELESCOPE

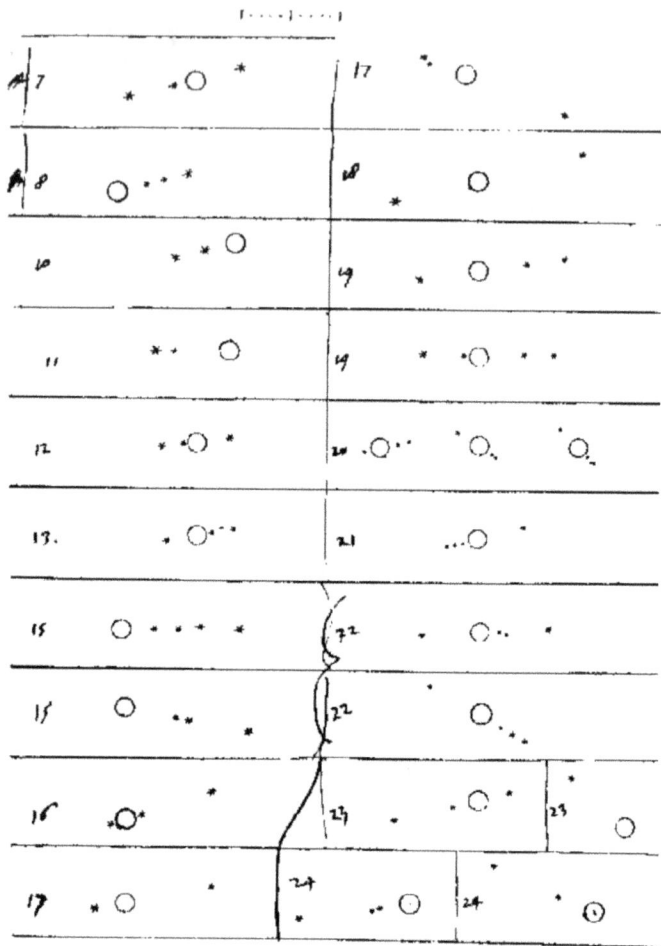

FOUR MOONS OF JUPITER
(January 7-24, 1610)

THE SEMINAL SOCIETY

Thomas A. Edison
Phonograph
1847-1931

Ernst Chladni
Acoustics
1756-1827

Sir Isaac Newton
Greatest Ever Scientist
1643-1727

Galileo Galilei
Father of Science
1564 to 1642

Leonardo da Vinci
Artist- Inventor
1452-1529

Oswald Von Wolkenstein
First Song Composer
1376-1445

ONE

DETECTIVE LESLIE HODGES suppressed a yawn as she rolled to a stop in a parking lot two blocks east of the Lee County morgue. It had already been a long day and was promising to become even longer. Crossing the street, she found the small coffee shop Medical Examiner Margarete Van Deere had suggested.

"Four-thirtyish'll work for me," the middle-aged ME had said. "Don't worry if I'm a bit late. There's always one last thing to do when I try to leave a few minutes early. Order anything you want. Judging from the last time I saw you, treat yourself to a cinnamon bun—or two. Tab's on me."

Indeed, the cinnamon buns were tempting, as were several other pastry items in the display case. But Leslie's self-discipline was fully in control. "Black coffee," she said to the barista. "Medium. To stay."

"Anything else?" the young woman behind the counter asked without looking away from the machine she was apparently trying to adjust.

"That'll do it."

"Okay. Just be a moment," the woman replied, looking up briefly to project a frustrated half-smile in Leslie's direction. "This brewer's acting up. Take any seat you want. I'll bring it to you."

Leslie zeroed in on a small table in a far corner, settling herself in with her back to the wall allowing her an unobstructed view of the entrance. The coffee arrived almost simultaneously with the medical examiner.

"I'll have coffee as well, please," Van Deere said to the server, "and one of your cinnamon buns, while you're at it."

"A bun for me too, please," Leslie added, her resolve fading.

"The bun's an indulgence for me," the ME confided, "I daresay you can use the calories."

Leslie forced a smile, swallowing her discomfort at yet another all too frequent and unwelcome comment about how thin she was.

The server returned with the second coffee and two buns, her demeanor much cheerier, now that she had apparently been able to fix the brewer. The ME took a tentative sip, then drained half her cup before saying, "Been a long day. Let me get right to the point. I don't know if we have anything yet or not. Preliminary finding is suicide. But..."

"Wait. Do I know this case?"

"Oh. Sorry, Detective. Male, forty-five. Bullet to the brain, seemingly, as I said, self-inflicted."

"Late Tuesday night," Leslie interjected, nodding that she now knew the case. "Heard the nine-one-one report. Called in by an eyewitness passenger on the Key West to Fort Myers ferry. Correct me if I'm wrong. The caller and her husband were returning to Fort Myers from a few days down in the Keys. Saw a guy shoot himself and fall overboard just before the ferry docked. Call came in at nine-twenty-three. Body was located about one a.m."

"One-ten to be exact. But how on earth do you do that? Have details like that in your head just from hearing it once? You weren't even assigned, so why would you even remember the call?"

"A gift, I suppose," Leslie shrugged. "I think 'Detective Cox caught the shooting. Shouldn't you be talking to him?"

"I can explain, but this is off the record."

"I don't know if I..."

"Relax, Detective. I've cleared it with Boots," the ME interrupted, referring to Leslie's boss, Captain Karen Stetson. "Karen and I go back a long way. Here's the thing. What I'm about to tell you is as far from scientific as it gets. The only verified *facts* that we have are that we have a dead man with a 9mm bullet in his brain and that his name is Derrick Franklin."

"An eyewitness reported he shot himself," Leslie reminded the ME. "That's a fact as well."

"Maybe. Maybe not."

"Thought you said that the witness saw this Franklin guy shoot himself. Did the witness get it wrong?"

"Like I said, maybe. Maybe not. "

"I dunno. Sounds open-and-shut to me."

"I know. Based on what the witness reported, it would seem that a guy on the ferry puts a gun to his head, pulls the trigger, then tumbles off the boat into the water. And, in fact, the ferry video shows him holding the weapon at his side as he comes out of the shadows."

"But?

"But on the other hand, he was out of the surveillance frame at the point in time when he would have lifted the gun to his head.

Next thing that the video shows is him going over the transom. Although the witness insists he fell after the shooting, he possibly could have jumped. For now, we're going with the witness's version, but the video is inconclusive."

"Still sounds like a suicide to me."

"I'm not ready to pronounce it, but just between us girls, and off the record, I'm thinking homicide."

"Homicide! But the witness...."

"No, listen. Two things bother me. First, forensics says the shot was fired with a slight downward angle. In a bullet-to-the-head suicide, the trajectory is almost always upward."

"Never downward?"

"Hardly ever."

"And second?"

"The dead guy's name?"

"Derrick Franklin?"

"Yes, the name, Derrick Franklin, rang a bell. Took me a while to put it together but, believe it or not, Franklin works, worked, for my husband's cousin who runs a marine salvage business. Employs divers, welders, those types of trades. And Franklin was the diver who discovered a treasure aboard a ship that went down almost due west of Key West four hundred years ago. Instant wealth. All of them. There was so much treasure, mostly from Venezuela, aboard that ship that the sinking is said to have taken down the Spanish Empire. Gold bullion, pearls, you name it. Worth billions."

"And you can believe this or not," Leslie added, "but I actually know the name of the ship. The *Buen Jesús y Nuestra Señora del Rosario*, right?"

"How do you..."

"Like I said, near-perfect recall for anything I've read. Anyway, I think you're saying that a man who came into such wealth wouldn't shoot himself."

"That, coupled with the wrong trajectory and the fact that point-blank shots to the head kill instantly, which this one did not. Doesn't add up all's I'm saying. I asked Lang Williams to go deep on this one."

"Lang's one helluva investigator, that's for sure. I worked with him on the Edison, Chladni and Newton matters."

"Yup. Best investigator in the state, you ask me. Blessed to have him. He interviewed the couple who called in the nine-one-one. According to them, there wasn't anyone close enough to have pushed him. Or for that matter, shoot him. They said that he went off the stern awkwardly, with arms flailing."

"A bothersome detail, indeed," Leslie said. "Inconsistent with a bullet-to-the-head instant death theory. What else do you know about Franklin?"

"Not much, actually. Great diver. Loved being under water more than above it."

"Fascinating, but why are you telling me all this? It's Cox's case, after all."

"His case or not, it has your name written all over it."

"How's that?"

"You'll see in a moment."

Trying the ME from a different angle, Leslie asked, "Any idea why Franklin was on the ferry?"

"No. What we do know is that he bought a round-trip ticket. Went down to Key West on the morning ferry. Back north in the evening."

"Video confirm that?"

"Coming home, yes. Going down not so much. But..."

Here it comes, Leslie thought, the real reason Van Deere had reached out to her. "But what?"

"Don't have a decent frame of Franklin on the Tuesday morning ferry south to Key West. But we do have a clear shot of one of your friends on the ferry south that morning."

"One of my friends?"

"Un-huh. Pete Jakowski."

"Jakowski! What the... But not coming back north?"

"Inconclusive. Nothing clear enough to say he was on the northbound ferry."

"What about on Key West? Know what Franklin did down there for the day? Or, for that matter, Jak?"

"Nothing on either of them. No hotel, motel, bike or car rentals in Key West under the names Franklin or Jakowski, at least so far. No credit card activity either." The ME sat back and signaled for a coffee refill, content to remain quiet until her cup was again full. "Assume, if you will," she continued after taking a sip of the freshly poured coffee, "Franklin was indeed murdered with people watching."

"That's a reach, given that a witness claims no one was close to him when he went into the water," Leslie responded, still confused. A medical examiner as experienced as Van Deere didn't usually color outside the lines. "You're thinking homicide because why? Because the guy just became rich and had everything to live for?"

"Look, Detective, I'm as confused about this as you are. Yes, I'm thinking homicide because Franklin had too much to live for to have killed himself. And, as I said, ballistics argues for homicide as well."

"Okay, but where's the motive?"

"I'm thinking perhaps diversion. Something else may be going down and someone didn't want it noticed."

"Anything in particular in mind?" Leslie asked, although skeptical of the whole homicide theory.

"Here's where my husband's cousin comes into play. Where science meets coincidence, if you will. His cousin is a retired Navy admiral, Makenzie Madison Masters. Actually, cousin-in-law, but close enough. She insists on being called Admiral Makenzie Madison Masters. Behind her back, everyone refers to her as Big Mack. They call her Three M to her face."

"Admiral, huh?"

"Fleet commander at the time she retired. Had aircraft carriers under her command. Trained as a Marine as well. The whole nine yards. Founded Masters Marine Salvage & Rescue, a naval salvage company raking in huge amounts of money working almost exclusively on contracts from her old friends at the Navy Department. Anyway, Makenzie, or as my husband is prone to call her, Big Mack, was over to the house last weekend. The two of them spent most of the day by the pool tossing down beers. I joined them late. By then, neither of them was feeling any pain. Three M wasn't so far gone, however, that she didn't notice my arrival and clam up right in mid-sentence."

"Was that unusual? I mean did she normally cut you out of conversations she had with your husband?"

"Not that I'm aware of. I asked him afterward about it and he said it had to do with billionaires and some society."

"The Seminal Society!" Leslie exclaimed, loud enough for any number of people to glance in their direction. Lowering her voice, Leslie asked, "The same Seminal Society that..."

"Yep, one and the same. That's precisely why you're here and not Cox. You're our Seminal Society expert. That cult of billionaires who believe that certain dead geniuses share a common soul. From von Wolkenstein in the fifteenth century, through da Vinci, Galileo and Newton in the sixteenth, seventeenth and eighteenth, to Chladni and Edison in the nineteenth and twentieth, those wealthy folks crave 'Firsts' from that group of geniuses. As you unfortunately know all too well, they'll stop at nothing to own those exclusive artifacts. And they get what they want."

"Does your husband know what happened to Edison's First phonograph, Chladni's First euphon and Newton's First published book?" Leslie asked, only half-kidding. Those were the three homicide cases Leslie and Van Deere had worked on together. Clearly, Leslie now realized, the Seminal Society was why she was sitting across from the ME.

"Apparently, cousin Makenzie had brought him up to speed on the antiquities that had gone missing. He said that she had mentioned all three of them. Then he added that she had said that some telescope was worth maybe a billion dollars!"

"A billion-dollar telescope, huh? Interesting. I presume it was a telescope found on the *Buen Jesús*—exactly the kind of thing that would be ravenously sought after by the billionaire collectors of the Seminal Society who collect so-called 'Firsts' and will stop at nothing to get what they want."

"In my husband's telling, Big Mack conveniently left out the murders associated with 'Firsts' from Edison, Chladni and Newton. She knows I worked on those homicides. I assume that's why she went silent when I was within earshot."

"According to what you said earlier, Admiral Three M Big Mack is a billionaire herself. Do you think she's become a Seminal Society collector?"

"All I can say on that front is that my husband also knew that a telescope Galileo peered through to view the moons of Jupiter, making him the first person to ever do so, had recently been stolen from the *Museo Galileo*. I can't imagine where he would have learned that little tidbit other than from his cousin. It's not exactly cocktail party conversation."

TWO

DRIVING HOME FROM HER UNOFFICIAL MEETING with the ME, Leslie's thoughts turned to retired Admiral Masters and the treasures Masters had recovered from the sunken ship. Money had never been central to Leslie's life, but with so much of her detective work focused on the billionaire Seminal Society collectors, she found herself musing on what she would do if she was suddenly wealthy—really jaw-droppingly wealthy like they were. Money, she quickly realized, would no longer define what she wanted, where she lived, what she did. A private jet with a dedicated crew could be minutes away, always ready to whisk her wherever in the world she wanted to go. Where would that be? Where would she live? How many homes would she have? Where would she vacation? What would she do with her time? Questions came faster than answers.

And how would she behave? Police officers are trained to treat every person humanely and with respect. Practically speaking, that doesn't always happen. Wealthy people, to Leslie's observation, despite their rhetoric to the contrary, are no different. In fact, she would argue, again from observation, the more wealth a person had, the less attention that person paid to the down-and-outs. It frightened Leslie to think that her human values could degenerate in that way if her fantasy ever became a reality.

No, she thought. That would never happen. She saw herself funding a foundation that would help distressed teens, similar to what Bobby Jo, the actress she had met during the Newton investigation, had done. Perhaps, she thought, traveling with unmotivated teens, allowing them to broaden their horizons and to see first-hand how others in the world lived, would be something she would enjoy.

The thought of traveling brought to mind the wonderful time she had had in the U.K. on assignment with Pete Jakowski, the former Pittsburgh Steeler defensive lineman turned detective. She smiled thinking of their time together; how comfortable she had felt with him; how he had made her feel special. His passion for life had consumed her.

And then thinking about her meeting with medical examiner Van Deere, Leslie couldn't help but replay her conversation of the previous evening with Jakowski and the article from the *L'international* he had sent her.

L'INTERNALIONAL

LYON, France – Despite constraints imposed by COVID-19, the year 2022 saw a dramatic increase in the theft of, and illicit trafficking in, cultural goods. It is estimated that as many as 100,000 archaeological objects, furniture, coins, paintings, musical instruments and sculptures have been reported missing. Topping the list is the unconfirmed substitution/theft of a Galileo Galilei telescope from the *Museo Galileo* valued conservatively at 750 million Euros.

Customs and other law enforcement authorities around the world have been working with Interpol in an attempt to locate the missing property and find the perpetrators. Innumerable searches have been carried out in airports, ports and border crossings, as well as in auction houses, museums and private residences. As a result, more than 300 investigations have been opened, and 67 individuals arrested. An anonymous source believes Galileo's first telescope is in the possession of, or on its way to, an individual now living in southern Florida.

The international operation was initially led by Spain's Guardia Civil, with international coordination supported by Europol, Interpol and the World Customs Organization. The operation is being carried out in the framework of the European Multidisciplinary Platform Against Criminal Threats (EMPACT) and is now headed by a U.S.-based task force under the jurisdiction of the Department of the Treasury.

Jakowski, she knew, had been feeding valuable information to the federal task force—as he had to Leslie as well—pertaining to the timing of art heists. Of particular interest to investigators was information about money transfers in and out of secret offshore accounts. Jakowski was privy to that kind of information as a result of his moonlighting for Morris Dexter Stratis, a billionaire cultural arts collector.

"I'm guessing you sent me that article," Leslie had commented to Jakowski, "because Stratis has the Galileo telescope in his sights? Or what?"

"Yes. And probably every other Seminal Society collector as well. But not just any Galileo telescope. He hand-crafted many of them and gave them as gifts to curry favor and buy good will among the Italian elite. From popes to kings to dukes."

"If I recall, and this is all very vague, he was found guilty by the Inquisition."

"The Inquisition *did* find him guilty. You're right on that. But his telescope gifts seem to have worked because he was allowed to keep his head attached to his neck. A far better outcome than for others found guilty by the Inquisition."

"You said 'not just *any* Galileo telescope.' Does that mean that not all of Galileo's telescopes are equally sought after?"

"Right. The grand prize—the most valuable one—is the one Galileo was using when he first saw the moons of Jupiter. He named them the Medician stars and gave the telescope to Grand Duke Cosimo II de' Medici."

"Never heard of the Medician stars."

"They're now called the Galilean moons of Jupiter. The telescope is known as the Medici Telescope and is valued—at least to the Seminal Society collectors—at roughly a billion dollars."

"You haven't answered the question. Is Stratis focused on this stolen Medici Telescope?"

"First of all, the rumor of the theft is just that: A rumor. Second, and more relevant to me, is that, frankly, I don't know what Stratis has in mind. The man's gone silent on me. Either he has nothing going on, or…"

"Or what?"

"Or he no longer trusts me, which I'm afraid might be the case. The chance that he's decided to sit this one out is just about nil, and if I was still in his good graces, he definitely would have clued me in on his game plan."

"Does that mean Stratis doesn't believe the Medici Telescope was stolen? Or, if it was stolen, maybe he's already got it?"

"Either's a possibility, Leslie. I just don't know."

"But then back to you for a second. Wasn't Stratis paying your son's medical bills?" Leslie was hesitant to bring up Jak's family situation, but her curiosity—and, in fact, her concern for his son—made it impossible for her not to ask.

"Truth is, Les, his monthly retainer is still being deposited in my son's account." The son the big detective was speaking of was in a special needs home. Jakowski running errands for Stratis, being his 'advance' man, as Jakowski called himself, paid the bills that would have been impossible on a cop's salary.

"You'd think with all their money and all the rest of it those billionaire collectors would be satisfied to leave well enough alone and not get involved in a potentially shady situation, like a stolen telescope."

"You would think that. But it's an addiction like any other. Seems to me, the shadier the better. For someone who can have anything he wants at any time, there needs to be something just out of reach. Something that requires more than money to get ahold of."

"You were such an important part of Stratis' pre-planning operation—or whatever the hell you did for him—in the past. Why cut you out now?"

"He was rattled that I had showed up at the bank on the Isle of Man at the same time the money transfer for the Newton was occurring. Couple that with my being with you, a Lee County sheriff's deputy, and it was all too much for him. Without my Stratis connection, the federal task force'll be flying blind from here on out I'm afraid."

"Blind as a bat," Leslie agreed. "According to you, there isn't even consensus that the original telescope was switched out of the *Museo*."

"Nowhere close to consensus. Sometimes a 'theft' is staged, in this case to make the Seminal Society collectors believe the Medici Telescope's in play. Happens more often than people might think. Drives the value—as well as museum visitors—up. Win-win for everyone."

"What makes you think that?"

"For starters, the museum insists they still have the original and Interpol's documentation supports that. According to the investigator, the thieves never made it to the display case. The video footage I saw supports that."

"Isn't that conclusive?"

"Task force believes that even the video was staged. Thieves anticipated that the museum would cover up the theft and circulated their own footage showing the substitution. I'll send it to you."

"Battle of the videos, I suppose," Leslie had replied. "Classic he-said-she-said. What does the underground network say?"

"That's just it. Utter silence! And the underground is never silent. Always some rumor or another. Or almost always. For the last several months, nothing, zip, nada! The Society collectors are playing it close as well. If I was a betting man, I'd put my money on the Medici Telescope being in play."

"Why so quiet then?"

"From what I gather, another Galileo telescope was found together with treasure in the hull of a sailing ship that sank in the Gulf of Mexico. If so, the availability of the Medici Telescope could significantly affect the value of the one just recovered."

"So how will the task force know what's changing hands and where? Could be anywhere in the country. Or the world for that matter."

"Could be. But there are undercurrents of Florida being where the telescope will change hands."

"Listen, Jak. I have another investigation to run to ground. At least for now, all this Seminal Society talk is fascinating, but not exactly relevant to my focus."

"I hear you loud and clear. But keep in mind that transport is critical. Private transportation. FedEx won't cut it. Then there's the matter of payment. Cash won't work. With all the sanctions going on, too much visibility."

"Jak, what are you telling me?"

"Only that characters in southwest Florida would satisfy both requirements. And down here, you have lots of hidden swampy spaces to conduct business."

"May I remind you, alligators live in those 'hidden swampy' spaces."

"What's an alligator or two among friends? Or among thieves, for that matter?"

Sensing she was being primed, Leslie asked, "What should I be on the lookout for?"

"Before everything went silent, there was talk of an auction— a public auction, where one of the objects is the telescope in some sort of a…well, for lack of a better word…a disguise. They can't very well present it as the Medici."

"This auction you speak of, is that like a storage shed auction? *Storage Wars* type of thing?"

"Les, your guess is as good as mine on that."

"If there's no publicity about the telescope, how will the billionaire collectors know to bid?"

"The minimum bid will be a clue. At the first whiff of a high-value auction, the Seminal Society collectors will swoop in like mosquitoes to blood—and so will the federal task force."

"Is that why…" Leslie had begun to ask his involvement but thought better of it. "…you're still up north?"

"You got it."

Like mosquitoes to blood. Jakowski's words were now playing in Leslie's head as she pulled into her driveway, thankful for an early end to an otherwise uneventful day.

Except the day wasn't exactly over, as Leslie learned a moment later when her cell rang. "You coming back to the office?" Cox asked, the usual jovialness in his voice all but gone. "Been waiting for you."

"It's after six. Long day. What gives?"

"So, what? You get a job as a banker and now you get to keep banker's hours? We're detectives, remember?"

"You get a job as chief asshole?" is what Leslie wanted to respond. Instead, she said, "You obviously got something on your mind. What's up?"

"You home?"

"Suppose I am? What's that got to do with you?"

"Be there in fifteen. I'll stop and get hamburger meat and buns."

"Don't bother! You won't be here long enough to get hungry."

"Don't be so sure, my dear Leslie," Cox teased, his voice playful again. "Fire up the grill. Hey, can I count on you for a cold one? Or should I bring my own?"

"You come here, cold is all you're gonna get."

———————

"Just so you know, I'm here 'cause the brass said to brief you," Cox announced at Leslie's front door almost exactly fifteen minutes later, a Publix bag in hand. "Not my idea. So, how's about pretending to enjoy the company?"

"Do my best," Leslie rolled her eyes, handing him a Yuengling, one of several left over from Jakowski's last visit. "Brief me on what?"

"Man overboard. Fell from the Key West ferry right at Fort Myers Beach after shooting himself in the head. Couple from New Jersey, visiting family, called it in. And the ferry video shows at least some of what went down."

"Sounds straightforward," Leslie said, deciding to not yet tell Cox about her conversation with the ME.

"Thought so at first. But it doesn't add up."

"I'll bite. You wouldn't be here if it 'added up'. What's bothering you?"

"Hey, can't I convince you to fire up the grill? I went to the trouble of picking up the meat and everything." Cox winked. "Even got some great-looking buns."

"What are we? Back in high school? Told you not to bother! Talk fast," Leslie instructed, wanting to be left to her own thoughts. "It'll give you time to get home and cook your own dinner."

"Okay, Sport. Have it your way. Here's where I am. Guy that went overboard was a professional diver. Name of Derrick Franklin. Spent his life on boats and under the water. Assuming he shot himself, he wasn't likely to have done it so close to the edge that he'd land overboard—unless he wanted to be found in the water for some reason. Troubling's all."

"Not buying what you just said," Leslie argued, playing devil's advocate. "If he loved the water as you say, I can see him wanting to spend eternity at the bottom."

"Everything's possible I suppose," Cox conceded. "But if he wanted to spend eternity under water, wouldn't he have shot himself further out in the Gulf where he would never be found? Or at least somewhere more...more remote than under the Matanzas Pass Bridge."

"Good point. What do you have on him?"

"Boarded the southbound ferry at seven-forty-five Tuesday morning. Have him on video. Here, take a look."

Leslie accepted Cox's cell phone and watched as a tall man wearing a long-sleeved, baggy shirt, jeans and sneakers, a red slicker over his shoulder and a floppy hat covering his face, walked slowly up the boarding ramp and disappeared inside. The man had the same height and build as Pete Jakowski and the way the man in the video moved and carried himself was strikingly Pete-like. The time displayed for the last frame of the video was 07:27:23. "That it? That's what you got?"

"Keep going. Next, you'll see Franklin leaving the ferry in Key West. Camera caught him walking southwest."

"That's important because..."

"Because I called and texted photos to every bar and restaurant along that street. There sure are a ton of them. Nobody acknowledges seeing him."

"You haven't had time to look at all the surveillance footage from all the street cameras. He had to have been spotted. He didn't evaporate."

"Keep going. You'll see him go back aboard."

The man, known to Leslie as Derrick Franklin, appeared. This time he was wearing the red, foul weather slicker, a floppy hat partially obscuring his glasses. There was something different about his gait. *Too much alcohol*, Leslie guessed. She noted the display time as 17:28:05. Franklin made his way up the ramp and disappeared inside the boat.

Cox advanced the video time to 21:10:12. The sun had set, and lights from land off to the right cast quivering shadows onto the water ahead which was relatively calm. As Leslie watched, the background slowly changed as the ferry rounded the northern tip of land and progressed past what she recognized as Bowditch

Point Park. The Matanzas Pass Bridge came into view dead ahead. The video time stamp now read 21:26:19.

Franklin's red slicker now appeared pink in the dim light as he walked to the bow of the boat, his silhouette framed by the bridge. With the bridge directly overhead, Franklin moved to the right and disappeared from the video, obstructed by the stern of a rescue boat strapped to the ferry's structure. Leslie noted the time as 21:28:18.

Less than a minute later, at 21:29:08, the same man came into view; this time the stern of the ferry was visible. The camera angle was off center. Instead of pointing straight back, it pointed toward the right, catching at best only half of the rear deck. The man was standing with his body against the back rail, facing away from the camera. He moved sideways, briefly disappearing from the video. Suddenly, the left side of his body came back into view.

His left arm abruptly flew upward. His body then flipped over the rail and was gone. Time 21:29:38.

"Now do you see why our conversation'll take longer than a few minutes?" Cox asked, interrupting Leslie's thoughts. "Any chance of…"

"Talk faster. Your beer's getting warm."

"Have it your way. Pushed, shot, jumped or fell?"

"Didn't fall on his own without something else," Leslie concluded. "I'll lay odds on that. Man spent far too much of his life on boats to fall off even with violent motion of the boat, which we have no evidence of. Something external got him."

"Agreed. Pushed, shot or jumped?"

"Indeterminate. Tell me again what the witnesses said?" Leslie was still not yet ready to disclose she had been briefed.

"Couple from New Jersey. Saw about what the camera saw. He put the gun to his head and shot himself."

"You follow up with them on that?"

"That's where you come in. Called your buddy Jakowski. See what he knew before I called them."

"Jak? Why would you ever connect a man overboard on the Fort Myers ferry to Jak?"

"He was on the ferry south to Key West. That's why."

"But not on the northbound ferry?"

"Video doesn't show him coming north. No."

"And what did Jak tell you?"

"Nothing of any consequence. Thanked me for calling him and said he'd follow up with the couple who called it in."

"Did you ask him if he was on the ferry?"

"Thought about it but decided to hold back a bit. Get your read first."

Leslie was surprised. Both at Cox's restraint, and with Jakowski for not saying anything about this when he had spoken with her on this subject the previous night. "And?"

"And what?"

"And did he follow up?"

"Wasn't five minutes before Stetson was on the horn instructing me to brief you. Seems we're working this one together. Something about your Pittsburgh connection. Said you'd take the lead." His smile broadened. "You need to confess anything, dinner's a perfect time. If you don't want burgers, I can run out and get steaks—even lobsters if you want."

"How many ways are there to say no? No hamburgers! No steaks! No friggin' lobsters!" She stopped short of saying, "*And no sex!*" Cox had a reputation as a womanizer and Leslie had no intention of playing into his constant maneuverings.

"It's just dinner, Leslie," Cox retorted. "I had and have every intention of keeping my hands to myself, if that's what's bothering you."

"Damn right you will!" Leslie snapped, tired of what she perceived was his game playing. "Your hands ever end up in the wrong place, I'll bust your wrist! And that's on a good day!"

"Hey! That's uncalled for! You've given me high ratings to the brass. You said yourself we make good partners. What the hell gives with the hostility tonight?"

Leslie couldn't determine if the wounded look in his eyes was real or an act, but she had had enough cat and mouse for one night. Truth was, it was Jakowski who had gotten under her skin and not Cox. "I think you better go, before…"

"Before what?" Cox challenged.

"Before we're both sorry. This conversation's officially ended. Don't let the door…" Leslie turned her back on Cox and headed for the kitchen, listening for the front door to open and close before reaching for the last of the Yuenglings, Jakowski's beer of choice, and resolving, not for the first time, to deal with the Cox situation. Of even more importance, she knew she had to resolve her relationship with the big Pittsburgh cop, who somehow had managed to penetrate her defenses in a way she didn't fully understand.

THREE

LESLIE DIDN'T UNDERSTAND WHY COX exhausted her so much. He was a good detective with friends everywhere, all willingly doing him favors. What he gave them in return was also a puzzle.

The two of them had worked the Chladni euphon matter as a team when her original partner, Daryl Fischer, was on medical leave recovering from a bullet he took in the arm. It was during the Chladni investigation that she had gotten the chance to fully appreciate Cox's ability to put people at ease with his good-ol'-boy, over-the-top personality. While being interrogated, subjects were led to believe that Cox was not on top of things. His questions, however, were steel-trap lethal. Not much escaped him as he relentlessly tracked down even the tiniest of inconsistencies.

That Leslie admired Cox's skills as a detective was undeniable. But on the flip side was his obsession with her private life. Continually prying into what she was doing, where she went, when and with whom. His seeming obsession with her relationship with Pete Jakowski was particularly irksome. She suspected he had called Jakowski using the ferry incident as an excuse to pump the Pittsburgh detective for information about what had gone on between her and Jak on their recent trip to the British Isles. Cox behaved as if he was a jilted lover—which he was not.

Leslie fixed herself a bowl of oatmeal to go with her beer and unwound over a partially finished jigsaw puzzle that hadn't been touched for weeks. She managed to find places for only a handful of pieces over the next two hours while awaiting a hoped-for call from Jakowski. A call that never materialized. Growing tired, she carried out her nightly ritual in something of a blue funk, flopping into bed just past eleven.

———————

Leslie reached out to answer her ringing phone, noting through a sleepy haze the red numerals reading 3:15. "Hodges here," she growled, not bothering to look at the screen to see who was calling.

"You alone?" the caller asked. It was Cox.

"As if it's any of your business! I'm actually shacked up with...with Chris Evans, you want to know. What the hell do you want? It's three-frigging-fifteen in the morning!"

"Caught a hot one. Only about a mile from your place. Domestic. Man's down. Perp's in the wind. You want to work this with me, or should I call Fish?"

"Now that you've got me up, why not? We've only got two other active murders, so what's the problem with taking on a third. Or maybe even a fourth at this rate."

"Okay, then. Make your amends to Mr. Pacino there and get your ass out of bed. It's Thursday, if I'm not mistaken, so jump into your gray outfit and I'll meet you there. Address on dispatch site."

"Whadda you got so far?"

"Only lead is a red SUV. Neighbor thinks Honda, not certain. Shooting occurred about an hour ago, give or take. Got the Real Time Intelligence Center on it. Nothing so far."

Cox had been right on with his gray outfit comment. It was Thursday after all. Part of Leslie's bedtime routine was to lay out her clothes for the next day according to a color scheme she had established long ago. Yellow on Sunday, red on Monday and then green, tan, gray, aqua, blue. Made it easy. It also made it obvious when she didn't make it home to change clothes. A small price to pay for efficiency.

The streets were essentially empty as Leslie drove the dozen or so blocks to the crime scene. She could see red and blue lights glancing off buildings even before she turned onto Severn Street, an older neighborhood with residences above and businesses below—barber shop, bakery, hair salon, coffee shop. None of the businesses were open at that hour, of course, but Leslie thought she saw a light on at the bakery. A sheriff's deputy was positioned in front of a door midway down the block in the same building as the bakery. The door, no doubt, was the entrance to stairs leading to the residences above the bakery.

Leslie parked down the block on the opposite side of the street from the deputy. Taking a moment to survey the scene, she stepped out of her car, just as Cox rolled to a stop in the middle of the street and jumped out of his car, his hand on his holster.

"Didn't you say the perp's in the wind?" Leslie asked. "Who the hell you thinking of shooting?"

Cox shrugged his shoulders. "You're right. Force of habit, I guess." He climbed back into his car and repositioned it close to the curb. A moment later he appeared beside Leslie. "Just heard.

Victim was DOA at the hospital. If we're going to be out here a while, mind if I round us up a pastry or two? Looks like someone's working in the back over there."

"Hold that thought. Let's see what the scene looks like first."

"Don't you ever get hungry?"

"On my own time, I do. But we're on the clock and I need to concentrate." Cox shrugged and followed Leslie to the deputy at the door, a young Latino male with Sanchez displayed over his shirt pocket.

"Detectives Hodges and Cox," Leslie announced, as they flashed their detective shields. "You controlling the log?"

"Don't know anything about any log," the deputy replied. "All I know is I was told to not let anyone in except for the medical examiner."

"Go online and pull up a crime scene log," Leslie instructed, "and mark us in at..." Leslie checked her watch. "Three-fifty-eight. The only other people allowed in will be the ME team. Who's been upstairs?"

"So far as I know, only me and the paramedics."

"You were the responding officer?"

"Yeah. I responded to the dispatch and took the stairs behind this door. Found the vic on his back in a pool of blood. Called for transport. With all that blood, I figured he had to be dead, but one of the medics said she thought she detected a faint pulse. Whisked him off to Lee Memorial."

"Well, faint pulse or not," Cox reported, "our vic was DOA at the hospital. Just got the word."

"Anyway," Leslie said, "what was the timeline from when you got here?"

"I got here about three-oh-five. Called in to Central at about three-ten. Medics arrived three-twenty, more or less."

Cox checked his phone. "That jives with me being pinged at three-twelve. Could you see where the blood came from?"

"Plain as day. Cut throat."

"You're sure?"

"Gigantic hole. I'm sure, yeah."

"Okay. Thanks," Cox said, pulling on latex gloves. "We're going on up. And like my partner said, no one else comes in except for the ME."

Reaching the top of the stairs and entering the apartment, the detectives were confronted with a scene just as Sanchez had described it, but without the body. The blood was mostly on a throw rug on the living room floor. Two sofa pillows lay on the floor between the mostly coagulated blood and the sofa, which to Leslie seemed to be the kind that opened to form a bed.

"Who called it in?" she asked.

Cox again checked his phone. "Guy named Clancy Lowry. He lives…"

"Lowry Bakery," Leslie said, "You're in luck. About to score your breakfast buns. Light's on the back of the bakery. No doubt it's our Mr. Lowry making bread and bagels for the morning crowd. But before we go down and pay the baker a visit," she added, glancing around, "let's figure out what we can about our victim."

"Yeah, we don't even know if he lived here or what," Cox agreed, walking toward a desk off in the corner.

"Don't touch anything," Leslie reminded him. "Gloves or not. Let the ME team do their thing."

Cox shot an "Oh, please," look in Leslie's direction. "Not my first rodeo, partner." And then, "Hey, here's something." Cox motioned toward an unopened envelope. "It's addressed to Mr. and Mrs. Chase Montrose at this address, and here's some return address stickers for Binita and Chase Montrose. Same address."

"So probably safe to assume that Chase is the vic," Leslie surmised. "At least until we know otherwise. Wonder where Binita might be?"

"That's the million-dollar question," Cox replied, heading for the door, "but for right now, it's time to speak with baker Lowry."

"Right behind you. Not much more we can do here until the ME releases the scene."

Giving a passing nod to Deputy Sanchez on their way out, the detectives turned right and in a few steps were at the bakery shop front door. Cox slammed his open hand on it several times but there was no response from inside. He pounded again, this time with enough juice behind it to rattle the glass. A large man, with a prodigious belly, appeared from a back corner, frantically waving his hands and mouthing, "Go away!"

When the detectives didn't move, he reached for the door, cracking it open only wide enough to send a scolding voice through the narrow opening. "It's the middle of the night and we're not open!"

"We're not customers; we're sheriff's deputies," Cox replied.

Noting Cox's shield, Lowry lowered his voice. "I gave my number to that officer Sanchez. Expected detectives to call at some point, but not break down my door! Anyway, come out back. Stuff's coming out of the ovens and I gotta be there. I'm alone this morning."

Leslie and Cox followed the baker through the customer area into a space that was easily five times as large. Ovens covered two walls and massive refrigerators lined a third. Stainless steel tables, some with sinks, were stationed in the middle, with an impressive array of pans, trays and mixing bowls suspended above, along with an equally impressive number of long-handled whisks, ladles and spatulas. The smell of cinnamon filled the air. Several of the tables held large trays of what appeared to be unbaked pastries.

"You're Clancy Lowry, I presume," Cox said to the big man. "You called in the matter upstairs."

"Right. Now please step back. Buns need to come out."

Cox did as he was told, watching the baker quickly remove several trays from the middle oven and deftly slip them into individual slots on a mobile cart. Whereupon Lowry wheeled the cart off to the side and restocked the oven with new trays from the table.

"Help yourself," Lowry said, nodding in the direction of the hot buns. "Plenty more where those came from. Don't burn yourself."

"Don't mind if I do," Cox said, tentatively touching the bun closest to him and quickly withdrawing his finger. "Better give it more time to cool."

"How about telling us what you saw and when?" Leslie said, having become impatient with all the baking goings-on. "I mean with respect to what happened upstairs. You can start by telling us why you were up there to begin with."

"Chase—he's the husband—is known to get himself...let's say...a bit over the top. Comes home and is...abusive to poor Bini...Mrs. Montrose. She been known to end up in the hospital. I heard the fight start and thought I'd go and break it up. I heard a thud, and the yelling stopped. 'Intermission,' I told myself. But it didn't restart like it usually did. I tell you, when they got to fighting, they fought! The silence got to me. That's when I went up. Got there too late, I'm afraid."

"After the initial shouting, you say," Cox said, following up, "you heard nothing. Nothing at all?"

"Can't be certain, but if pressed I'd say, someone going down the steps?"

"Running down the steps? Or walking?"

"Well, now that I think about it. There might have been two people on the steps. The first came down fast. The second, normal walking. I think that's what made me go up. Seemed odd."

"Got it," Leslie said. "But now going back in time for a minute, when did you arrive at the shop today?"

"Around two-thirty. Same time as I do every morning. Shop opens at seven. For the early birds."

"You have a helper? Or do you do it all by yourself?"

"Can't do it all by myself! We have three bakers. I work until after lunch. Joanne's here when the store opens. She supervises the counter staff. Max Clement starts when I leave, and he closes up. He's the one who prepares everything you see out here. Likewise, I prepare everything he bakes."

"That's all for now, I think," Leslie said, glancing over to Cox for a confirmation.

"Actually, just one more thing," Cox said. "Was this the first time you went up there to break up a 'fight', as you called it?"

Before Lowry could reply, Leslie's phone buzzed. The screen displayed Jak. "Gotta take this," she said, turning her back on the interview and moving into the front of the still-empty store. She touched the green accept button and put the cell to her ear. "What the hell are…"

"Sorry to wake you, Les. I need…"

"Been up a while. Make it fast, I've…"

"It's four-thirty in the morning! You having trouble sleeping or…hey, is that Cox I heard in the background?"

"Matter of fact, it was. We're…"

"We can talk later," disappointment apparent in Jakowski's voice. "Wouldn't want to disturb your…plans. Call me when it's more convenient."

The line went dead just as Cox appeared from the back, a fresh bun in his hand. "Not much more we can do down here," he announced before taking a bite. And then noticing the sour look on Leslie's face, he asked, "I do something wrong? I hope you're not upset I accepted the pastry."

"Nothing to do with you."

"Bad news phone call?"

"You could say that."

"You wanna talk about it while we wait for the ME team? We could go to my car. Or yours."

"Never mind. Just brief me on what the bakerman said. That you can do right here."

"Guy said he heard yelling. Louder than normal. Said he usually ignores the two of them fighting. But this…"

"Husband and wife?"

"This time the fight sounded serious, he said. Heard Chase threaten to cut Bini's nose off."

"Anything more?"

"Nope."

"Okay. I have a call to make. I'll meet you up there when forensics shows."

Leslie walked to her car, locked the doors, and dialed. Jakowski answered on the first ring. "I hope that wasn't a bout of jealousy I detected just before," she began. "Cox and I caught a domestic. Husband dead. Wife in the wind. When you called, we were interviewing the witness who had reported it."

"Sorry. Cop's mind always assumes the worst. And I was on high alert, Cox-wise, wondering what the real reason was that he had called me earlier asking about a couple who called in the ferry shooting."

"I was briefed on that. Yes."

"He could have developed the information himself, but I went along with it. Dug around a bit and learned that there was another witness, named Jennifer Longworth. She..."

"I hadn't heard that name. Not in the file, I don't think."

"Didn't call Lee County. Called Dexter Stratis—directly."

"Stratis? What the..."

"Hear me out. The name Longworth sounded familiar to me. I connected it in my mind with an art exhibition that Stratis holds every year. It's the social event of the season. People kill to be invited. A woman no one recognized appeared at his last party. Managed to get her picture taken next to several notables, including former mayor, Bill Peduto. Naturally, people wanted to know who she was. The official party register given to the Post Gazette society editor listed her name as Jennifer Longworth and that's the name they went with. However, she was subsequently recognized by a reader as being Celeste Greenslee, a nurse at the University of Pittsburgh Medical Center."

"Why the different name?"

"Spokesperson for Stratis claims it was all a mix-up. Names transposed. That kind of thing. The paper seemed satisfied and dropped it. All forgotten. Until I got that call from Cox. Ran a few traps and here we are."

"Where are we? I'm not following."

"Sleep deprivation, Leslie? This Longworth—or Greenslee—is obviously being used to run errands for Stratis. Keep track of people, that type of thing."

"Instead of you?"

"I suspect she's asked to do what they know I never would do. How long she's been doing it, though, is anybody's guess."

Leslie thought for a long moment. "Based on what you just told me," she finally said, "it's pretty clear that our deceased diver, the man Derrick Franklin, is somehow connected to Stratis."

"What? I haven't even told you what Greenslee said that she saw. Just because she was an errand girl for Stratis doesn't mean that there's any connection between that fact and the fact that she happened to have witnessed a suicide."

"Possible suicide," Leslie corrected.

"Okay. Possible suicide."

"But don't you see the linkage?" Leslie continued. "Greenslee purports to have witnessed the death of a man who is believed to have discovered a lost Galileo Telescope which, I must assume, is coveted by Dexter Stratis."

"And if Franklin is connected to Stratis in that way, then most likely his death also has something to do with Stratis—or at least somebody—wanting to get their hands on that telescope."

"All of which is why I'm on my way to the airport," Jakowski replied. "Plane lands at nine oh six this morning. Pick me up, okay? American."

FOUR

PETE JAKOWSKI WALKED OUT of the airport and climbed into Leslie's waiting car. "You're a welcome sight for a weary traveler. For a woman rousted from her bed at three in the morning, you look pretty chipper."

"I'll take that as a compliment. Matter of fact, I've managed several hours of sleep. All of it right in this car over in cell phone parking."

"Know a good breakfast place? Treat's on me."

"Haney's is about the best. Can sit outside if you like."

They drove in silence several minutes before Leslie said, "How long's it going to take before you answer the question?"

"And what question is that?"

"Is there more than one? What the hell's Stratis doing sending a woman down here to follow a guy who apparently shoots himself before falling overboard?"

"Hey, we don't actually know that Stratis sent her or that, in fact, she was following him at all."

"Cut me a break, would ya."

"Les, you mean you won't buy the idea that Celeste Greenslee just happened to be on vacation at the same time and place as the death of a man who discovered the Sunspot Telescope that her sometime boss Dexter Stratis would do anything to get his hands on?"

"Bingo. You'd have more luck selling me a bridge."

"You're right, of course. Just confirming that we're on the same page. As I told you the other night," Jakowski continued, "I've been cut out of the loop. I'm speculating here, but from what I can piece together, I'm thinking there was something on the *del Rosario*, the sunken Spanish galley that diver Franklin located last year. Are you familiar with the *del Rosario*?"

"Vaguely," Leslie hedged, playing her cards close to the vest. "Fill me in on what I need to know."

"Back in the early sixteen hundreds, Spain had its eye on Italy. Particularly siding with the Vatican in Rome. This was a power thing. France, to counterbalance Spain, backed the Venetian government. Galileo built the first telescope at a time

24

when he taught at the University of Padua. He demonstrated the telescope to the Venetian Senate and then presented it as a gift to his patron, Leonardo Donato, the Doge of Venice."

"Why the doge? Why not the pope?"

"The city of Padua was part of the Venetian republic at the time. From what I understand, Galileo had been chipping around the edges of how the universe worked, following the lead of somebody-or-other Copernicus, who a hundred years earlier espoused the idea that the planets and the earth rotated around the sun. This went against religious dogma that the earth was the center of everything. Is it any surprise the pope and Galileo were not on good terms?"

"How did that ever start? I mean, the idea that everything rotates around earth?"

"It seems that three hundred years before Christ, Aristotle 'proved' that the earth didn't move or rotate. According to him it was fundamentally too heavy."

"And just how did he 'prove' that?" Leslie was fascinated.

"When he rode a horse, he felt air move across his face. When he stopped moving, the air also stopped moving. 'How,' he asked, 'could the earth be rotating if there was no air moving?' The idea that he didn't feel air movement when he was stationary because both the atmosphere and the earth were rotating in unison had totally escaped his thinking. Aristotle was also misled into thinking that the earth was stationary by the fact that when a person throws a rock upward into the air that rock always lands beside the person who threw it. He reasoned that if the earth rotated while the rock was in the air, then the rock would land a finite distance away."

"I should have been paying more attention in science class," Leslie joked. "Where did you learn all that stuff?"

"Got it from the task force."

"And you're about to tell me Galileo's first telescope was on that sunken ship."

"Not exactly."

"I feel as though I'm interrogating a reluctant witness! If you're not going to fill me in, thanks for the breakfast offer, and where can I drop you? I've got work to do."

"Grouchy, aren't we?" Jak replied. "As it turns out, Galileo had a few false starts and made several 'first' telescopes as he worked to get the optics right. Only had magnification power of ten in the beginning. But that was enough to convince the people that he was onto something. He gave the early telescopes away to gain favor in his continuing quest to have his teaching salary increased. Apparently, the man was perpetually broke and used his facility for all things scientific—coupled with his cutting wit—to advance his prestige. Galileo became an expert in military maneuvers, rampart breaching, directional compasses, medical devices, you name it. He once even gave a talk on the size of Dante's Inferno."

"If it isn't his actual *first* telescope that has captured the Seminal Society collectors' attention, then what has?"

"The first *thousand* power one! That was the telescope he used to first see the four moons of Jupiter. He named them the Medicean Stars after the Medici family who were his patrons. But that's yesterday's prize telescope."

"And if he saw moons, why did he call them stars?" Leslie asked, struggling to follow.

"A bit of P.R., I suppose. Boost his patronage. I'll let the historians deal with that."

"So where exactly is this Medici Telescope now?"

"That, my dear Leslie, is the sixty-four-thousand-dollar question!"

"Do you know?"

"Not exactly."

"Seems we're going in circles."

"Not exactly."

"Can you please stop that! It's damn annoying."

"Conventional wisdom has it that Galileo gave that telescope, the one he first saw Jupiter's moons through, to Cosimo II de' Medici, the Grand Duke of Tuscany."

"Seems straightforward enough."

"You'd think so. But... I'll finish the story over coffee," Jakowski promised, as Leslie eased her car into a parking spot beside a bright red Lexus in front of Haney's. "Coffee better be good."

"Can't go wrong here. Haven't been disappointed yet."

Entering the restaurant, Leslie ushered Jak to a corner table. "Two coffees, black," she requested of the waitress who had followed them to the table. "And a menu for my friend, please."

"So back to the telescopes," Leslie directed after the requested menu had been delivered.

"Right. Well, it seems that Galileo gave a second telescope to il signore Medici some years later. This was the one that he first saw sunspots through."

"So, there are two Medici telescopes? Now I'm really confused."

"The plot thickens. Old Cosimo, himself playing politics, sent the second telescope—the one now referred as the Sunspot Telescope—to King Philip IV of Spain. Only it didn't get there."

"Wait! The Italian Medici sent the telescope to a Spanish king? What am I missing here?"

"Reason is that Spain pretty much controlled Naples, Sicily and the island of Sardinia at that time, and Medici, who was up north in Florence, was currying favor to protect his holdings along the southern Italian coast. He was, after all, the self-proclaimed protector of the Catholic Church—and he needed military help. Medici was never one to miss an opportunity to solicit favor. So, when the *Buen Jesús* sailed into Sardinia, he had the Sunspot Telescope placed aboard the ship for delivery to Spain in honor of King Philip IV's coronation. The king was a great patron of the arts, and superstitious to boot."

"Superstitious? What's that mean?"

"It turns out the number four had great significance to him, symbolizing the Sun as the fourth planet encircling the earth. Medici's bribe didn't work, as his gift to the 'Planet King' never made it to Spain. Perhaps if Philip IV had received the power to see far into the heavens, it would have given him a better perspective of his foreign political situation. Unfortunately, more than a historic telescope was ultimately lost to Spain during the 'Planet King's' rather tumultuous reign during Spain's Thirty Years' War."

"Are you saying the Sunspot Telescope meant for the 'Planet King' was on the sunken treasure ship? You're getting too mystical for me."

"All I'm certain of is that Derrick Franklin was the lead diver on the *Buen Jesús*. He found both the telescope, and, as I understand it, sealed papers that identify what it was. It was also listed on the ship's cargo log."

"Franklin's dead. And you're thinking it's not a coincidence."

"That's exactly what I'm thinking," Jakowski confirmed. "My guess is he removed the telescope before the treasure was brought up and buried it at some location near the sunken ship known only to him."

"What now? You're not down here for no reason."

"Gonna track down the Sunspot Telescope. Franklin was going to be the starting point. Need a plan B."

"For Stratis?"

"Like I told you, I'm not working for Stratis on this one. This is one hundred percent task force."

"You referring to the federal task force headed up by Treasury Agent Maxine Ghana?"

"None other."

"Am I to assume I'm part of that 'task force'? Or what?"

"You, Detective Hodges, have a murder investigation to conduct. I suggest you concentrate on solving Franklin's homicide and leave this telescope business to the feds."

FIVE

A MILLION QUESTIONS FLOODED LESLIE'S MIND, but a call from dispatch interrupted her thought process.

"Deputy Cox has a message for you," the dispatcher informed her.

"Ten-four. Go ahead with the message."

"He's located the missing wife, a Binita Montrose, from this morning's incident. She's believed to be armed. Flamingo Estates. On Via Italiano."

"Ten-four. ETA about six minutes from present location."

"Be advised, tactical squad's been dispatched. ETA twelve minutes."

"Ten-four. Hodges out." Leslie looked down at the still-seated Pittsburgh cop. "I need to…"

"I heard. Go." Jakowski urged. "I'll finish here and Uber to my hotel. Catch you later."

Impulsively, Leslie bent down and kissed him. "I'll call when I can," she promised.

Leslie jogged to her car, flipping the lights and siren on as she worked her way out of the large parking area and onto northbound Route 41.

Seven minutes later she turned into an entry drive at the sign FLAMINGO ESTATES, WHERE DREAMS COME TRUE. Proceeding into the gated community, she followed a Lee County sheriff's vehicle that had arrived just before her. Hers was the fourth official car on the scene with five uniformed deputies standing in front of a four-story condo, several of them directing people coming out of the building to what appeared to be a clubhouse midway down the block.

Leslie spotted a sergeant standing just inside the door speaking into his mic. "I suppose you're Hodges," he challenged, looking in her direction. "What the hell's wrong with your partner? Scared hell outta these people; him yelling to evacuate the building and all!"

"It seems to be working," Leslie answered, instinctively defending Cox. "Haven't heard of any injuries. No report of gun fire."

"That's just it, no gun fire. No reason to evacuate!"

Changing the subject to avoid further confrontation, she asked, "Any idea of how many more people are left in the building?"

The sergeant shrugged. "This may be the last of them, but don't know for sure."

"How long ago did Cox go up?"

"Cox?" the officer asked. "Who's..."

"The detective up there with..."

"Didn't know his name. Been up there about ten, twelve minutes. Tactical's about here."

"I'm going up. Has a perimeter been set?"

"Just seeing to it when you interrupted."

"Leslie. Behind you." It was the voice of Daryl Fischer, her regular partner.

Startled, she turned. "What are you..."

"Heard your dispatch. Thought I'd..."

"Cox caught a homicide early this morning. Asked me to help. Husband was slashed and bled out. Wife fled. Cox located the wife. Fourth floor."

"Know where he is?"

"Upstairs," Leslie answered as she dialed his number on her cell phone. "Cox," she said when he answered, "what's your ten-twenty?"

"Fourth floor. Second door on right," came the immediate reply. "You coming or what?"

"Be right up."

"That asshole went in by himself," Fischer yelled, when she hung up. "He's going to get himself—and you— hurt, he keeps up this cowboy shit!"

"My money's on worse!" Leslie replied, breaking into a run toward the stairs. She had to wait before starting up to allow an elderly couple to pass. She, using a walker. He, shuffling, his hand firmly on the railing for balance. Confusion was written across their faces.

"Help these two," she instructed the nearest uniform. "Get them to a safe place." Into her mic she said, "Detective Hodges at Flamingo Estates. I'm in the building, going up to the fourth floor. I'm told Detective Cox is up there with an armed female."

Almost instantly, she heard, "Detective Fischer is going in with Hodges. No one leaves without escort to the rec building. Begin identification, we will interview all residents and guests."

"Perimeter's set," came a reply from a voice Leslie did not recognize. "Believe all but the fourth floor are accounted for." Once again, she was thankful Fischer had her back.

Reaching the fourth floor, adrenalin now pumping, Leslie noted that the second door on the right was open a crack. Steading her weapon in front of her, she kicked the door open. Fischer was a few steps behind, his weapon also drawn.

"Sheriff's department!" she yelled. "We're coming in!"

Nothing moved. No sound was heard.

Leslie took several steps to her right, Fischer to his left, their senses on high alert, trying to assess the danger. Anxious as to where Cox was, Leslie glanced over at her partner. Based on Fischer's negative head shake, she feared the worst. Assuming Cox was down, having walked into an ambush, she crouched even further and started toward the kitchen.

"Kitchen clear," she shouted a moment later.

"Front bathroom clear," shouted Fischer almost immediately after that.

The remaining area was open, allowing them to proceed across the living room to a narrow bedroom hallway. Fischer nodded toward a door on the left.

"Before we proceed, let me call Cox."

Fischer again nodded, pressing himself tightly against the wall next to the door.

"That's not good, no answer."

Fischer, using his fingers, counted down from three. At zero, Leslie pushed the door open, only to discover an empty sewing room.

A second door on the left proved to be a guest bedroom. Nobody there either.

The guest bathroom door was open far enough for the detectives to ascertain that it also was empty.

They positioned themselves on either side of a last door, on the right side of the narrow hallway. Leslie nodded her readiness. Fischer flashed three fingers. Then two. Leslie took a deep breath.

One finger. Then none.

Leslie turned the knob and at the same time pushed the door, which flew inward.

A woman sitting in a chair to the left of the door jumped upright, shrieking as she did so. Instinctively, Leslie's gun rotated toward her chest. A larger form off to the right also stood. Leslie's head swiveled in that direction, her weapon following.

"Hold!" Fischer screamed from behind her. "It's Cox!"

"What the hell's going on?" Leslie demanded, when she realized she had come close to shooting her partner. "Why didn't you shout out you were here?"

Cox was on the far side of a bed in which a woman was lying propped up by several pillows. She was holding a dish rag against her left eye, the corner of a plastic bag peeking out from the frayed cloth. "Didn't hear you out there," he said. "My bad. I was concentrating on the ice pack."

"And your phone! You didn't hear that either?"

"Battery's gone. Doesn't work. And you can put your weapons away," Cox announced, "got everything under control. Wife's the one in bed. This woman," Cox continued, pointing to the heavy-set woman standing in front of them, shaking uncontrollably, her hands high over her head, "is her sister, Audrey Canard."

Leslie and Fischer holstered their weapons, and with a mix of anger in her voice with Cox for not being clear on the phone about what was going on and relief that the scene was under control, said to the sister, "You can put your arms down and sit if you want. Sorry for frightening you."

"Cox," Fischer said, "why don't you bring us up to speed here?"

Judging from the tone of the question, Leslie concluded that Fischer had the same reactions as she was having. No doubt, she thought, it was the same feeling a parent might have upon finding her children hiding under a desk after having frantically searched the house for them. Scold or hug? But Cox wasn't a child.

"After you so abruptly departed this morning," Cox began, "I learned that the wife has a sister."

"And just how did you find this sister?"

A sly smile spread slowly across Cox's face. "I checked the Florida driver's license records to see if Binita here listed an emergency contact. Canard's name popped. Called her and here we are."

"I didn't..." the woman in the bed sobbed. "I...I swear I didn't kill him!"

"He was beating you, wasn't he?" Cox said. "That's where that black eye came from."

"He was drunk. More than usual." She lowered the ice from her face revealing a bloody eye socket. "He normally just punches me in the chest. This time he aimed for my face."

"What did you do then?" Leslie asked, realizing the woman's nose was twisted to the right, most likely broken.

"I yelled for him to stop. When he didn't, I…I grabbed a knife. I think I got his hand."

"His hand?" Leslie said, perplexed. "I thought he…" She caught herself, remembering her instructor's admonition to never lead the witness. 'Don't ever give them facts. Don't put words in their mouths. Let the perps hang themselves using their own words. You're nothing more than the scribe.' "You cut his hand. What happened next?"

"He threatened he was going to kill me! He hit me again, this time on the nose. I fell backward. He fell on top of me. I think he tripped. He may have hit his head, I don't know. He lay there long enough for me to get up and run for the car."

"Where did you drive to?" Leslie asked, thinking she could confirm the story by examining traffic cam video.

"I don't know. Just drove. Audi took me in."

"Audi?"

"My sister here, Audrey."

"What time was that?" Fischer asked. "What time did your sister let you in?"

"Don't know exactly. I drove around until the sun came up and I knew Audi would be awake. Maybe around eight."

"Eight-ten," the sister corrected, her voice small, tentative. "I just came out of the shower."

Leslie turned toward the sister. "What did she tell you?"

"Just that her louse of a husband came home drunk again and hit her."

"Did she tell you about cutting him with a knife?"

"No. I was concerned about her eye. I wanted to take her to the hospital, but she just wanted ice on it. Said they ask too many questions."

Turning to Cox, Leslie asked, "Call for a bus?"

"That's what I was doing just before my phone died." Turning to Fischer, Cox asked, "And to what do we owe the honor of your presence?"

"Where my partner goes, I go," Fischer retorted with a scowl.

"I'm Leslie's partner on this one," Cox corrected.

"You're just the temporary stand-in. I'm her actual partner! You got a problem with that, take it up with Boots!"

"Hodges and I are working this…" The remainder of Cox's sentence was unintelligible over the noise made by the paramedic team, led by several black-clad tactical squad members, entering the apartment.

A deep voice commanded, "Police! Drop your weapons! Hands in the air!"

"It's under control!" Fischer called, adding, "We're deputies." He reached for his shield.

"Don't make another move! Get your hands up!" came the immediate reply.

"Everybody's hands where we can see them!" the second man to enter the room barked. "Back away from the bed! All of you! Now!"

"You heard my partner!" Leslie interrupted, turning to face the tactical team. "We're Lee County detectives! And this is my scene! Cox over there is the arresting officer!"

"I said, hands up. Won't say it again!" the lead man repeated, leveling his Glock at Leslie's chest.

"I don't know who dispatched you—and frankly, don't give a shit! We announced our presence! Male and female plainclothes! Never requested assistance. Now, put your weapons down!"

"I didn't hear…"

"She's right," the second tactical officer interceded. "I did hear that. Three deputies are on scene."

"I didn't…" the first man repeated, his hand now wavering.

"This woman here in the bed," Leslie said, taking charge, "requires supervised medical transport. I suggest you step aside and let the medics do their thing."

"Who in the hell…?"

"Deputy Leslie Hodges! That's who! As I said, this is my scene, so get a move on! And put those weapons away before you hurt someone. Scene's secure."

The lead man glared at Leslie, giving himself time to go over his options before issuing the stand down order. The black-clad squad evaporated even faster than they had arrived.

"Transporting to Lee Memorial," one of the paramedics announced by way of information.

"One's the same as the next," Cox replied. "Go for it."

SIX

FISCHER AND HODGES WERE WAITING outside Captain Stetson's office, having both been summoned by her assistant. "If that's her TV I'm hearing," Fischer commented, rolling his eyes, "we're in for it! Boots only uses it to review possible disciplinary videos."

"Who you suppose's being disciplined?" Leslie asked, not grasping what her partner was trying to communicate.

"Unless I miss my guess, that's your voice. Either that, or a very good imitation."

Leslie moved nearer to the closed door and heard herself say, "We're Lee County detectives! And this…" The rest was muffled.

"What the hell! That was when the black knights stormed the sister's apartment. Damn near shot us! What's Boots doing with…"

Stetson suddenly appeared in the doorway. "Get in here and find out! The two of you! Where the hell's Cox?"

"'Detained', all's he said," Stetson's assistant called from her desk across the small waiting room.

"Send him in when he manages to get here!" Stetson ordered, closing the door before turning her attention to the two detectives. "That video came over from the tactical commander. You must know how I dislike getting videos of my detectives from anyone, especially from the tactical commander. What the hell was that about?"

"We're as surprised as you are," Leslie answered. "Neither Fischer nor I called for their help. "

"I was hoping you could shed light on it. And Fischer, why would you even be in that apartment in the first place?"

"Backing up Leslie."

"Not your case! You had no business even responding."

"Leslie's my…"

"Normally, yes. But not on this investigation. You notify dispatch?"

"I confirmed with dispatch I was following up regarding a possible armed suspect wanted for murder."

35

"You do know," Stetson continued, turning her gaze on Leslie, "that when tactical is on scene, they have full command."

"I do know that, yes." Remembering that dispatch had advised her about tactical, Leslie braced for what she anticipated was coming from her boss. Taking the offensive, she ventured, "There was really no reason for them to be there. We had a medical situation and the last thing we needed was further delay. I had the faster ETA."

"It's still their scene! And until they say so, you follow their lead. That clear?"

"Yes. But..."

"There are no buts! They are in charge. Period! End of discussion!"

"All's well that ends well!" Cox announced, coming through the door. "You talking about the wife, Binita Montrose? Happy to say she's out of surgery. Other than a nasty scar down the side of her face, they say she'll make a full recovery."

"Nice of you to join us, Detective," Stetson said. "I was just asking how tactical got involved. Did you..."

"I called for tactical backup. Believed the wife to be armed and dangerous. It's a multi-family building. Didn't want anyone hurt."

"Armed with a gun or knife?" Stetson asked, the sarcasm hanging in the room.

"I suppose a knife," Cox confessed, looking suddenly deflated. "Didn't think much about it. Sorry if I caused..."

"You called tactical for a knife? Evacuated a building you didn't have to. And didn't notify your partner? God knows what other problems you caused. You think that's good police work?" Directing her attention to Leslie, Stetson asked, "And where were you when Cox went to the sister's?"

"We were separated. Before all this, I got a call pertaining to another case and I left Cox to follow up with witness interviews."

"Something you and Fischer are working?"

"Not exactly," Leslie demurred, trying to avoid discussing her conversation with Jakowski. "Just clearing up loose ends."

Stetson guessed what Leslie was referring to and backed off. But it sparked curiosity in Fischer. "Loose ends on what case?" he asked.

"I'll fill you in later. Just paperwork stuff." Leslie hadn't yet made up her mind how much of the drowning case she was prepared to share.

"Fischer, if you and Hodges weren't working together," Stetson contemplated, "why in the world did *you* show up at the sister's building?"

"As I said, I heard my partner respond and went to have her back."

"I'll put that down to partner loyalty, not to good old-fashioned chauvinism."

"May I ask," Fischer said, changing the topic, "why are you reviewing the video of the apartment in the first place?"

"Complaint by tactical of interference by Hodges."

"They serious?"

"Who the hell knows with that bunch. Far as I'm concerned, since none of you drew your weapons on them, and no shots were fired, matter's behind us. Cox and Fischer, out of here. Hodges, a word, please."

When the door closed, Stetson turned to Leslie, "Just be careful with tactical. They play fast and loose—a bit of the old wild west, I suppose. But when we need them, we need them. Period. There's a reason they have command at the scene. Remember that."

"Ten-four, Captain."

"New subject. Van Deere briefed you on the dead diver. I told Cox to do the same. Has he…"

Rolling her eyes, Leslie responded, "He showed up at my home last night, and…"

"Say nothing further. If he goes beyond harmless, then let me know and I'll deal with him. By the way, I saw your assessment of him and I agree. He's a natural detective. Who were you following up with today, then?"

"Jak. He and I have been…"

"I know about your time together with Jak in Europe. Just watch yourself. I'm surprised he's in town. And I'm surprised he's involved with the diver."

"That's just it. I don't know what he knows and doesn't know. He claims not to be working with—or for—Stratis on any matter. Yet, he knows more about a missing Galileo telescope than he should. Unless, of course, he was briefed by the task force."

"Telescope? What the hell's that about?"

Leslie reminded her boss about the Seminal Society—Edison, Chladni, Newton, Galileo, da Vinci, von Wolkenstein—all sharing the same soul over the centuries. "We've had deaths related to the first three. If I follow Jak's thinking, he's tying a telescope rumored to be on the sunken ship to the billionaire collectors."

"By implication then," Stetson commented, "the telescope is tied to the homicide."

"Has the ME posted..."

"An hour ago. It's now official. That's what I wanted to speak to you about. Partner with Cox or Fischer? Your call."

"That's a tough one, Cap. Fischer and I work well together. He's quiet, but thorough. Cox, well Cox drives me crazy. But he's a natural. Man never stops. Chases every loose end no matter where it leads. Nothing escapes him."

"Would you be upset then if I said Cox?"

"As long as I don't have to select."

"Cox it'll be."

"Will Fischer be upset? If this is a Society case, it'll be high profile."

"He's beyond that. He's focused on retirement. Getting shot didn't help. Just be careful out there. You need eyes around the corner. Cox's eyes are everywhere but."

"Do I tell Cox? Or..."

"Give me 'til morning. Don't want it looking like we discussed it."

"That works for me."

"Oh, and one more thing about Jakowski." Stetson paused, waiting for Leslie's full attention. "We both know he's been working with the IRS Task Force and doing so with the blessing of his management. Well...well here's the thing. He may have slipped the tether."

"What does that mean?" Leslie asked, realizing her captain was choosing her words carefully. "Is there more I should know?"

"That's just it. I don't know whether to counsel you to break it off with him until we all get a better handle on his involvement with the Seminal Society collectors, or...or to stay close and see what you can glean from him. I'm of two minds on this one."

"To tell you the truth, so am I," Leslie confessed. "So am I."

Stetson uncharacteristically touched Leslie's shoulder. "I trust your instincts. Don't disappoint. Dismissed."

———◆———

Leslie ducked out the back entrance, not wanting to answer questions about her extended stay with Boots. There was nothing she could do about water cooler talk, but evasive answers would only fuel the gossip. A mile from the sheriff's office, she pulled into a Publix parking lot to pick up dinner. Grilled chicken is what she had on her mind. She rounded out her menu by adding a potato for baking and a green salad.

Checking her phone, she found two voice messages. Jakowski and Cox. Jak's first, she thought, feeling the excitement build within her, tempered now by Boot's warning. "Dinner, your house," the tinny-sounding voice said. "I'm buying—and cooking. Thinking of chicken, Jakowski family style."

She hit the RETURN call button, and he picked up almost immediately. "What the hell's Jakowski family style?" she inquired.

"Need to invite me over to find out."

"You're invited, of course. But tell me what I'm about to eat?"

"You either live dangerously, or you don't. Have I steered you wrong yet?"

"May I remind you; you haven't cooked for me."

"No time like the present. It's five-thirty now. What time?"

"I'm on my way home. Twenty minutes."

"Knock off early?"

"Tell you about it later. I'm sitting in front of Publix. Need anything?"

"Only thing missing is you."

"See you soon."

"Cox," she said into the phone a moment later. "What's up?"

"I suppose you're not about to tell me why you were detained?"

"You just renewed my faith in your deduction skills."

"Thought as much. Timeline's wrong on the Montrose homicide."

"What the hell are you talking about?" Cox's immediate transition into the case they were working threw her. Recovering, she added, "Oh, sorry, I wasn't following. You mean the husband wasn't stabbed when the wife said he was? Or what?"

"That part's right. She claims to have cut him on the hand—or wrist. Man died from blood loss from his neck. Crime scene photos appear to support that fact. Autopsy's not in yet, but I believe that's what we'll find."

"What timeline you concerned about?"

"Clancy Lowry's. Our bakerman. When we went downstairs, the first pastry was just coming out of the oven. According to his work schedule, he should have been turning out product long before that."

"Your thought?" Leslie asked, still not following.

"Bakerman was upstairs enjoying a bit of wife Binita's goodies when her old man stumbles home from the bar. Baker's out of sight, maybe struggling with his pants, when the fight breaks out. Husband goes down, bakerman cuts his throat. Possibly, the wife saw it all. Possibly she ran before he came out of hiding. Haven't worked it all through yet."

"Assuming all that to be true, what do you want from me?"

"Meet me at the bakery around three. Let's document his typical schedule. Bet the ovens are busy long before then."

"Do we need to do this tonight?"

"You got better things to do with your nights? Tell me. I'm all ears."

Holding her temper, Leslie stated calmly, "See you there at three."

"Any chance of din…"

Leslie hung up.

SEVEN

EXPECTING TO SEE A RENTAL in her driveway, Leslie stepped from her car mystified, her attention suddenly refocused on motion off to her right. Her neighbor, a large man whom she had seen many times but never met, was walking toward her. Judging from the eighteen-wheeler cab often parked in his yard to the side of his driveway, she assumed he was an over-the-road trucker. Leslie had observed him occasionally perched on a step stool bent over the engine compartment of the big rig, his upper body lost under the open hood.

"Hey, neighbor," the man called, his voice more southern even than hers. "Strange that after all this time we've never formally met. Name's Lord. Sam Lord. Friends call me Sammy." His voice was strong but seemed labored.

"Leslie Hodges," she replied, walking toward him, her hand extended in greeting. "It's nice to finally meet you. I've seen you out here working on your truck."

"Hope it's okay. You being a sheriff and all. I know it ain't proper to keep my truck there, but you know how it is. Trying to make a living and all."

"No problem," Leslie said, curious as to why he had made it such a point to let her know that he was aware of who she was.

"Do all my own work on 'er. Got three quarter of a million miles on the old gal and she's still goin' strong. Can't afford no down time."

"Forgive me if it's too personal, but you seem to be having trouble breathing. You doing okay?"

"Thanks, but I'm okay. Been deal'n with this for years." Sammy paused a moment, took several breaths, then continued. "But I did want to come over 'cause I just wanted to let you know, neighborly like that, well some guy came by your house twice in the last hour. The last time he even went around back and looked in your windows. Then he went and dug around in the trunk of his car before he left. Got me worried. Somebody did that around my house, I'd sure want to know."

Leslie pulled out her cell phone and scrolled to a picture of Jakowski. "Is this the man you saw?"

"I believe that's him, all right. Big guy."

"He's a friend. Police officer in Pittsburgh, actually."

"Oh. Sorry for getting up in your business. I just…"

"Just a friend. Wasn't expecting him this early."

Before Leslie could say more, a car slowed in front of her house and turned into her driveway, coming to a stop behind her car. "Here he is now."

"Yah. That's him, all right!"

Jakowski walked up to where they were standing. "Pete," she said, "this is my neighbor Sammy. Sammy, this is my friend Pete."

"Pleased to meet you," Sammy said, reaching his hand out in greeting. "You're from Pittsburgh I'm told. I get up there a lot. Love Primanti's. Matter of fact, I'm scheduled to haul grapefruits tomorrow up to Giant Eagle. Big warehouse up there. Well, nice meeting you both."

"Likewise," Jakowski said.

"Safe driving," Leslie called to Sammy's back as he trudged across the lawn connecting their respective properties.

"What was that all about?" Jakowski asked, following Leslie into the house after having retrieved two large shopping bags from his car.

"Came over to introduce himself and say hello. I've seen him working on his truck but hadn't met him."

"Seems a nice enough guy. Been working on that truck for hours. Saw him earlier when I came around, hoping you were home."

"I *do* work for a living. Case you forgot."

"That's why I'm here," Jakowski replied, ignoring the dig.

"What's that mean?"

"I told you Cox called with the name of the woman who saw that diver Franklin go over the side. Wanted to know what I knew. Told him I'd look into it."

"Why do I get the impression you're dancing on a dime?"

"Now it's my turn to ask, what's that mean?"

"Just because Cox called you with a question is no reason for you to fly down here."

"Franklin's suicide raises questions. For starters, before he died, like I said, there were background rumors of an upcoming Seminal Society auction for a Galileo First. Nothing concrete. Got the task force's attention."

Leslie wasn't comfortable sharing information on an ongoing investigation without prior approval, so she refrained from informing Jakowski of the ME's findings. "I suppose," she said noncommittally. "We better get on with dinner. Going to be an early night." Leslie then went on to brief Jakowski on Cox's theory of the homicide they were working on together.

"Let me get this straight. Cox woke you up last night in the middle of the night. And he's doing the same tonight. I sense a pattern forming."

"Sense what you will, I'm meeting him at the bakery. How about firing up the grill?"

"At your service," Jakowski declared, smiling broadly and bowing from the waist. "Don't need the grill. Coming up, the best roasted chicken you ever ate."

"You'll have to go some to outdo my daddy," she said, recalling how much her father loved to cook.

"His grilled or roasted?"

"Grilled."

"Forget it, then. Apples and oranges." The big guy proceeded to spread the contents of his shopping bag on the counter.

"Vodka!" Leslie objected. "Afraid not! Not with meeting Cox and all."

"Not for drinking. Set the oven to three-fifty and get out of the kitchen. It'll take me fifteen minutes to prepare, then two hours in the oven."

"We won't be eating until…" she checked her watch. "Almost nine!"

"Hey, I'm not the one scheduling middle-of-the-night stakeouts."

"I didn't schedule it. Is that jealousy I'm hearing?"

"Should it be?"

"You have nothing to fear from Cox. He's my partner. Nothing more."

"In that case," Jakowski winked, "two hours'll give us plenty of *quality* time. Don't want to waste a minute of what little time we do have."

Leslie kissed him, stood for a moment watching while he mixed paprika with salt and pepper, then turning to chop the onions and whatever else he had brought, his hands moving faster than her eye could follow. Not for the first time, she asked herself what was it about this man that excited her. Not normally one for flights of fancy, she felt herself drawn to him in a way she couldn't put words around. She left him to his work and went upstairs to shower.

———◆———

Getting on top of her emotions in the middle of the night proved more difficult than Leslie could have predicted. Less than four hours of sleep hadn't helped the situation. With concurrent homicide investigations on her plate, this promised to be a long day. She was beginning to share Jakowski's disdain for Cox and his squirrely methods. But she had to admit, the guy got results.

Pulling up outside Lowry's Bakery eight minutes early, Leslie was surprised that Cox was nowhere in sight. A moment later a loud rap on the window next to her head startled her into reaching for her weapon. But it was, in fact, only Cox, who walked around the car and slipped in beside her.

"Get yourself shot, you scare me like that," Leslie snapped after he pulled the door closed behind him. "Where the hell you come from? Didn't see you anywhere."

"That's a plus, my dear partner. Give a guy credit where credit is due," he laughed. "Over there," he said, pointing to a dimly lit alley almost directly across from the bakery, several large trash cans blocking the view. "Saw our subject roll in. He lit the ovens. A moment ago he put several trays in."

"How the hell you know what he did in the back of the shop?"

"When he opens an oven, the flare backlights him. The first one caught me by surprise. Here's a video of the second and third ovens being loaded." Cox held his phone so Leslie could see the baker loading pastry trays into two ovens. "Took this one just before you got here. From two forty-three to two forty-four."

"Proving what?"

"Not exactly proof. It confirms that his routine is just like he said. He gets in around two-thirty and begins the day's baking."

"On the morning Montrose died," Cox continued, "nothing went into the ovens until just before we arrived at his place. Closer to four than to three. And his helper, I think his name is Clement, wasn't there. Coincidence?"

"You liking Lowry as the perp? On what? Him not getting your breakfast into the oven on time? Circumstantial at best."

"Thin, maybe. Add in my interview with the bartender down there where Chase Montrose liked to tie one on."

Leslie turned in the direction Cox was pointing but saw only houses. "Down where?"

"You can't exactly see it from here, but there's a pocket bar, a little place, been there forever, just a few buildings down. Below a walk-up boarding house. Whorehouse, you ask me. Ol' Chase would tie one on and they'd point him home. When he was really bad, someone would call the missus, warn her."

"What about last night?"

"Chase was really into it. Said he had enough of his two-timing wife. Threatened he'd 'fix the old broad so no man ever looks at her again!' And that's a direct quote."

Before responding, Leslie took a moment to process what she was hearing. "Bakerman did say he heard Montrose yell something about him cutting off her nose. Sounds like Binita was stepping out."

"Been known to happen." Cox gave one of his winks, indicating he knew more than he was saying.

"Now all we need to do is prove it," Leslie challenged, silently acknowledging that Cox was probably right in his assessment. "You got a plan?"

"Happens, I do. Guy parks his car in a little private lot two doors down from the bakery, then walks down an alley and goes in the bakery's back door. There appears to be a traffic camera on the corner just before the alley entrance. Maybe we'll get lucky and that camera caught the time of his arrival yesterday."

"Can't get lucky if you don't buy a ticket. Go for it. Meanwhile, let's set up a neighborhood canvas. I learned years ago when I started out in Tampa, that the husband is always the last to know. We may find that the street knows who she's seeing."

"Wouldn't that be nice," Cox said. "Come on. I'll buy you breakfast. There's a little place a couple blocks from here."

"At this hour? My God, it's four-thirty!"

"Opens early for the fishing crowd. Never too early to fish. Bet the place is already going strong."

"I know better than to get between you and eating. Meet you there."

———————

Cox was dead on. The place was packed and twenty minutes before they could get a table, they were told. Leslie shook her head as if to say, *"Let's move on"*.

He looked up from his phone long enough to chide, "You got someplace better to be?"

She glared at him, saying nothing until he slipped the phone into his pocket. "What's so friggin' important this early in the morning?"

"Luck's holding. Night desk says they have a male, about two hundred pounds, entering the alley at two-thirty-five. No facial, but good profile."

"Anything the night before?"

"Not that lucky. Not yet anyway."

"Deputy Cox," the hostess called, "we've found you a table."

"Deputy Cox," Leslie teased, *"we've found you a table.* I take it you've been here once or twice before."

"Touché. You made your point."

Leslie accepted the acknowledgement with an inner smirk, glanced at the menu and ordered oatmeal when the waitress appeared.

"No brown sugar? Fruit? Something?" Cox chided. "No wonder you're so sk...slender."

"Cox, I told you to stay out of my personal life! And I mean it. Stay out!"

"Just caring for you. One partner to another."

"Let's just stick to business. I don't want to tell you that again. What I eat, who my friends are, what I do on my own time—off limits. You hear me?"

"Ten-four. Speaking of business, boss posted that we'll be working together on the Derrick Franklin drowning."

"Two homicides at once? Isn't that a bit much?"

"I suppose everyone else is busy. We do make a good team. You have to admit that."

"Any idea where we start?" Leslie asked, ignoring his implied question and steering the conversation away from her personal feelings.

"How about we go see the owner of Masters Marine Salvage & Rescue. A retired admiral, goes by Big Mack."

"That's where Franklin worked."

"How'd you know that?" Cox asked, regarding her suspiciously. "You been briefed on this case?"

"Curious is all. After you called this morning—I suppose that was actually yesterday morning—I looked him up. Company's owned by Makenzie Madison Masters. Retired Navy. Admiral, actually"

"Business press, when they want to be snarky, calls her Big Mack. She prefers Three M."

"It's too early to call and set something up."

"Okay. So, we finish up breakfast, I'll stop home, freshen up. See you at her house at nine. Take our chances." Cox hurriedly finished his waffle before reaching for his cell. "Here, I'll text you her address. See you at nine." He stood, tab in hand, and headed for the door.

Looking down at her phone, Leslie saw that the address was in Miromar Lakes, an enclave where even the most modest homes cost well into seven figures. It was an area she was getting to know all too well from two prior cases, each involving the Seminal Society.

EIGHT

LESLIE FOLLOWED COX ONTO THE MASTERS' curving driveway, almost slamming into his car when he stopped abruptly to avoid hitting a silver Bentley that had materialized from under an opening garage door and begun backing out. Cox's car rocked to a stop inches from the Bentley's back bumper, whereupon the driver's door flew open and a scowling woman marched directly toward Cox.

Leslie stayed seated behind her steering wheel, taking in the scene while recalling what ME Van Deere had said about this woman—her husband's cousin. The woman was even more imposing than Leslie had expected: Square chin and hard eyes evincing no trace of humor. Tall and broad-shouldered. And with work-hardened hands that were now firmly planted on her surprisingly trim waist as she confronted Cox through his driver's side window.

"What the hell are you doing in my driveway?" she screamed. "Damn near wrecked my car! And you!" she demanded, her flaming eyes shooting in Leslie's direction, "What the hell?"

"We're sheriff's deputies, Admiral Masters" Leslie asserted, getting out of her car and facing the angry woman. "We have a few questions about your employee who just died. Derrick Franklin."

"Hey, you want my time, you set up an appointment! Now out of my way if you damn well please! I have a company to run! Hell, I'm late already!"

Cox, for his part, having no intention of being pushed around, threw his car door open, forcing Masters to take a quick backward step. "Like my partner said," he interjected, "we'd appreciate a few minutes of your time to get your take on the Derrick Franklin situation. Unfortunately, death investigations don't run by the clock."

Cox, Leslie noted, was being careful not to call it a homicide investigation—or even suspicious. There would be time enough for that after receiving Big Mack's statement.

At this second mention of the deceased diver's name, Masters' eyes softened just enough to clue Leslie in so that despite her annoyance, she was listening. As fast as the acknowledgment had come, her command face was reset. "I'm late! Get your cars out of my way. Now!"

Leslie nodded to Cox, asking, "When will it be convenient for you?"

"My office can handle all that. Call and set something up."

Cox slowly climbed back into his car, waited for Leslie to do the same, then backed out of the driveway, following Leslie's lead. The Bentley accelerated past them, slowing at the corner intersection an instant before resuming speed. It was quickly lost from sight.

Cox pulled alongside Leslie, their driver's doors beside each other. "You going to set the meeting up, or should I?"

"Someone wants to talk to us." Leslie pointed to a man walking toward them from the direction of the Masters' house.

"Did I hear you say you're deputies?" the man asked, when Leslie approached. "I'm Henry Masters. This about Franklin?"

Unlike his wife, this Masters smiled openly. Leslie knew from long experience that appearances could be deceiving and there was no reason to think that Henry Masters was an exception. "We came by to speak with your wife about him," she began. "We understand he was an employee of hers."

"I can't imagine why Derrick would kill himself. He had everything to live for. Poor man. At least he didn't leave a family."

"So then, you knew him?" Cox asked.

"Of course! He was our chief diver. And a friend."

"By 'our' you mean Masters Marine Salvage and Rescue?"

"Yes. We usually refer to it just as MMS&R."

"I take it you're part of the company?" Cox said.

"Own it. Along with Kenzie. She's the president. I'm vice president of HR. She's not much of a people person as I'm sure you just gathered. Leaves that part of the job to me."

"Mind answering a few questions?" Leslie asked, sensing Masters wanted to talk about his friend. "We're trying to piece together what happened."

"What happened is Benny shot himself and fell off that ferry."

"Benny?" Cox and Leslie queried simultaneously.

"Derrick. In his early days, or so I'm told, he got the bends so many times it stuck. Been known as Benny long as I've known him. About twenty years, give or take."

Leslie glanced toward the house. "Is there a place we could sit?"

"Sorry. I thought this would be quick. Come around to the pool."

Masters led the detectives around the side of the house and into a two-story lanai that appeared to be larger than Leslie's entire home. The pool extended toward the horizon and seemed to blend with a lake, blurring the demarcation as to where one ended and the other began. Masters pointed toward a far corner where several padded chairs surrounded a fire pit. "Can I get either of you coffee? I've just made a fresh pot. Or if you prefer something stronger, I can..."

"No thanks," Leslie answered, taking a seat facing the lake.

Cox declined as well, taking a chair separated slightly from Leslie.

Masters sat opposite them, squinting to keep the sun from his eyes.

"Mind if I record our conversation?" Leslie asked.

"No problem. Do what works for you."

"What was Franklin's job at MMS&R?" she asked, clicking her phone into record mode and placing it on the table between her and Cox.

"Director of diving operations," Masters responded.

"Does that include sunken treasure ships?"

"Everything below water was his domain. Benny—Derrick— was a real pro and he'll be greatly missed. We're already feeling the impact. That's where my wife was off to this morning. A dive gone wrong."

"Was he worried about anything you know of?"

"Nothing at work."

"Personal life?"

"Wasn't married. No girlfriends that I know about. Benny was all about diving. Loved the water."

"Do you have any thoughts—any theory at all—as to why he would shoot himself?"

"Can't think of any reason whatsoever. He had everything to live for."

"What's that mean?" Leslie probed.

"You know about the *Buen Jesús*?"

"What's that?"

"Spanish sailing vessel sank in sixteen-twenty-two in the Gulf of Mexico off the Florida coast, west of Key West. Ship was full to the gunwales with treasure. Gold, jewels, you name it. Was on its way back to Spain from South America. Historians claim the sinking caused the collapse of the Spanish Empire."

"I understand your company recovered that treasure. That right?"

"We did."

"How does that work?" Cox broke in. "I mean, who exactly does the treasure belong to?"

"Great question. Every situation is different. If the Archaeological Resources Protection Act applies, as it did in this case, then the feds get involved. So does Florida. The whole question of who was entitled to what was in litigation for several years before the lawyers were able to negotiate a workable settlement."

"I take it MMS&R came out okay in the end," Cox said.

"Can't really complain. But my opinion, not as much as we should have. After all, it was Benny who found the vessel. Mostly buried. He and his crew carefully dug out and catalogued the antiquities over a two-year period. It was his work that allowed for the settlement."

"I suppose he was well compensated for his work," Leslie guessed.

"Handsomely."

"Mind telling us how much?" Cox asked.

"That's private information."

"What was MMS&R's share?" Cox insisted.

"That's also private, I'm afraid." Standing, he continued, "Now, if you're through here, I do have to get to work. I hope you got what you came for."

"Thank you for your time, Mr. Masters," Leslie replied, also standing. Taking one last glance out over the lake, she held her phone in front of her. "Please, for the record, state your full name and address, if you will."

"Henry Van Deere Masters and I live at...."

"Van Deere? Any relation to the medical examiner, Dr. Margarete Van Deere?" Cox asked.

"Her husband Sam is my cousin."

"So, you took your wife's surname when you married?" Leslie commented. "Don't see that happen all that much. Well, thank you for your time. We'll call for a time to see your wife."

"She's a busy woman. Didn't I just give you what you're looking for?"

"We don't yet know what we're looking for. Just gathering facts. Everyone sees things differently." Leslie's finger poised over the STOP RECORDING button. "That catalogue you mentioned earlier. The one Franklin compiled. Do you happen to have a copy you could give us?"

"As a matter of fact, I was just looking at it when you pulled up. I'll make a copy for you. Wait here, please."

50

"Surprised he's giving us the catalogue," Cox said after Masters had left. "With all the fuss over compensation, I expected him to turn you down flat."

"Always pays to ask. It's in the court documents in any event. Just take us that much longer to get it."

Cox had walked to the back of the lanai and was looking out over a lake, his eye following an attractive woman with white hair walking her little white dog on the white sand beach. "A Portrait in White. That's what I'd call it. A Portrait in White."

"Call what?" Leslie returned, confused by Cox's reference.

"The scene from this backyard. Everything's white."

"Not really. The water's blue. The trees are..."

"Everything important is white. The woman's hair, her dress, her dog. Even the sand she's walking on."

"I look out and see trees and sky and the water. You only see the woman. You need help."

"We all have our priorities, Leslie. Even you."

"What's that supposed to..."

"I'm sorry to disappoint you," Masters called, stepping into the lanai from a side door, "but our lawyer said to give you nothing more."

Leslie slowly walked around the pool to where Masters was standing and when she was less than a foot away, her face set hard, said, "Don't know what hole you're trying to cover, but it sure just got a lot deeper." She turned to leave, but not before she said, "You said Franklin didn't have any girlfriends that you knew about. What about men? Any friends?"

"Last question I'll answer. His life was diving. When he wasn't working, he was out on or below the water for pleasure. I think he had one or two buddies from his college football days who'd go out on the boat with him. Hey, all this for a suicide?"

"A man died," Leslie said, "It's our job to know why."

NINE

LESLIE CHECKED THE TIME, NOTING IT was exactly noon. Only four minutes had passed since she had last looked, but it seemed much longer. She had started working shortly after three in the morning, with minimal sleep, and was now having a hard time concentrating. She called Jakowski to see if he wanted to meet her for a quick lunch.

Her call went to voicemail, and she hung up without leaving a message.

Through a foggy cloud, she heard Cox's voice. "What do you make of Masters?"

She shook herself back to consciousness. "Which one?"

"You okay?"

"Nothing sleep won't cure."

"Knock off and go home. You've already worked a nine-hour day."

Ignoring her partner, she asked, "What have you found?"

"Franklin—Benny—was doing okay for himself. Salary looks to be two-fifty a year. Not too shabby. In the past few weeks, several deposits were posted. Totaling a bit over three mil."

"You're right. Not hurting for money. Total assets?"

"Working it."

"What about Masters? And which one are you talking about?"

"Admiral. Not enough for a court order. But I'm thinking multiples of Benny."

"Based on?"

"I pulled the court docs. And…"

"What court…?"

"Remember Masters said there was a court settlement?"

"Sorry. Go on."

"And the inventory Benny wrote up had numbers scribbled near many of the items. I'm guessing those numbers are someone's estimates of street value."

"Go on."

"Total is…wait for it…close to a billion dollars."

"You're kidding me! Shit! How close?"

"Does it really matter how close? What's a few million when you're in the billion range? Rounding error."

"Up in Tampa, the mob calls a million or so 'walking around money'. You're talking a billion. And Benny only received three million? Hey, as I think about it, maybe he really was despondent?"

"Les, give me three million, see how despondent I'll be."

"You got a point there. You have a copy?"

"Of the inventory? It's in the file."

Leslie pulled up the document and studied the list, now wide awake. A few minutes later she exclaimed, "I can't believe all that gold! And Inca jewels, pottery. The list is endless! Where did all that stuff go?"

"Sotheby's, from what I can determine."

"Auction?"

"No evidence of an auction. I believe they sold it privately. They gave me the 'confidential' crap when I called."

"I don't see a Galileo telescope listed."

"There isn't. What makes you think there should be?"

Holding information away from a partner was not something Leslie did lightly. But she still wasn't ready to come completely clean. "I see there's some sort of a letter from Galileo explaining the dimensions of the telescope he used to confirm sunspots. From what I know, that was what convinced him he could no longer deny that the earth went around the sun, leading to him eventually being found guilty of heresy by a Papal Inquisition. With Galileo involved, you know what this could be, don't you?"

"The Seminal Society!" Cox said. "Has all the markings!"

"Certainly, the telescope Galileo used to first see sunspots would qualify as a Seminal First," Leslie added, concealing the fact that she had already known of the linkage.

"Combine that with documentation of dimensions that could be used to prove authenticity, and we have a perfect artifact to pique the interest of those billionaire collectors."

"Big Mack could possibly now qualify as a Seminal Society collector," Leslie suggested, remembering her conversation with the ME. The telescope in question was the one Galileo used to first see the moons of Jupiter. The one he named after the Medici family. Leslie didn't recall any discussion of sunspots.

"What about the dimensions document? How much is that worth?"

"Seventy-five million," Cox immediately spit out, having memorized the values.

"If the document is worth seventy-five million, what the hell would the telescope go for? Assuming there even was a telescope."

"Half a billion," Cox said. "Or maybe even more."

"How about this for a hypothesis? The missing telescope is central to Franklin's death."

"If there really is a missing telescope," Cox replied, his voice suggesting doubt.

"You don't think..."

"My problem is, why then shoot himself? And shoot himself so close to the stern that he'd fall overboard? Frankly, if he was intent on taking his own life, I'd think he'd shoot himself when the boat was in deep water. Not within sight of land."

Rolling her tired eyes, Leslie groused, "That's the problem. Everybody has questions, nobody has answers."

—————

Leslie awoke shortly after five the next morning, fully expecting Jakowski to be in the bed beside her. She had called him twice more yesterday, once on her drive home from the office at three, and once more before she fell asleep shortly after eight. Both times her calls had gone to voicemail. She had even texted him, asking for a return call. She now studied her phone and noted that the text message had not been delivered.

Her disappointment with the big Pittsburgh detective dissolved into concern for his well-being. She promptly dialed his number, and again her call immediately went to voicemail. She then accessed the National Trauma Data Bank to see if by chance he had been involved in an accident.

Nothing came up.

Without thinking about the early hour, she called the hard-nosed head of the Department of Treasury task force, Agent Maxine Ghana, who had been heading up the tax fraud investigation of the billionaire Seminal Society collectors. "Ghana here. Leave your callback number. I'll get to you when I can." The crisp, brusque voice of Ghana's voicemail vividly called to mind the solidly built, black woman with wide-set eyes, high cheekbones and short curly hair that made her face appear round. The woman was taller than Leslie and from Leslie's point of view, built to be effectively aggressive.

"This is Leslie Hodges. Lee County sheriff's deputy. Sorry to call so early in the day. I've been trying to reach Jakowski since yesterday afternoon. He's not returning my calls. Do you happen to know where he is?"

Thirty-five minutes later, as Leslie was finishing up in the bathroom after a hot shower, her phone sounded and displayed the name GHANA. "Sorry to have called so early," Leslie said into the phone. "Thanks for calling me back."

"I'm an early riser," Ghana replied, her tone friendlier than Leslie had anticipated. "Thought I'd do some checking around before calling you back. Truth is, we also lost track of your friend. Last we have him is at your house."

"Thought I'd check. I've called his phone several times. Goes to voicemail. No response to text either."

"If we locate him," Ghana volunteered, "we'll let you know."

"Is he working with you on a missing Galileo telescope?"

"You know I can't discuss task force operations," Ghana chided, her tone containing what in her case passed for a smile. "Care to tell me what you know about that subject?"

Leslie's first instinct was to decline the invitation. Perhaps with a colorful expletive thrown in for good measure. *"Bad idea,"* she told herself. "I suppose I should repeat to you what you just told me about not discussing ongoing investigations. But I came to you for information, so I suppose sharing's called for. We don't have much, other than speculation. A man, Derrick Franklin, a diver, apparently shot himself and fell off a ferry from Key West. We recovered his body. One theory is that his death has something to do with an extremely valuable telescope."

"And you believe this...this *'theory'* that a telescope caused his death. Is that it?"

Something in the agent's voice triggered Leslie's instincts. "Agent Ghana, you want to tell me something, tell me. You don't, don't. But don't toy with me. I'm not much into games, so don't play with me!"

"And neither am I, Detective, into games. Neither am I. If telescopes are important to you, go talk to Professor Hammerschmidt. You met with him in Fort Smith at the..."

"University of Arkansas. Sir Reggie is the world expert on Newton's *Philosophiæ*. How the hell does that help with telescopes?"

"Newton's not all he's an expert in. Newton, Galileo—and even da Vinci—fall within his purview. I suggest you look up your friend."

"If you're suggesting I fly to..."

"How about a two-hour drive to Miami. Think Setai. Good luck with your criminal investigation."

Ghana dropped the connection with her accustomed abruptness. It was immediately replaced by Cox. "Leslie?" he asked, surprise in his voice. "Didn't..."

"Who'd you expect to answer my phone?"

"Not you. Thought you'd be sound asleep. Or otherwise occupied."

Now it was her turn to terminate the connection. When Cox immediately called back, she was tempted to allow the call to go to voicemail.

Instead, she answered it on the fourth ring. "What's so important it can't wait?" she barked into the phone. "These early morning calls are becoming a nasty habit!"

"Thought you'd want to know. I woke up at two. Decided to go stake out the bakery, see what the bakerman's up to."

"Learn anything we didn't already know?"

"Sort of. First, there's an alarm on his back door where he enters. I'm thinking we could get records of the times he's gone in and out in the past few days. That might place him at the scene."

"Problem is, as you know, the surveillance video we have of the entrance to the Montrose apartment only shows the deceased, Chase, entering. Nothing puts the baker up there."

"Well, here's the thing about that," Cox answered, his voice upbeat. "In the back alley there's a fire escape leading up to the Montrose apartment."

Visualizing the scene, Leslie agreed. "Yes, I recall the fire escape. But it's folded up, rather high. Designed to lower when a person's weight's applied—from the top. It'll be hard to access from the ground."

"Yes, but not impossible to pull down from the alley."

"It's too high for even a tall person to be able to jump up and grab it. A good fifteen feet."

"Any chance of you having a rope handy?"

"I can manage that," Leslie answered, thinking of the unpacked boxes from her years in Tampa. The boxes were mostly her deceased husband's 'toys' as she had always called them, stored in the backyard shed awaiting the day when she could bring herself to deal with them. "Junior had lots of ropes. Just have to go out back and get one."

"I'll be in the alley behind the bakery when you get here," Cox instructed. "Better to do this sooner rather than later."

Leslie was tempted to ask what the hurry was, but she thought better of it. Cox was always anxious to do what was on his mind. "Get there as soon as I can," she answered, hanging up before he could issue any more orders.

———

There was just enough visibility for Leslie to make her way from her house the few steps across the back lawn to the shed. It had been over a year since she had last been inside and she was anxious about what she would find. Working the combination, she thought she heard movement inside. Visualizing a swarm of rats feasting on the cardboard boxes, she pulled the door open and quickly stepped back out of the doorway.

Using her flashlight, she cautiously peered inside, expecting the worst, but discovering the best. Nothing had been disturbed and nothing was moving.

It took Leslie longer than she had anticipated to find a rope long enough. Junior, her deceased husband, had taken up boating in Tampa where they both had been on the police force. He was a detective first-class, and she a patrol officer. They would spend their leisure time, the little they had, exploring Tampa Bay in a small boat driven by a 20-hp Honda outboard motor. Most of the boating stuff had been sold, but not all. Problem was, the box of ropes had been mislabeled, causing her to go through several before finding the right one.

Turning to leave, she instinctively ducked at movement in her neighbor's yard. A minute passed and nothing more was seen. Concluding that what she had sensed must have been a momentary headlight, Leslie walked out of the shed, saw nothing unusual, closed and locked the shed door. She then proceeded to her car, unaware that Sammy, her neighbor, was crouched in the shadows, less than ten feet from the shed.

TEN

THE DRIVE TO MEET COX TOOK LESS than fifteen minutes, during which time she replayed what she knew of the 'telescope murder', as she had begun to think of Franklin's death. She knew next to nothing of Franklin, the person. What his hobbies were, who he hung out with, where he lived, what he drove, lifestyle, were all blanks. Had he ever been married? What about children? Did he prefer male friends over female? Music? Sports? Gambling?

Leslie's growing wish list for knowing the deceased diver was cut short when she turned the corner into the narrow alley, the morning light just bright enough to see a silhouette of Cox leaning against a fence between trash cans.

"You sure took long enough," he said when she rolled down the passenger side window. "Got the rope?"

"In the trunk."

"Pop it. Then park down there," he instructed, pointing to an open area between two construction containers. "I'll wait for you."

A moment later Leslie found Cox standing under the horizontal section of the fire escape looking up in puzzlement. "I was planning on throwing the rope up over the railing and pulling the ladder down. But..."

"There's nothing for the rope to grab onto," Leslie acknowledged. "When I saw the fire escape when we first were in the apartment, I thought about the safety of living in a place where someone could easily climb up the ladder. That's why I knew this one was high." She reached into a plastic bag, producing a brick. "Here, I brought this from my yard. I think the neighbor's dog dropped it. Tie the rope around the brick and heave it up over the rail."

"That'll make a racket. Wake everyone," Cox commented, taking the brick in his right hand. "I'm not sure this is a good idea."

"Got a better plan?"

"Okay, stand back," Cox warned, tying the rope to the brick and double-checking the knot to make sure it was tight. "Here goes. Never was good at baseball."

The brick sailed over the railing and landed on the metal scaffolding with only a small ping.

"Good throw," Leslie said, genuinely impressed.

"I lucked out on that one. I really did."

"Looked like an old pro to me. Makes me wonder how many times you've done this before."

"Never. Would you believe..."

"Watch out!" Leslie suddenly swung her arm out to push Cox back into the street to keep him from getting hit by the descending ladder.

Cox luckily had taken a step back when he yanked on the line, so that the ladder barely missed him when it thudded onto the sidewalk. "Didn't think it would come down that fast or that easy. Like it was just greased. Smooth. I barely put any muscle to it."

"You thinking what I'm thinking?"

"I'm thinking, fire escape's being used on a steady basis. That your thought as well?"

"Appears that way. Let's get the crime scene folks back out here. Take prints. See if we can figure out who's been using this puppy."

"Good idea, Les. I'll call."

"Shit!" Leslie exclaimed. "Don't know why I didn't think of this sooner! Remember when we first interviewed the bakerman?"

"Sure do. He was baking great-smelling stuff."

"We had no reason to inventory his work area, but I'm visualizing the back door. Do you recall what was leaning in the corner near that door?"

"Can't say as I do. What do you mean, 'visualizing the back door'?"

"Usually, if I see something, anything, the image burns into memory whether or not I consciously know I've seen that image."

"You mean like photographs?"

"Like photographs you don't even know you have."

"How cool is that? What do you see?"

"Leaning up against the back wall in a corner is one of those telescoping poles. The kind used to change light bulbs."

"Everyone having lightbulbs in high ceilings has one."

"Except, the lights in the bakery are LEDs. No need to change them."

"Possibly just an old one hanging around."

"Doubt it," Leslie replied. "He didn't strike me as a man who keeps things around. That place was spotless."

"Time to get a search warrant?"

"Let's hold off. See what forensics finds on the fire escape. You have him on record claiming never to have been up in the Montrose apartment before this last time. A couple of errant fingerprints will give us all we need for a warrant."

Tempering his impatience, Cox changed the subject. "You up for breakfast? Back here smelling the bakery got my juices running."

"Is there anything that doesn't get you hungry?"

"How do you smell that cinnamon and not get hungry?"

"I must admit, the scent is calling to me. And besides, we need to discuss diver Derrick. I know nothing about the man. Same place as yesterday?"

"See you there. Their pecan pancakes are to die for. Trust me."

"Food is perhaps the *only* thing I'll trust you on. Now give me back my rope and don't forget to push that ladder back up. I assume it's on a balance mechanism. See you at the restaurant."

———◆———

"There's not a crumb on your plate," Cox pointed out. "That's not your style. Tells me all I need to know about the pancakes."

"My trust was well placed," Leslie acknowledged. "Let's go over what we know about Derrick Franklin. He's a long-time diver, tops in his field I believe. We know he worked for Masters for about twenty years. Salary somewhere around two hundred K."

"Plus a percentage of the salvage value of what comes off the bottom. Forensics accounting believes his average yearly income for the last four years is around a million. Give or take. That's consistent with him having an estate over on the Caloosahatchee River. You gotta see the place."

"What does he drive?"

"Six cars registered to him. Five are vintage. Two are at his home. Three in storage. He drives a Lamborghini Huracán EVO. The one we found in the ferry parking lot."

"Any video of him driving into or out of the lot?"

"Ferry company's been slow to produce the surveillance video. If we don't have it by noon today, I'll get a warrant. It's footage of the outside public area covering the lot. Can't see an issue getting the warrant."

"How about footage from county cameras? Surely, he was picked up at least on *one* camera between his 'estate' and the ferry.

In fact, let's try to find him on tape for, say, a week before he died. Get a pattern of his life. I'd like to know where he went, who he hung with, you know the drill."

"On it. Anything else bothering you?"

Leslie looked at Cox with a puzzled expression. "What makes you ask?"

"You're pretty good—I'd say the best I've ever seen—at reading people. I'm not all that bad myself. And right now, you're debating telling me something you know. I'll find out eventually, so let's get it on the table."

Leslie had to acknowledge Cox was indeed good at reading her. She hadn't told him about her conversation with Agent Ghana and the reference to Professor Reginald Hammerschmidt. He was right, she was duty-bound to enter all that into the file. Her concern was explaining why she had contacted the task force. She also knew that the longer she held out, the worse the situation would become. "You're reading me right," she acknowledged. "Spoke to Agent Ghana. You know who she is?"

"DHS task force. Your friend Jak works with them. What about Ghana?"

"For the record, I believe the task force is Treasury, not Homeland Security, for what that's worth. They play everything so close, it's hard to tell what they're up to—or who they even work for."

"In my mind, they're interchangeable. Wouldn't be surprised to learn they have two-sided badges. Tell me about Ghana."

"She knows we're investigating Franklin. To me that means Franklin's death is somehow tied to that Galileo telescope supposedly on the sunken ship. Won't tell me anything about that telescope, but pointed me to Professor Hammerschmidt, from…"

"Ol' Sir Reggie! World's expert on Newton, Galileo, Da Vinci and all those Renaissance rock stars. You met with him up in Arkansas. You and your…" Cox took a long second to come up with the right word. Finally settling on, "… good buddy, Jakowski. Well, this time it'll be yours truly with you over in Miami, not him."

"And just how'd you know Reggie would be in Miami?" Leslie asked, unable to suppress her surprise that Cox knew the whereabouts of the artifact expert.

"That's what I'm paid to do." Cox continued, "Don't know if you've seen it, but forensics posted what they found in Franklin's car and home."

"What time was that? Didn't see it."

"Late yesterday. Around midnight. They're still going through his computer. Tons of files on Dropbox. Man was a life-long journaler. On paper, and electronically."

"Shit! Not like me to miss it!" Leslie was angry with herself for taking her eye off the ball. "Anything suggest suicide?"

"Nothing yet. Much of what they found is coded. Some of the codes are easy. But some...some are proving difficult."

"Example?"

"Well, not coded at all was a copy of the manifest from the sunken ship. It had on it the telescope and a notation, SS."

"Seminal Society!" Leslie guessed.

"My take as well. Got me thinking."

"One that *was* coded?"

"The coordinates for the ship that sank in sixteen-twenty-two, the *Buen Jesús y Nuestra Señora del Rosario*, were essentially not coded. Twenty-four, sixteen point seventy-six and eighty-two, fifty point sixty-six. He simply combined the degree and minute numbers and omitted the N for latitude and W for longitude."

"Where is that exactly?"

"Due west of the Dry Tortugas."

"I was told west of Key West."

"Pretty far west."

"Gulf of Mexico?"

"Barely."

"Mind if I study the file a few minutes?"

"Take all the time you need. We're not going anywhere for a few hours."

"You have plans?"

"Thought we'd go examine Franklin's car. Then check out his digs. Get a feel for the guy."

"I have the car on the screen now. That's some piece of machinery! Quarter mil?"

"Over three hundred. Dig that blue. Think he had it specially painted? Never seen a color that...that intense. In a good way. See him coming a mile off."

———————

"That's one gorgeous car!" Leslie acknowledged when the vivid blue Lamborghini came into view in the otherwise drab chain link-enclosed county auto pound. "The picture doesn't do this puppy any favors. Never seen this shade blue!"

"Stands out all right. Especially among these clunkers." Cox waved his arm in a circle as if to include all the cars on the lot. "He certainly wasn't one to hide under a barrel."

"I saw in the file where he played professional football for Tampa Bay. Starter for several years until he was injured. Surprised a big man like that could even get into something so sleek."

"You'd be surprised. At that price, I bet they'll custom make the seat to fit any size butt."

"I suppose."

"Wasn't Jakowski a football player? He doesn't have this kind of money. Not from what I know of him, anyway."

"Cox, if that was a question, the answer is I don't believe so. Jak was injured early in his career. He might have had a nice signing bonus, but never a follow up—or whatever it's called—contract. Seems Franklin did okay for himself. Even before he hit it big with the diving."

"We're in the wrong profession. All's I can say."

"You planning on taking up diving? I'm thinking you're beyond football."

"Never was much for sports. Got the height, not the weight."

Leslie refrained from stating the obvious; lack of discipline. "From something Jakowski said a while back about his time in Tampa when the Steelers played the Bucs, he caught up with some college teammates. I wonder if he and Franklin knew each other."

"Says here," Cox said a moment later after consulting his phone, "that Franklin played for Pitt."

"So did Jakowski."

"Assume then, they were friends," Cox said, slipping his phone into his pocket.

"Makes sense," Leslie agreed, dodging the real issue as to why Jakowski hadn't told her. Pulling on her gloves, she opened the door and popped the trunk. Peering inside, she was surprised to find a massive 630-hp pristine engine. "Where the hell's the trunk on this thing?"

"Up front, under the bonnet," Cox called from within the sleek vehicle. He reached his hand down and touched a lever.

"Not much room for luggage," Leslie commented a moment later. "I'd say less than four cubic feet. Nothing here but a leather bag. Empty," she called to her partner, holding it open for his inspection. "Appears to have a whitish stain on the bottom. Almost as if liquid evaporated."

"Don't remember any stain from the report," Cox replied, easing himself out from inside the luxurious car and joining her at the front. "Bag yes. Stain no."

"Other than this bag, the cargo space is empty."

"I would have thought we'd find diving equipment, goggles, a spare regulator, that sort of thing. Means he must use one of his other vehicles for diving."

"A boat at least, I'd think," Leslie said, thinking back to the file report. "I didn't see any boats listed, but there is a truck at his house. Two garages. One for his *fun* cars. One for his boats and other diving vehicles. According to the report, that garage is packed with diving gear."

"Let's go see for ourselves," Cox said. "I'm checking boat registrations."

"While you're on with CIA Hillard, have Beth look carefully at video footage she uncovers of the area around any boat in his name. There's an off chance we'll see which car Franklin used for his boating activities. Particularly if those activities included non-work-related activities."

"You thinking women?"

"Or whatever. Doesn't always have to be a woman."

ELEVEN

THE TWO DETECTIVES STOPPED AT the headquarters building to pick up the Franklin house key. The fifteen-minute trip north to the Caloosahatchee River, with Leslie driving, was mostly silent. Pulling to a stop in a circular driveway that bent around a miniature lighthouse, she commented, "Guy spent his life on the water, under the water actually, so I don't suppose it's surprising his house is on a river—with his own private lighthouse and all."

"Can't wait to see the inside. File report says it's decorated in something they termed 'Old Shipwreck'."

"What's that mean?"

"I called Beth. All she said was, 'Gotta see for yourself!' My guess, the decorations came from salvage Franklin recovered."

"I'm happy to hear Hillard's working this case." Criminal Investigative Assistant Lizbeth Hillard was Leslie's favorite CIA. Not only did she have a double masters from Florida Gulf Coast University in Math and Criminal Justice, but she had also proven unshakable in court. "I don't know if you know this, but in preparation for the Edison phonograph trial, Beth took several forensic courses in art theft and fraud."

"She and I are...friends," Cox confessed. Even though his face was turned away, she could see the smug smile. "I'm the one who suggested the courses."

"I suppose I should have..."

Her sarcasm was lost on Cox, he was already out of hearing range halfway toward the front door of the sprawling house.

"Hold up a moment," Leslie yelled, hurrying to catch up. "Let's walk the perimeter before we go in. Get a feel for the place."

"Good idea. I'll follow," Cox apologized, slowing his pace. "Can't wait to see the sunken treasures inside—or whatever 'Old Shipwreck' means."

"A dock, but no boat," Leslie announced a moment later from the murky river's edge.

"That's surprising," Cox shrugged, distracted by his cell. "Hey, speaking of the devil! Hillard just posted several new entries. Found a boat registered to Franklin. Docked down on the

Matanzas Pass about a mile south of where the ferry to Key West docks."

"Anything else?" Leslie asked. "What about surveillance?"

"Jackpot! Blue Lamborghini!" Cox crowed victoriously a moment later. "No visible license plate, but how many blue Lamborghinis could there possibly be? Location a quarter mile north of the ferry dock, heading south at oh-four, thirty-eight on Monday. Car next seen, same location, heading north early Tuesday morning at one oh five. Then, get this, six hours later, at seven-twenty, again going south. That's the same morning he supposedly rode the ferry south to Key West. Then on the trip back north, he shot himself."

"That's consistent with him catching the eight o'clock ferry on Tuesday. Without knowing anything further, I'd say he went for a long boat ride Monday, got back after midnight, went home, came back and took the ferry south Tuesday morning."

"Tuesday evening, he gets back on the ferry, rides it north to Fort Myers and shoots himself just before the boat docks. Why am I not buying the timeline?"

"Can't argue with the facts, Cox. Timeline is what it is. And it *is* consistent with what we've seen so far."

Cox thought for a moment. "Based on the surveillance, I'd say that was about a twenty-hour ride on Monday, give or take a little. So, where did he go?"

"And did he go alone?" Leslie added.

"You can add that to our growing list of questions. You ready to go inside now?"

"Let's do it."

Cox inserted the key in the back sliding door, and the massive structure glided open smoothly, revealing what at first glance appeared to be the inside of a wooden ship. "This is creepy!" he observed, wrinkling his face. "Is this real wood, or..."

"From old ships. Smell the mildew? Appears we stepped backward in time. The furniture, if you can call it furniture, looks to be salvaged from the bottom of the sea. The drawer pulls, in fact all the metal, are shades of green. Copper or brass. Friggin' room looks like the inside of an old pirate ship. Weird, you ask me."

"The kitchen over there's in the form of a ship's galley. That oak table must have come from the captain's quarters of some big-ass ship."

"I'm surprised the windows aren't round," Leslie called from a room off to the right. "This is the crew's bedroom. Bunk beds and all!" A moment later she announced, "And here's the crew's

66

mess hall! This place is more of a roadside attraction than a home. Wonder if he gave guided tours."

"Where do we begin?" Cox questioned, his voice trailing off as he spoke.

"From the little I know about ship captains, and it's all from the movies, they kept everything of value in their quarters. Let's start there."

"According to the CIA report, that's exactly where his diaries and notes were found."

The captain's quarters turned out to be a single room with a bed bolted to the floor in one corner, a head area off to the side, with a small shower inside. Oak chests along one wall held his clothes, and a roll top desk occupied the opposite wall.

"Here's the round window you were looking for!" Cox called, pointing to the desk, above which was a polished, circular brass frame held to the wall with several brass bolts. The frame surrounded a thick glass window. Cox leaned close to the glass. "Not surprising, I suppose! It looks out over the river."

"Must have been an add-on," Leslie said, joining her partner. "I bet the real window is behind that seascape over there. Place wouldn't pass code without a window he could climb out of in case of fire. Before we dig into his papers and things, let's survey the garages, see what else we find. I know everything's catalogued, but doing it ourselves helps me digest it all."

"I'm following," Cox said, "lead the way."

The first garage they walked into, the one on the right as they had come up the driveway, was brightly lit, with a sparkling epoxy spotless floor. The walls were lined with silver-framed workbenches and cabinets with bright blue drawers. A yellow convertible sat on the far side; its hood open. "This is the first air-conditioned home garage I've ever seen," Leslie noted. "Looks like he did his own work on his cars."

"According to the inventory, that's a sixty-six Porsche. Looks to be pristine. Cost about a hundred fifty big ones. Maybe even more."

"I suppose everything in these drawers and on these shelves were catalogued. Is my assumption accurate?"

"Right on," Cox replied. "It's all in the file."

"Anything unusual?"

"Nothing I could see. But truth is, who the hell would know if a tool, or anything for that matter, was missing?"

"Only if he kept track of his purchases. I'll check to see later." Making a mental note to follow up, Leslie added, "Now let's go see what awaits in the left garage."

"That one's identical, only it's used for diving gear and not cars."

Indeed, the garages were essentially the same, with the exception that white pegboards filled the far side and back wall. Diving gear of every description was hanging on supporting hooks. The outline of each piece was carefully drawn in blue paint so there would be no mistake as to where an item belonged. "I read the report," Cox confessed, "but I don't have a clue what some of these devices do. I recognize the helmets and the goggles, even some of the regulators, but there are so many other gadgets and things I wouldn't know where to begin."

"These two open spaces," Leslie said, pointing to blue outlines down near the floor in the middle of the side wall, "appear to be air tanks. The tanks aren't anywhere around. I didn't know they came in different sizes, but these four next to the blanks appear much smaller."

Cox pointed to an area midway up the pegboard along the back wall. "Looks as if two face masks are missing from over there as well."

Leslie took several pictures of the pegboards, noting, "Let's keep a lookout for these items. Not likely to have disappeared."

"What's that going to tell us?" Cox inquired. "I suppose things break, get misplaced, all the time. My stuff sure does."

"Whoever knows? Just putting the jigsaw together. The less pieces gone missing, the clearer the picture. Humor me."

"Done out here?" Cox asked.

"Since everything's been catalogued, we don't need to make an inventory. Let's go inside and see what's what. Truth is, the house makes me feel..."

"Claustrophobic! At least that's my sense, Les. Feels I'm trapped on the Titanic. Let's get it done and get the hell out of here. We can always come back if we overlook something."

———◆———

It took slightly over two hours before they were satisfied everything had been properly recorded. "That's why I like it when Lizbeth heads up the CIA response team. It's all in the file," Leslie commented on their way back to the car.

"You appeared intrigued by that photograph on Franklin's desk. Three men."

"Sure was. The guy in the center is Jakowski! Appeared to be in his mid-twenties."

"Almost thirty years ago! Wasn't he playing for the Steelers then? Guy's held his body well. Lot of football players let themselves go. Not him."

"I don't know when he played for the Steelers. Never talks about it. On the left, that's Franklin."

"I saw that. So, who's on the right?"

"I sent a picture over to Beth with a note requesting facial identification. I'm assuming they were buds back then. Football at Pitt perhaps?"

"Grab a bite and head over to Franklin's boat?" Cox asked, checking his phone. "Beth just sent a note saying her team is finishing up at the boatyard. They'll be out of the way by the time we get there."

"Anything important?"

"Only thing of consequence is that everything was wiped clean. Other than a few smudged prints of doubtful value, nothing of interest. We don't have to go if you don't..."

"Oh, we'll go all right. We need to get a feel for the man. And besides, there's a restaurant over there I like. The Parrot Key Caribbean Grill."

Leslie's phone began vibrating. Glancing down, she noted it was the same number that had come up several times earlier, always with the label UNKNOWN. This time Leslie pushed ACCEPT.

"This is Sheriff's Deputy Hodges," she answered, impatience in her voice.

"Leslie, I've been..."

"Jak! I've been trying to..."

"Sorry," Jakowski apologized. "My cell didn't charge last night. Bought a burner. You okay?"

"Why shouldn't I be?"

"I've been calling. I thought..."

"It's been coming up UNKNOWN. Didn't see a message. Where've you been?"

"Visiting an old friend over on Sanibel. Can you talk?"

"This is not a good time."

"Over dinner then?"

"Pick me up at home, seven-thirty. Surprise me." Before Jakowski could respond, she hung up.

"So where was he?"

"Visiting a friend. Not your business."

"Be that way." The remainder of the drive to the boatyard was spent in awkward silence.

"This about Benny's death?" the parking lot attendant asked when Cox flashed his badge.

"Any particular reason you're asking about Benny?"

"Others from your office left a few minutes ago. Just missed them, he said, adding, "We'll surely miss that dude. Loved those cars of his. Not to mention the tips."

"When'd you see him last?"

"Didn't see him when he went out. He called me late Sunday about...about midnight it was. Told me they were going out early the next morning. Needed the spare tank topped."

"They?"

"He and a friend. A guy I don't recall seeing before."

"You working when he left?"

"Came in early. As I said, he tipped well."

"Were you here when he got back?"

"No. Knocked off at ten. DeChristo was working."

Cox held up his phone, a picture of Jakowski displayed. "Recognize this man?"

"Yep. Goes out on the boat a lot, but not this time. He's a big guy like Benny. Cop from up north. Pittsburgh, I think it is. The guy I saw the other morning I never saw before."

Cox brought up a copy of the picture that had captured Leslie's attention at Franklin's house. The yardman studied it a long time before saying, "This was taken a lot of years ago. I can't say for certain, but I think that's Benny on the left. And the middle guy's the cop. But...yeah, that third guy, the one on the right, I'd say that's who went out with Benny early Monday."

"Know where they went?"

"I know they went over three hundred miles."

"And how do..."

The attendant's face broke into a smile. "He used over half the spare."

"I take it that doesn't happen all that often."

"Just the opposite. In the last year or so, almost every time he went out, he used that amount. Just under two hundred forty gallons."

"Ever tell you where he went?"

Again, the big knowing smile. "Figured it out after all that publicity over the sunken ship." The man reached under his shirt and produced a gold chain. Hanging from the end of the chain was a gold coin. "See this Spanish coin? Present from ol' Benny. From the sunken Spanish ship he salvaged. Where else you think he went all those times?"

"After they salvaged the ship, did he continue going back there?"

"I'd bet on the ship site. Unless he found *another* sunken treasure ship. Now that I think on it, this was the first time in a while he used over two hundred gallons for one trip."

Cox started to say something, changed his mind, and instead said, "Here's my card. Call me if you think of anything else. I'll have a CIA investigator take your statement."

"CIA? Sounds serious! Why them? Am I in trouble?"

"Works for us. Criminal Investigative Assistant. Just want to get what you know in the file. Just tell them what you just told us. And anything else you may think of."

"Aye, aye," the man said, throwing what passed for a salute. "Oh, thinking of things I just remembered, one thing was odd."

"And what's that?" Cox asked.

"The person who went along with Benny didn't dive."

"And how do you know that?"

"They only had one mask on board."

TWELVE

"YOUR PHONE WAS DEFINITELY TURNED OFF!" Leslie said to Jakowski when she slid into the front seat, purposely not leaning over to kiss him. "That much I'll grant you. I'm not buying that 'not charged' bull!"

The big Pittsburgh cop didn't immediately answer. Instead, he focused on the traffic coming at him from several directions. "Is it always this busy?" he asked, "or is something special going on?"

"You're ducking my question."

"Didn't hear a question. You made a statement. That's your prerogative."

"I've had a long day Jak, and I'm not up to playing games! Take me back home if this is how the night's going to go!"

"Remind me to never get on your bad side if this is how you treat someone taking you to dinner."

"I'll ask again. I think you wanted your phone off so I, or someone, couldn't follow where you went. So, where the hell'd you go you didn't want to be followed?"

Jakowski drove several minutes without responding, allowing the silence—and tension— to build, before saying, "If I said my travels were official business, would that satisfy you?"

"Only if it was the truth!" Leslie retorted. "What official business?"

"Not at liberty to discuss. A mix, actually. Phone was off because the location's sensitive."

"Task force business?" she said, her tone softening.

"Good assumption."

"Can you at least tell me where you went? In Florida? Out of state?"

"Assume I never left the state."

"Miami?"

"That's certainly in the state. But no, not Miami. And I'm not playing twenty questions."

"Cut to the chase. What *can* you tell me?"

"Visiting an old friend on Sanibel Island."

"You have a nice visit?"

"As nice as can be expected with an empty house."

"What the hell's that mean?"

"Friend was off to Vegas. As the British would say, he has a wee wagering problem."

"So, you spent your time with…"

"His wife. Been friends with her since college."

"Let me get this straight. You spent the last couple days holed up on Sanibel Island with a long-time lady friend. And your cell was off for *security* purposes."

"That's one way to look at it. For the record, we weren't exactly 'holed up'. They have a ten-million-dollar home on the beach. We talked. And they're happily married."

"Is there another way to look at it?"

"Wife's worried about her husband. Gambling problems usually go from bad to worse. This one's no exception."

"This friend have a name?"

"Herco."

"Herco? Herco what?"

"Hank Hoyos. Goes by Herco. Known him since Pitt days."

"Play football?"

"Actually, no. Soccer. Quite good, I must say."

She held up her phone. "This the guy?"

"So, you've been to Benny's house—I should say land-boat. Unusual place, to say the least."

"'Unusual' is one way to describe it. I'd say eccentric."

"That's Herco, all right. Picture was taken a year or so after graduation. He was a soccer player in Colombia. Already a national hero down there."

"Married then?"

"This was at his wedding. Married a Peruvian woman who had moved to Colombia when she was two. Thinks of herself as Colombian."

"Name?"

"Valeria López. Goes by Val."

"And you spent how many days at her house?"

"I was working, Les. End of that topic. Okay?"

Leslie knew her choices were to drop the subject and enjoy dinner or press on and have Jakowski take her home. He was too good to reveal anything of value he didn't want her to know. "Where we going for dinner?" Leslie asked, signaling that she would honor his request. "I haven't had a decent meal since…since your wonderful roasted chicken."

"So, whose fault is that?"

"Work gets in the way."

73

"A place...a little place...I've never been to. De Adriatico. Mediterranean. Over near Miromar Lakes."

"How do you find these places?"

"Friend suggested it. Said it was the best Italian he had ever eaten." Jakowski concentrated on the traffic for several minutes.

In the silence, Leslie's mind wandered from thought to thought.

"Hey," he said, jarring her back to the present, "you said you had a tiring day. What's going on?"

"Franklin's death primarily. Oh, and a second homicide. Domestic—the one Cox and I were working when you called. Husband comes home drunk, his neck gets slashed."

"Wife? Boyfriend?"

"Looks like the wife. Cox's not sure. Wife doesn't seem the type."

"What type is that? Guy beats on a woman long enough, never know what'll happen. Hate domestic cases. Who the hell wants to arrest a woman for fighting back the only way she can. Law never helps."

"Can't say as I disagree."

"Any more on Franklin? Autopsy come back?"

"Nothing conclusive as of yet. Ferry surveillance seems to confirm he shot himself."

"But you have your doubts?" Jakowski remarked, as if reading her thoughts.

"Am I that transparent?"

"When you want to be, yes."

"Why would I want to be?"

"I can't imagine. Now who's playing games?"

"I'm troubled. Let's leave it at that. Been thinking of the Galileo Sunspot Telescope being on that sunken ship and wondering if that's what you're working on for Stratis. I know you told me you were cut out, but..."

"Working on it. I'll say that. But not for Stratis. My involvement is in a very limited capacity."

"And that is...?"

"Leslie! No more on that topic."

"You're hindering a homicide investigation."

"I thought you just said he shot himself."

"He did."

"So, if he shot himself, wouldn't it be a suicide?"

Changing the subject, Leslie asked, "By chance do you know where that Galileo Telescope is currently located?"

"I believe I do. Yes."

"And where would that be?"

"That, my dear, is something I cannot divulge."

"Even if it were part of a criminal investigation?"

"And just what investigation might that be?"

Jakowski was right. She had nothing yet to tie the death of the diver Franklin to the telescope, other than the telescope was believed to have been on the sunken ship, but not recovered. He had completely turned the tables on her, getting from her more than she had planned to say. A tribute to exactly how skilled Jakowski was at eliciting information from reluctant witnesses. "Just speculation on my part," she admitted. "Curiosity. Getting out over my skis."

———————

"Do I understand correctly that your boyfriend's again running errands for that Pittsburgh window magnate, Morris Dexter Stratis?" Cox asked, appearing at her desk in the Pit a moment after she arrived. He had obviously read her file notes.

Ignoring his smirk, Leslie said, "He's not working for Stratis. But we need to assume that several of the Seminal Society collectors are vying for a Galileo First telescope. I'd expect that Texan, William 'Little Billy Bob' Bishop, to be in the mix as well. But I haven't found anything to suggest that's accurate."

"Don't forget that couple we had lunch with up in Tampa when you and I worked the Chladni euphon case."

"Sanjay and Riya Kumar," Leslie acknowledged. "He's into electronics. GPS and satellites. A Galileo First telescope would definitely be of interest to him. How about tracking them down?"

"I'll get Hillard to see if any of the collectors are in the vicinity. What about calling that Great Southern Insurance guy? Name's Silver if I recall. See what he knows."

"Jack Silver's the CEO. And yes, his company insures artifacts such as the telescope."

"That's who I'm talking about. If there's a Galileo telescope's in play, he'll have a piece of it. That's what his company specializes in."

"Good thought," she said, reaching for her cell.

The call went directly to voicemail. Leslie explained what she was calling about and asked for a call back. She then called Agent Ghana and the result was the same.

"Cox," Leslie said, changing the subject, "what do you make of the two oxygen masks missing from Franklin's garage? Only one was found on his boat."

"Perhaps there never was a second mask. He appeared to live alone, so maybe that open space is nothing more than future planning. Hey, gotta run. Have a few loose items to follow up on with the Chase Montrose homicide. Catch you in a bit."

"Before you run off," Leslie called, "we've got two homicides going at the same time. That a no-no? Should we be passing Montrose off? I think it's time we brief Boots."

"Nothing much to report. It's all in there," he balked, pointing to the computer. "With your partner, Fish, on reduced hours and with everything else going on, everyone's pulling double duty. I say, let sleeping dogs lie. Both deaths are with us to the end, I'm afraid."

Cox was referring to the fact that Senior Detective Daryl Fischer had been shot in the arm working a previous case with Leslie. It was now common knowledge that his wife, Jessica, had been pressuring him to take his well-deserved pension and retire. His compromise was to work part-time. Trouble was, homicide investigations are full-time. "What items are you chasing?"

"Prints of bakerman on that fire escape. And on the door out of the Montrose apartment. That kind of thing. Loose end stuff."

"Didn't see that in the file," Leslie muttered, scolding herself for not paying attention. "I must be..."

"It's not posted yet. Got a heads-up from Beth. Seems there are multiple sets of prints. According to her, all from different times. Some going back months."

"Jak was talking about that just last night at dinner. A new FBI technique."

"You're thinking of palmitic acid. Diffuses from fingerprints at a predictable rate. That only seems to work for a few days, maybe a week at best. No, Beth's talking about good old-fashioned street dirt. Layers on the prints. She believes someone's been visiting the Montrose household on a regular basis."

"Using the fire escape. That's interesting. Probably why it came down so easy. When will the prints be processed?"

"Later today, I believe. I'm still liking Clancy Lowry for the Chase Montrose murder. He's a big guy to fit through that window, but 'love will find a way'. Hope the prints confirm. Les, you agree?"

"Can't argue with you. Next steps?"

"I was just fixin' to prepare a search warrant request for the bakery."

"Go for it. Mind if I brief the boss on both investigations? We're overdue with her and I'm getting antsy."

"Do what you think best. But I repeat, sleeping dogs are best being ignored."

———

Leslie's phone rang as she made her way to her captain's office. JACK SILVER appeared on the screen. The CEO of Great Southern Insurance Company was calling. "Jack, thanks for returning my call," she said into her phone. "Good to hear from you."

Almost simultaneously, Captain Stetson's assistant said, "Boots is out for the day. Emergencies go to Hud." Leslie nodded and headed back to her desk, the phone pressed to her ear.

"I anticipated your call, Detective," Silver said. "You're in luck on this one. I'm free to discuss what little I know about the Galileo telescopes. And I must tell you, it is very little indeed."

"Telescopes! Plural?"

"That's the confusing part. Certainly, there is one. Possibly two. Some say three, but I seriously doubt that. In fact, two is unlikely, you ask me. You need not comment, but I assume the death of that diver prompted the call."

"Good assumption."

"Recently, there has been an uptick of what I call 'restored treasures' coming to us for insurance coverage. What is not widely realized is that more than a fair share have proven to be either fakes, or so severely damaged, that value is questionable. This is especially so with artifacts pertaining to the Seminal Society. And coming off the ocean bottom! That's why Great Southern is sitting this out. At least until there's clarity in the subject matter."

"What do you mean by 'questionable'?"

"Something might be of high value to a particular individual, or group of individuals, yet that artifact has no market value outside that group. Too speculative for us, I'm afraid."

"Do I understand you to mean Great Southern is no longer insuring Seminal Society Firsts? Who is?"

"Depends. If there is only one, or possibly two, investors who value an item, Great Southern won't insure it. If we determine there really is a market, then we'll consider. As to who else will insure, I'm afraid I must leave that to your investigative powers."

"So the telescopes fall in the category of your non-insurance?" Leslie followed up, assuming she already knew the answer.

"Up to now, yes."

"Sorry, I'm confused. Up to now, the telescope in question—or possibly telescopes—was in a sunken ship under water. Am I right about that?"

"So far as it goes. We are aware of only one on the sunken ship. Any others have been either in private collections or museums. In some cases, substitutions have been made. You must appreciate that at times authenticity has been difficult to achieve."

"What do you know about the telescope on the sunken ship?"

"Admiral Masters has laid claim to several extensive sunken treasures over the years. In some cases, she's proven to us the value of the cargo, even before she completes the salvage. In those instances, we've gone along and insured what she can document."

"What about the *Buen Jesús*?"

"The Spanish-flagged ship sank off the Dry Tortugas in sixteen-twenty-two. Little over four hundred years ago. We insured some items from that find."

"But not any Galileo telescopes."

"Not exactly. Until recently, they couldn't prove which of Galileo's telescopes was down there."

"Just how many are there?"

"He made dozens. Maybe hundreds. Cut and polished the lenses to his specifications depending on what he was searching the heavens for. There is a series of islands off Venice called Murano, where artisans have been blowing glass since the thirteenth century. Galileo himself became pretty good at it, as well. The telescope supposedly on the *Buen Jesús* was the one he used to find the sunspots that led him to accept Copernicus' theory that the earth travels around the sun, and not the other way around. That's what got him in trouble with the pope."

"I thought at first it was the one he used to find the moons of Jupiter," Leslie interrupted. "The ones he called the Medician stars after the Medici family. But then I learned about Galileo's sunspots discovery, and...and...well, it's all so confusing!"

"That's what I mean by us not insuring unverified artifacts. Stories abound. Facts are...well, as I said, facts are hard to verify."

"You seem to be certain currently, though, that the telescope on the sunken ship is this Sunspot Telescope. What changed your mind?"

"Two things. Derrick Franklin found among the artifacts a sealed container housing a diagram drawn by Galileo simultaneously with a telescope discovery. In sixteen-thirteen, it appears Galileo sent that Sunspot Telescope, along with the diagram detailing its exact dimensions, to his patron, the Grand

Duchess Christina of Tuscany. As I said, it was the discovery of those sunspots that led to his eventual conviction by the Inquisition."

"And?" Leslie said, hoping Silver would elaborate on his comment. When he remained silent, she prompted, "You said two things made you comfortable insuring the Sunspot Telescope. What's the second reason?"

"That document Franklin recovered is in perfect condition and has now been authenticated."

"And where are these two items now?"

"I'd tell you if I could. Best I can do is suggest the east coast of Florida."

"Miami?"

Again, Silver didn't answer.

"Okay, then is it safe to assume Great Southern has insured the..."

"Not yet. There are conditions."

"Such as?"

"Actual physical possession by our client after the auction. And both items, the telescope *and* the documentation, again being verified."

"Auction? What auction?" The when, where, how questions were coming faster than Leslie could articulate them. "When will the auction take place? Where..."

"Whoa! Slow down, Detective. The man you need to speak with is Professor Hammer..."

"Sir Reggie!"

"I forgot. You visited with him about the Newton *Principia Mathematica*. Nice piece of detective work on your part. Tell you what. I'll get it set up with Sir Reggie. Suggest you head over to Miami. He's at the Setai Hotel. I'll text you the time. Ask him about the auction. He owes me one."

"Doesn't everybody?" She said to herself when the line disconnected. "Doesn't everybody?"

"Detective," Boots' assistant, Marge, said when Leslie put her phone down, "Shall I put you on Cap's calendar for late today, or in the morning? I'm sure she'd want..."

"Cox and I are headed for Miami. Hope to be back late but may have to stay the night."

"Cox and you?" the woman nodded, a knowing look spreading across her face. "Bet that'll be fun."

"Not going to happen!" Leslie retorted. "Not what you're thinking, anyway."

Leslie picked up her phone to call her partner, but not before she heard Marge mumble, "Office money says otherwise. Can't wait to see who's right."

———————

"You have quite a reputation in the department, you know," Leslie said to Cox, as they drove Highway 41 through the desolate Everglades. "You better watch yourself."

"What's that supposed to mean?" Cox grunted, without lifting his head from his computer screen.

"I told Marge we'd be traveling to Miami. She all but said the office is betting on you and I having a relationship."

"We do have a relationship," he smiled broadly. "We're partners."

"Playing dumb doesn't do you justice, Cox. Suggest you work on cleaning up your reputation."

"Can't help it if I'm a friendly guy. Gets me tidbits of information here and there; a report one day early; a heads-up on an investigation; an early preliminary fingerprint match, that sort of thing. Surprising how it all adds up."

"I'm all for the early warning system. It's just the method that..."

"What's wrong with friendly? You should try it sometime. Works wonders."

"There's friendly—and then there's going too far."

"If you're suggesting I'm doing anything improper with anyone, then say it. Give me names and times. Otherwise..."

"It's not me saying it!" Leslie snapped back defensively. "That's what the office's saying. I'm just the messenger."

"Didn't your mommy teach you not to throw stones—or even not to deliver them—when you live in a glass house?"

It took Leslie several seconds to process what Cox had just implied. When she did, her foot hit the brake pedal with such force that without the seatbelts snapping tight, they both would have been propelled into the windshield. Or worse! Luckily, there was no car behind them. He had hit a raw nerve; her relationship with Jakowski, a married man. It had begun quickly after her breakup with Assistant Prosecutor Allen Smith. A breakup seemingly precipitated by her involvement with Jakowski. Cox was right in one respect. Her relationship was out in the open. His dalliances were mere speculation.

"What the hell you doing?" Cox screamed, as the car swerved onto the narrow dirt berm that separated the roadway from the alligator-infested swamp that crowded in from the side.

Leslie sat rigid, struggling to calm herself. A moment later she opened her door and walked down to a murky creek, barely noticing the shadowy movement and the ripples in front of her where several alligators slid into the water. Others, their long snouts lying flat in the dirt, silently observed the approaching creature.

When Leslie hadn't returned in several minutes, Cox went down the embankment to find her. It was early afternoon, yet the heavy foliage cast a deep gloom over this desolate piece of swamp. This certainly was not the place for either of them to be with nothing separating them from the gators.

"Leslie," he called, "it's not safe here. Come back to the car!"

Other than the sounds Cox expected from a swamp, he heard nothing. He took several steps in the direction he had last seen his partner and again called her name.

Behind him in the vicinity of her car, he heard a noise, as if someone, or something, was moving along the path. "Leslie, is that you?"

Cox waited for a response that did not come. *"The car! Oh my God!"* a voice in his head suddenly shouted. *"You're a dead man walking if she drives off!"* He ran up the embankment as fast as he could, ignoring red eyes that seemed to be everywhere.

THIRTEEN

LESLIE WALKED INTO THE SETAI HOTEL several steps ahead of Cox. The remainder of the ride to Miami had been accomplished in silence, the tension between them not abating.

"You, young lady," Sir Reggie boomed when they entered his suite, "I remember you from...from Arkansas, wasn't it? Lovely Fort Smith." Turning to Cox, he extended his hand. "And you, young man, I don't recall having had the pleasure."

"My name's Simeon Cox. We spoke briefly on the phone when I set up the meeting for you to review Newton's *Principia*."

"Oh, yes. Now I recall. You're a detective as well. But you didn't come out to Arkansas."

"Good memory. I did not. Detective Jakowski took my place."

"Oh, yes, I recall. Big fellow."

"What brings you back to the States so soon, Professor?" Leslie asked, "I thought your lecture tour had ended."

"It is not often that something as rare and precious as the telescope Galileo used to discover sunspots turns up."

"I'm a bit confused," Leslie began. "You, I know, are a Newton authority. The telescope in question is attributed to Galileo. Am I missing..."

"I can understand your confusion. You came to me the last time because of my expertise on the Newton manuscripts. I am also versed in Galileo di Vincenzo Bonaiuti de' Galilei. He pioneered the scientific method. To understand Newton, one must understand what came before. It's as though they are a continuum. Beginning, of course, with da Vinci's notebooks."

Leslie thought of the Seminal Society collectors and their belief that da Vinci's spirit passed through Galileo to Newton. Sir Reggie was seemingly confirming that connection. "Are you suggesting Newton's work was an extension of Galileo's?" she asked, genuinely interested in what he had to say on the subject.

"Galileo, as had da Vinci before him, made fundamental contributions to science in several areas. You most probably know about Galileo's passion for astronomy and his revolutionary telescopic discoveries. He first used the telescope to confirm, at least in his mind, that all the planets, including the earth, orbit the

82

Sun in elliptical fashion. He proposed some simple laws that govern the motion of the planets and other objects. Newton quantified those laws. Galileo was also a pioneer in material strengths and battlefield logistics, especially attack angles of cannon balls, all pioneered by da Vinci a bit over a hundred years earlier." Sir Reggie paused a moment to be certain the two detectives were following him. "I credit Galileo as the forerunner of the scientific method as we know it today, all based on da Vinci's notebooks. Newton's laws of motion follow directly from the Great One's writings. Is it at all surprising that to know one is to know the other?"

"From what we've learned," Cox said, entering the conversation, and determined to set the record straight, "the telescope you're talking about is the one salvaged from the sunken ship. Is that correct?"

"You're thinking of the *Buen Jesús y Nuestra Señora del Rosario*. The original inventory, taken long before anything was recovered, listed the telescope as one of the seventeen thousand objects on board. Based on the date the ship sailed from Spain, and its ports of call, conventional wisdom would suggest that the telescope listed on that inventory was the one Galileo gifted to the grand duchess of Tuscany, around sixteen-twelve. Some scholars speculate that, in point of fact, that same telescope was presented to her son, Grand Duke Cosimo II de' Medici. But that is incorrect."

Cox blurted out, "From what we've been led to believe, that telescope, I mean the one given to Medici, was the one Galileo used to discover Jupiter having several moons. I believe he at first thought of them as stars and named them the Medician stars."

"Cox!" Leslie admonished, "please remember we're here by invitation. The professor is doing us a favor. No need to cross-ex..."

Sir Reggie held up his hand. "I understand your confusion. You certainly have done your homework, I dare say. Yes, today those 'stars' are known as the Galilean moons of Jupiter. And yes, I now believe the newly retrieved telescope is the Sunspot Telescope."

"So," Cox pressed, "the telescope on the sunken boat was the one used to find sunspots, not moons!"

"To my mind it is. But, my dear man, who believes what depends upon where the information has come from—and when. The telescope supposedly residing beneath the Gulf of Mexico since sixteen-twenty-two was rumored to be the one the Great

One was using when he first noticed the sunspots. That much I believe to be certainly true. Some are of a different opinion."

Leslie summarized, "So the Medici Telescope is in Italy and the Sunspot..."

"Fact is, no one today *knows* exactly where the Medici Telescope really is. A while back, some cracksman purportedly removed it from the *Museo Galileo* in Florence. Naturally, the museum denies it was ever stolen."

"Was it stolen or not?" Cox, not in the mood to mince words, asked. "Bottom line?"

"Not so fast, my son. Not so fast. With artifacts at this level, it is not easy to separate the fakes from the genuine. Often sophisticated electronics, spectrographs and the like, are used. Even then, questions remain. That's how good these people are. When hundreds of millions of dollars are in play, you can imagine how elaborate the schemes can become."

"Well, now I'm confused. So, you're saying," Leslie clarified, "that two important Galileo telescopes are in play."

"Indeed so. At least the Medici is."

"The Medici?" Cox doubled down. "Not the Sunspot?"

"I cannot vouch for the Sunspot. Only that the one on the sunken ship is—was—genuine. Where that one is now is anybody's guess."

"But you *can* vouch for the Medici?" Leslie asked, more puzzled than before. "How is that..."

"Simple, my dear. I saw with my own eyes the Medici Telescope."

"And just when was that?" Cox asked.

"Just this week. Here in Florida. I was asked to validate a telescope believed to have been recovered from the wreckage. Of course, I assumed it was the Sunspot Telescope, the one not seen since sixteen-twenty. Lo and behold, the one I examined was the Medici! Imagine, if you will, my surprise."

"Please pardon the question, Professor," Leslie leaned in, "but I would be remiss if I didn't inquire how certain you are that the one you recently studied is the original Medici and not a fake, or...or the Sunspot?"

"It certainly is not the Sunspot. Wrong length. I would not be so cavalier as to stake my reputation on my analysis, but from all observable aspects, the one I saw is the authentic Medici."

"What, in particular, makes you so certain?"

"Lens measurements, along with barrel length. Galileo was constantly changing each to account for different distances, different light values. Everything physical is correct. I was unable to perform material analysis, so, as I said, there is always doubt. Galileo had his own method of polishing lenses, and the one I saw bore his marks."

"What about the telescope in Florence?" Cox challenged. "If the Medici Telescope is on display over there, then how do you explain the one you saw here in Florida?"

"Of course, my dear sir, one of them—or possibly both—are fake."

"Then, according to what you just said, the telescope you recently authenticated could not have come from the bottom of the Gulf of Mexico. Am I understanding you correctly?" Leslie probed, making certain there was no uncertainty as to what Sir Reggie was telling them.

"Correct, my dear woman. Or, should I say, as correct as one could be in this field of study. I will, however, venture so far as to stake my reputation on the fact that I have never personally seen the Sunspot Telescope. I hope that is clear enough."

Taking a moment to digest what she just heard, Leslie followed up by asking, "Did you inspect the Medici here in Miami? Or somewhere else?"

"I can't be certain where I examined the Medici."

"Mind explaining?" Cox was nonplussed. "What's that mean?"

"A car picked me up at this hotel. I was handed a mask and instructed to wear it while I was driven to a storage facility. I was allowed to remove the mask only upon arrival. We had stopped directly in front of one of the sheds in a storage facility. Shed six-oh-one to be exact."

"You saw the number?"

"Indeed, I did," the professor answered, agitation creeping into his voice. "They wanted me to see it. And remember it. That was critical to their plan—or so they had led me to believe."

"What plan is that?" Cox immediately asked.

"There will be an auction. Something called the Great Shed Steal. Whoever bids on—and wins—shed six-oh-one obtains the Medici Telescope."

"What's to prevent someone from emptying shed six-oh-one before the auction?"

"I trust their word when they say it is under continuous armed security. In addition, it is safeguarded by two locks. A key lock that someone else controls and a combination lock. I set the combination and only I know the numbers."

"There are thousands of storage sheds numbered six-oh-one," Leslie debated. "How does the bidder know..."

"Sorry, my dear. I have now communicated to you all the information on the subject that I have. Further interrogation will prove most unfruitful."

Cox, not to be cut off, changed the subject. "Any idea as to where this shed is located?"

"We drove north for about an hour. Then a bit east as best as I can piece it together."

"Hear any unusual sounds? Airplanes? Highway noise? Maybe a train?" Cox asked.

"Boat whistles. Sounded like steamships. I'd say less than a mile away."

"Anything else?" Leslie asked, feeling as though she was overlooking something important. Normally, she fed off Cox during the interview process, but ever since she allowed him back in the car, any chemistry they might have had was non-existent.

"Afraid not," the professor shrugged, looking first at Cox then at Leslie.

"Can we encourage you to speculate on the going price for the Medici? Ballpark is all we need at this point," Leslie asked.

"That's a more difficult question to answer than you might imagine. The street value, I mean excluding the billionaire Seminal Society collectors, would perhaps be in the ten-to-fifty-million-dollar range. As a Galileo First, I can easily expect someone from the Seminal Society collector crowd to bid in the hundreds of millions. But..."

"For a telescope?" Cox practically hooted. "A piece of tubing and a couple of lenses! Gotta be joking."

"I don't joke, young man. Not about my field of expertise! Here's the thing with Galileo's telescopes; there are many such. The most important one is the Medici and a close second is the Sunspot. To a Seminal Society collector, exclusivity is the key to value. If only one telescope existed, the value easily would be hundreds of millions. If they both exist, well then it is difficult to think of either as a true First. Certainly not an exclusive First. In that scenario, I can easily visualize the value falling dramatically. Perhaps, even to the point of not bidding."

"Not bidding?" Cox's face showed how hard he was trying to grasp this. "If both telescopes came on the market, then *neither* has a high value? Is that what I'm supposed to understand?"

"Exclusivity is the Seminal Society collectors' trigger point. If they can't have an artifact all to themselves, they don't want it. Please understand, I'm not attempting to explain their behavior, just to report the facts as I see them."

"What makes the Medici Telescope more valuable than the Sunspot Telescope?" Leslie asked, being careful not to imply, as Cox had, that she saw little value in a couple of lenses inside a tube.

"Good question. That 'tube' as you call it, is carefully constructed from wood strips wrapped in a paper covering over which leather is stretched. The diameter, as well as the length, are critical. So are the lenses at either end. A true First. Simple, but elegant. As are most truly remarkable inventions. Trust me, the Medici Telescope's value is over five hundred million as a stand-alone." Sir Reggie paused a moment, lost in thought. Then he added, "There is a possibility I am incorrect with respect to the diminished value of multiple telescopes. There could possibly be a collection value, in that the telescopes represent a body of work that resulted in the Great One being found guilty by the Roman Inquisition for propounding the heretic notion of the earth not being the center of the universe."

"Was Galileo the first to suggest the earth circled the sun and not the other way around?" Cox asked.

"A hundred years earlier, a man by the name of Nicolaus Copernicus came to that conclusion. It wasn't until Galileo observed the Jupiter moons, and other phenomena, such as elliptical planet orbits, did he come to believe the Catholic teachings were wrong. He was warned—and behaved as if he agreed—to stop publicly talking and writing about the earth traveling around the sun."

"I assume he didn't really stop," Cox said.

"For a while he did. Then he became friends with the new pope, Urban VIII. Galileo then came to believe that the truth would prevail. Pope Urban, being sophisticated culturally, was quite interested in Galileo's ideas. The Great One was given tremendous leeway for the time, with but one caveat from the pope: That Galileo treat his findings as hypotheses, and not scientific fact. However, sixteen years later, in sixteen-thirty-two, he published a book titled, The Dialogue Concerning the Two Chief World Systems. The pope, furious, in part because he believed Galileo was mocking him, ordered another investigation. Galileo was found guilty and sentenced to death. His life was spared, but he was confined to quarters where he continued his astrology and mathematics studies. He eventually published his masterwork in physics, a book called Dialogues Concerning Two New Sciences. The two sciences are tensile strength and motion in which he discussed torrential kinematics, strength of materials and generally laid out a systematization of the science of motion, including the law of falling bodies."

"Was he punished further for that book?"

"Good question. He died four years later. But I truly believe the Church didn't understand what he was saying. That, in my mind, is why he wasn't punished further. It took Newton to complete what Galileo—and da Vinci before him—began."

FOURTEEN

THE SILENCE BETWEEN LESLIE AND COX continued during the two hour and twenty-minute ride back from Miami to Fort Myers; neither detective willing to initiate a conversation, even though proper procedure called for them to distill what they had heard and observed. Their silence continued the next morning as they approached Captain Karen Stetson's office in response to a summons from the boss.

Leslie, hearing footsteps behind her, turned to see Sergeant Hudson Oakmore turning the corner, walking quickly in their direction. "Hodges," he called, sounding out of breath, "what the hell's going on? Marge says she hasn't heard Boots this agitated in years. You two step in it?"

"Go right in," Stetson's assistant announced before Leslie could answer her immediate supervisor. "Boss's waiting for you," arching her eyebrows as if to say, *This isn't going to end well.*

Without preamble, Stetson said, "I understand you two drove over yesterday to Miami to see Professor Hammerschmidt."

"We did," Cox began, "to inter..."

"I wasn't asking a question, Detective! I was making a statement! I know exactly what you two did—and didn't do. Leslie, you gave him your card and asked him to call you if he remembered anything further. Well, he called earlier this morning. You weren't at your desk, and he demanded to speak to your supervisor. The call came to me instead of Hud. His exact words were, 'Tell those two detectives that I also recall low-flying planes. There was a major airport just west of the shed.' Does his message make sense to either of you?"

"It does," Cox quickly answered. "Very much so."

"And what about you, Hodges? Make sense to you as well?"

Boots' accusatory tone caught Leslie off guard. It was as if she was about to fail—or had already failed—a test of some sort. "Now we have a narrow area to concentrate on to find a storage shed where the Medici Telescope is being held."

"Good. At least you were both paying attention!"

Leslie tried to see how Cox was reacting to Boots, but his body was sideways to her, his head facing away. Swallowing hard, Leslie said, "Cap, I sense a problem. Care to..."

"Damn right there's a problem! First off, you were in Miami investigating a homicide without notifying the Miami authorities!"

Leslie was about to say she had come by to brief Boots only to find the captain out of the office, when Cox said, "We were gathering information on a telescope we believed had been recovered from a sunken ship. The one we believe the Seminal Society collectors are jonesing for. That wasn't exactly a murder investigation. A fact-finding trip, if you will."

"Did you advise the federal task force?"

"Didn't know we had to, Cap," Cox replied, confusion spreading across his face.

"Frankly, I don't give a good shit about them! I'm taking crap from the sheriff, who's taking crap from Miami. But truth is, between us, that's his friggin' problem. Not mine."

Cox said, "So what is..."

"You!" Stetson said, looking him straight in the eye. She then turned her penetrating gaze to Leslie. "And you!"

"What did..." Leslie began.

"Look at the two of you! Standing almost back-to-back! I've seen couples in the midst of hotly contested divorce proceedings show more empathy towards one another than you two. What the hell's going on?"

"Did Professor Hammerschmidt...say anything?"

"How stupid you think I am? One look at the two of you and it's obvious. The tension between you is overwhelming." Stetson glared from one to the other, then looked briefly at Oakmore before continuing. "Your personal problems are your personal problems—until they're not! And right now, they're my problem! Sir Reggie wasted no time informing me of the lack of professionalism you both showed in his interview. Said he had never seen two people who, in his words, 'thoroughly despised each other'. He said you didn't have to be a body language expert, as he happens to be, to pick up on it. He also said the only reason he continued the interview was his previous interaction with you, Leslie, up at Fort Smith. He found you engaging and, again," Stetson glanced down at a note card, "in his words, 'bright, tough and perceptive'. My observation of you two this morning bears him out. You agree with that, Hud?"

"These two haven't looked at each other until just now. You're right about divorced couples. Last time I saw partners with this much contempt for each other was...let me be blunt here...when she found herself pregnant and he announced he was staying with his wife of twenty-two years."

Stetson looked from Leslie to Cox, then back to Leslie. "We have no union rep here, so I don't want either of you saying anything. You both know department policy and I expect full compliance. You both understand me? The two of you have some sort of relationship, end it now! Or one of you transfer your ass to another county. You hear me?"

"That's not our situation," Cox immediately answered.

Stetson aimed her fury in Leslie's direction. "Is Cox's statement accurate?"

"Yes, Captain. It is," Leslie assured her. "We don't have..."

"Then going forward, can you two resolve your problem—whatever the hell it is—and work together? Or should Hud reassign you both?"

"I know I can," Cox replied. "It was just a misunderstanding."

"I'm okay with Cox," Leslie added. "I let my emotions get the better of me. Won't happen again. We're good."

"Hud, you okay with that?" Stetson asked, her demeanor softening.

"Let's have no more misunderstandings—or wayward emotions," their sergeant said. "Either of you have a problem, I want to hear about it directly from you. Not from the sheriff. Not from Boots. And worst of all, not from the public!"

"Yes, Sir," Cox and Hodges said with one voice.

"God help you if you're lying to me! Dismissed!" Stetson snapped. "Now get back to work! I need to take this call."

———————

On the way back to the Pit, Oakmore said, "Boots might not want to hear your personal problems, but I don't have that luxury. Each of you has twenty-four hours to put in writing any grievance you have with the other. If neither of you has a problem, I'll allow you to continue as partners. If not, I'll deal with it. Understand?"

Again, they answered, "Yes, Sir," in unison.

"Let me also make it clear, if neither of you give me anything, I'll put nothing on your record—this time. If I learn of problems between you from others there'll be hell to pay. Now go solve those two homicides you're working. I don't want to have this conversation with either of you again. Understood?"

Oakmore disappeared into his office before either detective could respond. They took several steps in the direction of the Pit before Cox said, "I need to apologize to you. What I said in the car was uncalled for. Last night driving home I realized how good a team we make. When we arrest the bakerman, hopefully later today, the two of us will have worked on, and closed, more homicides than anyone else on active duty, other than Fischer. That's what a good team does. We're a good team. Don't want to screw it up."

"Just stop poking me about my private life and all's good."

"It's hard when you're so over sensitive. Why I don't know. But Les, you are."

Leslie's anger instantly boiled over. Instead of lashing out, she walked to the end of the hall where she turned to face Cox, her neck and face hot. Forcing her voice to remain calm, she said, "In all honesty, I know I overreacted. Psychologists must have a name for it. All I want is to be treated equally around here. Keep my private life out of the workplace. That's all I ask."

"Fair enough. What if I asked for the same?"

"You saying I poke at *your* private life?"

"All the time. Every time I tell you I have a contact in some agency or another you either make a comment, or at the very least, roll your eyes implying I've been in some sort of a relationship with that person. I've spent years cultivating those relationships and..."

Leslie stifled the urge to say, "*I'll bet!*"

"...and...there, you almost did it again. I can see it on your face. Stop your sniping and I'll stop poking. Deal?"

"Deal," Leslie said. "Your private life is off limits, as is mine."

"With one exception," Cox added.

"And that is?"

"Your Pittsburgh cop friend."

Her face flushed. "What's Jakowski have to do with..."

"Everything, I'm afraid. He's prying around the edges of the telescope. He's in and out of Florida more times than Trump. One day he's working for the Seminal Society collector Dexter Stratis, the next day he isn't. Then he's working for the task force. Then he isn't. Tickles my suspicion bone, you wanna know the truth."

Leslie had been suppressing the same apprehension, beginning with her trip with him to Europe. They were compatible when together, conversation coming so easy, comfortable in each other's presence, causing Leslie to envision a nice life together, essentially a duplication of her life with Junior before he had been taken from her. That, she now realized, was the source of her agitation. She knew she had to put her relationship with Jakowski on hold until his marriage officially ended—and his status with Stratis fully vetted. Knowing what needed to be done, and doing it, were two distinct things. She couldn't seem to muster the resolve to do the latter. "How about you letting me handle Jak, okay?"

"Fair enough, Leslie. But you need to promise me that if his activities overlap our investigation in any way, I need to be read in."

Discipline prevented her from barking, *"Not on your life!"* Instead, she simply said, "I know where personal ends and business begins. You needn't worry."

Cox started to reply, changed his mind and said, "Let's talk about our bakerman. Here's what we know for certain. Husband's out drinking, as he often was. Tells anyone who'll listen that he's 'going home and settling this thing once and for all'. He leaves the bar earlier than normal. Gets in a fight with his wife. She ends up with a black eye, he ends up dead, his neck sliced with a kitchen knife. With me so far? Oh, and we find the bakerman in his shop with a late start on his baking for the day."

"With you." Leslie secretly rolled her eyes, but acknowledged he was right.

"We also have bakerman's statement that he hadn't been in the deceased's apartment, except a few times to fix leaks."

"We also have his prints on the back drop-down fire escape," Leslie added.

"Lots of prints on that fire escape. What we don't have is timing. All of those fire escape *visits* could have been sometime in the past. I've convinced myself they were having an affair. We need to find the missing knife *and* we need to place him up in the apartment when the husband made his way home."

"The bakery search found the pole possibly used to pull down the escape," Leslie added. "No fingerprints and no unexpected knives. What we need is proof of him going up there at the critical time."

"We're asking the neighbors for video. So far, nothing."

"What about street video?"

"Inconclusive at best," Cox replied, adding, "CIA Beth believes we have something at the right time. Trouble is, it's inconclusive."

"What's that mean?"

"Some sort of corruption in the data from the camera. Something about pixelation problems. They're working it."

"So, we hurry up and wait. As Junior always said, the hardest part is the waiting."

"At least that gives us a chance to concentrate on the Franklin matter. What do you make of what Reggie said about finding the Medici Telescope in that storage facility? And not the Sunspot?"

"According to him, it's impossible for the Medici to have been on the sunken ship. Assume that as a given," Leslie continued, "I had been working on the theory that the deceased had driven his boat from Fort Myers down to the salvage site, possibly to recover the Sunspot Telescope, intending to keep it for himself."

"I buy that theory. With the added proviso that Franklin was working for one or more of the billionaire Seminal Society collectors. Looking for a huge pay day."

"The auction— the 'Great Shed Steal' of all things—suggests he, or someone, was working with more than one telescope. Playing them off against each other."

"That would certainly drive the bidding up," Cox agreed. "Can you imagine billionaires at a storage shed auction? What about those guys who specialize in abandoned sheds? Imagine, bidding a thousand dollars or so and finding a telescope worth, say fifty, a hundred, million!"

"The average shed bidder probably would never know the real value of an old wooden telescope and possibly throw it out. Or sell it for a few bucks."

"Happens all the time," Cox said. "I'm thinking of driving over and seeing if I can locate the shed. You with me?"

"Not on your life! After that lecture from Boots! Not going anywhere *near* Miami. Sheriff'll be all over us! In fact, we need to call Agent Ghana."

"Do what you think best with Ghana. Personally, I wouldn't give her the time of day."

Without comment, Leslie picked up her phone and dialed Ghana's number.

Surprisingly, the task force agent picked up on the first ring, saying, "Just the person I wanted to talk to. Understand you visited with Sir Reggie. How..."

"Hold for a moment," Leslie interrupted. "My partner, Simeon Cox, is here and I'd like to put you on speaker. No one else can hear."

"Not happy. But go ahead, then." After a slight pause, the agent continued, "I assume Reggie told you about the Medici Telescope in the storage shed. That was an unexpected turn of events."

"How so?"

"We've known for a while now about the theft—disputed theft I should say—from the *Museo Galileo*. Interpol's been working with us on that. Without much cooperation from the museum, I should add. It's as if they don't want it recovered. Interpol's convinced the Seminal Society collectors are behind the theft, but we can't find a link."

"Which ones of the collectors? Can you give us names?"

"Stratis tops the list. Little Billy Bob's got tentacles out. The Indian couple, Sanjay and Riya Kumar, and new..."

"I thought the Kumars had financial problems."

"Problem's been resolved. They're hot after the telescope. At least they were when it was the Sunspot Telescope. The Medici might be out of range for them. That won't stop them from bidding at the early stages."

"Anyone else?"

"A recent addition. Your new friend, retired Admiral Makenzie Madison Masters. She's a real piece of work, that woman."

"Is that the whole list?" Leslie asked.

"There are several, as a matter of fact. Two Saudis, a man from Turkey, and one—possibly two—from Italy. We also have a few nibblers from China, Japan and Korea. Oh, and one from Mexico as well."

"I don't suppose you'll be providing their names," Cox commented.

"You suppose right, Detective Cox. Not one of those participants has set foot in Florida, either directly or indirectly."

"Happy to have you clarify that, Agent Ghana," Cox responded with undisguised sarcasm.

"Does that mean the four—five—you named," Leslie probed, "are *already* here?"

"That's a valid takeaway," Ghana conceded.

"What about Pete Jakowski," Leslie ventured. "How does he fit with all this?"

"Far as we know, he and Stratis are on the outs. Jak's been in and out of Florida over the past several weeks. He landed in Fort Lauderdale over a week ago, but no flight out."

Leslie was about to thank Ghana and hang up when a thought struck her. "If Jak wasn't working with the task force, and I trust you on that, then why would you track him at all?"

Silence met her question.

The saying, *he who speaks first, loses*, popped into Leslie's mind and she heeded the adage. Cox took a breath as if he was about to say something. She strenuously ran a finger across her throat as a warning to him to keep quiet.

He obeyed.

The silence mounted to the point where Leslie was tempted to hang up thinking the federal agent had terminated the call. Leslie resolved to wait until the line rolled over to dial tone.

"Off the record," Ghana finally said, her voice low, measured. "No recordings, no notes."

"Agreed," Leslie replied, after receiving a positive nod from her partner.

"You as well, Detective Cox. You as well."

"You have my assurance, Agent Ghana." Cox responded, rolling his eyes and shaking his head.

"Court order. Jakowski works for us from time to time, but he's not been read in on the telescope file because from all indications, Stratis has locked him out. When he flew to Florida, we asked the court to allow us to monitor his travel as well as the GPS on his rental. GPS was a bit too far. Judge pitched a fit, to say the least. In the end, went along. Gave us three days."

"I assume you're not tracking him now."

"As I said, we got three days."

"Anything of interest pertaining to my investigation we should know about?"

"Only that he spent about half his time with the deceased Franklin and the remainder at the home of a man known as Herco Hoyos over on Sanibel Island. Hoyos is a former Colombian soccer player. In his soccer days, you know, the team was owned by Escobar. We have reason to believe Hoyos is still connected to the active enforcement arm of the old *Medellín* cartel."

FIFTEEN

ARRANGING A MEETING WITH MAKENZIE Madison Masters, president of Masters Marine Salvage & Rescue, up to this point had proven to be difficult. The woman was in constant motion, didn't answer her own phone and never called back, all as noted in the case file by Criminal Investigative Assistant, Lizbeth Hillard. Cox tried working his magic to no avail. The best he was able to manage, after browbeating Big Mack's assistant for several minutes, was, "The boss'll be out of the country for several days. She's on her way to the corporate plane as we speak."

"What's that mischievous grin for?" Cox asked Leslie when he relayed the assistant's words to her. "And what the hell you lookin' up with such gusto?"

"Here it is!" Leslie exclaimed. "All I need now is..."

"What the hell you looking..."

"The tail number for the Masters' corporate plane! And now I'm looking for...Oh! Here it is! A flight plan was just filed! Her plane's taking off at twelve-twelve from Page Field and landing at twelve-fifty-five at...at, can you believe this? MIA!"

"She's flying across the state! Why not drive? Here to Miami, two hours. Bet flying isn't any faster."

"Shit! She's leaving the country! Miami may be her first stop, but it's not her last. Cox, you drive."

"Where we going? Over to Miami? Not a good id..."

"Page Field." Leslie checked her watch. "We'll just make it."

In the car, Cox exclaimed, "Shit! According to the GPS's ETA, they'll be gone before we get there."

"That's what lights and sirens were made for—along with a heavy foot."

"If you think I'm going to block an aircraft with this car, you better think..."

Leslie wasn't listening. She was waiting for Ghana to pick up. When the agent finally answered, Leslie wasted no time. "I need a favor. Actually, two favors. By any chance is Big Mack booked on a flight out of Miami today? No time for the whys now. Fill you in later."

Silence on the phone for a long minute. Then, "On an American flight leaving at two-twenty."

"Bingo!" Leslie exclaimed. "Second favor. Would you..."

"And lookee here," the agent said. "She's traveling with none other than Sir Reggie! Landing in Florence of all places."

"Interesting! I need to speak with Masters."

"I'm waiting for how I fit into that plan," the agent reminded Leslie. "Spring it on me."

"Use your magic to ground her plane here at Page. I'll release the hold only if she agrees to be interviewed by us on the flight over to Miami."

"If she doesn't cooperate after you take off?"

"I assume you can refuse to allow her plane to land."

"Remind me to never cross you."

The line went dead.

———◆———

"I protest this conversation!" Masters announced, leaning forward in her seat opposite the detectives, their knees almost touching in the compact cabin of the small jet aircraft. "This...this is coercion, pure and simple! You're only here because our takeoff clearance was cancelled. Now that I've agreed to talk to you, am I correct that unless I cooperate, we won't be allowed to land in Miami?"

"Let's just say," Leslie answered, refusing to go on the record with the actual circumstances of this interview, "we've been trying to schedule this interview for several days now and you haven't made the time for us. This is a homicide investigation, a homicide of one of your key employees and I'd like to know why you're refusing to discuss Franklin with us."

"I'm not refusing anything. Just very busy at the moment."

"Spin it how you like, Admiral, to us it appears as if you're withholding information vital to a fatality investigation. We understand you're about to leave the country, so that's enough for us to have your passport surrendered. I'd say we're doing you a favor trying to get this resolved before the plane lands. Give us straight answers and we won't inconvenience your travels."

"Still sounds like coercion to me."

"You want to spend your time bickering," Leslie said, "keep it up. We have a judge standing by," Leslie looked down at her phone as if to say, *"One call and you're not leaving the country"*. "So, what'll it be?"

Her host silently considered her options. The plane began taxiing, picking up speed as it went. Masters swiveled her seat around to face forward. Within minutes they were accelerating down the runway. Leslie felt the familiar pressure as she was pushed backward into her seat, the ground quickly falling away beneath the wings. Interstate 75 was already behind them as the plane banked to the right.

The plane leveled off and Masters' chair again turned so that the three were once more facing each other. Leslie said, "The interview is now beginning if you have no further objections." Not hearing a response, she set her phone to record mode and entered the date. Then she added, "Detectives Leslie Hodges and Simeon Cox aboard the private jet aircraft of Masters Marine Salvage & Rescue. MMS&R herein. We are speaking with retired Admiral Makenzie Madison Masters, president of the company. The deceased, Derrick Franklin, was an employee of MMS&R when he died."

Leslie looked over to Masters as if to say, *"Add what you like"*.

Masters gave a slight shrug and nodded; eyebrows raised.

"What position did Franklin hold with the company?"

"Chief of Salvage Operations."

"What did that entail?"

"We don't have enough time for all that he did," Masters equivocated.

"Granted," Leslie said. "How about limiting your answer for now to his responsibilities with respect to the recovery of the *Buen Jesús*. You can have your office send us a listing of other responsibilities, say over the past five years."

"Franklin—Benny to us—," Masters began, "was the one who found the *Buen Jesús* on his own time. He was diving off the Dry Tortugas, looking for...for God knows what. Because it was his find, he received a percentage of the salvage."

"Was a Galileo telescope one of the salvaged items?"

"Right to the heart of it, I see. A Galileo telescope, the one dubbed the Sunspot, was on the original salvage list. He—and I—did a ton of investigating. Galileo produced many, many telescopes in his lifetime. They each had different magnification and lengths, depending upon what he was looking for. He gave the one on the *Buen Jesús* to his patron in Florence, Christina..."

"Talk to us about what happened to that telescope. We know it didn't come up with the salvage. So where is it?"

"Wouldn't we all just love to know? There's an auction going on at a shed over in Lauderdale. Some say it's the Sunspot. Others say it's the original Medici, the one that's believed to be in a museum in Florence. Lots of confusion."

Glancing at her watch, Leslie realized that unless she prevented the plane from landing, she only had a few more minutes. Changing the subject, she leaned forward and asked, "Do you believe Franklin shot himself on the ferry?"

"Not by any stretch of the imagination, Detective! He wasn't the type to take his own life! Not that way anyhow."

"What's that mean?

"If he wanted to die in the water, he would have dove down and simply turned his regulator off—or allowed it to run dry. And it would have been miles from shore, not a thousand feet! Not buying it!"

"What *are* you buying?"

"The Sunspot Telescope was removed from the *Buen Jesús* before we brought the salvage up."

"You suggesting Franklin took it?"

"If the shoe fits, Detective."

"Shoes are funny, Admiral. Sometimes one style fits many feet."

"You trying to tell me something?"

"Just talking about shoes. So, tell us, why are you flying to Italy with Sir Reggie?"

"My travel plans are my private business! I don't answer to you—or to anyone."

"That's certainly your prerogative, Admiral," Leslie said, parroting back Masters' defiant attitude. "That doesn't stop me from speculating that since you're traveling with one of the world's experts on Galileo, you want his advice on something. What could that subject be, I ask myself. Maybe, just maybe, the telescope being auctioned off in that storage shed is not the Medici. Maybe it's the Sunspot? Or maybe it really is the Medici?" Leslie studied Masters' face as she spoke but saw nothing useful. "If I were trying to sell the Sunspot Telescope and the Medici suddenly came on the market, I'd want to know if the Medici in the shed was a fake or the real one. And what better way to make certain than to take Sir Reggie, the world expert, to confirm which it is? Am I close?"

"That assumes *I'm* in possession of the Sunspot Telescope, doesn't it?"

"Your company had possession. You just said so."

"As I said, it never surfaced!"

"As you said, Admiral. As you said."

Masters' eyes darkened and her face set hard. She clutched the armrests as if holding herself back from attacking Leslie. "How dare you," she seethed through compressed lips, "accuse me of..."

"I haven't accused you of anything. I'm merely trying to put the pieces together. If I'm wrong on anything I said, you're free to set the record straight."

"That telescope never came off that ship! Period!"

"Then where did it go?"

"I have no idea!"

"Have you thought about where it could have gone?"

"What I think about is not your business!"

Leslie leaned forward, their faces almost touching. "I'll tell you exactly what *is* my business, Ms. Masters. My business is a dead man who I believe had in his possession the Sunspot Telescope! And furthermore, I believe you share that belief."

The overhead speaker came alive, breaking up the tension permeating the cabin. "Please prepare to land," the pilot's voice crackled. "Position all seats forward and fasten seat belts. We will be on the ground shortly."

Makenzie Madison Masters' clenched hands relaxed slightly as her seat swiveled around, ending communication.

"Any time you want," Leslie called to the admiral's back, "please feel free to correct my beliefs." Leslie had no expectation of a response.

Nothing more was said until the plane rolled to a stop near the main terminal. While they waited for the door to be opened, Masters turned to face the detectives, all hostility now gone. "I must hand it to you Hodges, you do hold your own. As a new Seminal Society collector, I'd sure love to own that Sunspot. My plan is to bid on that shed, assuming I can satisfy myself the Sunspot's in there and not the Medici which I could never afford. So, you're right. I'm taking Reginald to Italy to verify that the Medici on display there is a fake, which, for the *official* record, he insists is not. And time is of the essence."

"Thank you, Admiral," Leslie said. "I wish you all the luck in the world with your bidding."

"To show there are no hard feelings on my part, please consider having Captain Mathews fly you back to Fort Myers. Take a detour if you wish and have him fly you over the wreck site. Nothing to see now, but it'll give you a perspective of the conditions we work under."

SIXTEEN

THE PLANE WAS FLYING LOW OVER the Gulf of Mexico. Leslie, her head pressed against the small port, focused on the barrier islands just offshore from Fort Myers. The pilot banked slightly. When the plane leveled off, it was directly over the bridge under which Franklin, standing on the rear deck of a ferry, had shot himself in the head. She struggled to wrap her mind around the relationship between Big Mack, the missing telescope, and Franklin's death. Nothing added up, yet she had the overwhelming sense they were all somehow connected, as was her friend, Jakowski.

Suicide or homicide? That was a threshold question. Despite the medical examiner's report, that question had not yet been resolved to Leslie's satisfaction. Suicide being 'out of character' for Franklin was not a valid reason for concluding it wasn't a real possibility. People were always doing things that were 'out of character', whatever that phrase meant.

The jet's left wing dipped as the plane began its descent into Page Field. The pilot, using the speaker for the first time since leaving Miami, announced, "We'll be on the ground in a matter of minutes. All seats forward, please."

Turning to Cox, she asked, "Learn anything from our air tour of the treasure site?"

"Don't know what there was to learn. Lots of water down there. Other than the Dry Tortugas themselves, very little else."

"You realize, don't you, that other than the fact of Franklin's death, we know very little other than he was in charge of the diving operation. But it was his job to supervise the recovery of everything down there worth recovering. Not adding up."

"Les, you thinking he hid the telescope?"

"If not him, who else? I can't picture anyone positioned better than the chief of salvage operations to set a little to the side for himself. Other than perhaps Big Mack herself. Who, I might add, appears to be a buyer and not a seller."

"There's nothing *little* about this Galileo telescope, Les. That instrument will sell for a hundred million, minimum."

"Much more if there is only one on the market. Hundred's only the price if the Medici is real. The Sunspot's worth much more to the Seminal Society collectors if the Medici's fake."

"Didn't the professor tell us the Medici was real? And in that shed."

"He did. And that's what's puzzling me. If he was so certain, then why travel all the way to Italy with Masters just to verify to her what he already knows?"

"Double-check?" Cox shrugged. "Just to make certain."

"Makes absolutely no sense. Junior always said that if it doesn't make sense, treat it as a lie."

"So, what're you thinking?"

"Say Sir Reggie's lying about the authenticity of the telescope in the shed. And if that's true, then there's no point for him to fly all the way to Italy to view the Medici. He—and Big Mack—are up to something else. What, I can't imagine. We both know that one way or another that missing Sunspot Telescope is worth enough to steal for—or to be murdered over."

"That moves Admiral Masters directly into the crosshairs," Cox acknowledged. "She's knee-deep into the Sunspot. But, as you pointed out, she's a buyer—a Seminal Society collector, if you will—not a seller."

"That goes against what logic tells us. It was her salvage down there. So legally, she owns the Sunspot. I'm thinking she..."

"... has it! In fact, she really *is* the seller! Then this buyer crap is a red herring!"

"That's where I'm going. Since the Sunspot never came to the surface, how did she obtain possession?"

"The sixty-four-thousand-dollar question! Assuming, of course, she even has possession."

"Oh, she does!" Leslie's voice held more authority than the facts warranted. "Or, at the very least, she knows where it is," she added to soften her statement. "I would bet..."

Leslie's thought was interrupted by a text message. GREETINGS FROM A TEXAS FRIEND. SAME PLACE, NINE TONIGHT. COME HUNGRY AND ALONE. YOU WON'T BE DISAPPOINTED. TRAVEL BACK IN TIME TO VISIT MOONS AND SUNS.

Leslie turned the screen toward Cox. "Just what I needed! Looks like Little Billy Bob has summoned me."

"That's a good thing. He's a Seminal Society collector, if I recall right. Didn't you meet with him in the Newton matter? Billy Bob Bishop. Authenticated a Newton book for you—or so the file says. Was prepared to pay over a billion dollars if it was the proper version."

"How the hell you know all that?"

"It's in the file. You take great notes."

"I worked that aspect of the case with Fischer. Why would you..."

"Insomniac. Read files to put me to sleep."

"There're better ways of falling asleep. You should..."

"Oh, really? Want to impart your wisdom? I'm all..."

"Don't go there!"

"So, what's the story on this Billy Bob character?"

"Bishop's grandfather, William Bishop, Sr., hit oil in Odessa, Texas when he was twenty-five. Old Billy Bob died in nineteen-sixty-two and his oil holdings went to his son, Bryant Bishop, who hit a bridge abutment a few years later going over a hundred miles an hour. Little Billy Bob was twenty and wasted no time selling his daddy's oil holdings for well over two billion dollars. He then began buying Texas land. 'When oil hits its stride again,' he told anyone who would listen, 'I'll cash out. I own it all!' Last count, the guy's worth upwards of a hundred billion."

"You met him at the penthouse of the Naples Ritz-Carlton. Right?"

"According to this text, I'm to meet him there again."

"You want me to go with...?"

"Alone, is what he said."

"I can wait in the car. Isn't that what Fish did?"

"I'm a big girl. I'll go alone. Nothing goes in the file until I give the word. Hear me?"

"Don't eat too much. Bring a doggie bag back if you can. I love ribs."

"I don't recall putting the menu in the file."

"Fish told me. He said you damn near slept the whole way back to Fort Myers."

"This time I plan to save room for the key lime pie, you want to know."

———————

"Nice of you to come, Deputy Hodges," Little Billy Bob said, bowing with a flourish as he opened the door to the penthouse for Leslie. "Lot of water has passed under the bridge since we last broke bread it seems."

"By 'lot of water'," Leslie clarified, "I assume you mean the arrest of the person who shot and killed the guard over at the university when I was working on the Newton manuscript case."

"That, and the recent death of that diver, Franklin. Keeping you hopping, I imagine."

"I've found that in my field of endeavor there's never a lack of work. If you invited me here to discuss police matters, Mr. Bishop, whether the case is open or solved, then we have mismatched expectations. I'm afraid I won't be able to..."

"Just as feisty as ever, I see. But you're wrong, my dear. So very wrong. Policing is what *you* do. I want no part of that world. Collecting is what *I* do—my vocation as it were." His eyes moved slowly from her feet to her face where they lingered, taking in her deep green eyes. "Can't a guy invite a good-looking woman—better than I even remember—to dinner with him just because he enjoys her company?"

"And can't a woman accept for the same reason—and because of the food? I confess to being addicted to your ribs, that special sauce. I've ordered ribs several times since, and nothing compares. I even tried making my own. Not even close." She took a moment to reappraise the good-looking Texan, then added, "You and I both know I'm not here for ribs. Or for that matter, sparkling conversation. I assume you have information on Franklin's death that I'd like to know. And I have...let's just assume...information that's pertinent to an art object you want to acquire. How'm I doing?"

"I don't know what tune you march to Hodges, but you're refreshing. I know exactly where I stand with you. I like that." He took his time before continuing. "Here's the plan—assuming you're on board, that is. First, we follow the agenda you just laid out. I tell you about the diver Franklin and his underwater exploits. Then you tell me what you can about the telescope that went missing from the *Buen Jesús*. Then we put aside all business talk and enjoy a rib dinner. The ribs I hasten to add, arrived from Texas just this evening. This time, save room for the key lime pie. I promise you won't be disappointed. Sound like a plan?"

"Sounds like a plan," Leslie acknowledged. "I make no promises as to what I can share."

"Fair enough." Bishop led the way across the entry to a corner with two facing upholstered silk armchairs separated by a small table. "Can I get you anything to drink?" he asked when Leslie was seated. "We have a fully stocked bar. Anything you desire."

"No, thanks. You can begin by telling me about the telescope."

"There's more than one Galileo telescope, but I assume you're referring to the one on the inventory of the ship."

"We're calling that one the Sunspot," Leslie volunteered.

"Would you mind indulging me while I show off a little Galilean history? I'd really like you to understand the importance to me of a First from one of the greatest minds ever. Truth is, I can't decide who was smarter, Newton or Galileo. In science, it was probably Galileo. But he was so foolish in his personal life. Taking on a powerful pope—and being found guilty by the Inquisition—is the height of arrogance, I would say. I do believe, however, that most of what Newton proved, Galileo already had guessed to be the case. Those two are so linked, they're almost singular."

"I can see, then," Leslie commented, settling back in the comfortable chair, "why you wanted to buy—or perhaps now own—Newton's original *Principia*."

"I won't comment on my ownership, but I do admit to a passion for Newton and certainly also for my favorite, Galileo di Vincenzo Bonaiuti de' Galilei. In sixteen-ten he discovered that Jupiter had several moons, and when he calculated their elliptical orbits he convinced himself that Copernicus, a hundred years earlier, had been correct. The earth was indeed traveling around the sun and not the other way around."

"Isn't it a big step from seeing the moons of Jupiter to concluding the sun is the center of the universe?" Leslie asked, comfortable enough with the Texan to voice the question that had been nagging at her.

"Who really knows how great minds work? As I said, scientists had been nibbling around the edges of the sun being the center of the universe for a long time before Galileo. According to the Catholic Church, the Bible said otherwise. Galileo believed the pope was reading the Bible incorrectly. The pope believed that views contrary to the Bible were heresy. Galileo, knowing the pope's rigid views, needed allies. He played up to the Medici family, even naming the moons after the Medici family and giving the powerful family the very telescope he had used to first see Jupiter's moons."

"That's the one currently in the *Museo Galileo* in Florence," Leslie commented, not ready to discuss what she had learned from Professor Hammerschmidt about the theft and shed auction.

"You've been doing your homework, I see. That's why you're calling the telescope found on the sunken ship the Sunspot Telescope. To differentiate from the Medici. Those sunspots further supported Galileo's belief that the sun was the center of the universe." Billy Bob paused, then added, "Don't ask me how sunspots correlate to the earth traveling around the sun. Above my pay grade." Bishop laughed, his eyes sparkling.

Leslie knew at that moment that no amount of money would stand between her host and ownership of the Sunspot Telescope.

"In sixteen-fifteen," Billy Bob continued, "Christina, the Grand Duchess of Tuscany, posed Galileo a question: How could the 'scientific' idea of a central sun be compatible with Scripture regarding an immovable earth? To which question he rather famously replied in a letter that turned into an essay, taking him months to write. Several years later, around sixteen-twenty, perhaps sensing he'd need more protection from the pope, Galileo delivered to his great friend, the grand duchess, the actual telescope he had used to confirm the sunspots along with a sealed document diagramming its exact dimensions."

"And she promptly gifted it to the King of Spain," Leslie added, her way of demonstrating she was following. "That's why it was on the *Buen Jesús*."

"An inauguration gift for King Philip IV that never made it to him." Bishop said, acknowledging Leslie's understanding of history. Standing, he announced, "I'm pouring some more Chianti in tribute to our discussion. Please join me."

Surprising herself, Leslie nodded. "That sounds good."

A moment later, holding the wine high in front of him, Bishop toasted, "To art. And to those who appreciate its true value."

Leslie, practicing not rolling her eyes, raised her glass but said nothing.

Breaking the silence, Billy Bob said, "Getting back to our story. This letter Galileo wrote to the duchess was meant to calm the pope. In the letter, Galileo explained the independence of science from religion and went on to dispute that his findings are contrary to the Bible. He stressed his belief in both the Bible and in what he had discovered through scientific means. According to him, it was a misinterpretation of the Bible to claim that his conclusions were against religion. To say the least, instead of having a calming effect on the pope it did just the opposite."

"I don't blame the pope for getting angry. Galileo's letter accused him of misinterpreting the Bible," Leslie added. "Not a good plan on Galileo's part, I'd say."

"Therein lies Galileo's downfall. It wasn't just the Bible that was under attack. It was the pope himself. That could never be tolerated, so the pope's Inquisition found him guilty."

"House arrest for the rest of his life," Leslie filled in.

"Only because the Medici family, including the grand duchess, came to Galileo's defense. Otherwise, he would have been burned as a heretic." Billy Bob took a deep sip, savoring the flavor. Closing his eyes, he held his glass high again. "We pronounce, judge, and declare, that you, Galileo, have rendered yourself vehemently suspected by this Holy Office of heresy, that is, of having believed and held the doctrine—which is false and contrary to the Holy and Divine Scriptures—that the sun is the center of the world. You are further suspected of believing that the earth travels around the sun and that the earth is not the center of the world."

"Is that a direct quote from the verdict?"

"Modified a bit. As best as my aging mind will allow."

"Your 'aging' mind is sharper than most anyone I know, regardless of their years," Leslie said, genuinely impressed with the man sitting across from her.

"Only with respect to my passions."

"Other than Newton and Galileo?"

"Let's hold that for a later time. Dinner will be served soon, and I must know what you have found regarding the Sunspot."

"Only that it's missing. As you certainly know, the telescope was listed on the inventory taken before the contents of the *Buen Jesús* were brought up. According to everything I've been led to believe, the Sunspot never surfaced."

"Is that what Masters told you?"

"Pretty much. But...but something's troubling you. What is it?"

"My sources tell me Three M has the Sunspot."

"I left out one fact," Leslie confessed. "Before his death, Franklin took his private boat for a long ride. Left Fort Myers early in the morning and arrived back at his dock about one in the morning."

"You suggesting he went to the dive site?"

"Likely."

"And he didn't come back with the Sunspot?"

"Not that we know."

"And the next day he killed himself?"

"Looks that way."

"And you're not settin' any great store by that order of events?"

"Should I be? Are you?"

"Bet my horse I'm not! Your speculation?"

"Said more than I had intended already. Can't get into those details. Sorry."

"If, as I am led to believe, Masters has the Sunspot, where do you go from here?"

"Can't discuss police business. But she does call herself a Seminal Society collector. That argues for her being a buyer, not a seller. If she already has the Sunspot, why did she fly off to Italy to verify the Medici? Oh...now I've actually said too much!"

"You certain that's where she went?"

"I can't discuss this!"

"Again, I ask: You certain she's on that flight?"

The challenge in Billy Bob's voice was too much to ignore. "I'll bite. What are you telling me?"

"There is no need to fly to Florence with the world's expert to know whether the Medici is real or a fake. The only way to know for an absolute certainty is to have it lab tested. The museum refuses. End of story. You need to test the one in the shed. Assuming there even *is* a shed."

"You know about the shed? And about Masters' trip to Italy? What don't you know?"

"Frankly, I don't know where the Sunspot is. I can only guess."

"Then, what did Hammerschmidt see in that shed?"

"He told you whatever he was paid to tell you. Nothing more—or less. That simple. Man's been bought."

"By whom?"

"By the same people who are buying up everything we value. The cartels."

"What am I missing?"

"The newest Seminal Society collector. A man by the name of Castro Estrada Jimènez."

"Name means nothing. Should it?"

"Does 'The Zs' ring a bell?"

"*Los Zetas*! East coast of Mexico. Fentanyl! You name it! They're into artifacts now?"

"Jimènez wouldn't know a piece of art if it fell on him! Money laundering all the way. They're using art to launder money."

"And Admiral Masters?"

"Classic front."

"And Hammerschmidt?"

"A stooge. She's taking the professor to The Zs so he can validate directly in front of them that the Sunspot she has is genuine. After that, Masters will bid in her own name, but for the ultimate account of The Zs. Essentially, she'll have a blank check."

"How much are *you* willing to pay for the Sunspot, if, just saying, the Medici is available?"

"Surely, you don't expect an answer to that question, other than for me to confess that money is only a marker. If I spend my money only on prudent stuff, then someone other than myself would have the pleasure of spending that money after I leave this planet. So, why shouldn't I enjoy myself with a Galileo First? Or whatever else I might enjoy?"

Before Leslie could venture an opinion, Billy Bob announced, "Dinner is served. No more shop talk. Time to enjoy ourselves."

Accepting her host's warm hand, she followed him into the adjoining room where a table for two had been formally set. Before sitting down, he said, "One more fact for you to consider. Your gentleman friend, the one you know as Jak, and I know as Esquire, no longer appears to be running errands for Dexter."

"Was that a question? Or a statement?"

"Possibly both. Okay, no more business. The ribs are awaiting."

Perhaps it was the wine Leslie had allowed herself. Or perhaps it was the intimate lighting and wonderful ribs, even better than she had remembered, that had relaxed her. Or just perhaps it was the easy manner of the good-looking, dark-eyed Texan sitting across the table from her, his leathery skin suggesting wide-open spaces and a carefree life. Whatever it was, she was thoroughly enjoying his company. That fact became abundantly clear when he reached across the table, touching her arm ever so slightly. She hadn't moved, both of them knowing what his touch suggested.

"What would your wife say, if she..."

"You haven't done your homework on *me*. I haven't been married in donkey years. Make that several generations of donkey's." Bishop considered Leslie a long moment before saying, "The more important question is, what will Esquire say?"

Leslie was still formulating her response, when he added, "I don't suppose we'll have long to wait before that becomes a moot question."

"And just what makes you think that?"

"For starters, your hand hasn't moved. If anything, the tension has disappeared. I know you to be a good judge of people, Leslie. So am I. And you're a good person. Just work out your relationship. Then we can..."

"I think this has..."

"Time for the highlight of the night," Bishop declared, his face again animated. He tapped his watch and within seconds waiters had placed generous slices of key lime pie in front of them. "Don't feel you have to eat it all. But I do warn you, even the way you watch your weight, you'll eat more than you think you will."

"Is it that good?" she parried. "Or are you suggesting my willpower is diminished?"

"Both, I venture to say. Both."

SEVENTEEN

BILLY BOB HAD BEEN RIGHT; THE KEY LIME PIE was by far the best she had ever eaten. Leslie had promised herself that each forkful would be her last, only to find that her normally infallible self-control had vanished. She had stopped eating only when her plate was clean. The last time she had consumed food with such abandon was on a dare from her college roommate. She had been sick the whole next day.

Now relaxed and dozing in the back seat of a Lyft heading north on I-75 toward her home in Lehigh Acres, she suddenly jerked awake remembering her phone, at Bishop's insistence, was off. Quickly retrieving it, she noted several messages from Cox, all pertaining to the Chase Montrose homicide. He had captioned each message as INFORMATION ONLY, not wanting to interrupt her meeting with Little Billy Bob. Skipping to the end, the message read: BOOKING THE PERP. NOT WHO YOU MIGHT THINK. DETAILS IN THE AM.

Clancy Lowry, the baker, was the person Leslie had focused on as the killer. So, who did Cox book into the county jail? And why? Cox purposely hadn't provided details. She checked the official file and found nothing more. A call to Cox's phone went unanswered.

Leslie, now fully awake, scanned her other messages and almost overlooked one that was labeled simply LORD. It took her a moment to remember that LORD was Sam Lord, her neighbor. Opening the message, she saw what appeared to be a building. The image had been captured in low light from a distance and it took her several seconds to see the back of a man, a tall man, frozen in mid-step approaching the side of the building. Zooming in on the image, she realized the building was a side view of her house. The identity of the man evaded her. On a whim, she blew up the photo to the point where only a portion of the face was visible. "Jakowski!" she yelped, causing the driver to glance in his mirror.

"Say what?" he called back to her.

"Oh, nothing. Sorry."

The message was without comment. The only other fact Leslie could glean was the time. An hour ago. Ten-ten. Most likely Pete would be waiting up for her. A wave of guilt flooded over her even as she affirmed to herself that she had done nothing wrong with Billy Bob Bishop. She focused her attention on what she was prepared—and not prepared—to share with Jakowski.

Thinking of the missing telescope brought her mind back to Franklin's suicide. And the images captured by the surveillance camera. "Oh, my God!"

"You okay, lady?" the driver said, pulling over into the right lane and slowing. "Need anything? You're not gonna be sick, are you?"

"Just keep going. I'm fine."

In fact, Leslie wasn't fine. The image Lord had sent of the man in her yard, who she was certain was Pete Jakowski, triggered a memory of an image of Franklin on the stern of the ferry just before he moved out of camera view.

There was no way to accurately judge, but her mind told her that Franklin, and the man in the image Lord had sent, were the same height. Build seemed off, but that could be distortion, or any number of factors. There were no good facials to compare. She visualized Jakowski's movements, comparing them with what she recalled from the video of Franklin. Similar enough, but not the same. The framed picture she had seen at Franklin's house, the one showing the three Pitt buddies, flashed to mind. All three roughly the same height and build. Figures could have changed dramatically in the thirty-some years that had passed since that photo had been taken. She knew firsthand that Jakowski's hadn't. Judging from the autopsy photos, neither had Franklin's. What about Hoyos'?

The questions were coming faster than Leslie could process them. "Enough," she blurted. "Enough!"

The car came to a stop, the driver turning to face her.

"Go on!" Leslie commanded, "I'm fine. Just get me home!"

"Lady, you *are* home. Need help going inside?"

———◆———

The house was unnaturally quiet when Leslie entered the living room. She had expected to see Jakowski sprawled on the sofa, a beer in one hand, the TV tuned to some sports channel, perhaps recapping the day. But the TV was off, no trace of Pete, not even an empty bottle.

Did he go back to his hotel when I wasn't here? The rental car in the driveway suggested otherwise. Going upstairs to her room, she found it empty. Puzzled, she tried the guest bedroom and was startled to find him sound asleep, naked, snoring softly. Quietly pulling the door closed, she retreated to her room and sat on her bed trying to put the pieces together.

Not fully understanding what Jakowski was telling her by sleeping in the guest room, she gave up, got ready for bed and within fifteen minutes, she too was sleeping soundly, something she rarely did since Junior's passing.

———————

"Sleep well?" Leslie inquired of the drowsy-looking man making his way into her kitchen slightly after seven-thirty in the morning.

She herself had been roused by a call from Cox who had begun the conversation by bursting out, "Curious to know who I like for the death of Chase Montrose?"

"All ears," Leslie had responded.

"All yawns, sounds more like it," Cox had quipped. "Okay, here goes. We had it all right, just the wrong guy."

"Hey, it's too early for riddles. Out with it!"

"Access to the apartment was via the fire escape, using the light bulb changer pole your photographic memory had spotted to pull it down. Only it wasn't bakerman doing the pulling."

"So, who was it already? Gotta pee, so make it fast."

"The assistant baker. Man by the name of Max Clement. Fingerprints all over the pole, as well as the fire escape."

"What about Binita, the wife? Any involvement?"

"Still working that. Fischer's taking it from here. We need to concentrate on the diver—and the telescope. See you in the office."

"Give me an hour."

"You got something going on?"

"Cox!"

The line was hastily disconnected.

"You look rested," Jakowski countered, giving no hint as to why he had chosen the spare bedroom over her bed.

"Wish I could say the same for you."

"Have a lot on my mind is all. I know you don't eat breakfast, or I'd whip up pancakes."

"Maybe another time. Coffee's ready. You want pancakes, go for it."

"What time did you get home? Waited up, almost to midnight."

"Didn't know I had a curfew," she snapped. Realizing she had come off too harsh, she added, "Must have just missed you. Rolled in about eleven-forty-five. Surprised to find you in the guest bedroom."

"Didn't think you'd appreciate an uninvited man in your bed."

"Hadn't thought of it that way. Here, speaking of men," she said, focusing on her thoughts from last night while fumbling to pull up the surveillance images of Franklin on the stern of the ferry, "who's this?" She held her phone up so Jakowski could get a good view.

"Franklin. On the stern of a boat. I'd say a ferry. This a pop quiz?"

"And who is this?" she asked, changing the image.

It took several seconds before he answered. "Me, it appears. Hard to make out, but I'd say that was me last night entering your house."

"The similarity between those two pictures has me going in circles. I agree, the second one's you. But...the first one could be you as well."

"That's impossible. I wasn't on the ferry. It's Benny. What makes you think..."

"Tired mind, I suppose. When the neighbor sent that pic of you, it reminded me of Franklin's all."

"In what way?"

"Can't pin it down. Franklin's death got me going. Too many loose ends for my liking. Mind's working overtime, getting nowhere."

"I don't know what's bothering you, Leslie. Something clearly is. Seems to me I've overstayed my welcome. I'll be gone when you return and... and let's keep it that way until you resolve the Franklin case. Probably best for everyone concerned. Thanks for the coffee."

———————

"So, tell me about your time with Little Billy Bishop," Cox asked when she arrived at her desk. "Get the key lime pie you were jonesin' for?"

"Ate it all as well."

"Not like you." Cox raised his eyebrows before continuing. "Ready to brief me? I saw there's nothing in the file." What he didn't say was that not annotating the file also was not like Leslie.

"According to LBB, our good buddy, Admiral Masters, is fronting for the Zs' cartel. He doesn't believe she went to Italy with the professor."

"Where then? We saw her meet up with Sir Reggie at Miami Airport."

"They went to see a guy named Jimènez. Billy Bob claims he's a Z. It's all a money laundering operation."

"Homeland Security put a bulletin out on him some time ago. Bad dude. She's got more money than anyone needs, why get involved with the cartels?"

"Nothing's adding up's all I can say."

"Where exactly are they meeting?"

"If Billy Bob knew, he didn't say."

Cox concentrated on his phone for several minutes before confirming, "Here's what I was referring to. Castro Estrada Jimènez. Home base, Progreso. Spotted in Cancun two days ago for what it's worth."

"Cancun. Always wanted to go there," Leslie confided. "Spring break destination. I'd think Jimènez would have better places to go. More private."

"Don't slay the reporter. Just giving you the facts. Seems that DHS is paying close attention to him. If this is money laundering, then Treasury is watching as well."

While Cox was engaged with the Cancun file, Leslie called Agent Maxine Ghana, who, surprisingly, answered on the first ring. "Just who I was thinking about," she said. "How did your meeting with Bishop go? Get to sample his pie?"

"How did you..."

"We're all over the Seminal Society. You certainly should know that by now."

"What's buying and selling artifacts, telescopes from Galileo to be exact, have to do with the feds? You folks confuse..."

"Money laundering. In this case, drug money to be exact. Buying and selling art is prime for them."

"You can't be suggesting Billy Bob Bishop's a drug dealer?"

"I wouldn't rule it out. But no, not LBB. But people around him."

"What people exactly?"

"Need to know only. Sorry."

"I'm working an active homicide!" Leslie snapped, her tone turning sharp. "Isn't that need enough to know?"

115

"Killing the messenger won't work, Hodges. Knock it off. Man shoots himself on video and goes overboard. Suicide in my book. You know something I don't?"

Now it was Leslie's turn to bargain. "Give and get? That work for you?"

"You first."

Taking a chance, Leslie filled Agent Ghana in on her theory that Franklin's death did not occur the way it appeared on video.

"Okay, I'll buy that, Hodges. For now. We have information suggesting that The Zs' cartel is trying to purchase a Galileo telescope at an auction. Someone is fronting for Castro Estrada Jimènez. From what I can determine, he's the current Zs kingpin. We like Bishop for their contact."

"Have you considered Masters?"

Silence for several seconds, followed by, "She's a lightweight. Never bought anything worthwhile. However, she *does* have access to the Sunspot. Working against your theory is that she's on a flight to Italy—with that professor, Sir Reggie. Watched video of them boarding the flight earlier today."

"Mind sending me the video? Say from the time Masters left her jet until the time she and Reggie boarded the commercial flight."

"You'll have it within five. Knock yourself out." And with that, Ghana was gone.

Turning to Cox, Leslie said, "I suppose you heard that?"

"Hate to bring it up, but where do you think Jak fits into the missing Sunspot?"

"Wish I knew," Leslie shrugged. "Wish I knew." She considered sharing her discomfort at the similarity between the images of Jakowski at her house and Franklin on the stern of the ferry. Before she said anything further, her phone beeped, indicating the receipt of a file. "Let's watch this on the computer. Ghana says she saw Masters and Reggie board the commercial flight to Florence. Bishop suggested she went to visit Jimènez somewhere in Mexico. Both can't be right."

"My money's on Ghana," Cox maintained as Leslie's computer screen powered on. "What the hell's a playboy from Texas know about Three M's travel plans?"

"See there," he said a moment later, "that's Three M walking into the terminal from the tarmac. And that's Sir Reggie over there in the corner leaning against the wall, waiting for her."

Leslie's eye followed Cox's lead and focused on the man at the edge of the video. "Can't exactly see his face, but same build— and height."

"She's going into the women's room. Reggie hasn't moved."

Several minutes passed and Masters emerged from the bathroom, nodded in the direction of Sir Reggie, who then caught up and the two of them hurried off down the concourse. The video then blinked several times. When it came on again, Masters, with Reggie at her side, was approaching the camera.

Leslie paused the file, allowing her to zoom in on both faces. "Shit! They're both turned away from the camera! Can't get a clear view!"

"Play it to the end, Les. Let's see where this leads."

A third camera caught the pair from behind walking down a passageway, ostensibly onto the plane. When the video ended, Leslie said, "I take it you're with me on this. I'm not buying what they're selling."

"A hundred percent! Except, frankly, I don't know who's selling what."

"Got something specific in mind?" Leslie asked.

"Masters came off her private jet and immediately went into the bathroom. That's odd."

"Do that all the time when I leave a plane. There's nothing...Oh, shit! You're right! She used the potty on her private jet on her way off. I even heard the toilet flush! And..." Leslie added, her eyes closed, visualizing something, "...when she left the jet she was wearing flats. Black flats. Let me find that on here." Leslie moved the cursor back to the beginning and hit PLAY.

Masters was clearly wearing black flats.

Fast forward to Masters emerging from the women's room and nodding in the direction of Sir Reggie. She was now wearing black pumps with a wide one-inch heel.

"Body double," Cox announced. "I'm willing to bet Sir Reggie's an actor as well."

"I can't believe the professor would go along with this. He has too much of a reputation to maintain."

"He most likely was told to meet her at a particular location, maybe a private gate somewhere. That's all he knows. The two people, actors I suppose, we saw get on the flight are not Masters and the professor. Masters changed her costume in the head, waited a while for the actress playing her to clear the area, then went off to meet the real Reggie. The two flew somewhere they, and by *they* I mean the admiral, didn't want to be traced to."

Leslie processed what Cox had just outlined, then said, "It all sounds a bit...hokey, you ask me."

"Worked, didn't it? Fooled Ghana. Masters is off in Mexico getting marching orders from The Zs. Any chance of us scoring a trip to Cancun? After all, you got the feds to pay for that Isle of Man jaunt with Jak." An oversized smile appeared on Cox's face. "Just kidding."

Leslie felt her face flush and was about to lash out but thought better of it. Cox was factually correct. In hindsight, the Europe trip was a mistake, for several reasons—not the least of which, she now felt compromised. Thinking back over her conversation with Jakowski earlier today, she should have pinned him down more than she had about the similarity between his image and the image from the ferry. "Shit!" she exclaimed, suddenly understanding why the two images blended in her mind. "Bring up the surveillance from the ferry!"

While Cox searched for the electronic file, Leslie found the image from her neighbor, Sammy Lord, and held it up.

"Same windbreaker," Cox proclaimed. "Can't see color on yours, but I wouldn't be surprised if it's the same. Same person?"

"This is Jak. Going into my house about ten-forty-five last night. Didn't see the jacket. Lightweight, foul weather gear I'd say. Play the video."

Leslie carefully studied the movements of the man on the ferry, trying to determine if it was Jakowski. "What's your take? That Jak or not?"

"Looks like him. But...but something's not computing. Movements are off. Possibly because of the ferry's motion. If I had to give a definite yes or no, I'd have to say, no. That your take?"

"I'm concerned I was forcing it. To be clear then, we both agree, the man on the ferry does not appear to be Pete Jakowski."

"Not in the video of the ferry coming north from Key West," Cox concurred, his attention returning to the keyboard. "Let's review the ferry going south earlier that day. See if we can determine who's on board."

"Thought you had a passenger manifest."

"They don't consistently record walk-ons."

"Amazing," Leslie observed, "how few faces they actually capture. What's the purpose of the video if...Hey! Isn't that Jak!"

Cox hit the PAUSE key, freezing the three images, two female and one male, in mid-step. "Face is turned, but I'll lay money on that being Pete. Wearing the same jacket as the rear deck shooter."

Leslie touched the name JAK on her cell phone, fully expecting her call to go to voicemail—or be blocked entirely. To her surprise, Jakowski answered on the second ring. "Mind answering a question for me?"

"Fire away."

"Cox and I are looking at the southbound loading Key West ferry video of Monday, and..."

"And there I am, boarding the ferry."

"You didn't think you being on the ferry that morning was important enough to tell me about?"

"Benny and I were going down to Key West. We had arranged a meeting down there. Only Benny didn't show."

"And you went alone?"

"What choice did I have? We had arranged to meet a man about a horse."

"Enough evasion, Jak. This 'horse' have a name?"

"Sunspot."

"And the man?"

"*Los Zetas* drug boss, Castro Estrada Jimènez."

"Found Franklin's boat!" an upbeat Lizbeth Hillard said when Leslie checked in with the CIA. "In a marina in Key West. According to the manager, Franklin often leaves his boat there for days at a time."

"That boat's a crime scene," Leslie said, stating the obvious. "We now believe Franklin was stabbed in the neck and died on that boat. Need a complete work up. I don't know if it's possible, but we'd like GPS readings for a week. When you're finished, have the boat trucked up to the Lee County Marine Unit. What do you have so far?"

"Marina guy says he's seen the man who docked the boat before. Confuses him with Franklin. Also gets him confused with another guy who comes in with Franklin. All three about the same size. I sent him a shot of your friend Jakowski. He confirmed he was one of the three. The other guy's name he didn't know exactly, but says it's something like Herb or Herbo. Definitely from south of the border though."

"Herco! Hank Hoyos. Picture's in the file. Get a confirmation. Find out which of them dropped the boat off this last time."

"On it, Detective," Hillard chirped.

"Any progress on Jak's whereabouts the night in question?"

"Forgot to mention it. It's in the report. A Pete Jakowski was registered in a room in a small B&B. Here's the thing. Best as I can determine, he checked in around five. Don't know if he stayed or left. I've asked a local uniform to go over and check, show his picture around, see if he was actually there. So far, no response."

"Good work Beth. Keep us posted." Leslie hung up and said to Cox, "Trust you got all that."

"I did. We only need *one* land-based sighting of Jak after the ferry left at six to satisfy ourselves he couldn't have been on that northbound ferry. What he did down there after the ferry left is not our concern."

"Unless he met with the cartel folks."

"That's a different investigation," Cox reminded his partner. "Let's leave that to the feds—for now."

"Speaking of the feds, we need to follow up with Masters. She knows more about the missing telescope than she's let on."

"Which one? The Medici or the Sunspot?"

"Both, I suppose. Only now I'm treating the Medici as a distraction, a decoy if you will. Sunspot is linked to Franklin, and most likely to his death. Went missing around the time he died. Sunspot's also linked to Jakowski. The Medici's important, but for our purposes it simply serves to change the value of the Sunspot. That your take?"

"Two Galileo Firsts coming available at the same time—and roughly at the same location—too much of a coincidence. I agree. Medici is a distraction."

"And remember," Leslie quipped, "There *are* no coincidences in murder!"

"Not where the Seminal Society lives," Cox grimaced, mostly to himself.

"You say something?"

"Nothing of importance," Cox assured his partner.

"Hey! Guess what I just found?"

"No clue. You been glued to that phone of yours for a while now. Must be interesting."

"Beth put me onto an app for my phone—goes beyond the regular airlines. Been tracking Masters' private jet after it dropped us off."

"I'm listening," Cox said, peeved, realizing their CIA hadn't sent him the flight-tracking app.

"Page Field overnight. Then filed a flight plan to...wait for it. Cancun!"

"Cancun? That's consistent with what Little Billy Bob told you. Meeting with Castro Jimènez you imagine? You thinking of asking the boss for permission to fly...?"

"Too late for that. The plane's due back at Page exactly two hours from now. I'd like to get Masters into the office for an in-depth interview. Any thoughts?"

"We could try giving her the choice of talking with us voluntarily or we spill her secret Cancun jaunt to the feds. Bet ol' Ghana wouldn't have any problem draggin' her ass in for questioning."

"That just might work. Masters went to a lot of trouble to hide her Mexican meeting from them. How about I see you out front in an hour. We head over to Page."

Both of their pagers simultaneously sounded.

"Hold that plan," Cox announced. "Need to get our butts to Boots' office ASAP!"

EIGHTEEN

"TREAT JAK AS YOU WOULD ANY OTHER Person of Interest," Captain Karen Stetson advised. They were in her office, Leslie and Cox standing awkwardly near the door while Sergeant Hudson Oakmore was in his customary seat across the desk from their boss. "From what you've told me, he hasn't lied to you. Of even more importance, both you and Cox seem to be in agreement he wasn't on the ferry coming back from Key West."

"We've gone over the footage several times. Someone built like him, and wearing the same-colored jacket, did come north. But we're pretty certain it was a different person." Leslie paused, then added, "But, on the other hand, we haven't been able to prove he remained in Key West either."

"And that person, you believe," Stetson said, "was either the deceased, Derrick Franklin, or a person presenting as Franklin."

"Officially," Leslie stated, "it was Franklin. That's consistent with the scenario that he shot himself and went off the stern of the ferry."

"Off the record?"

"Cox and I are toying with the idea that the ferry shooting was staged."

"Next steps?"

"Jakowski will be here in the office; probably here already. We plan to take a formal statement. Lock his story down. Then we've got an appointment with the ME. Go over her findings once more."

"Let Cox take the lead with Jak. You're too close. And...and I hope to God it doesn't come to this, but if you need to hold him, I'm to be informed first. Also, if you instruct him to remain in the jurisdiction, I'm to be informed of that as well. Leslie, I'd take you off the case, except that will send the wrong message to Jak and his management. Arresting him could, and most probably will, end his career. Play it straight. And need I tell you? Adjust your sleeping arrangements until this case is closed."

"Already done, Captain." Leslie didn't bother to explain that Jakowski had taken the initiative in that respect. "Already done."

—◼—

"I have to hand it to Jakowski," Cox said to Leslie while they waited for ME Van Deere to join them in the small briefing room adjacent to the ME's office, "he certainly came prepared to lay it all out. His statement was as complete as we could have wished for."

"I hope it was all true and he didn't just tell us what he knew we would uncover anyway."

"You have reason to disbelieve him?"

"Can't say as I do. I do feel...well...cheated. No, not so much cheated, as duped."

"According to him, he and Franklin were buds; went fishing together out in the Gulf often. Franklin told Jak about the Galileo telescope he had found on the sunken *Buen Jesús*. Jak, seeing an opportunity to free himself from running point for that Seminal Society collector Stratis, volunteered to broker the telescope to the drug lord Jimènez. To that end, Franklin was to run his boat down to the site, retrieve the telescope, come back to Fort Myers and the two of them were to take the ferry down to Key West to consummate the deal."

"According to Pete, Franklin never showed," Leslie quickly added.

"That squares with not seeing him on the surveillance video going down. My question is logistical. We asked Jakowski why Franklin didn't just pick up the telescope from where it was hidden and go directly to Key West. Why drive the boat all the way north only to turn around and go south on the ferry? You buy what he said?"

"Yes and no. According to Jak, Franklin didn't want his boat identified as being in Key West at the time of the transfer because that would have been a sure giveaway that he had stolen the treasure. Plausible, I suppose. But then why get on the ferry at all?"

"So he could transfer the Sunspot to his best friend in a place where he would be certain not to be surveilled," Cox responded. "Most likely, a men's room on the ferry."

"As I say, plausible. Was Jakowski working for himself to get rich? Or for the task force?"

"My money's on himself. Ghana appears as confused as we are."

"Since when do you trust *anything* a fed says. They're born with an overactive liar gene. Truth is, and I hate to say it, but I

123

share your thought as well. Now the big question is: Whether either of them, Jakowski or Franklin, was on the ferry coming north?"

"Les, a more important question as far as the death is concerned is whether it was Franklin on that ferry, or a Franklin imposter? With respect to Jakowski, we'll check the motel he claims to have stayed at. We'll also go over ferry videos for Tuesday. Of course, Beth Hillard and her investigative team are all over that now. Les, your agitation is misplaced. Jak's too smart to trip himself up."

"For facts we can validate, I agree. But the speculation troubles me."

"What are you speculating on?" Van Deere asked, coming into the room. "You two need a few minutes? You seem to be..."

"Oh, we're fine, Doctor," Leslie responded to the ME. "Thanks for taking time to see us. We're going round and round on this Franklin case, sorry to say. To be perfectly honest, we've come around to your way of thinking. Not a suicide."

"You're not alone. One of our interns, young doc by the name of Miguel Flores, born in El Salvador, went to medical school in Mexico City, took it on himself to review the file and to perform additional procedures. He's convinced me that my initial instinct was correct. We have a definite homicide."

"And his theory is?" Cox asked, anxious to hear what the ME had to say about Franklin's death.

"Hypovolemic shock brought about by a puncture of the right carotid artery."

"Bullet wound?" Leslie asked, confused over the last image captured by the ferry camera showing Franklin, or an imposter, shooting himself in the head.

"Diameter much too small for a bullet, even a twenty-two."

"Maybe a pencil, then?" Cox pressed.

"Perhaps a spike of some sort? I'd guess a pick. Likely a pick with a handle."

"You mean like an ice pick?"

"With a fine shaft. Yes, an ice pick would fit the profile," Dr. Van Deere acknowledged.

"Was he stabbed above or below the water?" Leslie asked, trying to visualize the crime scene.

"Above. I presume, on his own boat."

"And he died of the stab wound? Not the bullet?"

"That requires speculation."

"If you were to speculate, what would you say?"

"Don't quote me, but I think the entire underwater crime scene was staged. You might recall the preliminary report indicated evidence of an air hose becoming wrapped around his leg?"

Leslie nodded and Cox, a puzzled expression beginning at the corners of his mouth and spreading to one eyebrow, leaned forward but said nothing.

"The markings on Franklin's body suggest that he was on a boat, diving. Not that he fell from a ferry. If he was on a boat, his or any other, he was just too good a professional to allow himself to be caught by an air hose. And besides, why on earth would he even be diving that close to shore? Makes no sense. From lack of water in his lungs, I'd say he died out of the water and then placed where he was found after death."

"How long would death have taken?" Cox asked.

"Assuming the pick had been removed instantly, and judging from the size of the wound, death would be measured in minutes at best. Maybe two, three."

"He died of blood loss," Leslie clarified, "and not asphyxiation—or a bullet through the brain?"

"He was stabbed in the neck and died from that wound. Before he passed, he was also shot in the head. Head wound didn't kill him, but only by seconds."

"Same assailant? Or do we have two killers?"

"Could be two people, but if so, they worked together because the timing is too close. Dr. Flores has a theory. Hey, I've got to run. I've asked him to stop by. He was finishing up a case and should be here within a few minutes. I've given you all I can. Always nice to see you. Sorry I can't stay."

"Likewise," Cox called to her back as the medical examiner hurried through the door.

Within a minute a tall, slender, early-thirties man entered the room, his lab jacket open down the front, revealing a black T-shirt that proclaimed in white letters: EVEN DEAD LIVES MATTER! His eyes were lively and bouncing from one to the other of the detectives. "I'm Flores and you're here about Franklin," he announced in almost accent-free English. "Nothing official and I'm not allowed to be quoted. Haven't earned my spurs, as they say in Texas."

They weren't in Texas and even if they were, Leslie wasn't so certain they said that in the Lone Star State. She let it slide. This young doctor's exuberance was refreshing.

"At first, we assumed the slug to the head took his life. Changed my analysis when I found a tiny, but deep hole in his neck. Question is, what came first? The bullet hole or the pick."

"So, you think it was a pick. An ice pick?"

"I'm convinced it was a pick. An ice pick was found on his boat."

"According to the file," Cox added, "cleaned of any blood or prints, if I recall right."

"You recall correctly. Too clean, in fact. No salt spray, nothing. So, yes, I'm convinced it was the ice pick. Dissected the carotid. Found evidence of a bleed. On the other hand, the bullet trauma was essentially clean, with minimum blood seepage. And why, I ask myself, would someone shoot somebody in the head and *then* stab that person with an ice pick? I suppose it could happen in that order, but less likely."

"I'll ask that question backwards," Leslie said, probing. "Why would that somebody use an ice pick on the carotid and then a bullet to the head?"

"You put your finger on what has had me scratching my head for a few days."

"And?"

"And I think the shooting was panic. Stabbing with the ice pick might have occurred in a moment of rage. Without thought. Pick was in his hand, perhaps for some other purpose, and he swung it."

"Go on," Cox coached. "We're interested."

"Franklin falls, blood is spurting, killer panics. Wants it over fast. Goes for the gun and fires. Can't take a chance of pulling up to a dock with a dead body, boat full of blood, even late at night. I went down to the docking area at three this morning and sure enough there were several fishermen. Perp couldn't risk it. Threw the body overboard under the bridge. I'm thinking he himself went down, perhaps wearing diving gear. Leaves the gear under the bridge, line tied around Franklin's foot. Perp then cleans the boat, returns it to the slip and disappears. He gets himself to Key West and takes the ferry north, pretending to be Franklin. Pretends to shoot himself in the head on the ferry conveniently under the bridge."

"What's the purpose of that?"

"To make us believe Franklin's death was a suicide," Flores said with a flourish, clearly pleased with himself. "To prevent a homicide investigation would be my guess as to why such an elaborate undertaking."

"Time of death?" Cox asked.

"Waiting for you to ask. If we go by the eyewitness account, TOD would be Tuesday, nine twenty-three p.m. If we go by the theory that he died on his boat, the time would be around midnight, Monday."

"That's roughly a twenty-one-hour difference," Leslie commented. "Surely, forensics..."

"He was under water. Brackish water to boot. Not a lot of damage from fish. Some, but not much. This man had spent a considerable amount of time under water and who knows exactly what that does to death calculations, so defense counsel will have a field day with rigor, or any other analysis."

"What are you trying to tell us, Doctor?"

"My time of death, the time we have agreed to put on the death certificate, will be Monday, midnight. But...but just know there are a lot of assumptions in that assessment. I'll be uncomfortable defending it."

"Anything more you care to tell us?" Leslie asked. "You seem to have done a remarkable bit of detecting already. I, for one, am impressed."

"I studied the tapes from the ferry and nothing I saw was inconsistent with what I have said."

"Thank you," Cox said. "I join my partner in being impressed."

"One more thing," Flores began. "Pure speculation on my part, but I had the distinct impression there was something off with the imposter's gait. Can't pinpoint it, but for some reason it seemed off. Inconsistent, that's what it was. Inconsistent. If anything further comes to mind I'll let you know."

"Please do, Doctor. Anything you think of," Leslie offered before Flores, as his boss had done a few minutes earlier, disappeared through the door.

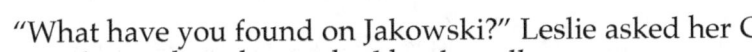

"What have you found on Jakowski?" Leslie asked her CIA a moment later when she reached her by cell.

"Nothing definitive, I'm afraid. As the file timeline shows, Jak spent time in the bar. At five, actually, four-forty-nine, he walked several blocks to a small overnight place, called The Raven's Nest, and took a room. He went directly to the room and that was the last the proprietor saw of him."

"First floor room, or...?"

"First floor. One B to be exact."

"Was the proprietor in position to see him leave or what?"

"Not exactly. She lives on the second floor. In the back. Her son had a basketball game at school. She left shortly after Jak checked in. Wasn't back until after ten."

"Have you found anyone who saw him in Key West after six?"

"Not yet. I reviewed the port captain's surveillance footage. The angle isn't perfect, but it does capture everyone going up the ramp onto the ferry. The man we saw shoot himself and go overboard was wearing a red, foul weather jacket when he boarded. The last man to board, at five-fifty, just as they began pulling up the ramp, was built almost exactly like Jakowski. Same height, shoulders, and from what I could guess, weight. But I can't be positive it's him. Sorry."

"I'll have a look," Leslie said.

"Like I said, at first I thought it was a match. I've watched it a dozen times and if you twisted my arm, I'd say it wasn't him."

"Why?"

"Intangible is the best I can tell you. Didn't move the same. Don't really know. Also, we have a confirmed sighting—actually, several—beginning at seven-forty the next morning."

"From?"

"The boarding house proprietor. Heard his alarm sound at seven-thirty. Saw him leave the house ten minutes later. There's a small breakfast place around the corner. Owner says he served a large pancake stack and a double order of bacon slightly after eight to a man fitting Jakowski's description. He confirmed Jakowski's picture."

"Good job," Leslie praised Hillard. "Keep working it." Before hanging up, Leslie briefed her CIA on her upcoming interview with Admiral Masters.

"Want support from us?" Hillard asked. "Search warrant or anything?"

"Premature for that at this stage. Keep a log of her plane's activity." Leslie confirmed the tail number before disconnecting to meet Cox in the parking lot.

"Any update on Jakowski?" were her partner's first words.

"Apparently took a room in Key West, but no sightings that night after about five. He was a possible ferry passenger, but inconclusive. He *was* sighted by the landlady in the morning, and later by the owner of a restaurant who served him breakfast."

"Then we can rule him out from being on the northbound ferry."

Leslie didn't respond for several minutes while she processed all that she had heard. "Jakowski, and that task force crowd he runs with, are good enough to plant decoys. Just like Masters fooled Ghana at the airport, if they want us to believe Jak was in Key West, then by God they will make it easy enough for us to believe it! Especially when we want to believe it. I'm keeping an open mind." Leslie sounded more certain of herself than she felt.

"I suppose you're right, Les. For what it's worth, he could have been on the ferry, killed Franklin, then when the ferry landed in Fort Myers, got in his car and drove back to Key West. Takes about four, five hours. Plenty of time to be back in bed, wake up in the morning and parade around town making certain he was seen."

"That's certainly a possibility," Leslie acknowledged. "But speculative at best."

"Everything's speculative at this point. I take it you haven't talked with him."

"Didn't answer," she said, looking away as if to indicate that this topic was now off the table.

Cox, to his credit, changed the subject. "Our timing's spot on. Masters' ETA is seven minutes from now and we're two minutes out. I called in a favor with a buddy working Page. We'll be parked at the terminal when the jet pulls up. How's that for full service?"

Ignoring the gloat, Leslie said, "Here's what's troubling me. If I could find Masters' plane, so could Ghana. I feel we're being played. But I don't know the game—or the rules."

"Assume the feds knew her jet flew to Cancun, presumably to pick her up. So what? It's after the fact. Too late to monitor her activities in Mexico—or to do anything about it."

"Suppose so," Leslie conceded, still agitated at not knowing what role she and Cox were playing. Adding to her discomfort was Jakowski's involvement. There was no denying the big cop's shadow fell over every aspect of the homicide.

"Right on time," Cox announced. "Plane's on the ground, not at the terminal yet. You work out how you plan to get her talking? Leaving the country and going to a destination other than the one that was claimed is not our concern—or our jurisdiction."

"What about reentering without going through customs?"

"First of all, you have no jurisdiction over that. And second...second, that won't work."

"We can always bluff?"

"Take your eyes off your cell and you'll see for yourself what your problem is."

Leslie looked up in time to see a car bounce to a stop at the base of the steps that had been extended downward from the jet, U.S. CUSTOMS AND BORDER PROTECTION clearly visible on its door.

Two uniformed officers, a female from the driver's side and a male from the passenger seat, got out and headed up the steps.

Leslie's hand was on the doorknob when Cox said, "Let's give them time to do their jobs and clear the area. I have no doubt all is in order, or Masters wouldn't have called ahead. Won't take Customs but a minute or two."

"How do you know they called ahead?"

"The app you're following clearly told you the plane was coming direct from Cancun. It's illegal to enter the country without being cleared in by customs."

Leslie rolled her eyes at the thought that the borders appeared to be open to non-citizens but not to citizens. She began to respond, thought better of it and sat back. Cox turned out to be right. Only it was almost ten minutes before the agents reappeared and the car disappeared across the field.

A moment later, when the detectives entered the cabin, Masters called out, "Hodges and Cox! Just who I was about to call! Come on in."

Not expecting such a greeting, Leslie said nothing. Cox broke the awkward silence by asking, "And just why is that? Why were you going to call us?"

"Hammerschmidt went missing!"

"On his own?" Cox inquired, "or kidnapping?"

"And where?" Leslie sputtered. "Cancun?"

"Cancun International. We were in a private hangar. He left the plane. Said he had to stretch his legs. Didn't reboard. We were ordered to leave without him."

"Who ordered that?"

"I'd prefer to not disclose that information," the Admiral demurred.

"You brought the subject up," Leslie told her, back in control. "You want help? We need all the facts possible. And I mean *all* the facts you have."

"Estrada Jimènez."

"The Z drug boss? Directly?"

"Directly."

"Is that why you flew to Mexico? Deception and all?"

"I wanted that crazy Treasury lady, Ghana, off my ass, you want to know the truth!"

"Nothing crazy about an IRS agent wanting to collect taxes," Leslie reminded her. "Just doing her job."

"I have a right to be left alone! Travel where I want without being hounded for taxes! I pay my taxes! Know what I just paid?"

"I've haven't a clue," Leslie confessed.

"North of two hundred million!"

Leslie's police mind immediately flashed, *motive*. Motive for what, she could only guess. The taxes on the sale of the Sunspot, assuming it sold for two hundred million, would be in the range of...forty million! *That means the object she sold, if indeed there had been a sale, was into the billion-dollar range!*

"That's a lot of money," Cox spoke up. "But as I see it, if you make a billion then..."

"Screw that!" Masters snapped. "Where the hell does the government come off taking so friggin' much money! That's why I wanted Ghana out of my business."

"And just what business is that?" Leslie asked, managing not to choke at the gall of the woman.

"That Galileo telescope we found on..."

"The Sunspot or the Medici?"

"That Medici, the one over in the shed, is a fake! The original is safely where it belongs in the *Museo Galileo* in Florence. The only telescope in play right now is the Sunspot."

"Professor Hammer...Sir Reggie...himself told us the Medici was about to be auctioned from a storage shed near the airport in Fort Lauderdale."

"Sir Reggie, it would seem, has been co-opted by drug money. He's now owned by drug chief Jimènez, or so it appears. That is, if he's still alive."

"Let's start at the beginning," Cox demanded, settling into the seat across the aisle from where Masters was standing. "And leave out nothing."

"I don't appreciate your tone, young man! I'm voluntarily telling you what I know. I haven't waived my right to remain silent."

"You certainly have that right," Leslie agreed, her voice calm, trying to reduce the sudden tension. "Remain as silent as you like, but please keep in mind Cox here, and I, are investigating the death of one of your employees, Derrick Franklin. From what we gather, he was also a good friend. Possession of the Sunspot Telescope may be at the center of his death. That puts you directly in the crosshairs. And at this point in time, makes you our chief suspect. Need I say more?"

Admiral Masters, who had been standing tall and rigidly straight, slumped into a seat, motioning Leslie to do the same. When Leslie complied, she began, "You know about the sunken treasure ship we located. The *Buen Jesús y Nuestra Señora del Rosario*. It contained the Sunspot Telescope which, as you also well know, did not come off the bottom when the cargo was brought up."

"We do," Cox impatiently confirmed.

"The deal was, Franklin and I had arranged to sell the telescope to Jimènez for, as you rightly said, just under a billion dollars. Sir Reggie was to validate the telescope, for which he was to be paid a percentage. That's why we went to Cancun. "

"Why the business with the auction? What's that about?"

"Apparently some ruse by a rival gang to distract the Seminal Society collectors. With the Medici possibly available, why bother with the Sunspot? That's why Reggie was being paid well. His life as a trusted artifact evaluator was essentially over."

"You were to take Sir Reggie to Cancun. I assume," Leslie said, working through the logistics, "someone else was to bring the telescope?"

"The man who arranged the deal with Jimènez in the first place. Our third, but silent, partner."

"And the name of that 'silent' partner is?"

"A friend of Franklin's from their football days. Cop by the name of Pete Jakowski."

NINETEEN

LESLIE AND COX WERE A BLOCK FROM headquarters before their first words were uttered. Leslie broke the silence. "I must admit, all roads lead to..."

"Your friend, Jak. Maybe there's a good explanation for that?"

"I'd love to hear it. Jak's been running interference—that's his word, not mine—for Dexter Stratis for many years. He's very familiar with the Seminal Society collectors and how they operate. He's also knowledgeable about international money flow and mega dollar deals. And he's been dealing with valuable artifacts, including Society Firsts, for many years now. If anyone could pull off drug cartel money laundering, Jakowski can. That's for sure."

Turning into the parking lot Cox added, "You're right on with that, sorry to say, Les." Trying to soften his partner's obvious distress, he added, "But...but there could be an explan...Hey!" Cox exclaimed, interrupting himself and pointing in the direction of the only civilian car parked at the front of the building. "Isn't that Ghana? In that car over there! What the hell?"

They didn't have long to wait. Just as Cox came to a stop, Ghana emerged from her vehicle and positioned herself directly in front of their car.

She walked to the door behind Leslie and motioned for them to pop the lock. Once inside, the door closed, she said, "I don't get duped often, but I gotta confess, Admiral Masters fooled me, all right. Convinced me she was going to Italy. Interpol's arrested the two imposters—local Florida actors—in Florence. They're a dead end far's we're concerned. Unless *you* want them held, we're about to release them."

"Can't imagine they have anything for us. Just get their contact info, we'll follow up if need be."

"That's what I thought you'd say, Leslie. What do you know about Sir Reggie?"

"Didn't come back to the States with Masters. Disappeared from the hangar in Cancun," Leslie tentatively answered, sensing Ghana knew more than she was letting on. *Give to get.*

"If I tell you he's in Acapulco, would that surprise you?"

"It sure surprises me," Cox confessed. "Happy to hear he's not dead. How the hell did he get from the east to the west coast?"

"That, I believe," Ghana replied, "is the salient point. He didn't hop a commercial plane and fly. That we know. Not enough time to drive, so it had to have been by private plane. There's nothing registered, leading us to the conclusion that some player wants—needs—him on the west coast."

"Go on," Leslie prodded when Ghana stopped talking. "Why Acapulco? And who's he with?"

"Not likely on vacation, I'll venture that much. Doubt he's there by his choice."

"You didn't answer my question. Who's with him?" *Hope to hell it's not Pete.*

"This is embarrassing, Leslie, and I'll deny it if asked, but we have no eyes on him and likely will not while he's there."

"Then how do you know he's even in Acapulco?" Cox demanded.

"Would you believe a little birdie?"

"Only if the birdie has a name," Leslie mimicked the agent's coy tone.

"Woman by the name of Riya Kumar. I believe you..."

"Had lunch with her and her husband," Cox said, "Up in Tampa when we were working the euphon case."

"Apparently, she and her husband are Seminal Society collectors and hot after the Sunspot Telescope."

"Current location for the Kumars?" Leslie asked.

"Opal Key Resort, Key West."

"So, what else you have for us?"

"Isn't that enough?"

—————

Leslie approached Captain Stetson's office with trepidation. Requesting permission for her and Cox to go to Key West was only part of her anxiety. Her inability to produce evidence that Jakowski, a cop who had a brief relationship with Boots long ago, and who Leslie herself was currently in a relationship with, had remained on Key West after the northbound ferry carrying Franklin home to Fort Myers had sailed, weighed heavily on her. As it stood, and until it could be proven otherwise, Jakowski had to be considered a Person of Interest—a major Person of Interest.

"Close the door behind you," Boots directed when Leslie entered the office. "Cox is already here, and Hud's been briefed and won't be joining us." Stetson waited for Leslie to approach and take her place standing beside her partner in front of the captain's large desk. "Sheriff about had a canary when I ran your request up the flagpole. 'Be glad they didn't ask to go to Cancun,' I told him. Here's the thing. That resort the Kumars are staying in is over a thousand a night. I can't even imagine what one gets for that kind of money. You have the boss's okay for two nights, three hundred per night, max. You'll need a car down there. Take an unmarked. You need more time, ask. I'll see what I can do. No promises."

"I'm thinking," Leslie began tentatively, "that once we're finished with the Kumars, we could poke about, see if we can clarify Jak's timeframe."

"That's exactly what I had in mind. We need to definitively place him on land after the ferry left, or...or place him on the ferry. His management's been briefed and has put his investigation in our hands. Jak's career's on the line, to say the obvious. Warning: He is not aware of our investigation."

"Noted," Leslie assured her boss. "Good news, we have some evidence of him being down there the next morning. Unfortunately, that's in question because video shows that Jak could have been on that ferry along with the man we saw on the video."

"We'll cross that bridge when we get to it. Jak was down in Key West for a reason. We need to know the reason—as well as the time frames. Jak's prints are all over this mess. Frankly I'm not putting much faith in the Kumars. That's how I sold it to the boss; that Jakowski's movements are key to us solving Franklin's death. Make no mistake, you two are going down to clear—or indict— Pete Jakowski. I don't give a crap if he's working for the feds. If he's involved—or even withholding evidence—he's going down. Understand me? I'll personally see to his indictment."

"Indict?" Leslie yelped involuntarily, unable to mask her surprise. "I thought..."

"Something you don't yet know. Beth Hillard just traced a text message sent from Jak to Agent Ghana at ten the night Franklin supposedly shot himself in the head and went over the side of the ferry."

Leslie sucked in her breath, let it out slowly, then asked the critical question. "Do you have a location for him at that time?"

"Twenty-five-point eighty-four north, eighty-two-point zero-three west. Don't bother looking it up," Stetson said to Cox who was busy plugging numbers into his cell phone. "Location's roughly eight miles south, southwest of Marco Island."

Closing her eyes and visualizing the Gulf of Mexico at that location, Leslie, in a barely audible voice, said, "If I'm not mistaken, that's about where the ferry would have been on its trip north."

"Roger that, Hodges. Roger that."

———————

"This is sure comfortable-looking," Leslie confessed to Cox when they entered the Opal Key Resort & Marina. "From the picture, I thought it would be old and...well, stuffy." Scanning the bright blue cushions covering the brown wicker furniture, she added, "What an inviting atmosphere."

"For a thousand big ones a night, you too can be pampered. Better satisfy yourself with Motel 6," Cox, his eye following a shapely woman carrying a canvas bag, joked.

"We have some time before lunch, let's go out by the pool."

"I'll meet you there," Cox replied, moving in the direction of the woman, "I'm going down to check out the boats."

Leslie stepped out onto the large patio, her eyes taking in perhaps a dozen women lying face down on flattened lounge chairs, several with their bikini tops undone. The large pool, its shimmering water reflecting the sapphire blue of the sky, was devoid of people.

"Oh, there you are," a voice with a familiar British accent belonging to one of the world's most beautiful—and wealthiest—women, called. "I was hoping to catch up to you before lunch. Where's your partner?"

Leslie pointed in the direction of the boat dock. "Exploring the scenery," she answered, refraining from rolling her eyes. "How are you, Mrs. Kumar?"

"Riya, please dear, call me Riya. Come and sit with me. We can speak in private over there."

When they were both seated, Riya wasted no time getting to the point. "I know you are investigating the death of Derrick Franklin. Poor man. He had so very much to live for. The world was his to take." Riya looked off into the distance for a long moment, then turned her attention back to Leslie. "In case you are wondering, we—my husband and I—were in discussions with him for a Galileo First. The Sunspot Telescope to be exact. I suppose you know that a Galileo telescope was found on a ship that sank not all that far from where we now sit." Riya waved her arm in the direction of the water. "That precious artifact did not make it to the surface with the other treasures Franklin and

Masters brought up. But of course, you know that. That's why you're here."

"Franklin's unfortunate death is why we're here. With that in mind, may I ask, were you in contact with him directly? Or with Masters? How did that all work?"

"An intermediary."

"Name?"

"In due course, my dear. In due course."

Leslie knew that in this instance 'in due course' meant that the name would only be forthcoming if Leslie agreed to some condition. She forced herself to remain calm even as the words 'quid pro quo' came to mind.

"We had settled on a figure. All was going smoothly, until...until the Sunspot vanished!"

"Vanished? Can you please elaborate on that?"

"The agreed-upon plan was that I was to meet the courier here in Key West this past Monday afternoon. I was here with the money—in this case an authenticated, guaranteed, and untraceable bank deposit."

"Did you meet with the courier?"

"Indeed! Both my husband and I met with him."

"You're angry. Remind me of a person's been duped. Wasn't it what you wanted?"

"It was authentic all right! That's not the problem. There can be no satisfactory resolution. We had our hearts set on owning that artifact, and now...now I'm afraid we'll never have that chance again. That, to us, is a devastating loss."

"I'm now confused. I can't begin to imagine your loss, but how..."

"Please wait for my husband to join us. He'll be along in a moment. I get too emotional."

"So, Riya, just why are you still here in Key West?"

"For us collectors, 'hope springs eternal'."

Sensing this phase of the conversation had run its course, Leslie asked,

"How much did you agree to pay for the Sunspot?"

"Private," Riya said, her voice barely above a whisper. "That's a very private matter."

"Between us only," Leslie said. "I won't put the number in the file." Before Riya answered, Leslie added, "On second thought, I may be required to tell my partner. If the amount becomes critical to the investigation, I'll have to put it in the file."

Riya again looked away. When her eyes returned to meet Leslie's, she said in a barely audible voice, "Let me just say north of three hundred and leave it there. In the end, the amount really isn't important."

A thought struck Leslie. "What time were you to meet this...this courier?"

"Four-thirty."

Before Leslie could ask her next question, Sanjay appeared beside his wife. "Oh, Sanjay, there you are," Riya said, taking his hand. "I was looking for you. You remember Detective Hodges, don't you?"

"Who could ever forget such green eyes? I certainly do remember the detective. We had a lovely lunch at the Columbia Restaurant with her and her mate—partner. Didn't much care for the lad, if I recall right."

"He was okay," Riya corrected. "You hadn't expected him to join us. Caught you by surprise, that's all."

"Surprise seems to be the order of the day. I take it this...this conversation with Hodges was preplanned and not an accident."

"Now what would give..."

"Riya! Look over to the dock and you will see for yourself. Now tell me Detective, that *is* your mate, is it not?"

"It is, sir. We have an..."

"I invited them to lunch," Riya interrupted. "Derrick Franklin died, suicide it appears. The detectives have questions for us."

"Franklin is dead! When did it happen?"

"Monday," Leslie answered, surveying Sanjay's face intently.

"What could we possibly know of such a tragic event?" Sanjay demanded. "That's when we flew here from Jamaica. Landed just after eleven-thirty in the morning."

"Our questions pertain to the Sunspot Telescope," Leslie laid out. "Not about the death of Franklin."

Riya turned to her husband. "In light of what transpired in Acapulco, I thought it would be best the sooner we cooperate and set the record straight the better it will be for us with the next First."

"Riya," Leslie interrupted, a thought suddenly coming to mind. "I assume you've been in communication with the IRS then."

"Agent Ghana set up this meeting with you. We cooperate, they close the file. Tax investigation over."

Leslie silently thanked Agent Ghana. The quid pro quo for this meeting was coming from the feds. That meant Leslie need not promise anything. That was good to know.

Sanjay smiled. "It is certainly about time they dropped..." He thought better of what he was about to say and turned to Leslie,

"It seems we are committed to talk to you about our...our little adventure. Let's not spoil lunch. We can eat and after lunch conduct our business right here by the pool. It is private enough. Will that be acceptable?"

"I see no reason why not. Please allow me a few minutes to bring Detective Cox up to speed and we will rejoin you."

"Riya and I will be having a nice chardonnay. Should I order something for you and your partner?"

"Water will be fine, thank you."

TWENTY

LUNCH WAS OVER. THE GROUPER HAD BEEN grilled to perfection. The two detectives were driving out of the resort parking lot when Cox said, "Let's find a beach and walk lunch off."

"We need to canvas Duval Street, check out Riya's timeline. This isn't the time for 'walking off lunch'."

"Both are possible. Kumars weren't scheduled to meet the courier until after four-thirty. It's only two-eighteen. Hour on the beach should work out fine."

"Go for it," Leslie announced, magnanimously giving in to Cox, mentally adding a chit to the 'he-owes-me-one' ledger.

A moment later Cox said, "What's the chance the person who gave the Sunspot to Riya was Jak?"

"For starters, Riya knows Jakowski and said it wasn't him. Why lie to us and put their IRS release in jeopardy? I'm leaning toward believing her."

"Could she be covering for him?"

"Why?"

"That, I don't know. Truth, it appears, doesn't seem to be a fundamental tenet of these folks. Money seems to be their prime motivation. Also, there isn't an abundance of mid-fifties, six-five men running around with, what did she call it, a 'tight figure'. That argues for Jak."

"I sensed tension between husband and wife. My take is that he isn't happy how their IRS mess, whatever it is, got settled."

"Think about it, Leslie. If one—or both—of them are ardent Seminal Society collectors, they would have wanted to walk away with the telescope. As it turns out, they were used embarrassingly as pawns. According to what Riya told you, they paid over three hundred million to some mystery person to *buy* the telescope. They then were, in Sanjay's words, 'coerced' into flying to Acapulco to personally deliver the newly acquired telescope to the Andrews Sisters who run the *Pishtacos*, a vicious Peruvian gang."

"*Artista* Sisters. Sofi and Chio," Leslie interjected. "Thought they were dead. Killed by rivals over a year ago. I saw it on TV."

"TV's not a good source of vital information. I've asked Hillard to run it. Assume for now the sisters are alive and kicking and met with the Kumars. Apparently, Sir Reggie was also there for validation. The sisters then paid the Kumars four hundred million for the Sunspot. That's a hundred-million-dollar profit in less than a day! Not a bad gig if you can get it."

"Les, aren't you the one who told me that when it comes to a First, it's the object that counts, not the money? You got that from that Texas billionaire dude buddy of yours, Little Billy Bob. Kumars had it in their possession—and ownership—just long enough to make the pain of loss all that much greater."

"You thinking that's why Sanjay's so down? Losing a First?"

"I'll take the money any day," Cox laughed. "The puzzling part to me is why in the hell the boss of the Peruvian gang even cares about a Galileo telescope?"

"Been thinking about that in the context of my conversation with Little Billy Bob."

"Any conclusions?"

"Nothing concrete. What if the *Artista* Sisters, in turn, flipped the Sunspot to someone with a much heavier wallet? Such as Little Billy Bob? Or for that matter, Morris Dexter Stratis?"

"Thought you said LBB would only commit to four hundred?" Cox's eyebrows raised in confusion. "My money's on money laundering. But I don't see how it's done?"

"You know, now that I replay my conversation, Billy Bob never really committed to a number. The four hundred figure was my interpretation. In answer to your question, as always with drug lords, money laundering is the big problem. Having tons of money without an obvious channel to making that money causes governments to come after you for their *fair share*, whatever that means. Or for criminal behavior. Or both."

"In this case, how's that work?"

"On *paper* LBB pays the Sisters, say a billion, maybe even more. The Sisters dutifully deposit the money—ostensibly received from LBB—in a U.S. bank, producing for the bank the legal Sunspot Telescope purchase documents, along with Sir Reggie's appraisal. Perhaps they added a few pictures as proof of the transaction. At that point, it would be hard for the IRS, or anyone else, to claim the deposit was drug money. That would give the *Artista* Sisters legal currency of a billion dollars in the United States to work with."

Cox digested Leslie's analysis in silence. He parked the car in a beach parking lot, got out and took a few steps toward the sand, still not saying anything. Turning to Leslie, he finally acknowledged her analysis. "Makes sense. If, and only if, LBB, or whoever the buyer was, only paid four hundred million, or thereabouts, and gave a receipt for a billion. The six hundred million difference between the billion and the four hundred million actually paid came from illegal activity." Cox bent down, sent his shoes sailing toward the car, and called, "See you in an hour," as he turned and jogged off down the beach.

———————

Leslie resisted the urge to follow her partner's lead. Instead, she walked to the water's edge where tiny waves were lapping onto the white sand. After carefully placing her shoes above the water line, she sat with her feet stretched out in front of her. The warm water gently rolled over her ankles, coming halfway up her calves. She leaned back and replayed, word for word, the entire conversation she and Cox had had with the Kumars poolside.

"I don't know what my wife has already told you," Sanjay had begun when the lunch dishes had been cleared, "so let me go back to the beginning. Beginning, I suppose, is a funny word for an ongoing activity, such as our love for collecting Seminal Society Firsts which we have been doing for many years. We..."

"Mind telling us which Firsts you own?" Cox interrupted.

"Sorry, Detective, Riya and I make it a policy to never, ever, discuss which ones we own, or which ones we would like to own. We made an exception in this case in the interest of...helping you—and the IRS."

"Someone approached you for the Sunspot? Who was that?"

Sanjay looked away, as if making up his mind. Turning back to the detectives, he answered, "The man we know as Esquire."

"Go on," Leslie encouraged, mentally equating Esquire to Jakowski. "I know who you are referring to."

"Esquire showed us an image of a sealed, waterproof tube that had writings on it. There also was a signature on the tube belonging to a man named Derrick Franklin."

"Did you recognize that signature?" Cox asked.

"Neither of us did," Sanjay confessed. "Esquire also presented us with a document from the world's expert on Galileo, a professor known as Sir Reggie, certifying that the tube with Franklin's signature contained a genuine Galileo telescope known as the Sunspot Telescope. Riya spoke with Hammerschmidt, that's Sir Reggie, and satisfied herself that the Sunspot was indeed inside that tube. She also learned that the tube was then at the bottom of the Gulf of Mexico, but would soon, under Franklin's direction, be raised. All of this coincided with what Esquire had told us."

"Why had this Esquire fellow contacted you?"

"Riya knew him from past Seminal Society dealings. We also know that others had been informed of the telescope."

"What, if anything, did you agree with Esquire to do?"

"Purchase it from him."

Questions had flooded Leslie. She picked one. "For how much?"

"Is all this necessary?"

"We believe it is."

"Three hundred million," Riya answered.

"And how were you to gain possession of the Sunspot?"

"We were to be in Key West Monday afternoon and would receive a call shortly after noon."

"Did you receive such a call?"

"Yes and no," Sanjay equivocated.

"He means," Riya added, "we received a call from Esquire. He told us there was a problem and the Sunspot was not yet available."

"Did you get another call?" Cox inquired.

"Again, yes and no," Sanjay said. "We got a call from another man, not Esquire, several hours later telling us to go to Willie T's bar. That's on Duval Street."

"Name of the man who called?"

"Don't have one. Sorry."

"Description?"

"Don't have that either."

"Can you explain?" Cox had asked, "why you can't give us a description of the man you met at Willie T's?"

"Please hear me out. When we arrived at the bar we were ushered into a small booth near the far wall. A short while later, a man's voice—possibly a woman's—spoke to us from the booth directly behind us. It was a hoarse voice and Riya believes it was a woman. The voice asked if we were prepared to transfer three hundred million dollars to an account in exchange for the Sunspot. You might imagine the questions that inquiry provoked. The short version, which took us a bit of time to work through and get comfortable with, was that we were being used simply as couriers. Highly compensated couriers—but couriers nonetheless."

"What does that mean?"

"I'll make a complex transaction simple. We paid three hundred million for the privilege of taking the Sunspot Telescope from Key West to Acapulco."

"You said you were highly compensated. How highly?"

"Hundred million. Paid three hundred. Sold it for four—in Acapulco."

"Think of the bright side," Riya quipped. "We exclusively owned a Galileo First for six hours!"

TWENTY-ONE

WHEN LESLIE OPENED HER EYES, COX WAS standing over her. "Nice snooze?" he asked. "Good thing I have no evil intentions."

"That is a good thing—for you," she bristled, quickly getting to her feet. "Sun knocked me out. Have a nice run?"

"Didn't get far. Met a friend."

"I won't even ask her name."

"You're certain it's a female."

"For you, are there any other kind?"

"You'd be surprised."

"Okay, surprise me."

"You win. I'm guilty. Known her since high school."

Leslie said nothing until they were almost to the center of town. "Let's head directly to Willie T's. This is about the same time of day the Kumars say they were there."

"You have doubts?"

"Don't you? I don't put the Kumars down as anyone's couriers."

"Hundred million heals a lot of wounded pride."

"He's a billionaire. They behave..."

"A billionaire in tax trouble. Isn't that what they said the last time?"

"That's what we were led to believe," Leslie conceded. "Okay, I'll buy it."

"On the other hand, drug lords have other very effective ways to get what they want. Knife against the throat can be very persuasive."

"The stakes are too high for the Sisters to chance it. If we're right about the transaction, it's all designed to move money safely into the States so they can use it here. A slit neck can make things messy. No pun intended."

The bar was mostly empty when the detectives came through the front door. A single customer sat at a corner table, his head hanging over a half-gone beer. Several empty glasses off to the side. Cox walked over to the bartender, a middle-aged, pudgy man with a full head of curly hair, flashed his badge with his left hand and held a picture of Jakowski in his right. "Ever see this man?"

"Can't say as I have," came the immediate reply.

"Hey! Don't walk away! Look carefully. We have reason to believe this man was in here last Monday. What name you going by?"

"Donny."

"Donny, you working that day?"

"Depends on the time."

"This same time?"

"Yep. This's my shift. Three 'til closing."

"You still telling me you haven't seen this man?"

"Don't recall him. No."

"What about this couple? You ever see them?"

"Oh, hell yes!" Donny's eyes came alive. "Who could ever forget that Indian woman? Gorgeous is all I can say about her. Drop-dead gorgeous! That's *gorgeous* with a capital G! And elegant."

"When was she here?"

"On the day you said. A woman came in shortly after I started, said an Indian couple would be here about four. Wanted them put in that back booth over there, next to each other with their backs to the door."

"And you did that?" Leslie asked without taking her eyes from the sole customer whose attention seemed to focus on Cox.

"Hundred-dollar tips don't come easy these days. You do what you have to do."

"You were paid a hundred dollars to save a seat?"

"Two booths. That one and the adjacent directly in front. I was told a couple would come in and sit in the booth in front of theirs."

"Is that what happened?" Leslie asked, taking over the questioning.

"The Indian couple came in almost exactly at four. Another couple came in a few minutes later and went directly to the booth next to the Indians."

"You serve them drinks?"

"Told to stay away. So, stay away I did."

"You overhear anything?"

"Nothing. They were here almost an hour, maybe a little longer."

"Did they speak with each other?"

"Not that I could hear. But, as I said, I wasn't close to them either."

"Was anybody?"

"That guy over there. Comes in every day, drinks five beers, adds a double of Guaro as a chaser to his fifth, and wobbles outta here. Answers to Larry. Doubt that's his real name. He was here that day. And every day since. Gone by five-thirty. Never saw him before that."

"Guaro," Cox repeated. "Never heard the name."

"Had to look it up on the Internet. It's the colloquial name for aguardiente, the drink of Colombians."

While the bartender was talking, Cox consulted his phone. "Here it is. Claims it's 'distinct with soft notes of anise layered over tropical fruit and has a perceivable sweetness'. I suppose I should try it sometime."

"I'll pour a shot for you."

"Can't now, I'm afraid."

"Who left first?" Leslie asked, focusing back on the Kumars. "I mean between the people in the booths."

"Indians were last out. They picked up a package from the seat where the other couple had been."

"What kind of package?" Cox inquired.

"Tube. About the size of a baseball bat. Maybe a bit longer."

"Can you describe the other couple?" Leslie pursued.

"Not really. Man was tall. Athletic build. Keeps in shape. Woman almost as tall. Good figure. Dark hair. Wearing sunglasses. Couldn't see her eyes."

Leslie scrolled through her cell phone, found what she was looking for, then held the phone up so the bartender could see. "Recognize this woman?"

"Ya. That's her. The woman with the sunglasses. Except in this picture, she looks more South American than I remember her." Donny looked toward his sole customer and reached for a beer mug. "That's his signal. Time for Larry's nightcap. Would you excuse me?"

"Anything further you should be telling us?" Cox asked.

"Like what?"

"Anything at all. You've got our full attention. You could start with the name of the woman who tipped you."

"Never saw her before," the bartender insisted, filling the mug with Yuengling and setting it aside as he reached behind him for the Guaro. "No name comes to mind."

"I don't know what to make from Valeria López being Colombian and that creep Larry drinking Colombian rum," Leslie commented when she and Cox were back in their car heading down Duval Street to begin their search for anyone who had seen Jakowski on Monday night. "One thing's for sure. The Kumars' story appears to check out."

"Add that to the Kumars delivering the Sunspot to the *Artista* Sisters. I looked them up. Sisters' names are Sofi and Chio del Rio."

"Except that the Sisters run the *Pishtacos*. That's a Peruvian gang," Leslie reminded her partner. "Valeria is Colombian."

"Peru and Colombia share a border. I thought she was originally from Peru. Close enough for me."

When the car stopped in front of Rick's Bar, Leslie said, "This place has been canvassed by the locals. We have, I think, everything we're likely to get from them. How about if I wait for you out here, do a little research?"

"Not a problem. Shouldn't take but a few minutes. Just want to get Jakowski's timeline confirmed. Be nice if we can find Jak was here on the island after six."

"Speaking of Jak, you think he could have been with Valeria back there at Willie T's?"

"Crossed my mind," Cox acknowledged. "Fits with the story of Jakowski brokering the Sunspot. But the bartender was definite it wasn't him. Not everyone is lying."

"Tell you what, while you're inside, I'll take a quick run back, press ol' Donny a bit more. Maybe get some details on his big tipper."

"Just don't go overboard," Cox cautioned. "Locals might pitch a fit. Remember, even if it was Jak, he still had time to make the six o'clock ferry."

"One piece at a time," Leslie called to his retreating back. "One piece at a time."

Two minutes later Leslie was in front of Willie T's searching for a parking space. Unlike an hour earlier, there was nothing available on either side of the street, forcing her to turn the corner onto Southard. Luck was with her. A car was pulling out halfway down the block and she slipped in when it drove off. Walking back toward the bar, she noticed a three-story house with balconies on the two upper floors surrounding a courtyard with several glass-topped, white-metal tables sprinkled about. A large wooden painted raven hung over the yard.

"*Raven? Raven?*" she repeated to herself. "*Where have I...Isn't that where Jakowski took a room? The Raven's Nest?*" Leslie played back Beth Hillard's report to confirm she was correct. She stopped to check out the house, only to realize that it looked almost

148

identical to the other houses on Southard, except an alley ran alongside connecting Southard to the adjacent parallel street. While Leslie stood taking in the scene, her street-cop eye spotted a man stumbling along the sidewalk in front of The Raven's Nest. She tensed instinctively, ready to help should he require assistance.

Then it came to her. This was the same man the bartender had called Larry. The same man who ended his day with a double shot of Guaro. Leslie carefully watched as he haltingly progressed along the sidewalk, his profile momentarily blocked by a parked car.

Suddenly, Larry's head was gone from her sight. Assuming he had fallen, she rushed across the street, arriving in time to observe him reaching for an object lying a foot beyond his outstretched arm. Blood ran from a deep gash on his forehead. She knelt beside him noting his eyes were clouded, whether from the alcohol or from the fall, she couldn't determine. She pressed her palm against his forehead to stem the bleeding while at the same time looking around to see if there was a bystander who could call 9-1-1. The only person in sight was running away from them down the alley.

Leslie momentarily released pressure, pulled out her own phone, dialed 9-1-1, set the phone to speaker mode and resumed the pressure. She provided the 9-1-1 operator with the pertinent information, then put her ear to the fallen man's chest and listened to his shallow breathing. His heart rate was slow, but steady.

Her phone, now lying on the ground beside her knee, sounded. COX appeared on the screen. She touched the ACCEPT button. "Cox," she began, "I'm on Southard, half a block north of Duval! Man down! Need help!"

Cox's reply was unintelligible. The phone went dead, but not before a siren came into earshot. Her partner arrived just as the ambulance rocked to a stop in the street in front of her. "Grab that jump drive over there," she instructed Cox, nodding toward the object the downed man had been reaching for.

Cox threw her a quizzical look.

"Do it!" she commanded. "I'll explain later."

"What do we have here?" a deep male voice above her demanded.

"Man down. Been drinking. Forehead laceration. Pretty deep, judging from all this blood."

"You a cop?"

"Sheriff's deputy. Lee County."

"A bit far from home. He fall, or what?"

"I believe he fell. I was across the street when he went down. May have tripped. May have been pushed—or possibly hit with something. I don't know. Saw a man running down the alley."

"Lost a lot of blood, I see. I'll take it from here," the paramedic said, accepting a large pad from his partner and placing it over the wound. "Looks like you might have stopped the blood loss soon enough to save him. But it'll be close, judging from his blood pressure. He doesn't look to be in any too good a shape to begin with."

"From what I know, five beers and a double shot of Guaro. Every day I believe."

"Willie T's?"

"You got it."

"Bartender's a friend. Okay, we're taking him to Lower Keys. Is he under arrest or anything?"

"No. He's free to go."

Leslie walked over to join Cox, who immediately said, "Mind telling me what's going down—partner? Your arm's covered in blood."

Leslie filled Cox in on what had transpired. Adding, "It took me a while to figure out what Larry there dropped when he fell."

"You mean the jump drive?"

"Would you ever expect a derelict like this guy to have a jump drive?"

"Can't say as I would," Cox allowed. "What's bothering you?"

"All out of character. Why have a jump drive? More important, why carry it in your hand? Unless..."

"Unless you're about to hand it to someone," Cox added. "Maybe he was a messenger?"

"Bingo! Supporting that theory, I saw a man running down that alley. Now that I think about it, the runner tried hard to blend into the cans and junk and not be seen."

"Get enough for identification?"

"I'm processing it. Been concentrating on keeping Larry there alive. But something about the image struck a note. It'll come to me."

"You get anything confirming Jakowski remaining on the island?"

"Never made it that far."

TWENTY-TWO

THIS TIME ON THE TRIP HOME COX WAS driving. They were on U.S. Highway 1, two hours north of Key West, approaching Key Largo. "Have a good nap?" he teased.

"Needed that, I suppose," Leslie shrugged, doing her best not to allow Cox's constant poking to get to her. "Want me to drive?"

"Can I trust you in the Everglades not to leave me with the alligators?"

"Best way to prevent that is for you to sleep. At least then you're not busy agitating me."

"Grow a skin, partner. Yours is awful thin."

"Look, you know I'm sensitive about Jakowski," Leslie surprised herself by expressing her feelings. And to Cox of all people. "I probably shouldn't have gone to the Isle of Man with him. In my defense, it *was* business. We did make the arrest. To remain home would also have been wrong. Just leave it alone, will you? It's something I need to deal with."

"Sorry," Cox relented, his tone conciliatory, "Speaking of Jak, we didn't get positive confirmation he *wasn't* on that ferry going north from Key West. That would make it a lot easier for you. Want off the case?"

"Hell no! You're not going to suggest that to the boss. Are you?"

"Shit no! But I wouldn't be at all surprised if Boots pulls the plug. Jak's in the middle of this. For all we know at this point, he could have been the guy in the video who 'shot' himself. Or even the guy in Willie T's who passed the telescope to the Kumars. His paw prints are all over this thing."

"That's what has me going. In all honesty, I don't think that's him on the tape. Doesn't move right."

"What about the guy running down the alley? Could that have been him?"

"Same problem. Didn't move right."

"What's that mean? 'Didn't move right'?"

"Jakowski is light on his feet. He's a big man, but moves like a basketball player. Light and efficient. No excess movements. The man in the alley was herky jerky."

"Could have disguised his movements. Been known to have been done."

"Perhaps that's what I'm seeing." Leslie was lost in thought watching the fishing boats move lazily on either side of the causeway bridge. "What do you make of the jump drive we found?"

"Besides the fact that a drunk had it in the first place, to find it encrypted makes even less sense. Can't wait for Beth Hillard's report. Never known her and her team to not be able to decode anything."

"Might take a while, but they usually come through," Leslie agreed.

"Hey," Cox said a moment later, "we're coming to my favorite eating place down here. Let's break. You can drive from here. Besides, this is the home of key lime pie. Best anywhere."

"Go for it," Leslie said as her phone suddenly made its presence known, "Speaking of the devil!" she said into the phone. "Cox and I were just talking about you." She turned the phone so Cox could see she was talking to Hillard. "Got something for us?"

"Indeed I do," came the upbeat reply from their Criminal Investigative Assistant. "You won't believe this, but you hit a gold mine with that drive!"

"I'm putting you on speaker," Leslie said. "We're in our car, so it's secure. Go ahead."

"First, the encryption was primitive, not at all what we see from the cartels these days. Second, we have a list of names, twenty-two female; eight male. Along with pictures. None over twelve."

"What's that..." Leslie began to ask, but was cut off by Hillard who tersely said, "Sex trafficking. Children!"

"Sex..."

"That's not the end of it. A ship, the *Viru*, that's the flagship of the Inca Lines, is due into Key West at eight tomorrow morning. We have reason to believe those poor kids are aboard."

"How much, if any, of this have you confirmed?" Leslie asked, knowing how thorough Hillard was.

"Because of the nature of this information, I didn't want to send up flags. The only thing I know for certain is that when the *Viru* went through the Panama Canal, they listed a school class of twenty children, five teachers, on the manifest."

"Have you briefed Boots?"

"Holding off. Waiting for instructions from you."

Looking over to Cox, who was nodding affirmatively, Leslie said, "Brief Stetson and ask her to call my phone when she's read the file. Oh, and Beth, great piece of work. Thanks."

"You're the one who found the drive! I just read it." With a rushed, "I'm on my way!" Beth concluded the call.

Leslie turned to Cox. "Still hungry?"

"Even if I was, the boss'll be on the line within ten minutes. Let's just sit here. We may be going back south."

———

Leslie's phone rang in exactly six minutes. Without introduction, Stetson asked, "Tell me what your plan is."

Cox began to answer. "I was thinking of..."

Leslie interrupted by saying, "We, with your blessing, plan to call Ghana. This is best handled by the feds. We have no real jurisdiction and who knows..."

"Good plan!" Stetson confirmed. "Fact is, I already instructed Hillard to send the file to Agent Ghana. Call and brief her personally. Then get your asses out of there and back home. Sheriff'll be real unhappy to learn you were anywhere around there when those children are brought off the ship. Shit's going to hit the fan!"

"What the hell she mean," Cox asked, "about shit hitting the fan? Didn't we—you—do a good thing finding that drive?"

"Don't know for certain, but my guess is people have been paid to turn a blind eye with respect to those children. Whoever made those payments won't be happy when the children are returned home. Can't imagine the boss wants us rolled up in that in any manner."

"You certain they'll be returned?"

"No call to be cynical," Leslie said, waiting for Agent Ghana to answer.

A moment later the federal agent came on the line. "Just got the file from Boots. Good work, Deputy. Give me the background. How did the drive come into your possession?"

Leslie outlined her and Cox's time in Key West, ending with, "And while I was kneeling on the ground applying pressure, I realized the object he was reaching out for, the one he appeared to have dropped when he fell, was a computer jump drive. I had Cox secure it when he arrived."

"Leslie, tell me about the person you saw retreating down the alley," Agent Ghana asked. "Male, female. Tall, short. You know the drill."

"I told you all I have. Tall. I'd say around six-foot-three, four. As I said, male. I suppose the runner could be female, but I'm leaning toward male. Couldn't see the hair. Runner was staying close to the right side of the alley. I'm thinking so I couldn't get a good silhouette."

"Could you make out a color?"

"Initially I thought black. Like a black tracksuit. But now as I review the image, I'm thinking it was green. Dark green. Head covered with a cap. Everything the same color."

"That all you have?"

"Isn't that enough?" Leslie flung back, agitated at the federal agent's condescending tone.

"Just want the record complete, Deputy. You did good. Now let me feed you back some facts you wouldn't know. First, that guy Larry—real name, Luis Diaz—was a lieutenant in the *Pishtacos* Peruvian gang working for the *Artista* Sisters before his deterioration. Now he's a runner for the Sisters in Key West. My guess, after this incident we won't hear from him again. Delivers messages from the *Artistas* in Peru to the stateside operation."

"Are you saying Larry was passing information about the children to the stateside gang?"

"That's almost what it was, Leslie. Except, you have it in reverse. That stick was going *to* Larry, not *from* him."

"You mean, the man I saw in the alley was *delivering* information?"

"Exactly! The 'stateside gang' was to pick the children up in Key West when they got off the boat and distribute them along the east coast, from Florida to Maine. That much we know for certain."

"Then what *don't* you know?" Leslie asked, at a loss.

"Not what! *Who*. Who delivered, or tried to deliver, the drive to Larry?"

"From your tone I believe you have a strong possibility. You in a sharing mood?"

"Goes no further."

"Cox and I are good with that."

"Valeria López has been known to deliver messages wearing green. As you say, almost black."

Confused, Leslie repeated, "Valeria Ló..."

"Hank Hoyos' wife."

They were now deep into the Everglades. Night had landed hard, confining visibility to the arc of the car's headlights. In a state where one and a half million alligators call home, Leslie knew that a large number of them now surrounded their car. The good news, alligators don't go looking for humans. The bad news, they don't back down from confrontation.

Cox stirred himself awake, his eyes blinking several times as he slowly became oriented. "Hey, tell me we're not going west! We are, aren't we?"

"We're going home," Leslie asserted, bracing for the verbal abuse about to be launched in her direction. "I thought better of us going back down there. Not a good idea. Particularly since the boss said no."

"I thought we ironed all that out earlier," Cox said, keeping his temper in check. "I thought we were in agreement it would be good if we watched the ship unload, maybe see someone in the crowd that would trigger something. When I fell asleep, we were going south."

"That's just it," Leslie complained, "trigger what? We have no clue what we're looking for. I just happened to be in the right place at the right time to see that guy Larry fall. The jump drive has nothing to do with the Franklin killing as far as we know. Trafficking children, as horrendous as it is, is not our jurisdiction down there. I'm sure Ghana will have video for us to see if that becomes important to our investigation. And hey, if money is changing hands with the locals, the further away we are, the fewer jurisdictional issues will bite us in the ass."

"Should have consulted with me," Cox shook his head slightly, strangely calm for him.

"It seemed so...so clear cut. Sorry. Didn't want to wake you. It's been a long day, and..."

"And truth is, Leslie, admit it. When you make up your mind, there's no changing it. Hey, judging from that sign back there, we're almost across the Alley. I got forty-five minutes. Wake me when I make Captain." With that, Cox closed his eyes and either fell instantly asleep or pretended to do so.

TWENTY-THREE

AT PRECISELY TEN HUNDRED HOURS, LESLIE and Cox were standing at attention in Captain Karen Stetson's office with Sergeant Hudson Oakmore at their side as Sheriff Jamison Radclif, wearing a freshly pressed uniform, came through the door. "At ease," he said, smiling and pulling the door closed behind him. "Nice piece of work, both of you. Thanks to you, thirty children are on their way home to their parents."

"Was anyone arrested?"

"Nobody came for them. You disrupted their communication. For that impressive endeavor, you both will be the recipients of a Medal of Commendation. Congratulations on a job well done." Radclif then faced Leslie, saluted, and then turned to Cox and did the same thing. "Because of the ongoing investigation we'll be unable to publicly announce these awards, but just know your work is very much appreciated. Now, unless you have questions, I've got work to do."

The room maintained its respectful atmosphere with the four officers saluting their boss who then walked down the hallway toward the building's back exit.

Stetson looked to Cox and Hodges. "Don't read anything into his abruptness. Man's got a lot on his mind these days. Shit's coming at him from all directions. This was a bright spot for him, believe it or not. Just don't publicize the commendation until the investigation is over. Now, tell me about Key West. Hud, you're free to stay or leave. Your choice."

"I'll stay. Can't wait to hear what these two were up to down there."

Leslie nodded to Cox who did a good job of briefing their bosses on what they found. When he finished, Stetson commented, "I take it from the timelines, that you neither proved nor disproved Jak being on that fateful northbound ferry."

"The only thing we know for certain, is that Jakowski was wearing a red, foul weather jacket during the day. Several videos confirm that only one man with Jak's build and wearing a red jacket boarded the ferry. However, we can't say conclusively that man was him."

156

"So, he could have been on board," Hudson reasoned.

"Could have been. Yes," Leslie said.

"Cox, you look doubtful. You have another take?"

"Jakowski *could* have been on board the northbound ferry, I concur. I'm not in the camp of those who believe it was Jak was the guy who put the gun to his own head."

"About that," Hudson queried, "Hodges, what's *your* opinion?"

"I'm with my partner on the shooter. I don't believe it was Jakowski."

Stetson, who had just listened throughout the give and take, said, "On what do you base your conclusion, Hodges?"

"Motion is all wrong for starters. Maybe it's the boat rocking that threw his gait off. That's possible. Don't think so, though."

"For what it's worth, I've studied the video for hours and I agree with the two of you. But know this, until Pete Jakowski is proven to have been in Key West at the time of the shooting, he is a Person of Interest. How you plan to manage that, Hodges, is your problem. Don't spook him, but don't tiptoe either. He's capable of disappearing in an instant. Hopefully we've taken precautions against him fleeing, but with his knowledge of law enforcement and his contacts, he might slip away. Is that clear, Deputy?"

"Clear, Captain," Leslie answered uneasily, realizing that her instructions were anything but clear—and mostly impossible.

"I say we begin again with Admiral Three M," Leslie suggested to her partner when they were back in The Pit. "Work through everyone on our list, try figure out what we're missing here."

"Agreed. Let's get her overprivileged ass in here, do this right. Tired of chasing that woman all over hell. Hey, and while we're at it, we need to talk to her husband as well."

"You think he knows more than he's saying?"

"Leslie, one thing I've learned is that nobody tells the police everything. Why the hell you think they invented waterboarding?"

"I'll ignore that comment. You work on getting Big Mack and her husband in here and I'll concentrate on Franklin's friend, Herco. Three M handed you her personal card when we left her plane. Use it. See if it works like she said. We'll do Jak last."

"While you're at it, Les, get Herco's wife in here as well. She can provide alibi support for him if required. Maybe we'll learn if it was really her you saw in Key West. Speaking of Jakowski, I'm thinking you got it backwards. Get him in here while we're cooling our heels waiting for the Admiral. I'm betting he's more central than you give him credit for."

"Cox, hate to break it to you, I have no friggin' idea where he's at on all this. I'm thinking he knows a hell of a lot more than he's told me, that's for certain. I'm calling him right now."

To Leslie's surprise, the big Pittsburgh cop answered on the first ring. "Where the hell you been, Les? Went by your house, didn't see anybody home. On assignment or something?"

"Where are you?" Leslie asked, not answering his question.

"Holiday Inn."

"Mind coming over to the office? Cox and I want to go over a timeline with you."

"Still working the Franklin death?"

"We are. That a problem?"

"Don't be so defensive. I'll be happy to tell you what I know—again. See you in about twenty."

"What should I make of Cox escorting me back here to the interrogation room and not you?" Jakowski asked when he entered the small room and found Leslie sitting at the single table, her hands crossed in front of her. "Should I be worried?"

"I'll tell you exactly what you tell *your* interviewees. You only need worry if you've done something you're not proud of."

"Trouble is, Leslie, I only say that when I have my suspicions."

Ignoring his remark, she said, "Let's start with what your plan was. We know the Sunspot Telescope was found among the cargo on a sunken sailing ship off the Dry Tortugas. That ship, the *Buen Jesús*, is now owned by a retired admiral by the name of Makenzie Madison Masters. From what you told us so far, you were working with Derrick Franklin to...to do exactly what?"

Without hesitation, Jakowski answered. "Yes, the *Buen Jesús*. The Sunspot is owned by Masters Marine because her employee, my friend Benny, found the sunken hull on one of his private dives—or so he claims. Big Mack disputes Benny's claim. That telescope's worth a fortune and I was working with Benny to collect a little for each of us."

"What is your definition of 'a little'?" Cox asked, speaking up to remind Jakowski that he, Cox, was part of the interrogation team.

158

"On the assumption the Sunspot could be sold for two hundred, I planned to net fifty. That would be more than enough to end my dependence on Stratis."

"And start a new life?" Cox insinuated.

Leslie flashed her partner a "Back off!" look, but said nothing.

"If I was so inclined," Jakowski replied, his voice remaining friendly. "That indeed would be enough, way more than enough, to do anything I wanted."

"Let me get this straight," Leslie was firm. "You and Franklin were going to sell the Sunspot to a third party and keep the proceeds for yourselves. Not split with Masters?"

The big cop appeared lost in thought. The Lee County sheriff's detectives allowed the silence to go unbroken. Finally, Jakowski said, "I frankly don't know what Benny's arrangement with Three M was. Initially, I believed he was working with her, off the company books. But from a few things I observed, that might have changed."

"Mind providing examples?" Leslie probed. "Observations, conversations, anything."

"Feelings mostly. For example, when the cargo was brought up from the Gulf floor I was on the dock when the barges came in. That's when Three M learned the Sunspot had not been salvaged. She's not known for her calm demeanor, but she took the news as if it meant nothing. I mean, a two-hundred-million-dollar artifact gone missing and Big Mack doesn't blink!" Jakowski paused, then added, "And forty-five minutes later I was in the parking lot about to leave, when Herco, a friend I hadn't seen in a long while, rolls in. Before I could get out of my car and say hello, Big Mack comes racing down from the wharf and screams at him as only she can scream."

"What was she screaming about?" Leslie inquired.

"The missing telescope. Wanted to know what he knew about it. Questioned him about working with Benny."

"What was the result?" Cox asked. "I mean, how did the encounter end?"

"My friend, actually a mutual friend of mine and Franklin, calmed her down by saying he'd get to the bottom of it for her. He repeated several times to trust him, it would all work out."

"What did that mean?"

"Your guess is as good as mine. My take, he promised to take care of getting the telescope sold. Why Big Mack believed Herco could deliver on the telescope I don't know."

"Herco, you say?" Leslie stopped him. "Repeat for Cox what you told me about him."

"Hank Hoyos. Known him since Pitt. Hell of a soccer player. Took Pitt to the national championships. Played professionally for the *Atlético Nacionals*. That's the Colombian soccer team. National hero type of thing. Then he apparently developed a gambling problem and things went a bit downhill for him."

"Talking with this Herco character satisfied Masters, did it?" Cox clarified.

"Appeared to."

"Tell me," Leslie said, changing the subject slightly, "who were you planning on selling the Sunspot to? I assume you had a buyer lined up."

"Subject to verification."

"And that buyer was?"

"Off the record?"

"Sorry, can't go there."

Leslie glared at the big cop, trying to decide whether it was time to warn about him being a Person of Interest.

Reading her mind, Jakowski, his voice barely above a whisper, said, "*Sinaloas*."

"Drugs and money laundering!" Cox shook his head. "You kidding me? What the hell *you* doing working with the likes of those guys?"

Leslie turned her scowl on her partner before focusing on the man she had been sharing her bed with. "When you say *Sinaloas*, I assume Cox is right. You're referring to Guzman-Loera's organization."

"They're also known as the Pacific Cartel and the Blood Alliance," Cox added. "Currently based in Culiacán. With all the names they use, it's hard to keep track."

"One and the same," Jakowski agreed, turning away. "Look, I wasn't helping them move product or anything. Everything I did with them was above board. Just brokering a deal for a telescope. They wanted to buy, we wanted to sell."

Cox, his face portraying skepticism, leaned in close to Jakowski. "A telescope that just happened to be a Seminal Society First. And one you didn't own, I might add. Don't overlook that fact."

"I was the middleman. Broker, as I said. It was owned by Franklin. He found it."

"I thought the Sunspot Telescope belonged to Masters. More accurately, Masters Marine."

"And I thought Benny was working for Masters herself. I thought she was in on the side hustle. He and I were to meet on the eight a.m. ferry to Key West. He was to bring the telescope and we were to go down together and meet my contact. Benny never showed."

"And you went to Key West by yourself?"

"I did. And spent the day in Rick's Bar. As you know, Benny never showed."

"And you spent the night where? Or did you take the ferry north?"

"A little place just off Duval. Called The Raven's Nest."

"You were there all night?" Cox asked.

"Where the hell else would I be?" Jakowski shot back.

"Calm down!" Cox placated him "We're trying to pin down timelines. You know the drill. Just making certain we get it right the first time."

"Jak," Leslie interrupted, "any reason you picked that place? I mean there are tons of places to stay in Key West. You stay there before, or what?"

Jakowski took a long moment before answering. "I have to think what I'm at liberty to say. Look, as you know, I work on and off for a federal task force and..."

Leslie interrupted. "Were you working for the task force in anything you're telling us?"

"No."

"Okay, then, please don't waste our time by hiding answers based on your *federal* obligations. Please proceed."

"Runners for the *Pishtacos* hang out at Willie T's. They like to meet their contacts around the corner on Southard. The Raven's Nest is perfectly situated to observe their drops."

"So, Jak, you knew the *Pishtacos* were involved with the telescope? Even though you were set to broker it to the *Sinaloas*? It's hard to keep all the actors straight, but aren't they rivals?"

"I was keeping an eye on the *Pishtacos* for a task force matter, but rumors have been circulating for months that the *Sinaloas* were much more serious than any other cartel when it comes to the telescope. They're the ones set up that silly 'storage shed' baloney. They've been working this telescope thing for a long while now, trying to outbid The Zs; screwed up the Sunspot deal all right. Everyone wanted verification from the world expert. Made Sir Reggie a popular man in certain circles, say that much. Even Stratis got interested. Until he realized the shed was a scam."

"When did you find out," Leslie asked, "that the Sunspot was bought by the *Artista* Sisters? You have a hand in that, by chance?"

"Just as surprised as everyone else. Those cartels are often intertwined. I haven't been read in on that aspect of the business, but I do know Herco—and I —are...are screwed, to put it crudely."

"And your friend, Herco, was working for Masters in this Sunspot sale?"

"Assume so, but don't know for certain. Guy made a ton of money from soccer. Wife originally came from a top family in Peru. Wouldn't think he had money problems."

"You're dead-on target there. I'd never guess Herco and...and Mrs. Herco'd be in it for the money, would you?" Cox commented.

"Herco and I go back a long way. Seems I've known him forever. But something changed, about a year ago. Spends a lot of time in Vegas. I'd say he's taken up gambling."

"Maybe he's going out there for the girly shows," Cox commented, adding a nervous laugh to show it was a joke.

"That's totally out of character for him."

"Gambling problem?" Leslie asked.

"I'm not sure I'd go that far, but it's a possibility. Something's changed. That much I know."

"You have Herco's address?"

"When he's in the U.S. he has a home on Sanibel Island. Lives there with his wife Val."

"Her full name?"

"Valeria López."

"You say Valeria's from Peru?"

"She is—was. Now calls herself Colombian."

"What can you tell us about her?" Leslie asked.

"For one, she was Peru's Miss Universe winner. One of the world's most beautiful women. Still is. Tall. Elegant. Smart."

"She have her own resources?" Leslie asked, indulging her own curiosity about the woman.

"Very much so. Comes from a well-connected family. She was an actress, played in several movies. Marilyn Monroe of Peru."

"If she's got money, why doesn't your friend go to his wife instead of to the tables of Vegas?"

"Addictions, as you well know, run far deeper than just the money. Truthfully, at this point I'm speculating."

"Got a picture of her?"

Jakowski produced his cell phone, tapped the screen several times, then turned the device to face the detectives.

The scene appeared to be a backyard swimming pool inside a massive screened-in lanai, beyond which was a magnificent flowering garden sloping away to what Leslie guessed was the Gulf of Mexico. A sailboat was on the horizon. The bikini-clad woman in the lounge chair left very little to the imagination. Leslie had to agree with Jakowski's assessment, Valeria López was indeed one of the most beautiful women she had ever seen. It was hard to take her eyes off the woman whose legs seemed to extend forever.

"When Herco's not in the States, where would he be?"

"Colombia. I believe he's still involved with the soccer team."

"Didn't Pablo Escobar own the *Atlético Nacionals*," Cox asked, "before he died?"

"That was some thirty years ago. Lot of things change in thirty years."

"Lot of things remain the same," Cox retorted. "Just sayin'."

Jakowski, his fists clenched, stretched to his full height so that he towered over Cox, "If you're implying Herco and I have been...less than law-abiding, then you are very much off base. Our relationship has been clean—squeaky clean! I defy you to find otherwise!"

TWENTY-FOUR

RETIRED ADMIRAL MASTERS SAT IN INTERVIEW Room Two, her hands folded on the table in front of her. Susan Morehouse, a criminal defense lawyer and a principal of Morehouse, Young and Cohen, sat beside her client. The two of them sitting essentially motionless, reminding Leslie of predators waiting for their prey to land at the exact right spot before pouncing. "Don't underestimate Attorney Morehouse," Leslie whispered to her partner just before entering the room. "Remember from the Chladni case how nothing escapes her?"

"Remember her all too well. I spoke to her earlier today when I set this up, and she was surprisingly pleasant. Wasn't expecting that."

"Surprised she went along. Not like her..."

"I'd say, the child trafficking did it. She claims her client knows nothing about those children on the ship and is willing to do anything to help."

"We have no linkage between the telescope and the children, so how..."

"What she doesn't know doesn't hurt her. Fox News linked the trafficking to the cartel. I suggested we wanted to speak with Masters about her links to the *Artista* Sisters." Cox smiled broadly, bowed deeply while exaggeratedly swinging his arm in the direction of the door. "And voila!"

Leslie could not avoid laughing as she pushed the door open.

"Care to share your little joke with us, Detectives?" Morehouse asked as they seated themselves across from the women.

Ignoring the question, Leslie simply said, "Thanks for agreeing to meet with Detective Cox and myself on such short notice. We'll do our best to get you out of here ahead of rush hour. Of course, that depends as much on you as it does us. Let's get right into it. We understand an employee of yours—I suppose I should say, deceased employee—one Derrick Franklin, located a sunken ship, the *Buen Jesús y Nuestra Señora del Rosario*, in the Gulf of Mexico, near the Dry Tortugas."

"He did, yes," Masters replied.

"We also understand a manifest created of the contents of the *Buen Jesús* listed, among other objects, a telescope crafted by Galileo."

"The Sunspot Telescope, yes."

"We also believe that when the cargo was brought up from the wreck, the Sunspot Telescope, as you call it, did not come to the surface. Is that correct?"

"Correct. The Sunspot was not recovered as part of the official salvage."

"Can you speculate as to what happened to that telescope?"

"No speculation!" Morehouse cut in, holding up her hand to prevent Masters from answering.

"Sorry, my bad," Leslie said. "Let me correct the question. Do you know what happened to the Sunspot Telescope?"

"I believe I do," Masters hesitated, "but I..."

"Don't guess. If you know, tell the detectives. If you don't, say nothing."

"What I do know is that Benny, that's Derrick Franklin, supervised the salvage recovery. It was he who signed off on items brought to the surface."

"And since he didn't sign off on the Sunspot, it didn't come up. Is that what you're saying?"

"It didn't come to the surface during the salvage recovery operations. That I know."

"Did you have occasion to ask Franklin what happened to the Sunspot?"

"I asked him. Of course I did."

"What did he tell you?"

"Not to worry."

"What did he mean by that?"

"Speculation!" Morehouse interjected.

"What did you believe he meant by that?" Leslie corrected herself.

"The Sunspot would eventually come up."

"Off the books," Leslie suggested.

"Don't answer," Morehouse instructed.

"Did you have a conversation with a man named Hoyos? Hank Hoyos? Concerning the Sunspot."

"Yes. A friend of Benny."

"And what did Hoyos say about the Sunspot?"

"Exactly what Benny said. Not to worry."

"And you understood that comment to mean what?"

"The Sunspot would be recovered and become available."

"And did it?"

"Don't answer," Morehouse again warned her client.

Masters turned to her lawyer. "Afraid the cat's out of the bag on this one. These detectives know I traveled to Mexico, Cancun to be exact, to broker the Sunspot. Went there with Dr. Hammerschmidt, the world expert, to authenticate the Sunspot."

"Who were you meeting with in Cancun?"

"Castro Estrada Jimènez."

"Does this Jimènez have a title?"

"Nothing official, if that's what you mean."

"Unofficial."

"He heads *Los Zetas*."

"Known here in the States as The Zs," Leslie prompted. "A drug cartel."

"Don't answer!"

Leslie allowed Masters a moment to disobey her lawyer before moving on when Masters followed her lawyer's instruction. "Was Jimènez the potential buyer of the Sunspot Telescope?"

"Answer only if you know."

"That was my understanding. Yes."

"Did Dr. Hammerschmidt, in fact, authenticate the Sunspot to Jimènez?"

"He did not."

"Why not? What happened?"

"A man boarded the plane and took Sir Reggie, that's Dr. Hammerschmidt, off."

"Do you know where they took him?"

"Answer only if you know. Don't speculate."

"I'm told he was summoned by the *Artista* Sisters."

"And who are they?" Cox asked. "And why would they want to take the professor?"

"Speculation!"

"They run the *Pishtacos*," Cox made clear. "As we understand it, that's a Peruvian gang working the west coast of Mexico."

"I wouldn't know anything about that, Detective," Masters said.

"Seems to me, we're about done here," Morehouse said, standing and motioning her client to follow her lead.

"Please sit, Attorney Morehouse," Leslie instructed. "We have just a few more questions and we'll wrap it up." Leslie waited until the lawyer took her seat. "I assume you had a price in mind when you were in negotiations with Jimènez?"

"Two hundred fifty million was the number most often discussed."

"For the telescope alone?" Leslie asked. "Or, did other services come along with that?"

"I don't know what you're suggesting, Detective," Morehouse barked, "but whatever it is, my client is not answering! Come, we're finished here!"

Masters dutifully got up and followed her attorney toward the door. Before leaving, she turned and said, "I understand the Sisters offered four hundred."

"That's enough!" Attorney Morehouse ordered. "No further comments!"

"You're here today to talk with Detective Hodges and myself about Derrick Franklin, and the work he did for Masters Marine Salvage & Rescue," Cox said to Henry Masters. "You have been given the opportunity to have counsel present, and you have declined. Is that all correct?"

"That is indeed correct."

"The position you hold with the company is?"

"Vice President of Human Resources."

"And in that position, you get to know the employees and their job functions?"

"I do. At least for the top-level folks I do."

"You knew Derrick Franklin, both professionally and personally, did you not?"

"If you're asking were we friends, the answer is yes, we were."

"Please describe Franklin, if you would."

"I prefer to call him Benny. That's what his friends called him. Man loved diving. Overdid it at times, but he was as natural under water as a fish."

"Let me focus, if you will, on the salvage operation pertaining to the *Buen Jesús*. From the beginning to the end of the operation to bring the sunken cargo to the surface, how long did it take?"

"Many months. Twenty-seven to be exact. Permits had to be obtained. A myriad of paperwork had to be processed. Title issues, claims by the feds and by Florida, you name it. Everyone got in on the action. I chided Benny. Told him we would have been better off had he brought the stuff up without registering it. As it turned out, we had to work through titles. Litigation became necessary."

"I mean from the time you began hauling cargo to the surface. From that point until you had it all up, how long did it take?"

"Benny had it all organized. We had four barges and five dive boats, twenty divers in all, in place the day before. Divers worked in pairs from a pre-established manifest. Everything went like clockwork. First diver went down at exactly zero eight hundred. Last diver came up at zero six thirty-five. Twenty-three and a half hours."

"Pre-established manifest? Please explain."

"We spent almost two months carefully taking photos and itemizing everything on the *Buen Jesús*. Needed it for the permitting. As I said, when it was time to salvage the items, the divers worked in pairs. For each dive, the team had a goal. Sometimes it was a single item. Sometimes it was several items. Every item was again photographed and catalogued as it came up."

"Wasn't it a big surprise when the Sunspot Telescope failed to come to the surface?"

Masters glanced away. It looked to Leslie as if he was covering his embarrassment. "I hate to admit this, but at the time I was preoccupied with logging in the salvage items and creating an actual salvage manifest. Everything was going smoothly. I never realized that the Sunspot Telescope was not on that manifest."

"If I understand you correctly, two manifests were created."

"One was for permitting purposes. The other the actual recovery."

"Why two?"

"That's just the way we do it. Sometimes things break, get dropped, all manner of stuff goes wrong. It's not like walking into a warehouse and bringing things out. We compare the two manifests when the dive is completed."

"Is that when you found the Sunspot had not been brought up?"

"In this case, even before they were compared."

"Does that happen often?" Cox quizzed. "According to what you said a moment ago, cargo does go missing from time to time?"

"I did say that things happen. But truth is, we have very little slippage. That's my wife's department. And she does an outstanding job of getting everything possible off the bottom. She spends countless hours painstakingly putting it all together. She prepares a 'dive order' in which she assigns each item to the diver team she trusts the most with that type of item."

"Who was the Sunspot assigned to? Who did she trust with it?"

"I wouldn't know that for certain. Kenzie controlled all that, but I can't imagine anyone other than Benny. My job was to log it in—and inspect it—when it reached the surface."

"Would the telescope have been scheduled for early or late in the operation?"

"Scheduled for next to last. She wanted Benny on board the mothership when the last piece came up. Champagne and all that."

"What was last?"

"A set of pearl earrings, fashioned for the Queen of Spain."

"I take it nothing else was missing—other than the Sunspot? Everything else on the original salvage manifest was recovered?"

"It certainly was. To the very last gold nugget."

"When did it become known the Sunspot was missing?"

"The first I heard about it was just before we tied up at the dock. About five minutes out."

"How was it made known?"

"As far as I can determine, quite by accident. Kenzie wanted to see the telescope, to touch it. Perhaps she wanted to look through it, don't know. She asked Benny where it was stowed. He told her it had been removed from the dive order and he had assumed she didn't want it brought up when all eyes were focused on it."

"I can imagine her demeanor at that point! I bet she was angry with him."

"I wasn't there to observe. I don't know."

"Where did that conversation take place?"

"To the best of my knowledge, right there on the recovery ship just before we tied up."

TWENTY-FIVE

LESLIE SPENT THE REMAINDER OF THE DAY organizing the file and mentally digesting what she and Cox had learned from the interviews with Admiral Makenzie Madison Masters, Henry Van Deere Masters and Pete Jakowski. While nothing she had heard placed Jakowski on the wrong side of the law, she came away feeling less than pleased.

Cox had summarized it plainly. "That had to be painful for you, Les," he had commented after Jak walked from the interrogation room. "As expected, he didn't say anything that incriminated himself. But he also didn't say anything that indicated how the Sunspot managed to make it from the floor of the Gulf of Mexico into the hands of Seminal Society collectors Sanjay and Riya Kumar."

"For that matter, he didn't shed any light on how the *Artista* Sisters and their Peruvian *Pishtacos* gang got involved. He was well on his way to collecting a fortune and suddenly it's gone—and he's doing nothing about it. There's more to this than meets the eye."

"I can see how that bothers you, Les. What do you make of his denial of being on the ferry the night when whoever went overboard? You believe him?"

"That's a good way to put it, Cox," Leslie deflected, purposely not answering his question. "We don't know who went overboard, do we? The top-side visual evidence points to Derrick Franklin shooting himself and falling off the stern, but the forensic evidence places the bullet hole an inch or so forward of where the video suggests the muzzle was placed. Also, Van Deere believes Franklin died instantly, which is inconsistent with taking a step and falling overboard after being shot."

Cox listened, thought about what his partner was saying, then shrugged.

Leslie continued, "And to add a complication, perhaps a meaningless one as far as our investigation goes, we seemingly have Herco's wife Valeria delivering information to that Larry guy, the drunken *Pishtacos* runner, giving him, or getting from him, I don't know which, the cartel's stateside operational

170

information on the arrival of children to be used in sex trafficking. Dealt with sex trafficking up in Tampa and it never got any easier. I hurt for those children. Makes my skin crawl just thinking about it."

"Don't lose focus, Les. We have a death to straighten out—and hopefully solve. Trafficking is not our focus."

"This can't be purely coincidence. Herco, a good friend of Derrick, a man who died a suspicious death, has a wife who is running interference for a Peruvian cartel. For that matter, he's a good friend of Jak's as well."

"Let's concentrate on that for a moment if you don't mind. Three men, all athletes, remain friends for years. I think..."

"Nothing wrong in lasting friendships. Those three shared a common interest, so it's not surprising they remained friends."

"You're in step with my thoughts exactly. We need to concentrate on the three of them. Jak came clean about working with Franklin to sell the Sunspot to the cartel off Masters' books, if you will. As much as it hurts, your buddy is knee deep in alligators. He knows more than he's letting on. I'll bet on that."

Now it was Leslie's turn to process what her partner was saying. Working through the facts, she realized one fundamental truth. "You'd think," she said, almost to herself, "that by now, after seeing all that my husband Junior dealt with up in Tampa, it'd be second nature for me to realize that money corrupts. When the numbers get large enough, it's the special person who's strong enough to resist."

"And I'd say two hundred million leaves no one standing."

"You don't hold a very high opinion of your brethren."

"Les, prove me wrong. Just go ahead and prove me wrong."

"Thinking about juvenile trafficking, it just came to me we've never actually seen what's on that drive I recovered."

"CIA Beth Hillard read it to us."

"Not exactly. She said it contained pictures of some thirty children under twelve arriving Key West on the *Viru*, Inca Lines. Nothing more. I didn't see anything about that drive in the file."

"You make something from that?" Cox asked, a puzzled expression on his face. "It's not our concern. We know it was acted on. Hell, we even got commendations! Beth told someone."

"All the same, the contents should be in the file. Boots must be following instructions."

"From?"

"If I had to guess, I'd put my money on Agent Ghana. Everything to her is 'need to know'. Drives me crazy."

"Hey, who you calling?"

"Hi, Beth. It's Hodges. Need a favor. You know that jump drive we recovered in Key West, I..." Before Leslie could finish her sentence, and before the line went dead, she heard Hillard say, "L-6794".

"She knew what I wanted," Leslie informed Cox while at the same time pulling up file L-6794. "Oh, shit! These pictures break your heart! They're...they're babies! Landing time of the *Viru* is..." Leslie checked her watch. "...was eight hours ago! The only other notation in the file says, 'TRANS LORD LA'. What the hell you think that means?"

"Your guess is as good as mine, Les. As I've said, those children are not our problem. And thank God for that!"

"Would you still be saying that if you had a kid go missing? It's everyone's friggin' problem! That's what it really is!"

"Time to knock off. I see Hillard finally located Herco." Cox studied the file a moment longer, then said, "Scheduled for nine in the morning. Should be interesting."

"Herco, I assume that's who we're interviewing, holds the key to this. We need a tight timeline on him. As well as on Jak. See you in the morning."

"See you. Bunch of us are going over to Gus's. You joining us?"

"Not tonight. I got a few things to clean up here and then I'm going straight home. Frankly, I'm wiped."

———————

Fifteen minutes later, on her way out, the 'incident' alarm sounded, informing everyone in the building that something unusual was currently happening in the county. Leslie turned and headed to the Real Time Intelligence Center at the back of the building. The first thing she heard when she opened the door was a commentator describing a large group of children found in various states of distress. "Where is this?" Leslie asked a dispatcher. "Is it live now?"

"The far right screen is live, from Immokalee. But you won't see much. Most of the action happened forty minutes ago, over on twenty-nine. That monitor," the woman said, pointing to the one next to the live screen, "is a repeat loop beginning when the first car arrived on the scene."

Leslie studied the screen, noting a tractor-trailer, its right rear wheel off the roadway, rear doors open. What appeared to be duffle bags, or backpacks, were scattered inside. "What happened?"

"Truck blew a tire and the rear of the trailer fishtailed into a canal two miles north of Immokalee. Driver opened the rear compartment to get a tire iron and two of the older boys who had been locked in the truck jumped him. The others ran in all directions. A Good Samaritan called nine-one-one. First officers on scene gave chase to the children. Truck was gone when backup arrived. Wasn't even time to change the tire. Driver must have panicked. Couldn't have gone far because it hasn't come up on any of our cameras."

Leslie recognized the area. It was southeast of where she lived in Lehigh Acres and very close to the intersection of Route 82. Not more than fifteen—twenty minutes, tops—from her house. "Catch any of the kids?"

"Most got away. Caught ten girls and three boys hiding in the swamp. None over the age of nine. The others scattered. According to one witness, there may have been a child still in the back of the truck."

The file pictures from the drive Leslie had retrieved in Key West flashed into view in her mind's eye. "How many children in all? Any good estimate?"

"From what we can piece together, around twenty-five."

Before Leslie could respond, Captain Stetson came through the door of the now very active monitoring center. "Hodges! Just the person I was looking for! About to call you. We believe those children on that drive you found are the same ones inside that trailer. Didn't get sent back home after all as we have been told!"

"Didn't Homeland Security turn them away at the port? Isn't that always the plan?"

"Guess someone else had other plans. Now it's full-scale our problem! I couldn't find that jump drive you listed in your notes. Not like you, Hodges! What the hell gives?"

"The drive was not in my possession. I thought it was..." Thinking better than to blame her boss, Leslie said, "...File L-6794. You'll find what you're looking for in L-6794."

Stetson marched to the nearest console, motioned for the operator to move aside, sat down, logged in and pulled up the file number Leslie had given her. "Here it is, all right! Here, Jackson," she said to the displaced console operator, "Send these pictures over to Immokalee immediately. These, I believe, match the children from that truck." She thought for a moment, then continued, "Post these for Lee, Charlotte, Glades, Collier, Hendry. Note to officers: Vulnerable children, proceed with due care. I will personally supervise this operation. I want every one of those children kept safe. Every last one of them. No screw ups!"

"What do you want from me?" Leslie asked. "I can't get those kids out of my head."

"You have enough on your plate as it is. You can't do much with this anyway. I'll arrange for a shelter—and meals."

"Will they be deported?"

"You're getting too far ahead of this. Right now, we need to find the still missing children, and by all means, keep the ones we do have safe."

"Let me go over..."

"Hodges! Stand down! You look beat. Go home, get a good night's sleep. And by God, now you better stay away from Jakowski. In this operation, he's toxic."

If there was one thing Leslie had learned since becoming a Lee County sheriff's deputy, it was not to cross Captain Stetson. Stories of those that had didn't end well. "Aye, aye, Captain. Heard you loud and clear," Leslie said, reluctantly leaving the RTIC. It seemed a longer walk than usual to her car, the images of the children following her the whole way.

On the drive home, Leslie forced her mind to work through the Franklin death, beginning, once again, with the autopsy report where the medical examiner had made it clear that Franklin had died, not from a shot to the head, but from a neck puncture. She mentally played the video of the man who supposedly was Franklin, the man coming north on the ferry who fake-shot himself under the Matanzas Pass Bridge. Was that man Jakowski? The mutual friend Herco? Or possibly even a third party? Someone still unknown to their investigation?

Leslie was so absorbed with her thoughts, that it wasn't until she was locking the living room door behind her that she realized there had been motion off to her right in her neighbor's yard when she came down the street before turning into her driveway. "Lord's often out in the side yard working on his rig. Nothing unusual about that," she convinced herself.

Thinking of Franklin naturally led to thinking of Jakowski. The question she then had to answer was whether to believe him about staying that night in Key West or not. The mere fact that it remained a question troubled her. "How," she asked herself, "could she possibly be in love with a man she didn't fully trust?"

She was mostly finished with her dinner prep and working on her second Yuengling, when she first saw the note from Jak explaining that he thought it best they cut off contact until, as he put it, "the Benny matter is resolved to everyone's satisfaction." Relief flooded her body now that she didn't have to be the one who broached the subject. "When you get this, please call," the note had ended.

"Dinner first," she promised herself, intending to call him when she was more relaxed.

It wasn't until she had sliced up the chicken and had it sautéing in the frying pan and was about to add the vegetables to what ultimately would become soup, that the image of the empty Immokalee truck popped into her mind. The image she had seen in the operations center before leaving work.

She froze dead in her tracks realizing that an identical truck image was also firmly in her mind as well. The second image came from what her unconscious mind had captured as she walked from her car to the front door of her house about forty-five minutes ago.

Leslie quickly processed what she knew about her neighbor. Essentially very little, except for his visit several days earlier, where he had said, "Hey, neighbor. My name's Lord. Sam Lord. Friends call me Sammy."

Then it hit her. One of the notations, 'TRANS LORD LA', in the jump drive that she had recovered in Key West could be translated as, 'TRANSportation from Key West for the smuggled children by LORD Trucking Lehigh Acres."

Leslie grabbed her weapon and bolted out the back door, her mind flooded with thoughts, mostly centered on the child that reportedly had remained in the trailer when it left Immokalee. She might now be alone and scared somewhere along the route. *Or perhaps, still in the truck?* Leslie's eyes scanned the path, but she saw nothing as she quickly approached the truck, confirming that it was the same vehicle she had seen in the video.

"Hey neighbor!" came Lord's deep distinctively raspy voice. "This is private property! You're trespassing!"

"You know I'm a sheriff's deputy," she yelled back, not stopping. "Here on official business! This truck was involved in...an incident! I need to examine it!" The trailer loomed twenty yards straight in front of her. A man stood with his back to her, a hose in his right hand, spraying water inside. Leslie leveled her weapon at the man. "Turn that water off and step away from that truck. Do it now!"

Leslie felt a hot poker rip across her thigh before the gunshot registered. The impact buckled her right leg sending her hard to the ground, her weapon skittering away into the wet grass. From where she lay, it was impossible to determine what direction the bullet had come from. She saw no movement and the man with the hose was now nowhere in sight. Blood ran from two widely spaced holes in her thigh. She instinctively applied pressure to stem the flow, using both of her hands.

Almost immediately, a cloth bag, or backpack, smelling of vomit, slid over her head and was clamped tightly in place. Hands under her butt and behind her back lifted her from the ground. She swung wildly, her fist coming into contact with what felt like an arm, only it had no give. Further flailing made no contact. A moment later she was dropped onto the wet, slick wooden floor of what she assumed to be the tractor-trailer. Before she could pull the bag from her head, she felt a sharp jab in her arm just before the truck door slammed closed, the locking mechanism clicking solidly into place. Everything immediately went pitch black—and deathly quiet.

Then the drug began to work. She felt faint, lightheaded, then dizzy. It was all she could do to pull herself to the side wall and try to prop herself up. She had the presence of mind to check her leg for blood and found it relatively dry. Thankful that she was no longer in danger of bleeding to death, she nevertheless pulled the bag from her head and positioned it beside her leg in the event she needed a tourniquet. She then sat as still as she could make herself, listening to the silence, moving in and out of consciousness.

She suddenly sat bolt upright, sensing, rather than feeling, that her right leg was dripping blood. How much time had passed, she had no way of knowing. But judging from the fact that her right pants leg was heavily soaked, it seemed that it had been more than momentarily.

Her probing fingers confirmed what she had feared. Blood was present over a wide area! Fumbling for the bag, she managed to tie it around her thigh. She recalled a situation she had witnessed years ago in Tampa with a shooting similar to hers. A tourniquet had remained in place too long, and doctors could not save the leg.

"Let me out! Help!" she yelled repeatedly. "Let me out!" Slowly it came to her that this trailer was used for hauling human cargo and was soundproofed. She could make all the noise she wanted, all to no avail. Her dying inside the trailer meant nothing to people such as Lord—or to the people he worked for. They dealt with human death every day of their miserable lives. She shivered, realizing that she had been living next door to this wretched excuse for a human. Hopefully, not for any longer.

Leslie reached for her cell phone only to find it had no cell signal! Then she recalled that often trucks, such as this one that had been modified for human cargo, not only had sound-deadening material installed but also used foil to prevent GPS tracking of victims. Her cell phone was useless.

She tried to stand, but a wave of dizziness, followed quickly by nausea, forced her back down. She sat with her back against the side of the truck knowing that energy conservation would be her best—and perhaps only—survival option.

She recalled the words of the dispatcher in the Real Time Intelligence Center. "Driver opened the rear compartment to get a tire iron and two of the older boys who had been locked in the truck jumped him." She certainly could not jump anyone, but she could make good use of the tire iron, which she knew from past inspections of trucks such as this one, was located in a holder directly behind her.

Hoping the driver had replaced it before escaping to hide the truck here, she carefully worked herself close enough to the truck wall where she made out a slight shadow. Reaching her arm as far forward as she could, she was able to feel the outlines of the holder. Nausea flooded her body as she forced her arm even further. It was all she could do to keep from vomiting on herself. Her fingertips made contact with the bracket, but she could not get purchase on the tire iron itself as her hand slid from the bracket and slammed to the floor.

"You can do it, Leslie," she heard Junior's encouragement as clear as if he was standing over her. *"Take a minute. Gather yourself. Make a plan of action. Then execute."* She let her head slump forward, expelling air from her lungs as she did so. Then she filled her chest to capacity, lifting her head at the same time. She repeated the procedure twice more just as she and her late husband had practiced.

She was now ready to try again; the plan being to slide her body tight to the wall and lunge for the tire iron in one continuous motion, the goal being to grasp the tire iron in her hand. She also knew that knocking it to the truck floor would work as well.

"Ready," Junior said, his tone confident.

Leslie nodded.

"Get set."

"Go!"

And go Leslie went. Her arm shot upward while her body folded forward. Her knuckles hit the bracket edge and Leslie felt her skin split open. Ignoring the pain, her arm continued forward another several inches until her fingertips felt the rounded metal of the tire iron.

"Grab the iron! Grab it!"

Leslie's hand closed—and locked—around the metal. Unable to sustain the bent position, her body straightened up. The tire iron, at first, resisted movement. But then suddenly it snapped free of the holder, causing Leslie to fall backward, her head glancing off the side of the truck and landing on the floor with a soft thud, the iron falling safely beside her.

Her only job now was to remain alive long enough for someone to open the truck door.

According to her training, the timeline for survival without water was three to five days, maybe a bit longer. The bullet hole in her leg changed all that. Mentally scanning the manual, she read, "Infectious-purulent complications from gunshot wounds to the lower extremities occur with fifty-two-point three percent lethality, often from gangrene or sepsis." Not a positive outlook.

"So much for the negatives," Leslie told herself, "I need to concentrate on the positives." The only positive she could conjure was the massive hunt she knew was now going on in Lee and surrounding counties for this truck. Even that tiny hope was tempered with the understanding that the search was confined to highways and known storage lots. One thing was certain, this truck was hidden from public view and private home lots would not normally be part of the search criteria. At least not for several days, by which time it would be too late to save her leg, to say nothing of her life.

TWENTY-SIX

TIME STOOD STILL FOR LESLIE. SHE REFUSED SLEEP as best she could, knowing that the only thing keeping her from bleeding to death was the tourniquet on her thigh. She knew about the conflicting views as to how often the pressure should be released. The range was from never, down to two hours. Amputation was not a good outcome, so she decided on three-hour intervals. Life had boiled down to focusing on the not-so-simple act of counting time. The problem, she soon realized, was that remaining awake was becoming nearly impossible as the hours steadily ticked by.

From time to time, she thought she heard faint noises, as if someone was about to enter the trailer. She listened intently, trying to discern human sound; voices, a cough, rhythmic pounding, anything. All to no avail. The lack of sound was deafening—and disorienting.

Several times she caught herself dozing. On each occasion she shook herself awake and checked her leg, only to find her slacks newly dampened even though the tourniquet was as tight as she risked making it. How much longer she could hold off sleep she didn't know. Judging from the decreasing time intervals between her eyes involuntarily closing, she didn't expect to remain awake much longer.

———◆———

Jakowski's eyes came open at exactly six o'clock. Light was just beginning to peek around the window shades. He fumbled for his phone, expecting to have missed a call from Leslie. The note he had left for her made him a loose end. And Leslie didn't do well with loose ends. Her mind required order, repeatability. Above all, *no loose ends*. Period.

He checked his phone again at six-fifteen, then again at six-twenty-five. At six-thirty he dialed her number and listened while the call went directly to voicemail. Not like her. He tried several more times with the same result. By seven he was in his car heading for her home, knowing she almost always left at precisely seven-thirty.

Jakowski turned the corner a block from her house at seven-eighteen and was happy to see her car in her driveway. He pulled alongside and got out, taking in the quiet morning. Deciding against using his key and surprising her, he rang the doorbell at the front door.

No answer.

He rang again. Same result. He again tried calling.

Again, the call went straight to voicemail.

Key time!

Inside, he called her name.

No response.

He started up the stairs toward her bedroom when the cop in him demanded he secure the first floor before proceeding. First, he cleared the powder room bath off the living room. Then he opened the coat closet and gave it a quick once over. The dining area was empty, and he proceeded toward the kitchen.

His heart skipped a beat when he saw a partially cooked, uneaten, chicken stir fry on the stove. Leslie would never, ever, do that voluntarily. He turned and ran up the steps, taking them two at a time. Leslie's bedroom was empty, the bed had not been slept in. He checked the bathroom, the guest bedroom, then all the closets just to make certain he hadn't overlooked anything.

"Karen," Jakowski said into his phone when Captain Stetson came on the line, "I'm glad you picked up! Got a problem here at Hodges' house." He quickly outlined his concerns. "I'm hoping she was picked up by someone, Cox maybe. If not, then..."

"Give me a moment to check. One thing I'll say about Hodges is she's thorough. If she was being picked up for a case matter it would be in the file."

Boots put him on hold, and while waiting, Jak anxiously scanned the yard around Leslie's house for anything unusual.

"I just spoke with Cox," Stetson reported, finally coming back on the line. "He said he expected her in the office at eight. He's heading your way. ETA sixteen minutes. I'll dispatch deputies."

"Tell them I'll be searching the grounds. Wearing a tan shirt and jeans."

"Ten-four."

Jakowski stepped into the back yard, using the kitchen door. He saw nothing suspicious. Walking around the yard yielded the same result.

"Hey, you there!" a deep voice called, "keep your hands where we can see them! Lee County sheriff's deputies! You the Pittsburgh cop?"

"I am," Jakowski replied. "Nothing out here I could find."

"Mind showing ID?" the second guy asked. "Lots of people could be walking around with tan shirts and jeans."

Jakowski did as requested. They handed back his credentials and he said, "We need to examine the grounds more thoroughly. She went somewhere. Not like her to not call it in."

"First we'll have a look inside," the second man said, "You can wait out here if you like."

"I already did that. Nothing."

"We'll do it ourselves, thanks. Wait out here."

Jakowski again circled the yard, this time looking outward toward the neighbor's property. He remembered meeting the neighbor, a truck driver by the name of...of...Lord. He turned in that direction, took several steps and stopped in his tracks, his heart racing! There, mostly invisible behind a stand of holly, stood a white trailer identical to the one on the news that had broken down transporting children.

Running back to the house, he opened the side door and shouted, "Out here! Something you need to see!"

The second man, the one who had been doing all the talking, appeared in the doorway. "This better be good."

"Over there," Jakowski yelled, pointing toward the opening where he had seen the trailer. "That's the trailer everyone's looking for!"

The deputy quickly crossed the yard, then cried out, "Yeah! That's it, okay!" He reached for his microphone and called it in, adding, "Haven't approached, so this could be a false sighting. But it appears identical."

The radio squawked, "Stand down! Tactical team is ten minutes out. Do not approach. Repeat. Do not approach!"

"You hear that?" the deputy said to Jakowski. "Hold here until the tac team arrives. Ten minutes. Any sign of Deputy Hodges?"

"I haven't seen anything," Jakowski said.

"We found nothing in the house," the first deputy said, joining the other two at the yard edge. "Didn't realize there was so much distance between the houses in this neighborhood. Nice piece of property Hodges has here."

"Settlement from her husband's death up in Tampa," the other deputy put in. "Line of duty thing."

Not being able to wait any longer, Jakowski declared, "I'm going in!"

"Hell you are!" the deputy with the name tag of HASTINGS pronounced, his hand on his weapon. "Sheriff doesn't brook shit from cowboys! Stand down!"

"One of your officers is..."

"You don't know where the hell she is! Could be anywhere."

Jakowski knew Hastings was right, but he couldn't just stand around. Time, in these situations, was always critical. "Time's critical!" he yelled. "We gotta go in! Cover me!"

"Like hell! She's either gone to ground or...or they got her! Either way, we'll let tac do this."

Before Jakowski could respond, a black van skidded to a stop just behind them and eight officers clad in black Kevlar poured out and ran toward them. "Where's the truck?" the leader called. "Gunfire?"

"Nothing since we've been on scene, sir," Hastings snapped briskly. "About fifteen minutes now."

"Nothing for a half-hour," Jakowski added. "Don't know when Les...Deputy Hodges...went missing. I'd guess about seven-eight last night."

"And you're who?" the tac leader asked.

"He's a Pittsburgh detective. Name's Pete Jakowski."

"Verona. Not Pittsburgh."

"Whatever. He thinks Hodges is over there. We haven't seen her yet."

"Does she know the neighbor?" the tac leader asked. "Maybe she went over there to talk with him about the truck?"

"Possibly. Makes sense. Met the owner myself. Appeared to be a nice guy."

The leader examined a small hand-held device, before announcing, "Samuel Lord. Holds a commercial license. No citations. No complaints. Clean record all around. That trailer matches the one we've been searching for. Okay, we're going over. Jakowski, you can join us, but for God sakes, stay out of the way. Truck could be wired, so don't approach until we've cleared it. For all we know, it could contain illegals, or dynamite—or both."

"You have an imaging heat detector?" Jakowski asked.

"Military grade. Getting it now. Often, they insulate the truck to keep the sound inside. Insulation messes with the image. This puppy'll see through all that shit. Tell us what to expect."

As he spoke, two black-suited figures approached the truck, each carrying a different device.

"Deputy Suskins, she's the one on the right, is our explosives expert. That tool she's using sniffs out explosives. Does a good job. Saved our butts any number of times. And Musgrove's got the imager. Shouldn't be a minute before..."

Musgrove's arm shot up into the air, and the tac team froze. "Maybe got one inside! Low temp if we do."

"Child?" Jakowski asked.

"Dying child—or adult. Could be a smuggler wrapped in a foil blanket waiting, ready to open fire when we breach the door. Never really know what we'll find."

Suskins rolled her arm in the universal motion to move forward.

"Seems it's not bugged," the leader announced, the tension in his voice now lessened. "That's good. Just stay out of the line of fire when we breach." He handed Jakowski ear plugs. "You'll need these. Don't have glasses for you, so put your hands over your eyes, or..."

"I know the drill," Jakowski reassured him, refraining from pointing out this wasn't his first rodeo.

TWENTY-SEVEN

LESLIE DIDN'T KNOW IF THE EXPLOSION WAS REAL, or a continuation of the on again, off again, dream she was having. Her head was pounding and suddenly she was blinded by the brightest light and sharpest pain she had ever experienced. Had she been standing she would have toppled over. Instinctively, she curled into a ball, forgetting for the moment the tourniquet around her thigh, and her now thoroughly blood-soaked jeans.

She was rolled up, struggling to understand what was happening around her. A man's face appeared. A stranger. Was she again dreaming or was it hallucinating? The face disappeared. Another face appeared. She was helpless to reach out; to speak. *Protect yourself,* she told herself over and over, pulling into an even tighter ball almost to where her face was buried between her knees.

A touch on her neck!

She forced one eye open. Lips were moving but no sound came.

Hands were on her legs pulling them down, exposing her vulnerable stomach. She tried to roll over, but strong hands forced her onto her back.

Rape! He's going to rape me!

She kicked out with as much force as she could muster.

The man jumped backward, his lips were again moving, this time with muffled grunts, pieces of words; nothing with any meaning.

Then a partial word? "Pul..." Then another, "...ong." The sounds were still unintelligible but coming in louder. She thought she heard the word, "blood," in conjunction with, "lot of".

Suddenly, the face of Pete Jakowski appeared. She blinked several times. His face was still there, floating above her, as if in a dream. She tried to understand, but nothing made sense. *Did I die? Did we both die?*

She was disoriented, confused, and again rolled into a ball, this time with her knees tucked against her face, the taste of blood on her lips.

"Les..." the voice of Jakowski said, breaking up. "...safe..."

184

She tried to speak, but the words died in her throat.

"...flashbang..."

She processed that word and her training kicked in. Things began making sense. The truck had been found. A flashbang device had been used to temporally immobilize any hostile occupants. She relaxed her body and turned onto her back.

Jakowski knelt beside her. "This is Jak. Can you see me?"

"Yes," came the tentative answer. "Is it really you?"

"It certainly is," Jakowski answered, taking her hand in his. "You're in good hands now. The team will..."

"Tell me we're not both dead."

"You're very much alive, Les. Thank God."

She pointed toward her thigh. "...been sh..."

Speaking was difficult, and when Jakowski failed to respond, she took his hand and moved it to her thigh.

His lips moved. "...know. ...ok."

"Blood," she managed. "...ding."

"Not you..." His lips continued without any sound.

"Boy's gone," came a voice from somewhere above her, "Twelve...fift... at most," the voice continued. "Bled....death."

Jakowski's lips again began to move. "He was shot...about the same...as Leslie, I would guess."

The good news with Jakowski's statement was the fact she heard most of it—and without distortion. Her vision continued to improve to the point where she could now discern worry on Jak's face. She again tried her voice. "I was shot," she began. "In and out I believe. In the thigh. Lot of blood. May have hit an artery. I've been using a makeshift..." Looking down at her thigh, she now saw that her blood-soaked jeans had been cut away, exposing a clean-edged hole in her thigh. "What the hell?"

"Worried for nothing," Jakowski informed her. "Medic says you'll be okay."

"But the blood!"

"From the boy on the shelf above you. It's his blood that's been dripping onto you. Soaking your pants."

"Then why am I so...so groggy? I thought it was from blood loss."

"How long have you been feeling that way?"

"Started, best I can tell, right after they locked me in the truck."

"Guessing drugs," Jakowski informed her. "A shot of something, I suspect. They'll know soon enough. Your ride'll be arriving within two minutes."

"On the grounds now, Detective," a disconnected voice from behind informed her. "Have you out of here and on your way in no time. You live right. I'm told that bullet didn't hit anything critical. Have you fixed you up in no time."

"Leslie!" A new, but very familiar voice called from the doorway. "What the hell's going on?"

Leslie looked in the direction of the sound in time to see Cox leap up and into the truck.

Spotting the Pittsburgh cop, he barked, "What the hell *you* doing here, Jakowski! Get your ass outta our crime scene!"

"Hold on, Cox," Leslie began, "He's..."

Ignoring Leslie's pleas, Cox turned to the tactical team leader. "Escort this man off the premises at once. Find out where he's staying." To Jakowski he said, "You have any plans on leaving Florida in the next day or two? Cancel them!"

"What's it your business?" Jakowski snapped back.

"Young boy's dead! Law enforcement officer's been shot! Vehicle being used for illegal transportation of humans! The list goes on. That enough for you? It's all my business! And until *I'm* satisfied as to how you knew this truck was on this lot, as well as what involvement you had in the shootings, you're a suspect! Can I be any clearer? Now answer my question."

"No. I have no plans on leaving your state in the next few days. Is that what you want to hear?"

"Only if it's the truth. See that you don't."

Jakowski flashed Cox a mock two-finger salute before sarcastically adding, "Aye aye, Sir." He jumped down from the truck, making room for the paramedic team taking Jakowski's place beside Leslie.

"Hey," Cox called in Jakowski's direction, "You know where the hell the owner of this truck, Lord, is?"

"Why in the hell should I know that?"

"If there's anything you know that we don't that will help us with this mess, I want it. Hear me?"

"I hear you. And I have nothing for you."

Cox was interrupted by the medic who had placed a stethoscope on Leslie's chest. "Everything sounds good. Nothing critical appears to have been hit. My guess, a couple of stitches, you'll be ready to go."

Leslie started to get up, causing the medic to hold her down. "Unless you plan on walking to the hospital, let us do our jobs. It'll go easier if you do."

"Glad to hear the bullet wound wasn't critical," Captain Stetson said two hours later, coming into the small room where Leslie had just finished having her thigh stitched. "Cox has briefed me. In case it's any solace to you, there's a warrant out for the arrest of your neighbor, Samuel Lord. We believe he's been involved in human trafficking for several years. Good work, Detective."

"All I did was spot the truck. Then manage to get shot."

"All in the line of duty. I've authorized as much time off as you need. You've earned it."

"I've got an open homicide, Captain. Can't be taking..."

"I've asked Fischer to work with Cox. You need..."

"Doctor released me. Said I was good to go. Fischer's got his hands full as it is. I need to stay on the case."

"I got to hand it to Cox. He called that right. Said you wouldn't take well to being relieved of the Franklin case. He said taking you off the case is a punishment. Well, I'm not trying to punish you, just giving you some well-deserved rest."

"Doesn't feel that way. Sorry."

"I heard the bullet passed through your leg. In and out. Lucky you didn't bleed to death. That happened to a partner of mine a while back. Didn't die but had to retire. Hasn't walked without a cane since."

"I thought that *was* what happened. It was so dark in there I couldn't see anything. Just felt the blood. Even the exit wound didn't bleed as much as is typical. Doctor called me lucky. I'll take it."

"So where did all that blood come from? The pants leg they cut off is soaked."

"Unfortunately, at some point they also shot a young boy. Put him on a ledge above me. Blood's his."

"Makes sense," Stetson exclaimed. "That's why the evidence bag is marked Blood-Juvenile Male One. Okay, Hodges. If you've been released, then go for it if you feel up to it. Please don't overdo it. Staying on the case'll make Fischer happy. He's all but retired anyway." Stetson thought a moment before continuing. "From the file notes, you and Cox are in nowhere land with this. Please tell me I'm wrong."

"Can't do that, Cap. Pieces of the puzzle aren't falling yet. But they will."

"Love your optimism, Detective. From what I see, one of those pieces involves Jak. Did so, even before he found you in that trailer. Was that coincidence or what?"

"You put a POI on him before. Let it ride. But I understand he called it in to you. Who knows what would have happened if it weren't for him. But..." Leslie's lips compressed into a grimace, "...if he's involved in the trafficking, then he knew full well I was there. School's still out. Cox put him on notice. Jak's agreed to remain in town at least a few more days."

"In all honesty, Hodges, that's one of the reasons I wanted you off the case. We need clear eyes where he's concerned."

"Until I can unequivocally place Jak on Key West after the ferry left, he's a suspect. In fact, he's prime. He spent the day down there waiting for someone. He took a room in a bed and breakfast place exactly where the messenger dropped the jump drive giving the particulars of the traffic drop. No one can convince me that wasn't coincidence. He has a story as to why he was there. But truthfully, Jakowski being Jakowski, I would expect him to have a good story."

"Keep working it. You need something, ask."

Stetson abruptly turned and vanished through the doorway, only to be immediately replaced by Cox. "Doc says you're good to go. Didn't want to disturb your little powwow with the chief, but we got work to do. You up for it?"

"Other than feeling like shit, I'm game." Leslie was exhausted, physically as well as mentally. But she wasn't yet ready to be alone with her thoughts. "What do you have?"

"How do you know I have anything?"

"Cox, you're as transparent as a freshly washed window. Reminds me of a giddy schoolboy. Out with it."

"I've spent hours, seems more like days, watching the boat video, and..."

"You need a drum roll? Spit it out already!"

"The man who shot himself and fell off the boat was an imposter, not Franklin. Whoever it was, most likely killed Franklin and dumped his body under the bridge prior to that. Probably tied an anchor to him to keep him in place. Explains the bruising on his ankle."

"My memory, the ME report calls it an air hose around the ankle."

"ME was speculating. I'm positive now. Did some measurements and it's conclusive, it wasn't Franklin on that ferry. Early this morning, I had the marine folks do some diving. Found an anchor about fifty yards from where the body was found."

"Must be more than one anchor down there."

"This one came from Franklin's boat. Rope size matches the wound. Checking DNA now."

"So, who was it? You have that worked out as well?"

"Too small for Franklin. About an inch too short. Exactly Jak's size. We haven't found one piece of evidence Jak was on Key West after the ferry left. Nothing." Cox paused, waiting for blowback from Leslie.

When none appeared, he continued, "Partner, you sure as hell *are* tired! I just accused your boyfriend of homicide, and you said nothing. Want a ride home? We'll pick it up tomorrow."

"You're right. Physically, I am totally beat. But that doesn't stop my brain from running in overdrive. Jak is troubling. He shows up at my house unexpectedly at a critical time. Coincidence? He directs the tac team to the trailer. Second coincidence? I want to believe him. Hell! He's one of us! But..."

"When the information in that drive you found failed to make it to that *Pishtacos* gang runner Larry, the question then becomes, how the hell did they continue with the operation? My money's on Jakowski! He was down there, wasn't he?"

"Human smuggling? Children! Pete might be into a con job here and there...hey, I'm not saying he is, or he isn't...but he's not into child abuse. I'll vouch for that."

"You're so sure of yourself. Based on what?"

"Knowing him," Leslie replied without hesitation. "Gut instinct."

"Sure you're not biased? You 've got every reason to be, you know. Need I remind you; a con artist can only survive as a con artist if he—or she—consistently fools people. The best of them can fool anyone. Just watch the news and you'll know that's true. I'm thinking of the bitcoin guru, but there's no end of examples of otherwise honest individuals pulling the wool over our eyes."

"I don't have to like Jakowski for human smuggling just because I like him for the telescope heist."

"Heist and homicide. Don't forget. They may be one and the same. I believe the fake suicide was the murderer's way of directing the authorities to Franklin's body. Implying a conscience."

"Or a close attachment," Leslie added. "You know, an anonymous call would have worked. Perhaps even better."

"I agree—about the call. By staging the suicide, the perpetrator not only told us to go down and check the bottom, but...but may have pointed us to the murderer as well."

"That's a bit of a leap."

"Factor in the gloves, Leslie. The perp wore gloves. Certainly not for temperature control. Air temp at the time was mid-seventies. Water temp not far below that."

"What then?"

"Hide something?"

"Like what?" The faded *Go Pitt* tattoo on the back of Jak's right hand popped up in Leslie's mind's eye. 'From my playing days,' he had confessed one night as they lay in bed talking, having exhausted themselves. 'Did a lot of foolish things back then. This is the least of them.'

Turning to her partner, Leslie revealed, "Jak has a tat. Back of his right hand. Would have clearly been visible, not for that glove."

"That's why he's top of my list. Height's right. Well, close enough. Movement's a bit off, I grant you that. Could be the ferry though, or nothing more sinister than poor-quality video."

"What about Herco, the soccer player? He have anything on his..."

"Looked at what seems a million images. Believe it or not, not one showed his right hand clear enough to make out. I think there's something there but can't be certain. Could have been a bruise. Soccer player and all that. School's out on him."

"You know, Cox, I'm suddenly more tired than I thought. I'll take you up on your offer of a ride home."

TWENTY-EIGHT

LESLIE ALMOST FELL ASLEEP in the shower. She continued to feel soiled even though the hot water had long since washed the blood and grime from her body. Her head touched her pillow two minutes after five in the afternoon, perhaps for the first time ever. Within a minute she was asleep and from that point until shortly past six in the morning when a dream began, she was aware of nothing. An observer might have concluded from her lack of movement and totally expressionless face, that she was in a coma—or worse.

That was before the dream. After the dream began, that same observer would have reported a woman possessed. The sheet covering her body entangled in her thrashing limbs, ultimately resulting in her sitting bolt upright, throwing her feet over the side of the bed, her arms continuing to swing wildly as if she were fending off a gang of attackers. Gradually, her arm movements slowed, then stopped almost as abruptly as they had begun. Her eyes fluttered for a moment before fully opening, her head turned from side to side as if searching for something lost.

Indeed, the woman she had been chasing was nowhere in sight, last seen in the shadows of the curtains bordering her window. In the dream, the curtains were the walls of an alley, and the woman was the person she had briefly seen in Key West. The woman who had been identified as Valeria López, Hoyos' wife.

Leslie fell back onto the bed, allowing her mind to clear and her heart to settle. She wasn't prone to dreaming and the few times she had, she had not experienced anything as vivid as this one. The clock read six-twenty-five when her sweat-soaked body finally made it to the bathroom and into the shower.

She took her time drying off, rebandaging her wound, making herself ready for the day. At precisely seven her original partner, Daryl Fischer, called. "Hope I didn't wake you," he began, apology in his voice. "Cox told me you'd be up. Said you'd be in the office by eight."

"No problem, Fish. What's up?"

"First, how you doin'? Quite an ordeal, I understand."

"Okay, I suppose. Considering everything. Other than a bad dream, a *really* bad dream, I slept well. Ready to go."

"Might be the drugs those rats gave you. Heard you were lucky. Bullet didn't do the damage it could have."

"My lucky day. Thanks for calling, but you didn't call this early for a social visit. What's up?"

"I caught the John Doe case."

"What John...? Oh, you mean the boy who died in the trailer. No name yet?"

"The children on the manifest—the ones from the drive you recovered—are numbered. I can't bring myself to refer to him as a number—a statistic."

"John Doe's not much better. Know the origin country?"

"Peru. It appears. Hey, you're right. It's not only a social call. What can you tell me about his death?"

"Nothing. I didn't even know he was up there on that shelf." Leslie closed her eyes as a shiver shook her body. The boy's blood had dripped onto her for hours and she hadn't done a damn thing about it! Is that where Fischer was going with his investigation? Her culpability? "The inside of the trailer was pitch black. Not a spark of light. I thought I was alone."

"He wasn't put up on that ledge while you were inside?"

"Unless I was out. Don't think I was, might have been though. Cox thinks I was drugged. Tox report's not back, as far as I know. I did doze near the end, just before..."

"From the amount of his blood on you, he must have been there for hours. We're thinking you both were shot just about the same time. Hear anything when you were put in the truck?"

"Nothing. I think it's all insulated."

"Here's the thing. There was very little blood on the floor, pointing toward him being placed above you *after* you were inside."

"Can't explain it. If the door had been opened, I would have seen light, or at least heard movement. I certainly heard it close after they put me inside. But that was only once—as far as I know."

"Okay, Les, I'll leave you be. If you remember anything, you know how to find me," Fischer chuckled. "Oh, and in the 'for what it's worth' category, Cox is zeroing in on your friend Jakowski for Franklin's death."

"Not surprised. The perp wore gloves and Jakowski has a tat on the back of his right hand."

"Better have a damn sight more than that. Everyone and his dog have tats these days. Won't get past probable cause, he goes in with only that."

"I don't know his full case, but I do agree with you. Jak claims to have been on Key West that night. We can place him there during the day. The ferry pulled out at six and there simply isn't anything putting him on the island after that."

"What's he claim?"

"That he was in a bed and breakfast. Sleeping."

"From five p.m.?"

"That's his story."

"And that's why Cox is hot to trot? Better cool his jets."

"Ever try to redirect Cox? Not easy."

"Sounds like you and Wonder Boy aren't doing so well as partners."

"I miss working with you, that much I acknowledge. Cox, aside from his few quirks, is okay. When he gets a scent, he's on it like a hound."

"All you need do is train him."

"Like my Daddy used to do with his dogs. If I recall right, that took him a lot of time."

"So, get started."

———◆———

Leslie finished dressing and checked her weapon for ammunition. Satisfied all was in order, she slipped it in her shoulder holster, walked down the hall to the staircase and took several steps down. Movement in the living room, a man's shadow, caused her to freeze, her right hand going automatically under her left arm. She drew her Glock 22, simultaneously yelling, "Don't move! Put your hands where I can see them! Now!"

"Holy shit! Leslie! It's me, Cox! What the hell's wrong with you?"

"What the fuck you doin' in my house? That's the only question on the table!"

"Put your weapon away before something happens," Cox admonished.

Leslie holstered the Glock and took a tentative step downward. "What the hell you think you're doing?"

"You don't remember me saying I was staying the night? I couldn't leave you alone, not in the condition you were in. Not with your neighbors shooting at you, I couldn't. Shit, you barely made it up those steps."

"What I remember," Leslie countered, "is you asking if I minded you staying the night. I told you what I thought of that in no uncertain terms!"

"You said, 'Not on your life, Bucko!', and that's a direct quote."

"And I meant it! And yet, here you are! Should arrest you for trespassing and all! Should have shot you a moment ago when I had the chance. Teach you to violate privacy."

"Knock it off already! I was standing—or for part of the night, sleeping—guard. Who the hell knows who shot you or why? Maybe you saw something you shouldn't have? Maybe your...hey, look, you know I'm right so drop the attitude. Okay?"

"Finish your sentence. You started to say, 'Maybe your...' but didn't finish your thought. Go ahead, get it out."

"Look, I'm thinking Jakowski's got more to do with all this than meets the eye. He's the one called it in. How'd he know you were in there? Maybe he was there all along? Maybe..."

"Don't you think I've gone over all that? After all, it's my relationship—and my life—that's at stake."

"Where'd you come out?"

"Truthfully? Not where I wanted. Not at all. Franklin, Jak and Herco were buddies since their Pitt days. Herco was a soccer star for the *Atlético Nacionals*, a Colombian team owned by Pablo Escobar who ran the *Medellín* cartel before his death about twenty years ago. The cartel's brutal enforcement thugs, *Oficina de Envigado*, The Office, are still operating, and heavily into money laundering. I believe Jak when he says the three of them planned to split, say, a hundred million by selling the Sunspot Telescope through Herco's former *Medellín* cartel contacts. Franklin was in on it for certain. I think also his boss, Admiral Three M, was involved as well. Why, I don't know."

"Cut to the chase, Leslie. Who killed Franklin? I say Jakowski. Motive. More cash dollars. The whole pie."

"I think we agree on one thing," Leslie reluctantly conceded, "Franklin took his own private boat south to the wreck site to retrieve the Sunspot Telescope that conveniently had gone missing from the recovery operation."

"On his way back," Cox added, picking up the storyline, "whoever was with him—and we don't know for certain if there was anyone with him—shot him, or as we now know, stabbed him with an ice pick, when they were under the causeway bridge to Fort Myers Beach, dropping both Franklin and the telescope over the side."

Leslie took a moment to consider what Cox had just said, then asked, "Why throw the telescope over? Just stab Franklin and push him off the boat."

"Who the hell knows? Maybe, just maybe, Franklin saw what was coming and threw the telescope over himself."

"Or," Leslie added, "a third accomplice was waiting on the dock and the killer didn't want to share with anyone so over it went. That would explain the fake suicide. The imposter staged the suicide, went off the back of the ferry to retrieve the telescope."

"That's a lot of work, when a rowboat would have worked just as well. Besides, diving gear would have been used and nothing points to such use."

"According to Jakowski, he was to meet Franklin on the Key West ferry, Tuesday morning. Franklin was a no-show. Didn't say anything about Three M or Herco, for that matter. Could the imposter be Three M?"

"The troubling part, Les, is we can't account for Jakowski's time Tuesday night."

"What about Herco?"

"Possible sighting late Tuesday afternoon, nothing conclusive. Hillard believes she has him on surveillance around three. Quality is, and I quote, 'piss poor'. She's working it. He says he was in Las Vegas, flew to Key West on a private plane, landing mid-afternoon. Can't yet confirm the flight, but he definitely *was* seen in a shop after the ferry went north. That sighting was confirmed."

"I assume Hillard's following up on his gambling?"

"Proving to be accurate. We now know he owes big money to an entity known as Cavanaugh. They use professional enforcers. Hillard thinks it goes further."

"What about Franklin? Jakowski? They involved with Vegas?"

"Not that Hillard's uncovered."

"I'd be surprised to find Jakowski has a gambling problem." Leslie nodded. "Police departments usually keep their ear to the ground for gambling problems of their detectives, especially in and around cities, like Pittsburgh, where casinos are located. Tell me about the confirmation of Herco."

"Claims he was in a Cuban coffee shop. They close at seven. Owner's on record stating they cleaned the tables around him and left together at seven-forty-five."

"Owner and Herco know each other?"

"Notes don't say."

"Herco's a rock star soccer player," Leslie reminded her partner. "Wouldn't be hard to get the owner—being Cuban, there's a good chance he's into soccer—to lie to the police for you. Happened all the time up in Tampa. What do we have on Franklin's boat after it docked early Tuesday morning?"

Cox consulted the file. "Boat left the dock shortly after nine. Full tanks. Nobody saw Franklin board. Hasn't returned." Cox searched the file intently for several minutes. Finally, he announced, "Found it. Knew I had seen this earlier. Franklin's boat. Gas log at Key West Marina shows the tanks filled at three-fifty. The boat was put on a mooring out in the harbor. Still there I suppose. Say, is it really time to get up? Feels like I just..."

"You up all night?"

"Told you, I was worried about you. Didn't want anyone sneaking past me."

"You're crazy! Know that?"

"Partners watch each other's backs. You'd do the same for me."

Leslie doubted that but kept her thoughts to herself.

Cox pulled the curtain back to see if it was really light out. "Shit!" he uttered, swallowing the quip he had intended to say about the moon being bright. "Your boyfriend's just getting out of his car. This'll get interesting fast. Want me to hide?"

Before Leslie could answer, the key turned in the lock and Jakowski, the former Steeler, stepped into the room.

TWENTY-NINE

"WELL, WELL, WELL," JAKOWSKI SAID, HIS brows rising in question, his lips smiling at the corners, "maybe I should come back later. I seem to be interrupting."

"Come in and join the party!" Leslie welcomed him, trying to keep her face neutral.

"The sofa's a mess," Cox said, when Leslie disappeared into the dining room on her way to the kitchen. "I'll sit there. Spent the night on it. A few more minutes won't kill me."

"Mind telling me why you're here?" Jakowski asked.

"Funny, that's the precise question I was about to ask you. Thought I'd wait for Les, but we can start without her."

"What can you do without me?" Leslie asked, reentering the living room. "Coffee'll take a moment."

"Wanted to know what brought your friend here so early in the morning. The morning after she got out of the hospital."

"Worried about her. Neighbor and all that."

"Got her back. Go on."

"Been thinking of all that's gone down. That child dying reached all the way to D.C. If I was a betting man, I'd lay a hundred on your governor having something to do with that. Task force reached out to me, see what I know."

"What *do* you know?" Leslie asked, beating Cox to the punch.

"Not much more than I told you. You do know I was planning on brokering the telescope using Herco's former *Medellín* contacts."

"Three M? Was she in on that transaction as well?"

"Don't think she knew about it. Might have."

"But, according to you, she ended up with *Los Zetas*. How'd that happen?"

"Don't rightly know. My information was that she was working with the *Pishtacos*. Then I found out about the Zs. I'm as confused as you are."

"Are you certain about the *Zetas*?" Leslie pressed.

"Truthfully, I'm not certain of anything. Other than I'm certain the *Pishtacos* are behind the child smuggling. Every one of those babies in that trailer was promised to somebody! DHS turns a blind eye. But I'll tell you this, your former partner Fischer has his hands full. He's got more than the death of that poor boy. He's been tasked with breaking up the trucking operation. And that begins with your neighbor."

"Lord. Samuel Lord. Guy seemed okay, when I met him."

"As in, shot-you-in-the-leg okay?"

"He do the shooting?"

"That's the word. Ask Fischer."

"I'll do that. Now that you're here, Jak, Cox has a few questions for you concerning the death of your friend Franklin. Any problem answering them?"

"What's going on? You all but just read me my rights. You think I killed him? That what I'm sensing?"

"Maybe not," Cox replied, getting up off the sofa and walking over to where the big Pittsburgh cop sat, "but I'm about half a step away."

"Tell you what," Jakowski said, "I'll take that coffee and you can fire away. I'm an open book. And you need not stand over me, I'm unarmed and going nowhere."

When they were all seated, coffees in hand, Cox suggested that Jakowski, seasoned detective that he was, start at the beginning and walk them through events as he knew them to be.

"As you well know, these things have no real beginnings," Jakowski explained. "Things just evolve from comments made over periods of time. Musings really. Then one thing leads to another, and another, and without any real planning, shit happens."

"Tell us about the shit that happened," Cox interrupted. "Even if you told us before, tell us again."

"Getting to it. You know about my involvement with Stratis. How I ran errands for him. Facilitated his purchase of Seminal Society Firsts."

"We know about the Edison phonograph and the Chladni euphon."

"And don't forget the most recent," Leslie added. "The missing *Philosophiæ Naturalis Principia Mathematica*, the book that brought Newton's laws to the world."

"We know about those three. Are there others?"

"None that resulted in a homicide, or other crime." When both Cox and Leslie looked unconvinced, Jakowski continued. "If you think it doesn't bother me to be working for a man like Stratis who thinks nothing of bribing officials to get what he wants, you're wrong. All that money changing hands, sometimes a billion dollars, started to play with my mind. 'A few million, Jak,' Herco would often say to me. 'A few million and he'll be out of your life. Your son'll get the best medical care and you'll be able to get away from Stratis for good.' Then about five months ago he came to me and..."

"And 'he' being Stratis—or Herco?" Cox clarified.

"Herco. He came to me with a story about a sunken treasure. I asked him what he was talking about. That's when I first learned of Galileo's Sunspot Telescope. The one in the Spanish galley that sank in sixteen-twenty-two. The *Buen Jesús*. Galileo had used that telescope in sixteen-twelve to confirm the sun rotated monthly by observing sunspots. That led to his eventual conviction by the Catholic Church in sixteen-thirty-three."

"You know your history, that's for sure," Cox commented.

"Got caught up in it. That's what happens. Anyway, Herco had this plan to work with Benny to separate the telescope from the other salvage and sell it privately. That's when they approached the Seminal Society collectors. The Sunspot Telescope would be a First and would bring in about a half billion dollars. Herco suggested I could score twenty million if I could arrange the sale. I believe he was thinking Stratis at that point."

"Did you," Leslie asked, "approach Stratis?"

"As things often happen, before I could, a rumor surfaced among the collectors that the Medici Telescope was about to be— or had been, depending upon which story you believed—stolen from the *Museo Galileo* in Florence and a fake substituted for the original. Needless to say, that got Stratis' attention."

"But you still went forward with Herco?" Cox said.

"He introduced me to a cartel buyer and my job, my only job, was to deliver the Sunspot to the buyer in Key West. I was to board the Fort Myers ferry, get the telescope from Benny, and deliver it to the cartel. I was on my own after that."

"Why couldn't Herco, or even Franklin, deliver the Sunspot directly? Why you?"

"Benny couldn't deliver it because he couldn't risk being seen with anyone. All eyes would be on him after it went missing. Herco because...well because he was into Vegas big time and he was afraid of being followed."

"And you were to receive how much?"

"Twenty mil."

"For being a delivery boy."

"Cox, you try dealing with the cartels and see how long your head remains on your neck! Twenty million is cheap for that risk!"

"So, what happened?"

"Benny was a no-show on the ferry. I remained on board, assuming he would drive himself, either by boat or car, to Key West. I waited for him all day but as you know, he didn't show."

"And you spent the night on the island? You didn't take the ferry north."

"Couldn't chance it. Thought for sure he simply missed the ferry and was driving down."

"And you have no proof of being down there past six o'clock when the ferry left?"

"Apparently not. But I was there."

"Not in any security footage we can find."

"Not so surprising is it? You think I can't avoid the cameras?"

"Public ones, perhaps. But with Ring, they're everywhere."

"You telling me you have private footage?"

"Not telling you anything," Cox smiled. "Only that you are not in any footage we have."

"My only explanation is that someone removed me from any recording you might have. I was there."

"Had to be someone sophisticated," Leslie commented. "Did a good job."

"Lots of sophisticated players when hundreds of millions of dollars are involved. That much I know."

"Any guesses?" Cox asked.

"The task force, for one."

"Any reason to think they would go to that trouble?"

"Only thing I can think about that, is someone on the task force has his or her hand in the till. As we already established, I'm sorry to say, money corrupts big time."

"We have been assuming," Leslie suddenly said, her face animated for the first time since being shot, "that it was an imposter who boarded the northbound ferry! What if it really was Franklin? Mind watching the video of the shooting, giving us your opinion?"

"Of course not."

Several minutes later when Franklin came into focus on the ferry, Jakowski declared, "That's definitely *not* him!"

"What makes you so certain?" Cox asked.

"I'll give you, it's his glasses. Distinctive, with those blue earpieces. Custom made to float. He was tired of his glasses going overboard without him."

"If those are his glasses, then what's bothering you?" Leslie asked, mentally scanning the inventory sheet from the ME and not 'seeing' the glasses.

"The blue surgical gloves. For the most part, blue gloves are nitrile."

"So?"

"So, Benny's highly allergic to nitrile, rarer even than a latex allergy. He'd never, ever wear nitrile gloves. That isn't him, I promise you. It isn't him."

As Jakowski was talking, Leslie again scanned the ME report. Franklin wasn't wearing *any* gloves. "You've convinced me of one thing. The person who we see going off the ferry is not the person found under the bridge."

"Or," Cox added, "the body has been tampered with."

"Who is it then?" Leslie pressed. "What about you? Same size and all."

"All three of us, Benny, Herco, and myself, are, at least we were, the same size, give or take a bit. People been confusing us since college days."

Leslie stood and walked toward Jakowski who remained seated. "If the person holding that gun is not Franklin, and not you, are you saying it's Herco?"

"Saying nothing of the sort. All I am saying, it's not me or Benny. Period. Nothing further."

"For now, we'll take your word for it," Leslie agreed, turning her back to Jakowski. "Let's move on. How much was your friend into Vegas?"

"Over seven mil. Maybe as much as ten."

"That's serious money," Cox said, cocking his head. "How the hell did he..."

"I don't know the whole of it, but from something he said, he may have been playing with cartel money. The telescope was his way out. Perhaps his *only* way out."

"What's he going to do now that the telescope's gone?" Leslie asked, visualizing Herco being thrown overboard from a fast-moving offshore boat, most likely his head already severed from his body.

"God only knows," Jakowski, looking into the far distance, murmured. "God only knows."

The moment the front door closed behind Jakowski, Leslie was on the line to Maxine Ghana. "Time you came clean with me," Leslie barked into her phone when the treasury agent answered. "I need to have what you know about Hoyos, and his wife, Valeria. Give it to me straight! I'm beyond..."

"Slow down, Detective. We're on the same side here. Heard you had a little...little mishap?"

"Got lucky. Clean through-and-through."

"Yeah, I know. Sorry 'bout that."

"What the hell's that mean?"

"What it sounds like. I'm sorry you were injured. As for Hoyos, he's a star soccer player. Was, actually. His playing days are over. Thought he would coach, but he got crossways with a Colombian drug dealer and that was the end for him. He's now getting jammed by Vegas, again cartel-related. Maybe that's the source of his soccer troubles, don't know. He hatched a scheme to sell the Sunspot Telescope to the Vegas bosses for significantly less than the going price. They, in turn, planned to sell it to the highest bidder. Big profits were in it for them. Hoyos got Jakowski involved. He cleared it with us. We asked Jak not to discuss it with his Verona management for reasons I can't go into now."

"Herco is working with the Mexican *Sinaloas* through his Columbian *Medellin* contacts," Leslie commented. "But the telescope wasn't sold to either of them. Herco's screwed!"

"He's screwed, yes, but not for the reason you think. Valeria, his wife, is a first cousin of the *Artista* Sisters, Sofi and Chio, who run, or ran, the *Pishtacos*. They have a family hold on her. She doesn't do exactly as they say, someone Val cares about is killed. Simple—and brutal—as that. And it works. It works the opposite as well. *Pishtacos* want someone kept alive, they usually live a long life."

"What about Herco? He lost his sale, how's he going to square with Vegas? And with all the other cartels involved."

"I can answer about Vegas. Val turned two hundred million for the sale. Gave her husband twenty. He's off to Vegas to settle—if he doesn't put it on the ponies first, as he's wont to do. Don't know about the cartels. They'll treat it as they do with any other business transaction gone bad. Truth is, they have their hands full with drugs and human smuggling. Don't need to be opening other fronts."

"What about the wife?"

"When that boy died—the one in the trailer with you—wife disappeared. Might have called in a favor with her cousin—or possibly the cousin had no more use for her. Either way, we can't find her. Those Colombians are experts in moving people in—and out—of our country. In a suitcase, under a tarp, in a fishing boat, any number of ways. If, as I suspect, the person delivering the stick turns out to be Valeria, she'll be charged with murder. Right now, the FBI has her number one on their wanted list. Not a good place to be."

"You check Sanibel Island?" Leslie asked, jealousy again stabbing her as she recalled the picture Jakowski had produced of Valeria in a skimpy bikini lounging by her pool, the Gulf of Mexico spread behind her.

"That home, as well as others, are under surveillance as we speak," Ghana quickly assured Leslie. "Trust me, breathing or not breathing, cartel's got her. Stake my career on it."

THIRTY

WHILE LESLIE WAS TALKING TO GHANA, COX was busy with Criminal Investigator Lizbeth Hillard, who was working to track down Hank Hoyos. "Try The Venetian in Vegas," he proposed. "Million to one shot, but one never knows. Flying in from somewhere in South Florida, Miami most likely."

"You nailed it!" the young investigator announced almost immediately. "Checked in yesterday."

"That's great! Let's..."

"Oh, crap! He checked out ten minutes ago."

"What the hell time is it out there? Got to be early."

"Seven-fifteen in the morning. My guess," Hillard added, "he's got a flight to catch."

"Know anybody in Vegas on the police force?" Cox asked, winking.

"Not personally, no," Hillard responded, not taking the bait.

"Okay, keep track of him best you can. Try to find that flight."

"Leslie," Cox called across the room, "before you get off with Ghana I need to speak to her."

"Just hung up. Sorry."

"Call her back. Need a favor."

When Cox told Leslie what he wanted, Leslie knew Ghana would be only too happy to comply by putting a tail on Herco in Vegas. In all likelihood, she had already done so. That would be consistent with finding his wife.

Sure enough, a few moments later when Agent Ghana was back on the line, she immediately confirmed that Herco was already under surveillance. "I can't believe he's in any hurry to leave Vegas. After all, the money he owed was transferred from one offshore account to another. He had no real reason to be there except to satisfy his addiction. Couple that with all the free liquor he can consume—and women he could have his pleasure with—and I ask, what can be bad?"

"What's your take on the glasses?" Leslie asked Cox when Ghana hung up. "Franklin's glasses."

Cox took a moment to collect his thoughts. "If Jakowski's right about the nitrile allergy—and we have no reason to think otherwise—and assuming those glasses are unique, which they appear to be, I'd go with an imposter. Someone who knew Franklin would be wearing them on the ferry going north—and someone with access to them."

"That's it!" Leslie cried. "Under our noses all along!"

"What the hell are you talking about?"

"Get Hillard on the line!" Leslie directed. While Cox was dialing, she brought up the images stored on her phone of the imposter. "I want her to review all the security footage she has from Key West, beginning when the ferry arrived from Fort Myers on Tuesday and extending until two hours after it left. Have her pay attention to the ferry, as well as all boats entering or leaving the harbor. In addition, have her view video from any street, building, or bar within a quarter mile of the dock. What I'm looking for is anyone wearing those glasses."

Ten minutes later Cox reported, "There's good news and bad news on the Hillard front. All told, she has over eighty hours of video."

"Is that the good or the bad?"

"Both, I'd say. But the real good news is that because of the boy's death in interstate trafficking, the sheriff's pulled a few strings and FBI's working with us. That means we have access to their computer matching software. Short answer, Hillard expects to have answers for us within hours, not days."

"That's good," Leslie acknowledged, still mostly distracted working the options of who killed Franklin in her head.

"You up to breakfast on the way to the office? I'm buying."

"For once, I'm famished. You drive."

Leslie shook her head, signaling to Cox she was having trouble hearing. He nodded, left money on the table, and they both walked out of Haney's Cafe. Once outside, Cox said, "Those bocce guys were sure worked up today. Something to do with their internet not working right. Or something like that. What were you saying?"

"I honestly don't know," Leslie answered as they walked toward their car, "if we're moving closer to a solution, or going in the opposite direction. Hopefully, Hillard will find something."

"It's always darkest before the dawn," Cox declared.

"Clichés are clever, but they sure don't help."

"Trying to cheer you up. You hardly said anything over breakfast."

"What with all that chatter about the internet being down, had a hard time concentrating. Been working the possibilities in my head."

"Come up with anything?"

"If Franklin wasn't on that ferry going north, then he was already dead and of course never went south. I now believe the ferry shooting was staged. Nothing else fits. You agree?"

"I suppose so. Can't believe Franklin got on that ferry and we can't positively identify him."

"Hillard's gone over the footage countless times. So have we. We only saw one person who even remotely looks like Franklin. He's a big man, hard to disguise himself."

"Anything's possible."

"Not likely though. I'm going with Franklin was dead under that bridge before the ferry left the dock on Tuesday."

"Where does that take you?"

"His killer staged the suicide."

"How do you know it was his killer?"

"The glasses. Franklin was never without them. My assumption is the killer took them. Why, I don't know. I suppose they just could have fallen off when he was shot and floated to the surface. But they were designed to remain on, so I'm going with the killer taking them."

"That means the footage we saw of Franklin docking his boat later that night wasn't Franklin, but..."

"Exactly!" Leslie interjected. "The killer. Pull over, let's go over it again."

Cox stopped the car in the far corner of a Publix parking lot and waited while his partner brought up the surveillance file she was looking for. She held her phone out so they both could watch.

1:05 a.m. Franklin's boat appears just outside of the marina pylons, moving slowly. Picture cut off at the waist of the only person visible. Head bent, looking at something in the boat.

1:07 a.m. Boat turns into a slip and the driver, wearing Franklin's glasses, moves to starboard and slips a line from an outside piling and ties it to a forward cleat. The boat slowly continues into the slip while the driver retrieves a second line from the piling and ties that one to a rear cleat.

1:07:25 a.m. Driver briskly walks forward and retrieves a line from a forward piling and slips it over a forward cleat.

1:10 a.m. Boat is in the slip tied to four pilings.

"Pause!" Cox called out suddenly. "See what I saw?"

"Sure did!" Leslie replied. "Gloves! That's why we only got Franklin's prints! Perp was wearing gloves. Same gloves as on the ferry?"

"Not certain they're the same gloves, but they're blue. Most definitely nitrile. According to Jakowski, this can't be Franklin."

"If not Franklin, who?" Leslie asked, shaking her head in frustration. "Sure looks like him!"

"We have footage of Franklin leaving the dock early—about six-thirty—in the morning. The only passenger was his friend Herco. I don't recall any gloves, although I wasn't looking for gloves at that time."

A few minutes later, after watching the images of the boat leaving the dock earlier that morning it was clear that only Franklin and Herco were aboard. Neither wore gloves.

Cox's phone sounded. It was Hillard. "Got some good news for you. Surveillance of the northbound ferry loading clearly shows the person we believe to be Franklin holding his ticket out to be scanned. That person is wearing the blue earpiece glasses you asked us to look for."

"What about gloves?"

"No gloves, but red, foul weather gear."

"Any further identification?"

"None so far."

"Okay, thanks. Send me what you have," Leslie said into Cox's phone.

"I'm not done," Hillard reminded Leslie. "This FBI software is amazing. And fast! We found a boat coming into the Key West fuel dock at fifteen-thirty-eight that same day. The driver of the boat is wearing those same glasses—and red, foul weather gear! And wearing gloves that appear to match the ones on the person going overboard from the ferry."

"Great work! Send it all to me ASAP." Turning to Cox, Leslie said, "We have our man! Now to roll him up. I'm calling Ghana, and..."

"Hold up a minute, Les. I think you got the cart before..."

"Stop with the clichés already."

"...the horse. Listen, Hillard said Herco checked into the Vegas hotel about midnight. Even allowing for the time change, what is it? Three hours? He didn't have time to get off the ferry that docked at eleven p.m., and race over to RSW and catch a plane."

"We can check the flights." Leslie sent a note to Hillard and almost immediately the answer came back. "Already done. It's in the file. Hank Hoyos flew out of Miami on the eleven o'clock—

eleven oh-four to be precise—flight. We've ruled him out of being on that ferry. Sorry."

"Back to ground zero!" Leslie said, slamming her phone onto the car seat, narrowly missing Cox's leg.

"Cliché?"

"Knock it off! I thought we had the bastard!"

"Look, we have evidence this Herco guy was on the boat with Franklin when it left the dock Monday morning. Franklin was alive then. When the boat docked, the jerk was wearing Franklin's glasses for God's sake! No sign of Franklin. Explain that."

"Dumped his body under the bridge, my take. Now to prove it."

"Glasses are a beginning," Cox acknowledged. "Build from that."

"I suppose he was wearing the glasses so the dock hands wouldn't start asking questions about where Franklin was. They left so early in the morning, the night crew most likely didn't even know Herco was aboard. It sure would be nice to get pictures of them both aboard the boat out in the Gulf."

"Cell phone picture could do that. Didn't see one listed in the evidence file, however."

"That would be Franklin's phone," Leslie said, her mood improving. "I saw a court order for access to Franklin's phone files. If he sent any photos, Hillard would have flagged them by now."

"Herco might have taken pics as well. We need his phone."

Leslie reached for her phone. "Who you calling now?" Cox asked.

"Get moving on a court order for Herco's phone," Leslie answered her partner.

"Hold up a moment." Cox advised. "Are you sure you want to warn him? He's out of jurisdiction now. Easy matter for him to slip into Mexico and disappear. Guy's a rock star in Colombia. Think we'll ever get our hands on him once he's out of the country? Like his wife; smoke in the wind."

"Killjoy," Leslie scowled. "Okay. Let's get back to the office, see what the day brings."

"Leave me alone!" Leslie shouted at the hapless clerk who was trying to document the details of her injury. "I'm fully capable of filling out the paperwork on my own! I have a homicide to investigate and no time for this nonsense!"

"But...but..." the young man protested, "I need..."

"Go tell Boots what you need! I have work to do!"

"Boots?" he repeated, confusion written across his face. "I don't understand."

"Captain Stetson. How long you work here?"

"This is my second week. I'm..."

"Didn't they tell you the rules for talking to detectives?"

"What rules?"

"You stand quietly at their desk, no three feet away from their desk, until they ask you to speak. You then have ten minutes to get done what you have to get done. You understand that?"

"Yes, Detective."

"Now go get what you need from Boots. I'm too busy to talk today."

When the clerk left, Cox said, "I've never seen you treat anyone like that. What the hell is it with those rules? You're busting his chops."

"You really want to start with me?"

"Just sayin'. Hey, this'll cheer you up a bit. The task force your pal Ghana runs, well they're working with Fischer on the John Doe. Anyway, since the wife, Val López, is in the wind, court issued warrants for the home, the car, and...wait for it...her phone."

"Why's the phone so important to you?" Leslie asked, puzzled by Cox's sudden enthusiasm.

"Communications with Herco."

"What's the chance of anything incriminating?"

"Slim to none. But hey, we're almost at a dead end and what do we have? A man wearing the glasses of a dead man. Hell, we can't even prove they're the same glasses. Imagine yourself on the stand and some weasel attorney says, 'Now Detective, if I understand correctly, your testimony is that the glasses Mr. Hoyos was wearing when that picture was taken belonged to the deceased. Is that correct?' Now what would your answer be?"

"Yes, that's correct."

"Please tell the jury how you came to that conclusion."

"The deceased owned a pair just like that with blue earpieces custom-made for him."

"Do you have those glasses in your possession?"

"No."

"Have you ever had those glasses in your possession?"

"No."

"Has anyone from law enforcement physically examined those glasses after Mr. Franklin's death?"

"No."

"Would you again tell the jury how you know the glasses in the photo are the same glasses Mr. Franklin was wearing at the time of his death?"

"They have blue earpieces that float."

"Are you suggesting that there is only one pair of glasses in the whole world with blue earpieces that float?"

"No, but..."

"Detective, if you didn't physically examine the eyeglasses, then how do you know the earpieces float?"

"Stop it! You've made your point! We're back to square one. We don't even have enough to get a search warrant, let alone an arrest warrant. Shit! Get out of my space! I need room to think!"

Cox, knowing not to tangle with Leslie when she was in this mood, retreated to his desk without a word. Leslie pulled up the file images, found the sequence from when Franklin's boat left the dock and studied it frame by frame looking for something, anything, she could use to demonstrate the glasses later seen on Herco were the same.

On the second pass, this time with a ten magnification, she noticed a small slice of material missing from the front right frame, she guessed about a half inch in from the hinge. Hurriedly, she queued up the images from when the boat was returned. The light was almost the same, but Herco's head was turned further away from the camera than Franklin's had been. What had appeared as a notch in the first series of photos, now appeared only as a scratch.

Not conclusive. But not to be overlooked either. Forensic analysis could do wonders with recreation. She flagged the 'before' and 'after' images for further review and analysis.

"Time for a walk," she told herself just as the clerk who had quizzed her on her injury came back.

"Detective Hodges," the clerk said, "I..."

"Oh, there you are. Hey, I need to apologize to you for the way I treated you earlier. You're just doing your job. Caught me at a bad moment. What do you need from me?"

"No more than fifteen minutes. I promise. I managed to get almost everything else from the file."

Leslie fell back into her chair. "Fire away. I'm yours for fifteen minutes."

The questions asked were easy for Leslie to answer. Exact time of the shooting: "Evening, between seven-ten and seven-fifteen." Light conditions: "Dark." Had she seen the shooter? "No". Describe the truck: "Normal fifty-five-foot silver/white tractor with nothing painted on the side." Describe the inside of the truck: "Didn't see the inside until the door was opened. Everything I saw is captured on film. No need to repeat."

"Focusing back on the shooter," the young clerk continued, reading from a checklist, "do you have a thought as to whether the shooter was male or female?"

"No," Leslie replied, "I just assumed it was a male."

"Thank you, Detective," the clerk said, already having taken a step away from her desk. "Only took twelve minutes and I'm out of your hair. Have a nice day." He then disappeared around the corner leaving Leslie contemplating the last question, the one about male or female. From the time Medical Examiner Van Deere had briefed her on Franklin's death until now, Leslie had focused on male perpetrators. Her friend Jakowski came to mind first, followed closely by Hank Hoyos, the second of the three close friends.

On the assumption that the person who staged the suicide was also the real killer, Jakowski remained a possibility. Hoyos was now ruled out because he was flying to Vegas at the time.

"Leslie," Cox's voice broke through the noise in her head, "Everything okay?"

"Yes, why?"

"You look like...well, you seem to be in a trance. Looking off into space."

"Just thinking. Going over the possibilities."

"Been doing the same. Seems we have two timelines. I mean, we don't know for absolute certain if Franklin died before the Tuesday morning ferry to Key West or on the way back north that night. I went back over the ME report, and she hasn't changed it. Death by puncture wound. Let's go with murder then."

"I may be off base here," Leslie replied, deciding to share her latest thoughts with Cox, "but we've been focusing on Jak and Herco as the shooter. What about Herco's wife, Valeria López? We know she's involved with child trafficking. If she could do *that*, she's certainly capable of homicide. She's almost as tall as Jak. A little clever 'bulking up' with clothing could very well fool us, particularly when we're thinking of a male perp."

"Hadn't considered her. But hey, makes sense," Cox conceded.

"If we assume the impostor was wearing Franklin's glasses, how did he/she obtain them?"

"And don't forget Admiral Three M," Cox added, "As well as a host of people we may not even be aware of. Perhaps your neighbor, that Lord guy?"

"Sammy? Hadn't thought of him."

"He's lower than scum! Piece of shit hauls human cargo! I'd as soon put a bullet in his head as say hello."

"Cox! You'll get yourself busted off the force, you say shit like that. Innocent until..."

"Don't start with the BS, Leslie! Those bastards near took your leg off. Killed that poor child! Too bad we did away with hanging. I'd get a front row to watch him swing."

"Don't get ahead of your lights on this, all's I'm saying." Leslie's phone sounded. "Speaking of the devil, here's..."

"Which devil? We've been speaking of several."

"Ghana. Be quiet while I answer." Leslie put the phone to her ear. "Just the person I wanted to speak with."

"Don't go getting your hopes up," Ghana said. "I don't have much for you."

"Anything to get us off dead center. I'm all ears."

"First, we've located López. She's still within the jurisdiction of the United States. My guess, not for long."

"Where?"

"Do not put this in a file. There's a possibility your files have been compromised."

"That's serious! For now, I'll follow your lead on the file compromise issue, but I need to advise Boots."

"Granted. Tell her to call me. Back to business. López is in a small boat anchored within the Dry Tortugas. We picked this up by a fluke. She's in a sheltered cove out of the way of everything. National Park Service doesn't have the personnel to patrol all the area, but one of their patrols had engine trouble and drifted into the cove. Took a picture which was routinely uploaded to DHS. Recognition software did the rest. For once, DHS did the right thing and responded to our APB on López."

"How do you know she's still there if they don't patrol?"

"No satellite images of her leaving. We played it backward and traced the boat back to Key West."

"Let me guess," Leslie said. "Boat belongs to our boy Franklin."

"Right on! How'd you know?"

"Why the hell else would you be calling me? Got anything more for us?"

"Matter of fact I do. Don't know if this'll make your day—or ruin it?"

"Out with it."

"Got a picture of Jakowski from a street cam in Key West."

"Tell me it was after six. After the ferry left."

"Leslie, if that's not rooting for him, I'll eat my hat. Nineteen hundred hours, thirty-three minutes, twelve seconds to be exact."

Cox, listening to only one side of the conversation, knew immediately from Leslie's sigh of relief what she had heard. Jakowski could not have been on the ferry.

"Okay," Leslie finally said, "one more time frame to clear. Tell me about Jak on Monday."

"Oh, if you're thinking he could have killed Franklin, skip it. He was on a conf call with us from about fifteen hundred to fifteen-thirty from his hotel in Fort Myers. Outlining the plans he had to sell the Sunspot Telescope using the *Medellín's* services. He was to meet Franklin on the ferry the next morning, obtain the telescope, and deliver it in Key West."

"He could have called from anywhere, perhaps Franklin's boat."

"Could have. But he didn't."

"You know that for a fact."

"As much as any *fact* allows. His phone was off, battery problem or some such thing. Called from the phone in his room. Had a devil of a time confirming it was him calling in."

"And where was his friend Herco in all this?"

"Hoyos went out on the diving boat with Franklin. I don't know if both of them were planning on meeting Jak on the ferry the next morning, or only Franklin. He wasn't exactly clear on that. We traced Franklin's boat back to Fort Myers and then down to Key West. Satellite doesn't miss much, I'll say that for it. Especially when you know what you're looking for. Arrived in Key West slightly after sixteen hundred hours. Tuesday."

"From where?" Leslie asked, sensing Ghana had more than she was letting on.

"As I said, From Fort Myers. Left the dock earlier in the day."

"How many people aboard?"

"Far as we could tell, one."

"Male or female?"

"Satellite's not *that* good."

"Don't bet on it!" is what Leslie wanted to say. Instead, she asked, "The driver wearing glasses?"

"Sunglasses. Why?"

"Tell you later. Know the color of the earpieces?"

"Now that *is* beyond the expectations of a camera from space."

"But you do know the answer to the question. I hear it in your voice."

"Went back and looked at security footage. As a matter of fact, the man who refueled the boat in Key West *was* wearing sunglasses with blue earpieces. I'll send you what I have."

"Why am I sensing you have more for me?"

"I just got off the phone with Boots and your former partner. Fischer's being picked up in thirty-five minutes at Page Field. Hopefully, we'll get to Madam López before she disappears. If we do, we want Florida law enforcement with us for sex trafficking and possible homicide."

"How does that affect me?"

"We have one more seat on the seaplane. Stetson says it's yours if you make it in time."

"What about Cox? He should..."

"Stetson has him working on linking Hoyos to the Franklin homicide. Good luck with that. Better get your ass outside, Fischer's waiting."

THIRTY-ONE

LESLIE, FOLLOWING FISCHER'S LEAD, DUCKED low to make certain she cleared the revolving blades of the DHS helicopter that had just landed. "Better hurry," one of the uniformed TSA officers who was acting as their escort, called. "This bird was diverted, and the pilot's pissed. Weather's building in the Caribbean and his window's tight. As it is, he won't make it home, or wherever he was going. Wouldn't be surprised if he aborted this flight south."

"Can he do that?" Leslie called over the whine of the engine.

"Pilots can do what the hell they want when weather's a factor. Wide latitude. Watch your head, up you go." He placed his hand on her butt, pushing her upward onto the steps.

With a sudden flashback of being shoved—helpless, shot and drugged— up into the back of her neighbor's tractor-trailer, Leslie whipped her head to face him. "What the f..." she began and caught herself. The man had already turned and was walking away.

"What was that about?" Fischer said when she sat down beside him in the cramped seats directly behind the pilot. "Looks like you..."

"Grabbed my ass! That's what!"

"Grabbed? Or pushed? Maybe he was just..."

"What the hell's the difference?"

"Never seen you get so worked up, Leslie. You okay?"

"Never been better!" She snapped, concentrating on the diminishing landscape as the earth fell away below them.

Wisely, Fischer dropped the subject, saying, "Heard you like that guy Herco for Franklin's death. Heard also he's last seen in Vegas."

Leslie spun around in her seat to face Fischer. "What do you mean, 'last seen'? We have him checking out of The Venetian and there's a tail..."

"Lost him, I'm afraid. Professionally done, I might add. Got in a cab. They followed the cab to the Bellagio. The man who got out was not the man who got in. They have watches on all modes of transit. From rental cars to buses. My guess, our side won't find him. Wherever he's going it's by private transport."

"You know how to ruin a person's day. What am I doing on this helo? You ask for me or what?"

"Miss working with you. I'm not blowing smoke, Hodges. I can honestly say you're the best partner I've ever had in thirty-two years of policing. My last case before I retire. Ever since I got shot, Jess's been after me to hang it up. It's time. On this one, the feds got ol' Val dead to rights. Just have to pick her up and bring her home."

"All from that drive she dropped. The one I found?"

"That was the last piece. They've been onto her for a while now. The death of that boy woke up the powers that be. That, and a few well-placed calls from Governor DeSantis."

"Know who shot the kid? For that matter, know who shot me?"

"I believe they do know. Ghana plays it close. I'm here to arrest López. You're here as backup. I was thinking you might hear something that'll help nail Franklin's killer. If it wasn't Jak, then the only three I know are López, her husband Herco, and..."

"Who, pray tell, is the third?"

"Admiral Big Shit!"

"Masters! We've just begun digging into her. But truthfully, if Franklin died on his way back to his dock, then it could only have been Herco, or..." Leslie paused, allowing a new thought to take hold. "Or a Herco impersonator!"

"Your friend the Pittsburgh cop could pass for Herco."

"Could, I suppose. But he was ruled out."

"By?"

Leslie thought about how much of what Ghana had said she could share with Fischer. "Jakowski's on a task force with the feds. He was on a call with them mid-afternoon. Couldn't have been on the call and out in the Gulf with Franklin."

"Why not?"

"Called from his hotel room. They confirmed the phone."

"When it comes to modern technology, who the hell knows what tricks people play. Maybe some kind of relay. Just sayin'. Food for thought."

"As if I don't have enough to think about as it is."

"Glad that's your case, not mine. Gives me a headache listening to you."

"Mind if I nap a bit? Still not fully back from the trauma."

"Took me months. Still not a hundred percent. Go for it."

Leslie opened her eyes as the helicopter touched down. She glanced out through the small window expecting to see the normal airport scenery—tarmac runways, terminal buildings, service vehicles. Instead, the landing surface was gray and lined with helicopters identical to the one she was on. Looking over the top of the parked aircraft, all she could see was water and sky, the sky being even darker than the water. "Where the hell are..."

"In the Caribbean, between the Dry Tortugas and Havana, Cuba. On a..."

"Aircraft carrier! How the hell..."

"Homeland Security operation, Leslie," Fischer informed her. "They do things a bit different from Lee County. Briefing begins in four minutes. Eleven hundred hours to be exact."

The pilot said nothing as the two climbed down the stairs to the deck of the carrier. When Leslie looked back up at him, he saluted, then turned away.

"Please follow me," a dark-skinned man wearing a short-sleeved khaki shirt and matching trousers with a gold belt buckle, said. "I'm Chief Petty Officer Brookings. The others are waiting. How was your ride down?"

"For me, uneventful. Slept most of the way," Leslie said.

"So did I," Fischer confessed.

"Probably for the better. Weather's making up. We're in for a...let me just say...less than optimal night. Here's the elevator. Room's five decks down." He checked his watch. "Get there just in time."

Brookings was right. Leslie and Fischer walked into the briefing room just as a tall balding man, wearing a starched white shirt under a freshly pressed navy-blue jacket with several rows of ribbons pinned to his left breast, and perfectly pleated trousers, strode to the front of the room. The jacket sleeves each had a single gold star positioned above a narrow gold band. Below the narrow band was a wide gold band. Leslie guessed the man to be some sort of an admiral. Following the admiral was a woman wearing almost the same uniform, except her sleeves held four slender gold bars instead of the wide bar of the man in front of her.

Chief Petty Officer Brookings led Leslie and Fischer to the back of the room before turning briskly on his heel, closing the door behind him. Leslie counted twelve others in the room, about half in everyday clothes, half wearing khaki shirts and pants.

David Harry Tannenbaum

"To the civilians in the room," the man in the Admiral's uniform began, "let me welcome you aboard the USS Wasp. I am Rear Admiral J. D. Walker and with me here is Captain Janet Barth, the vessel's commander. I have been informed that the DHS task force, headed by Treasury Agent Maxine Ghana, has done extensive work mapping out the details of drug smuggling and human trafficking by various cartels operating in the eastern Gulf of Mexico and Western Caribbean. In general terms, our mission over the next seventy-two hours is to intercept and disrupt, hopefully permanently, their operations. This is primarily a civilian operation, with the Navy providing transportation and logistics. That said, make no mistake, should we come under attack, we will respond in kind."

Admiral Walker paused, scrutinized the room, making eye contact one person at a time until every face had been studied. Satisfying himself that he held everyone's full attention, he continued. "I'm certain each of you are aware of the deteriorating weather. While normally weather, short of hurricane force, doesn't hinder us, for this operation because many of our targets are civilian in nature, we will delay the start until morning." He again paused, then added, "I have also been informed that much of this operation falls under a security classification preventing me from going into details. So, I'll turn the platform over to Agent Ghana. Before I do, because we have so many first timers on board, I'd be remiss if I did not point out that the Wasp is a small carrier, used primarily for launching and landing helicopters and other airborne assets. As part of its mission, on June seventh, nineteen-sixty-five, the *USS Wasp* scooped astronauts Edward White and James McDivitt out of the Atlantic when their spacecraft returned from a mission. The crew is justifiably proud of their heritage. You are free to walk the decks, observe the operations, but please obey all commands. Timing is critical. Agent Ghana, the room is yours."

Captain Barth followed the admiral to the back of the room where they stood on either side of Leslie and Fischer.

"I won't be detailing the entire mission," Ghana began, "other than to point out that if all goes as drawn up, four other boats, 'assets' as the admiral refers to them, will also be joining us in stopping several civilian ships, some of which are cruise ships, in order to remove drugs and humans. As most of you know, our current location is due north of Havana, Cuba. The operational range is from Belize on the south to New Orleans on the north. You may also know that north of us is a land mass, called Dry Tortugas. The area is more of a sand mass with a series of keys.

Navigation is only for small boats and bottom color is the primary method of navigation. Needless to say, we need sunlight for such a venture. At best, tomorrow the sunlight will be minimal. I am also informed that the cloud cover may not be in our favor until late morning. That presents a logistical question not resolved until then. The good news; if we can't safely navigate neither can our target. The bad news; they don't pay as much attention to maintaining life as we do. Any questions so far?"

The room remained silent.

"Okay. Anchored off Loggerhead Key north of Fort Jefferson is a diving boat. That boat represents a high value target for the two guests who just joined us. A little boy by the name of Juan Ramos Alverez was found dead in a trafficking trailer a few days back in South Florida. The woman standing beside Admiral Walker, who was also shot in the leg and locked inside that trailer, is Lee County Sheriff's Deputy, Leslie Hodges. Her partner, Deputy Daryl Fischer, is standing beside her. They're here because we have good intelligence that a woman wanted in connection with the boy's death is in that boat anchored off Loggerhead Key. Our intelligence is that a larger boat, operated by the *Pishtacos*, a Peruvian cartel, has been dispatched to pick her up. One of our missions is to intercept the cartel boat, which I understand has just been picked up by satellite. I'll say nothing further now, but we'll have a more detailed briefing at twenty-hundred hours. Here in this room."

With a voice that belied her size, Captain Barth, her words resonating in the room, announced, "You are all invited to dinner in the Captain's Dining Room at twenty hundred hours. Come hungry, there will be plenty to eat. Dismissed!"

—————■—————

"Hodges, Fischer. Hold a moment," Ghana called, hurrying to catch up to the two deputies. "Let's talk a moment," she said, nodding toward the back of the now-empty room. "Got a few things for you."

Leslie and Fischer waited while Ghana carefully closed the door. "Those two make a great pair. I'm talking about the captain and the admiral. They appear to be all business, all the time. But from what I'm told, that ain't so. This mission doesn't require a flag officer on site. Maybe the first time, but not now. More power to them, I say."

"So, there have been other operations of this sort. Is that what you're telling us?"

"This isn't the first 'round up' as the admiral likes to call these missions where we essentially relieve the cartels of their cargo, both human and otherwise."

"From your tone," Leslie commented, "I take it you think it's useless."

"Maybe not useless, but certainly disheartening. We gather up the drugs, and the people. I swear the drugs don't slow down for more than a week. As for the human suffering, God only knows what happens to those people."

"So why do it?" Fischer asked. "I mean, if it does no good, why do it?"

"Policy. If a child is murdered in the States, we do a 'round up'. Simple as that. Theory being it incentivizes them not to kill the kids."

"That working?"

"Not so much," Ghana shrugged. "Not so much."

"So why continue?" Leslie asked, knowing the answer.

"Ever try to change a government policy? Thing runs on automatic. Some higher-up has an idea, everyone around him or her says it's brilliant. That becomes the policy and God help anyone who tries to change it. Higher-up moves on, policy remains. That's the way it always has been—and the way I see it, always will be. Enough of that. The good news from your point of view is that I've permission to read you both in. So here goes."

Leslie had already stumbled upon much of what Ghana told them. What she hadn't known, or even guessed, was that Jakowski was in Fort Myers, not on vacation as she had been led to believe, but rather he was using his friendship with Valeria López to monitor their human trafficking operations. "Fort Myers? Why there?"

"There's an area between Fort Myers Beach and San Carlos Island that's perfect for landing human cargo—children. Mostly female. Seems the cartel's operating right under your noses."

"That area was devastated by Hurricane Ian. Can't believe..."

"Taking full advantage of the chaos over there, I suppose."

Fischer perked up. "Wait! Did I hear you correctly. Jakowski's friend Herco. His wife?"

"That's who I saw in the alleyway in Key West!" Leslie added. "Remember? The one who dropped the fob with the list of names! I just assumed that traffic—those people—were coming into Key West. You saying they're dropped off on Fort Myers Beach?"

"Maybe not on the beach per se. But it's a big area. Lots of confusion out there. Perfect for what they need." Ghana regarded Leslie thoughtfully before adding, "Got more for you. Remember those glasses you asked me to run through the system. The ones with the blue earpieces?"

"Franklin's glasses," Leslie answered. "The ones worn by the person staging the suicide. Find anything useful?"

"Video actually. Surprisingly high quality." Ghana held up her phone, fumbled with the screen a moment, then faced it toward the deputies.

A moment later, Leslie exclaimed, "Can't believe this! There's Val. Her husband's walking toward her. That's the ferry in the background. The glasses with the blue earpieces and the red, foul weather jacket are in his left hand. He's..."

Ghana stopped the video. "If you watch the left hand, you'll see him transfer the glasses and the jacket to his wife. But you'll miss the right, the real money transaction. It's mostly covered by her body, but watch closely."

Fischer leaned in close, his eyes glued to the screen as were Leslie's. In Herco's right hand, almost invisible to the camera, was a handgun, a Beretta. The hand slipped into Val's side pocket and when the hand was next seen the gun was gone. "The question is..." Leslie began.

She was interrupted by Ghana, who said, "The question is: Is this the same weapon that killed Franklin?"

"And the answer is?" Leslie asked.

"We'll know when we roll her up. Surveillance suggests she still has the gun. Truthfully, we're not certain of that. It might have gone over the side on the trip out to Loggerhead Key. I brought you two down to preserve the chain of custody, if we get lucky. Keeps me from testifying. Otherwise, we're wasting your time. I forgot to ask, how you progressing with arresting Hoyos out in Vegas?"

"Lost him!" Leslie glanced at her watch. "As of twelve hours ago, he's in the wind. Gone completely dark."

THIRTY-TWO

THE STORM INTENSIFIED TO A POINT WHERE ALL visibility was lost. Leslie had expected the ship to be rocking violently and was pleasantly surprised when she felt no real movement, other than a slow, almost soothing roll. The prime rib dinner was excellent, cooked to perfection. The rolls were freshly baked, as was the apple pie dessert. Leslie passed on the ice cream, but Fischer requested seconds. "Just eating what you didn't," he rationalized, undoing his belt a notch.

It wasn't safe to go out onto the flight deck, so after dinner they walked a hallway that felt like a mile in circumference. When they entered the briefing room, there were ten active screens in two columns of five. Each screen displayed a number.

Leslie said to Fischer, "I'm thinking, each of those screens is a ship in this fleet. And that big center screen with the seemingly random flashing dots shows where each is located."

"Partner, your guess is as good as mine."

The briefing was mostly technical with, as Leslie had correctly guessed, ten other ships participating. At one point, Ghana leaned close to Leslie. "See that center display? That's the *Wasp*. And that X, looks like a blur, but it's labeled twenty-five-dash-one, is the boat where Val's holed up."

"How do you know she's still aboard?"

"She's there, all right. SEALs planted a sensor on the side of the boat. Listening to them as we speak. Engine's been disabled. They're going nowhere."

"What happens if in this storm they drag anchor? Or worse, break loose?"

"I can give a glib answer such as who the hell cares. The real truth is, I want them tried for their crimes. And the weather up where they are has settled. They won't break loose."

"Does that mean the operation will start tonight?" Fischer asked.

"Main thrust is scheduled for noon tomorrow. That's when the weather clears south of us. Our squad deploys earlier. I'll meet you on deck three at zero seven hundred. Speed boat will be launched and ready. ETA at Loggerhead Key where López is

222

holed up is zero-nine-fifteen. I'm told it'll be a choppy, wet ride. Foul weather gear will be provided."

"You certain she's there?"

"Not much is certain in our business, Leslie. But she's there, I promise you. In fact, she received a text message about an hour back from the *Pishtacos* confirming her pickup time. Coincides with our satellite track. We'll be there waiting."

———◆———

Despite the small private room and comfortable bunk, Leslie had trouble sleeping. The surveillance video of Valeria López receiving Derrick Franklin's glasses from her husband, Hank Hoyos, as he emerged from the ferry, proved the tie between López, Hoyos and Franklin. That alone allowed her to obtain an arrest warrant for both Hoyos and López. With the right arraignment judge, she could satisfy probable cause and with Hoyos' cartel connections, have them both held without bail. That was the easy part. The hard part would be convictions. Sure, she could prove a Beretta was transferred from Herco to his wife. The ME would testify that a Beretta was most likely used to kill Franklin. But she had nothing to prove that the weapon in the video being transferred to López was the murder weapon. López would testify, assuming they could get around the spousal immunity, that she had no idea her husband was going to give her the weapon and had no idea what it had been used for. He, of course, would be exempt from testimony.

How to explain López's behavior of getting on the ferry wearing her husband's red, foul weather gear as well as Franklin's blue glasses? Obviously, to stage a fake suicide. Perhaps that's what the Beretta was to be used for? Assuming her husband killed Franklin, the question remained, why?

And then why would the wife fake a suicide by Franklin?

Questions, questions. What we need are answers!

Make up an answer, she told herself. You have the facts. Put them together and make up a plausible story.

She sat up. One scenario was easy to believe. Herco and his good friend Franklin went on Franklin's boat from Fort Myers down to the *Buen Jesús y Nuestra Señora del Rosario* wreck site to recover Galileo's Sunspot Telescope not recovered with the other items. Franklin dove down while Herco waited patiently on the boat. Franklin eventually came up empty-handed—or so it appeared to Herco. Eventually, they started back for home, and in the six or so hour trip Herco convinced himself that his friend was lying and somehow had managed to get the telescope aboard without Herco seeing it. As they passed under the bridge, Herco's patience ran out and he stabbed his friend and pushed him overboard. His glasses most likely fell off, or Herco purposely took them. Either way, when the boat docked, Herco was wearing the glasses and Franklin was on the bottom of the river. Herco was the man who the dock hand saw in the dim light.

Just when that theory seemed right, Leslie thought of another. Franklin dove down and couldn't find the telescope because his boss, Admiral Three M, had sold him out. She had beaten him to the dive site by taking a seaplane and retrieving it herself. Perhaps it was she who had set up the storage shed hoax with rumors of the Medici Telescope being auctioned off. All of that being designed to confuse the cartels, who ultimately relied on the Seminal Society collector husband and wife team of Sanjay and Riya Kumar to broker the sale.

Jakowski was caught in the crosshairs of three cartels, the *Medellín*, the *Sinaloas* and the *Pishtacos*, trying to make money brokering the telescope, all the while working for Ghana and her federal task force. A tangled web if ever there was one! He had expected his friend Franklin to hand off the telescope on the ferry to Key West. His plan had been to deliver the telescope to the *Medellín* contact and vouch for the legitimacy of it. When Franklin didn't show up, Jakowski was left to his own devices. He booked a room and did what? Did he do anything to facilitate the human trafficking? Could the dropped fob have been intended for him? Or was his presence in that location purely a coincidence?

More questions. No answers!

Just as she was dozing off, a new revelation struck her. Again, she sat bolt upright. The nagging question as to why the wife would stage a suicide. One possible reason. If human trafficking was taking place in and around Fort Myers Beach, it is easy then to suppose that drugs were also coming in via that route. The last thing a cartel would want was a concentration of law enforcement, especially dive teams, spending time looking for a body. The wife staged the suicide so that authorities would immediately go down under the bridge and find the missing body. That is exactly what occurred. Sure, an anonymous phone call would have served the same function. But with electronic traces, she couldn't be certain to avoid suspicion. Far-fetched, Leslie had to admit. But certainly possible. With Valeria's acting background, this would be a perfect final performance. A lifetime achievement type of performance.

THIRTY-THREE

"YOU LOOK LIKE SHIT!" GHANA SAID WHEN Leslie appeared at the hatchway on deck three at exactly seven in the morning. "I can't begin to imagine what kind of night you had."

"Not one of my better nights. Let's leave it at that. We were told to expect turbulence this morning, so I didn't eat breakfast. You think that's okay?"

"I'm not usually a breakfast person," Ghana confessed. "Cup of coffee lasts me for hours. My advice, for what it's worth, is expect it to be choppy out there. The less in your stomach the better. Be sure to get your foul weather gear tight around your ankles and wrists."

"Sounds like you've done this once or twice before."

"Let's just say, this ain't my first rodeo. And, if all goes well, it won't be my last. I'm counting on you to bring López in. I want to see her hang! It's the least we can do for that poor boy, Juan, as well as for the countless others whose names we'll never know. And Leslie, you're the exact right person to finish the job."

Before Leslie could answer, a man she hadn't seen before dressed in khaki pants with the name SEABASS pinned to a long-sleeved, blue work shirt, answered the breakfast question with authority. "My guess Sheriff, you won't want to eat for at least an hour. Maybe somewhat longer. Don't be fooled by the calm water and lack of wind when you first board. The transport is sitting in the lee of the Wasp and believe me, the water's churning out there. Life jacket's a must. You'll find them to your right when you step aboard. Put them on and secure the buckles *before* you move forward to your seat. There are five other transports down there all preparing to leave at the same time. If you go overboard, it'll be a mess to sort out. But don't panic, let the vest bring you to the surface. Electronics will find you, the team will do the rest. Those folks are highly trained. We leave no one behind! If you get queasy, move to the railing and barf over the side. Cleaning up's a bitch, you lose it in the transport. When you're ready to eat, we have provisions. Now, follow me."

Leslie, heeding Seabass' advice, took a seat next to the port side rail, Fischer was in the seat directly behind her. She turned to say something to him and in that instant the boat engines revved and the boat shot forward. She managed to grab the rail in time to prevent going overboard.

"Hang on," Fischer yelled. "Despite all their electronics, there won't be much to salvage if one of those boats back there chops you up."

"You're supportive this morning, I see," she snorted, her words mostly lost in a gust of wind.

The motion was surprisingly calm. She had experienced much worse on a lake back home in Gulfport the few times her father had taken her fishing. *Piece of cake.*

She was about to turn to see how Fischer was fairing when the boat hit a wave, causing the bow to fly upward, throwing Leslie back against her seat. The sudden increase of wind in her face made it difficult to breathe. Almost immediately, the bow fell, slamming against the water with such force that she envisioned the vessel breaking in half. It was all she could do to remain in her seat.

The wind increased even further until it was howling past her ears. Forcing her eyes open, she realized that the waves were above her head a good four feet. She had never seen water this angry looking. *Menacing!*

The bow slammed into the wave and again the bow of the transport was thrown up and this time to starboard almost dumping her over the side. Her knuckles were white from grasping the seat. Fighting off nausea, she told herself this wasn't going to end well. *Glad I didn't eat this morning!*

The up and down pounding, and the violent sideways twisting continued for what seemed an eternity. Leslie fought to hold the contents of her stomach, but knew it was a losing battle. Problem was, if she released the grip on her seat she'd be thrown overboard. *Cleaning up was a bitch.* The words of Seabass rang in her head. Leslie frantically looked around, hoping to spot a place where she could go to avoid this torture—go to die. Nothing looked promising.

Leslie spotted Ghana on the starboard side. Sitting calmly and talking on what appeared to be a satellite phone as though nothing were amiss. "Hate that woman!" she mumbled, struggling to hold down whatever remained from her dinner.

The loudspeaker crackled harshly. The crashing of the boat, coupled with the steady wind and wave noise made it almost impossible to hear. The voice, Leslie supposed it to be Seabass, was saying something to the effect that they would turn north in two minutes and when they did, the pounding would mitigate.

All Leslie wanted at this point was to be put out of her misery. Being thrown overboard and drowning would accomplish that desire faster. *The sooner the better!*

The two minutes seemed a lifetime. A million thoughts flew through Leslie's mind. None related to work, all focused on getting her own life in order. Her foremost concern, if she were to judge by the amount of time devoted to that subject, was what to do about her relationship with Jakowski. Assuming, of course, he would follow through on his divorce. Jak working with the feds to gather intel through Val, his friend's wife, on the cartel's stateside operation was a major chip in his favor. On the other hand, him trying to score with the Galileo Sunspot Telescope, was a huge negative. Brokering deals with cartels just wasn't something Leslie could condone. Lasting love, Leslie had come to understand, was not decided by an accounting spreadsheet of pros and cons, but rather it came from the heart. And her heart was compromised.

Suddenly, her total focus was on whether to end the nausea by unlocking her grip and taking her chances hanging over the side or barfing where she sat. Slowly, her fingers released one by one as her body began tilting to the left. Going over the side became a real possibility.

The boat slowly began to rotate. As it did, the motion mitigated and the wind seemed to fade. A moment later the chaos was gone. The bow settled and the violent sideward thrusts ceased. Unfortunately, the motion in Leslie's head continued. She gagged back the bile in her throat, uncertain if she could prevent an over-the-side spectacle. A long-suppressed memory surfaced. For her tenth birthday her father had taken her fishing off the Mississippi coast. She had caught a twenty-three-pound redfish. On the way back in, a squall hit and she had 'tossed her cookies' as her father liked to say. The thrill of the redfish had been lost to the embarrassment of the 'cookies'. She had vowed never again.

"Leslie," Ghana's voice slowly broke through Leslie's concentration. "Are you okay?"

"Working on it," came the honest reply. "I hope the rough stuff's over, all's I can say. I'm about to toss my cookies."

"Look up. Sky's blue. See that line above us? Marks the northernmost line of the storm. High's pressing it down. That's good for us and a few other of the transports. Those poor souls who drew the southern interceptions have their work cut out for them. Keep your eyes on the horizon. Works wonders."

"You're chipper. Considering the pounding we just took." Leslie turned around to Fischer and found him slumped back in his seat looking as green as a person can look. He hadn't vomited as far as Leslie could determine, but he looked as if he wished he had—and might yet do so. "The rest of us look like my partner there. And you? You look as if you're ready for a party."

"In this situation, I do have an advantage over you. My father was a fisherman. Went out every day, rain, shine, or storm. 'People have to eat,' he'd say. 'We have to eat. Got a job to do. Gotta do it.' He was sick once, the only day I recall he didn't go out. The 'grip' he had said."

"Where did you grow up?"

"I was born in Miami. Father lived his whole life in Trinidad. Sent my mother to have his baby in the 'great free country to the north' as he called the United States. I really didn't move here until he died fighting the Jamaat al Muslimeen coup attempt. I was twelve. The government of Trinidad and Tobago, to show their gratitude, honored his wish and allowed my mother and me to go to Miami. Since I was a U.S. citizen, it was the least they could do. That was over thirty years ago. Need to postpone this get-to-know-you bonding talk. Came over to give you an update."

"From the look on your face, it's not good news."

"Frankly, can't determine. They're working it, but I doubt it'll resolve before we get on scene."

Whether it was the calmer water, or focusing on the horizon, Leslie's nausea was now gone. She released her death grip on the seat and sat up straight for the first time since the transport moved away from the carrier. "Five minutes ago, I wouldn't have given a thought to what you have. Now let's get Fischer up here and hear what it is."

Fischer, his pallor still mostly green, stood and walked forward, holding the rail for balance. "Did I hear you say you have an update?"

"Radio traffic interceptions," Ghana said. "I suppose you know we're pretty good at that. You know that seaplane flying out of New Orleans Admiral Walker briefed us on? The one the *Pishtacos* contracted to pick up Valeria López? It was dispatched to Loggerhead Key where their boat is anchored."

"Disabled, I thought you said," Leslie commented, making certain she had the facts correct.

"Still disabled. That's right. Problem is, the plane left Lakefront ..."

"I thought the New Orleans airport was Louis Armstrong," Fischer interrupted. "What's with..."

"That's where the plane was supposed to fly out of. That's the problem. Plane flew out of Lakefront an hour early. Control believes the cartel knows about our interdiction operation and moved their time frame up. López, as you well know, has family ties to the cartel and they want her out of there."

"Can we get there in time?" Leslie asked.

"We'll be about fifteen minutes too late according to control's calculations. Seaplane arrives at eleven-oh-five. Our ETA is eleven-twenty. But..."

"There always seems to be a 'but'," Leslie commented, almost to herself.

"But—we intercepted another communication," Ghana went on, choosing to override Leslie's criticism. "A bit cryptic but believed to be accurate. This one from another seaplane, one that took off from Punta Gorda. Message is: ETA eleven-ten. WAIT!"

"Any idea who sent that? Who's aboard the second plane?"

"It was signed, PARTNER, ESQUIRE."

THIRTY-FOUR

GHANA WAS TALKING, BUT LESLIE HAD STOPPED listening several sentences back. The ramifications of Esquire, Pete Jakowski, being on a seaplane on his way to a rendezvous with Valeria López, both of them being evacuated by a Peruvian cartel, was straining her ability to coherently process. She didn't know what was worse, the legal consequences or the personal devastation. On the personal side, she had allowed herself to conclude that Herco had shot Franklin, when it now appeared that it had been Jakowski all along! True, she had been concerned that Jak had spent considerable time at Herco's wife's house, she a beautiful actress lounging around in an almost non-existent bikini. But that apprehension had been for personal reasons, not professional concern.

"Earth to Leslie!" Ghana's voice broke through. "You're in your own world. Mind joining us— here on earth? It's critical we get this right!"

"Oh, sorry, Ghana. I was...was working through what you said."

"About what?"

"Who was on the Punta Gorda plane." Leslie was unable to speak Jakowski's name. Betrayed was what she felt. Betrayed— and deeply hurt. Not only by the man she had been sharing her bed with, but by the woman in front of her. The woman who had vouched for Jak being only a *facilitator*.

"That's not the topic. Forget Esquire! We can sort that later! We're discussing the fact that the New Orleans flight will soon be landing at Loggerhead Key. We're still a good twelve to fifteen minutes out. Our transport's designed to be practically invisible on the water, but that's not foolproof. Good news. When the sun's behind us, as it is now, it takes special equipment to see us. Seabass believes that the plane not changing direction is indication we're invisible."

"It could also be," Leslie added, "they see us but also know we're not close enough to stop them."

"Good observation, Detective. That scenario only works if they don't wait for the Punta Gorda plane to land," Ghana countered.

"But," Fischer said, still pale, but gaining color in his cheeks, "I would suppose that the plane from Punta Gorda would have turned back if the first plane was planning to leave without waiting. They must be in communication."

"Another good observation," Ghana said. "It's nice working with smart people. That's what I figure. Truth is, we have no other option. Turn back and we miss them. Once that plane is in the air, short of shooting them down, we've lost López. Keep going and we at least have the possibility of capturing whoever is on the Punta Gorda plane."

"Assuming both planes are there when we arrive, what's the plan?" Leslie asked, beginning to focus on what her role would be in the arrest of Jakowski.

"Then we...Oh, hold for a moment. Seabass has an update." Ghana listened to a voice in her earphone, then turned back to the deputies. "Good news. The New Orleans plane has landed and López is now aboard. They just received instructions to remain in place. Whoever is controlling their operation believes a U.S. Coast Guard plane is overhead with orders to shoot."

"Is it real? Or a stunt on our part?"

"I'd bet on a stunt. We know they have military radios and access to secure frequencies. We're not above feeding them false info. But you know, sometimes you live right and get lucky. For all I know, there really is a Coast Guard flight overhead. Speaking of luck, we can use a bit right now and hope the Punta Gorda pilot doesn't spot us and turn around. Or if he does spot us, he won't realize what we are. From what we know of the pilot, he's not cartel trained. Just a local hired by Esquire."

Not landing is precisely what Leslie was grappling with. She didn't want to be the one to find Jakowski on that plane. His presence would prove conclusively that he was much deeper into illegal activities than previously known to her. The probability of conviction high, with first degree murder leading the list. Her stomach ached as she realized that his arrest was certain—unless the plane turned and headed directly to Mexico.

The hum of the transport they were riding in reduced and the boat slowly lost speed. "Now what?" Leslie asked. "I thought timing was critical."

Ghana listened intently for several minutes to the muffled sound coming from her earpiece, then said, "Okay, listen up. Here's the plan. We're slowing for timing purposes, and to launch two small boats. The Punta Gorda plane apparently hasn't seen us. They're descending, about to land. Unless something changes, it'll be at the López plane at eleven-eighteen. The incoming plane will taxi as close as possible to the New Orleans plane. Passenger Esquire will transfer over from the Punta Gorda plane to the New Orleans plane in the same lifeboat they used for López. The Punta Gorda plane will then leave. Their plan is predicated on the overhead Coast Guard plane following the Punta Gorda plane, clearing the way for the New Orleans plane to take off. You with me?"

Leslie turned her thumb up.

Fischer said, "Following."

"Okay then, as I said, we will be using two small boats, with a third held as backup. SEALs will be in the first boat; the three of us in the second. Both boats will circle around to the far side of the Punta Gorda plane—opposite the steps. The SEALs will be in the water and position themselves beneath the plane. When Esquire is in the lifeboat and on his way to the New Orleans plane, the SEALs will render both the lifeboat driver and Esquire unconscious. Esquire will then be transferred back to the second boat, minus his outer garments. That's when you two place him under arrest."

"Let me guess," Leslie interrupted, "a SEAL—or someone—will put on Esquire's clothes and board the New Orleans plane."

"You should be working for us, Detective! You're right on. A SEAL, posing as Esquire, will enter the New Orleans plane. A second SEAL will be close behind, as will I. My job is to subdue and arrest López. Their jobs are to subdue the pilot and any hired help. They'll have mics attached, so everything said will be heard. At the first sign of trouble, cavalry, the real cavalry, will be dispatched from this boat. Hope that's not necessary. Won't be pretty. Any questions?"

"What are we to arrest Jakowski—Esquire—for? We have a good case against Herco for murder one. But Pete, I don't..."

"Don't let your personal life get..."

"It's not that! It's that I don't have the supporting facts. Hell, I can't even place him at the scene!"

"Shit, Leslie! Do what you friggin' want! Arrest him! Don't arrest him! Hell, it's your case! Do with it what you will! He's not my concern, López is" Ghana walked away.

Fischer took her place. "For what it's worth, partner," he said, "I'm with you. I've been reviewing the file. You got a good murder one case on that guy, Hank Hoyos. The one called Herco. You got essentially nothing on Jakowski, except circumstance.

Strong circumstance at that. Just arrest him! With a bit of digging we just might get lucky. It happens."

"Fischer, what I want to know is what the hell's he doing on this plane? Meeting López in the middle of nowhere. A person wanted for murder no less!"

"Hate to break it to you, partner," Fischer said, "but you're not the first, nor will you be the last to be fooled by a guy like him. He's on that plane for one reason and one reason only. They're in it together. Start a new life south of the border."

"What the hell you talking about?"

"I saw that file photo of López. Need I say..."

"Shit! I'm the girlfriend. And the girlfriend's always last to know! That what you're telling me?"

"I suppose."

"Hell, if I let him go, Ghana, DHS, Boots, everyone, will think I covered for him. I'm screwed whatever I do."

"I'll make the call," Fischer offered. "Take the heat for it. They can't do much to an old, retired guy."

"Thanks, Fish. But Esquire's mine to deal with. I'll do what needs to be done."

"Just know I support your decision—whatever way you go."

They both looked up as the sound of a low-flying plane broke through the otherwise quiet morning. Fischer checked his watch. "Come, it's showtime."

———————•———————

The plan was working as drawn up. The original dinghy operator who had brought the small inflatable from the anchored boat out to the Punta Gorda seaplane was lying face up, bound and gagged in the back of the small inflatable where Leslie, Fischer and Ghana were waiting. Ghana was outfitted as if she were part of a SWAT team, firearms and all. The door to the Punta Gorda seaplane swung open and a man with Jakowski's build stepped out wearing sunglasses, his hat low over the glasses. He glanced around, took a step, hesitated, studied the dingy a long moment, then proceeded to descend the short flight of steps.

Leslie, sitting in the boat out of Jakowski's sight line, felt a sharp pain shoot through her body as if she had again been pierced by a bullet. She recalled that an actual sniper had once told her that if he had wanted a target dead, the target would be dead. Period.

This pain, of course, hadn't come from a bullet. Rather, it emanated from betrayal by the man she had been considering marrying; the very same man who was now fleeing the country he professed to love. Worse even, he was fleeing with one of the most beautiful women in the world.

"Hurry," the man in the dinghy called up to Jakowski, "time is critical."

Jakowski took another step down, paused as if he was about to retreat, then stepped into the small boat, being careful to land in the center to prevent tipping. The instant both feet were in the boat, a black bag was slid over his head and was pulled down and firmly secured under his chin. Jakowski's hands went up to release the bag and a rope instantly circled his arms. Two men, one taking the legs, the other his upper body, took him down. Big and strong as he was, Jakowski was no match for the well-trained Navy SEALs holding him.

The plane that had brought him began moving away, its engines coming up to full speed in preparation for taxiing and takeoff. The men holding Jakowski waited until the small plane had taken off before transferring him from the blowup to the dinghy and lying him at the feet of Leslie and Fischer. Ghana stepped over him and into the blowup heading to the New Orleans seaplane, whose engine had begun to rotate.

The SEAL who had taken Jakowski's place in the blowup was now wearing Jakowski's hat and sunglasses. He started up the steps to the seaplane, his head down. The plane door opened and Valeria López stood in the doorway, her arms open wide to greet her lover.

The Jakowski stand-in made his way slowly upward, being careful not to miss a step. Reaching the landing, Valeria pulled his body against hers, tightening her arms around him.

An instant later, confusion spread across her face as two SEALs flowed past her and into the plane. The confusion faded to panic when a third SEAL separated her arms from around her lover and pinned them behind her.

"You, Valeria López," Ghana said, having followed the SEALs up the stairway, "are under arrest for the murder of Juan Ramos Alverez while engaging in human trafficking. You have the right to remain silent. Anything you say can and will be used against you in a court of law." She looked to the man López had been hugging. "Cuff and search her. Search her belongings as well. Make certain she has nothing lethal in her possession. You know the drill."

In the boat below the seaplane, Esquire was lying face down. The two men rolled him over in preparation of sitting him up. Leslie reached down and grabbed his shirt as if to help lift the big man. In all honesty, if she could have thrown him overboard, she would have. Instead, she stepped back to listen to Ghana's excited voice in her earpiece.

"Leslie, hear this! We found it! The Beretta! I'm betting ballistics will find this a match for the gun that killed Franklin! The one we saw Hoyos put in his wife's pocket!"

At any other time, Leslie would have been ecstatic. Except, here she was, with Jakowski at her feet and no evidence whatsoever of his involvement in the killing. Hoyos was in the wind, and as well organized and connected as the *Pishtacos* were, likely to remain that way. "Shit!" she exclaimed. "Shit! Shit, shit, shit!"

She cocked her leg in preparation for kicking the big Pittsburgh cop as hard as she could. Her leg began forward, and she switched her focus to his face wanting to savor his expression when the blow struck home.

"Holy crap!" She heard herself scream. "Holy crap! What's this?" Getting command of herself, she shouted at the man below her, "What the hell's your name? Tell me your name! Now!"

The man, sitting on the floor of the boat, his hands cuffed behind him, started to stand. One of the SEALs pushed him down. "You want your collarbone broken; you do that again!"

"Esquire. I go by Esquire. You know me as Peter Jakowski," he said, perfectly imitating the Pittsburgh cop.

Leslie had to admit, now that she looked at him directly, he did look like Jakowski, except for the eyes. The eyes were wrong! Pete's were alive. This guy's eyes were dead! Black holes. "Like shit you're Jakowski!" she spat furiously, reaching down to grab the wrist buried behind him.

The prisoner twisted his arms away while at the same time violently nodding forward, his forehead coming within an inch of her chin.

Jumping back, she barked to the SEAL who had slammed Esquire's head back against the railing, "I need to see the back of his right hand!"

The SEAL immediately bent the prisoner forward.

Leslie slowly leaned in, hoping—praying even—that she didn't see the *Go Pitt* tattoo.

Seeing nothing but bare flesh, she triumphantly shouted, "Hank Hoyos. You're under arrest for the murder of Derrick Franklin. Anything you say..."

Turning to Fischer and smiling deeply, she said, "Partner, read him his rights. I might be tempted to add a few choice words, but you, I trust, are above that. We need to do this by the book. Even scumbags deserve that much."

The End

Thank You

As I have said before, I am blessed with several great editors. Brenda Goldberg Tannenbaum, Debi Bass and Lori Mercier. I deeply appreciate each of you.

My longtime friend, Ronald Slusky, has provided invaluable insight into all sixteen of my published novels. Even during the first draft I hear his voice in my ear criquing my "Pittsburgh" grammar and sentence structure. I don't know how I could publish anything of value without him.

Thank you again to my wonderful wife, Mary Tannenbaum, who is always there for me. Love you.

Books by
David Harry Tannenbaum

The Seminal Society Series

Edison's Phonograph

Chaldni's Euphon

Newton's Laws

Galileo's Telescope

General Fiction

Standard Deviation

Out of the Depths

Adventures in the Law

Mystery/Thriller (under the pen name David Harry)

Jimmy Redstone / Angella Martinez Series

the Padre Puzzle

the Padre Predator

the Padre Paranoia

the Padre Pandemic

the Padre Poison

the Padre Phantom

the Padre Phony

the Padre Pirate

the Padre Puppets

About the Author

David Harry Tannenbaum and his wife, Mary, have a home in Miromar Lakes, Florida. When David isn't writing, he enjoys swimming, bocce, model train building, walking Franco—and searching for characters to be exploited in his next novel.

In Memoriam

Lori Mercier, one of my editors, recently, and very much unexpectantly, passed away. She is the daughter of Douglas Madeley, a good friend who introduced me to the Tortulia group of men who get together once a week for breakfast and lively discussion. Lori had a unique way of looking at stories and language which I will sorely miss. May her memory be a blessing for all who knew her.